Woman at Sea

WOMAN AT SEA

Catherine Poulain

*Translated from the French
by Adriana Hunter*

JONATHAN CAPE

LONDON

1 3 5 7 9 10 8 6 4 2

Jonathan Cape, an imprint of Vintage Publishing,
20 Vauxhall Bridge Road,
London SW1V 2SA

Jonathan Cape is part of the Penguin Random House group of companies
whose addresses can be found at global.penguinrandomhouse.com.

Penguin
Random House
UK

First published in France as *Le grand marin* by Éditions de L'Olivier in 2016.

First published by Jonathan Cape in 2018

penguin.co.uk/vintage

A CIP catalogue record for this book is available from the British Library

ISBN 9781911214588 (Hardback edition)
ISBN 9781911214595 (Trade paperback edition)

Typeset in India by Integra Software Services Pvt. Ltd, Pondicherry

Printed and bound in Great Britain by Clays Ltd, St Ives PLC

Penguin Random House is committed to a sustainable future for
our business, our readers and our planet. This book is made
from Forest Stewardship Council® certified paper.

MIX
Paper from
responsible sources
FSC® C018179

O you singer, solitary, singing by yourself – projecting me;
O solitary me, listening – nevermore shall I cease perpetuating you;
Never more shall I escape, never more the reverberations,
Never more the cries of unsatisfied love be absent from me,
Never again leave me to be the peaceful child I was before what there,
    in the night,
By the sea, under the yellow and sagging moon,
The messenger there arous'd – the fire, the sweet hell within,
The unknown want, the destiny of me.

Walt Whitman

You should always be heading to Alaska. But getting there – what's the point? I've packed my bag, it's dark, then the day comes when I leave Manosque-les-Plateaux, Manosque-les-Sorrow. It's February, the bars are no emptier, there's smoke and beer. I'm leaving, I'm off to the ends of the earth, the limitless oceans, to glassy calm and raging peril, I'm leaving. I don't want to die of boredom or beer or a stray bullet. Of misery. I'm leaving. You're mad, they jeer – they always jeer. All alone on a boat with hordes of men, you're mad, they laugh.

Go ahead. Laugh. Drink. Get wasted. Die if you like. Not me. I'm off to fish in Alaska. See ya.

I've left.

I'm going to cross the big country. In New York I feel like crying. I cry into my latte, then walk out. It's still early. I walk along wide, deserted avenues. The April sky is very high, very clear between tower blocks that rear manically into the raw air. Small caravan stands sell coffee and cakes. Sitting on a bench opposite a glass building set aflame by the rising sun, I drink a large cup of insipid coffee and eat a huge muffin, a sugary face-sponge. And happiness gradually seeps back, a subtle lightness in my legs, an urge to pick myself up, to look round the street corner, and then further, to the next one ... And I get up and walk. The city's stirring, people appear, the giddy whirlwind begins. I launch myself into it till I'm exhausted.

I take the bus, a Greyhound bus with a racing dog on the side. I pay a hundred dollars to trace a route from one ocean to the other. We leave the city behind. I've bought cookies and apples. Hunkered

I

down in my seat, I watch the succession of highways, the arteries of the beltway meeting, splitting, coming together again, cutting across each other and disappearing. It makes me travel-sick so I eat a cookie.

My only luggage is a small army bag. I covered it with precious fabrics and embroidered designs before leaving. Someone gave me a down anorak in a washed-out sky blue. I mend it all through the journey: feathers drift around me like clouds.

'Where are you headed?' I'm asked.

'Alaska.'

'To do what?'

'I'm going fishing.'

'Have you done it before?'

'No.'

'Do you have a contact?'

'No.'

'God bless you.'

God bless you. God bless you. God bless you. Thank you, I say, thank you so much. I'm happy. I'm going fishing in Alaska.

We travel across deserts. The bus empties. I have two seats to myself – I can half lie down, my cheek pressed to the cold window. Wyoming is under snow. Nevada too. I eat cookies dunked in pale weak coffee at a rate dictated by the McDonald's and rest stops along the way. I stitch away and disappear in the clouds from my anorak. Then it's night again but I can't sleep. Casinos flicker on either side of the road, glowing wheels of neon, luminous cowboys brandishing pistols blinking on and off. Overhead, the slenderest crescent moon. We pass Las Vegas. Not a tree; loose stones, scrub burned by the winter. The sky lights up quickly in the East. Almost before you sense it coming, the day has dawned. Ahead the road stretches out straight, snow-capped mountains in the distance, and then, all alone on the desert plateau, a railway track heading off towards the horizon, towards the morning. Or to nowhere at all. A straggle of doleful cows watch us go by. Perhaps they're cold. And we stop again to have lunch, in a service station where chrome-heavy trucks stand with engines roaring. An American flag flutters in the wind, in front of a giant poster advertising beer.

I start to limp. I hobble uncomfortably in and out of the bus. God bless you, someone says, more concerned. There's an old man who's also lame. We make eye contact with something like recognition. In a roadside rest stop one night, tramps gather round me.

'Are you a Chicana? You look like a Chicana, you look like my daughter,' one of them says.

And we set off again. I'm a Chicana with my red cheeks, my blazing cheeks; a Chicana who limps and eats cookies in clouds of feathers while looking out at the darkness over the desert. A Chicana going fishing in Alaska.

I meet up with a fisherman friend in Seattle and he takes me onto his boat. Years he's been waiting for me, there are pictures of me on the walls, the boat's named after me. Later he cries. This great man who turned his back on me, now sobbing on his bunk. It's dark outside, and raining. Maybe I should leave, I think.

'Maybe I should leave,' I whisper.

'That's right,' he says, 'you go now.'

It's so cold and dark outside. He's still crying and I am too.

Then he says sadly, 'Maybe I should strangle you.'

I'm a little frightened. I look at his big hands, I can see he's eyeing my neck.

'But you're not going to?' I ask in a soft little voice.

No, maybe he won't. Slowly I fill my bag. But still he says I should stay, stay just for tonight.

We take a ferry, he stares off to sea with his reddened eyes, not talking. I look out at the water, at his unreadable face, at my own hands as I rub them together, again and again. Then we walk through streets. He sees me to the airport. He's ahead of me, I'm out of breath trying to keep up. He's crying. And I cry along behind.

Halibut Hearts

It's a glorious day in Anchorage. I wait behind a window. A Native man hovers around me. I've come to the ends of the earth. I'm frightened. Then I set off again in a tiny aeroplane. The stewardess serves us coffee and a cookie, and we head deep into the mist, disappearing into whiteness and blindness. Well, you asked for it, sweetheart, your ends of the earth. The island appears between two scrolls of fog – Kodiak. Dark forests, mountains, and the dirty brown earth emerging from beneath melted snow. I want to cry. I have to go fishing now.

I drink a coffee opposite a belligerent grizzly bear in the arrivals hall of the tiny airport. Men walk past, bags slung over their shoulders. Big-framed, their faces tanned, scarred. They don't seem to see me. Outside, the white sky, the grey hills, seagulls, everywhere, endlessly flying past, mewing.

I call. I say, 'Hello, I'm the woman who's friends with the fisherman in Seattle. He said you were expecting my call, that I could stay with you for a few nights? Then I'll find a boat.'

A man's non-committal voice – he says a few words to someone. 'Oh shit!' I hear a woman's voice reply. Welcome, Lili, I think. Welcome to Kodiak. Oh shit, she said.

A small, skinny woman climbs out of a pick-up, fine yellow hair, drawn face, pale thin unsmiling lips, porcelain-blue eyes. She drives, doesn't say a word. We're on a perfectly straight road between curtains of trees that open onto bare landscape. We drive along the coast, crossing fingers of water taut with frost.

'You can sleep there.' I'm shown a sofa in the living room.

'Oh, thank you,' I say.

7

'We make nets for the fishermen. Purse seines. We know everyone in Kodiak. We'll ask about work for you.'

'Oh, thanks.'

'So, anyway, take a seat, make yourself at home, the can's here, bathroom there and kitchen here. When you're hungry help yourself from the fridge.'

'Oh, thanks.'

They forget about me. I sit in a corner, carving a piece of wood. Later I go out, I'd like to find my own shack. But it's too cold. Brown earth and soiled snow, a grey sky over the bare mountains, so nearby. When I come back they're eating. I sit on the sofa, waiting for it to be over, waiting for night-time when they'll go to their room. Then I can unwind and maybe sleep.

I'm dropped off in town. I sit on a bench overlooking the harbour and eat popcorn. I count my money, the banknotes and the coins. I need to find work soon. A man calls to me from the dock. Under that white sky he looks as beautiful as an ancient statue outlined against the grey water. He has tattoos all the way up to his neck, under the dark curly mop of his rebellious hair.

'I'm Nikephoros,' he says. 'How about you, where are you from?'

'From a long way away,' I tell him. 'I've come to fish.'

He looks amazed. Wishes me good luck.

'Maybe see you later?' he suggests before crossing the street.

I watch him climb three bare cement steps on the pavement opposite, then open the door to an austere, square wooden building – 'B and B bar' it says on the front – with large single-pane windows, one of which is cracked.

I get up, walk down the footbridge to the pontoon.

'Are you looking for something?' a bulky man calls to me from the deck of a boat.

'Work.'

'Come aboard then!'

We drink a beer in the engine room. I daren't speak. He's kind and teaches me to tie three knots.

'Now you can go fishing,' he says. 'But whatever you do, talk confidently when you go asking for work. Let the men around you know who they're dealing with.'

He offers me another beer and I think of a smoke-filled bar from another life.

'I have to go,' I say quickly.

'Come back whenever you like,' he says. 'If you see the boat moored up, don't even think twice.'

I head off along the docks, asking from boat to boat, 'You don't need any help on board, do you?'

No one hears me, my words are snatched away on the wind. I have to keep repeating myself before getting a reply:

'Have you fished before?'

'No,' I mumble.

'Do you have papers? Green card, fishing licence?'

'No.'

I get strange looks.

'Try further along, you'll find something,' I'm told, still kindly.

I don't find anything. I go back to sleep on my sofa, my stomach full to bursting with popcorn. I'm offered nannying work – minding children for a couple who are going fishing. It's a terrible humiliation. I refuse with gentle obstinacy, lowering my head as I shake it from left to right. I ask where I can find basic accommodation but the replies are evasive so I go back and help my hosts make their nets.

And then I find something at last. I'm offered two crewing jobs on the same day: herring fishing along the coast on a seiner – or going out to sea for black cod on a longliner. I choose the second because longlining sounds better, because it will be tough and dangerous, and the crew will be made up of hardened seamen. The skipper, a lanky man called Ian, gives me the job and looks at me with a mixture of amazement and gentleness. He takes in my colourful bag and me standing in front of it, and says: Passion is beautiful. Then the softness in his eyes is gone.

9

'You'll have to prove yourself right away. We have three weeks to ready the boat, repair the lines and bait the longlines. Your only aim in life now will be to work for the *Rebel*, day and night.'

I want a boat to adopt me, I murmur into the windswept silence of the night.

We've been working for days in a damp lean-to, sitting at white iron tubs where the coiled longlines are kept. We repair the lines and replace damaged hooks and the missing gangions that connect the hooks to the line. I learn how to splice. Beside me a man works in silence. He arrived late, bleary-eyed. The skipper yelled. He smells of beer and is chewing tobacco. From time to time he spits into the irretrievably dirty cup in front of him. Jesús, sitting opposite me, smiles at me. Jesús is Mexican. He's short and stocky, round bronzed face, apricot cheeks. A man emerges from an ill-lit room, followed by a very young, very fat woman. She's Native. The man looks away sheepishly as he walks past.

'Steve got lucky last night,' sniggers the skipper.

'If you call that getting lucky,' the man next to me replies. Then without taking his eyes off his tub of line or even changing his tone, he says to me, 'Thanks for the statue.'

I look at him perplexed. His face is serious but his dark eyes seem to be laughing.

'I mean it's a beautiful statue ... Liberty. It was the French who gave it to us, right?'

The radio plays country music. Someone makes coffee and we drink it from cups perfunctorily wiped on a corner of clothing.

'We need to remember to bring some water back in jerrycans,' says John, tall and blond and very pale.

'My name's Wolf, just like a wolf,' my neighbour says quietly.

He tells me he's been fishing for fifteen years, that boats he's been on have foundered and gone down three times, and he'll have his own boat one day, maybe even at the end of this season, you know, if the fishing's good, if he doesn't do too much painting the town red. I don't understand.

'The town? Red?'

He laughs, and Jesús does too.

'It means going out to get drunk.'

I wouldn't mind going myself, to paint the town red. He can tell, and promises to take me, as soon as we're back from fishing. Then he gives me a wad of tobacco.

'Here, put it like this ... against your gum.'

I'm happy. I daren't spit so I swallow. It burns my stomach. You get nothing for nothing, I think.

Jesús walks me back in the evening. I'm frightened of the sea, he tells me, but I have to go fishing because my wife's having a baby. You don't earn enough at the canneries. And I really want to get out of the mobile home we share with a bunch of other people. Find an apartment just for the two of us and the baby.

'I'm not afraid of dying at sea,' I say.

'Don't say that, you shouldn't talk like that, you must never say things like that.'

I think I've terrified him.

Ian, the lanky man, has invited me to his place, a house on the outskirts of town, lost in dark woods. The others exchange funny looks: they think the skipper's going to get lucky this evening. His wife no longer lives with him, she was too bored in Alaska, she lives with their children in the sun, in Arizona. He'll join them after the fishing season, when the house is sold. It's already almost empty: there are just a few mattresses left in deserted bedrooms, a large red armchair – his armchair – facing a television set, a stove and a fridge, from which he takes two enormous steaks.

'Eat, little sparrow, you'll never make it otherwise.'

I leave three-quarters of my portion. He sends me back to the fridge of wonders where I find all sorts of ice creams. I lie on my corner of floor and look out of the window. Night over Alaska – and here I am, I think – with the wind, and the birds in the trees. Oh let it last, don't let Immigration ever catch up with me.

Every evening my skipper rents a film to watch while we eat – steak for him, ice cream for me. He's ensconced in his handsome red armchair, I sit on my mattress surrounded by cushions. Ian tells me stories, talking so much he doesn't seem to breathe, carried away by what he's saying, his face glowing. He has the long, sad face of a wronged teenager, but it comes alive and lights up at a remembered image or gesture. And then he laughs. He tells me about the beautiful boats he's skippered, a very pretty one called the *Tenacity* that went down in huge seas in February, on the Bering Sea, off the Pribilof Islands, but not one of his men was lost. She went down because they were too heavily laden with crab (too heavily laden with crab or cocaine? Opinion is still divided in town). He laughs at himself, his lack of experience, before he'd joined Alcoholics Anonymous, when he drank so much he'd be dragged out of bars, often by the feet.

Days go by. The work is relentless. Sometimes Wolf and I go for lunch in Safeway, the big local supermarket. On the way back he talks some more about the boat he'll have one day. He's serious, not smiling now. He asks me to come on board as crew.

'Yes, maybe, if you don't hate me after the season,' I say.

He also tells me about a girlfriend he loved and how she left him in the end. He's had trouble sleeping ever since, he adds sadly.

'All that wasted time,' he says.

'Yes,' I reply.

Then he spits out his tobacco and says in a brighter voice, 'You'll need a fishing licence to work on board. That's the law, there are frequent checks and the troopers won't ever let you get away with anything.'

That evening we go into town together, to the hunting and fishing shop. The salesman hands me a form. He doesn't seem to notice Wolf whispering to me, telling me my height in feet and inches, and a social security number he's just dreamed up. I put a cross in the box marked 'resident'. The man hands me my card.

'There you are, you're all set. That's thirty dollars.'

We go down to the harbour and walk along the waterfront to the B and B. The stark panes of glass reflect the sky over the harbour. One of them is still cracked. A man is standing at the top of the steps, his hefty arms cradled around his torso, broad chest, pot belly, waders rolled down to his calves, a felt Stetson pushed down over his red hair. His belt buckle gleams. He greets us with a nod, grimaces a smile with his cigarette between his lips, steps aside to let us pass.

'It stands for Beer and Booze,' Wolf tells me as he opens the door.

Men are sitting with their backs to us, elbows on the wooden bar, heads slouched between their shoulders. We find a couple of stools. The waitress is singing as we come in, a strong clear voice rising above the cigarette smoke. Her heavy black hair falls almost to her waist. She makes quite a show of slewing the dark weight of it over her back as she turns around. Then she comes towards us, swinging her hips.

'Hi, Joy,' says Wolf. 'We'll have two beers.'

A big man has come over to Wolf. He's holding a glass of spirits, vodka perhaps.

'This is Karl, the Dane,' Wolf tells me and then turns to him and says, 'and this is Lili.'

Karl has yellow hair hastily tied into a stiff little ponytail, a big face marbled with red and heavy eyelids filtering the liquid blue of his Viking eyes.

'We're heading back out tomorrow. If everything's OK,' he says between two clicks of his tongue, his glass hovering at his lips. 'We're ready. The fishing should be good, if the gods are willing.'

Wolf nods. My beer glass is empty. In the shadows at the corner of the bar a red-haired woman drains her glass. She stands, goes round to the back of the counter and comes over to us. The waitress with the black hair takes her seat.

'Thanks, Joy,' says Wolf. 'Same again with a little schnapps to go with it.'

'Are they all called Joy?' I ask quietly when she moves away.

'No, not all. The first one's Joy the Indian, this is Joy the Redhead, and there's another one, Big Joy, she's a very heavy lady.'

'Aha,' I say.

'And when the three Joys go out drinking together, men steer well clear. They can go off for five days in a row when they're on a bender. And they don't take any prisoners.'

Karl's tired. He finishes his drink, asks for another. Stands a round. Joy the Redhead puts a wooden counter next to my still-full glass.

'I met a guy this evening,' Karl drawls wearily, 'just back from the South Pacific, he was fishing for shrimp. They work in shorts and T-shirts out there. Shorts, did you hear that? And he comes here for cod! They don't know a thing, these little bastards. Working on the edge, they've never experienced it – working on the edge, that's us, that's just us, the North Pacific in winter, ice on the boat you have to break up with a baseball bat, and boats going down. We're the only ones who know that!'

He gives a thunderous roar of laughter, choking briefly before calming down, then his face breaks into a beatific smile and his eyes glaze over.

'So who's this little thing?' he asks, remembering me.

'We work together,' says Wolf. 'She's crewing on the *Rebel* for the black cod season. She doesn't really look it but she's tough.'

Karl gets to his feet unsteadily, puts two huge arms round my shoulders.

'Welcome to Kodiak,' he says.

Wolf pushes him away gently.

'We're off now. Don't forget your wooden nickel, Lili. Keep it in your pocket, you're entitled to a drink with that. There isn't a man in the world better than him,' Wolf says as we go outside, 'but I didn't want him to scare you. And don't let anyone touch you, that's respect.'

It's dark outside now. We move to another even darker bar, the Ship. In the back room men play snooker on dilapidated tables under the white glare of old neon lights. A fat girl pulls on a bell rope as we walk in, and the men cheer.

'We came at the right time,' says Wolf. 'A round for the whole house.'

We find ourselves some space in the scrum. Wolf is waking up, his eyes get brighter, his jaw tighter, his teeth gleaming in the half-light, two white canines.

'This is the last frontier,' he says in a half-whisper.

The waitress serves us two small glasses of colourless liquid.

'It's my own,' she says.

Her red lipstick has bled into the fine lines above her upper lip, the blue eyeshadow on her crinkly eyelids leaps out from her wide white face with its heavy, tired features.

'I'm Vicky,' she says when Wolf introduces me. Then she adds, 'This is a tough place. They're not all angels dragging their boots around here. Watch out for yourself – if you have trouble, I'm here.'

We drink three glasses. Then we leave the dark bar: the friendly waitress, the rowdy men, the pictures of naked women above the snooker tables, their silky rounded haunches seeming to protrude from the dirty walls, the old Native women, drunk maybe, impassive, sitting in a line at the end of the bar, the semblance of a smile occasionally playing on the aloof set of their mouths.

At Breaker's I'm asked for ID. I take out my fishing licence, but the waitress scowls.

'Need a picture.'

I dig out my passport.

'You now have the right to get drunk,' says Wolf.

'You know, if I'm lucky the boat will go down,' I tell Ian one evening, 'and you'll all get out safely, except for me.' Because I keep remembering Manosque-les-Sorrow, every day and every night. I don't want it to get me.

'You don't have to die. Just stay in Alaska.'

'Someone's waiting for me.'

'Don't go,' he says. 'I'd like to take the *Rebel* for the crab season on the Bering Sea this winter, I don't have my crew yet. If you prove yourself I could hire you.'

'You'd hire me to go crab fishing?'

'It'll be very tough. The cold, the lack of sleep, working twenty hours a day or more ... dangerous too. When rough seas hit and you got a thirty-foot sea, fog that confuses even the radars and then you risk running onto rocks, blocks of ice or another ship. But I think you'll make it. You'll love it, even, love it enough to accept the risk of dying.'

'Oh yes,' I murmur.

The tall black pines moan outside. Ian's gone to bed upstairs and I fall asleep on the floor with the wind whistling in from the sea. I'm always first to wake, when the sky's still dark over the trees. I get up and roll up my sleeping bag, then make coffee and fill a red thermos with it. I tiptoe upstairs, open the door to the bedroom where Ian sleeps, a bare room with a mattress on the floor. I don't like waking him, but when I put the thermos by his bed, he opens one dark eye. I slip away.

'I'm going to show you something I think you'll like, an old film that a crew member left on the boat. He made it himself when he was fishing on the *Cougar*. It's not exactly top quality but it'll still give you an idea of what crab fishing's like in bad weather. Well, bad weather ...'

The house is quiet, the wind has dropped. Ian takes an old DVD from a cardboard box and puts it into the player. Every now and then a branch rubbing against the roof makes a sound like wing beats, the furtive slither of a bird blown off-course. Ian turns out the light and sits back down in his red armchair; I hug my knees to my chest. We stare at the screen in the dark: at first there are only streaks of white that hurt our eyes, then the roll of the black ocean, the slow rhythm of the swell. The horizon pitches violently and we see the rail and the shining decks with sprays of water spattering over them. Droplets splash onto the lens. It's night-time. Faceless men move in the glare of sodium lights, dark shapes only partially lit up thanks to their orange rain gear. A streaming crab pot looms out of the water, and because the boat and these men are surrounded by dark foreboding depths, it looks like a monster from the abyss. The water opens and closes like a voracious mouth. The pot is raised into a ravaged sky, hanging from a cable, swinging heavily. The blunt mass of it appears to hover a moment before coming down, swaying between the deck and the water. Two men at the rail, slight supple figures, guide it towards a steel support that they've just raised into position. The crabs spew out of its gaping jaws, seething when a crewman lifts open the door and tips them into a tub, his body half inside the pot. He's holding a box of bait, unhooks the old one, slings it onto the deck, attaches the new one, comes back out, flips the door shut, the men at the rail retie the straps, and the crane is hoisted up until the pot tips overboard. The whole thing lasts less than a minute.

There's an intangible cadence and rhythm to this dark, silent, almost flowing choreography. Yes, that's it, the men are dancing on the wave-pummelled deck. Each knows his place and the part he plays. One steps aside with a lithe entrechat to avoid being struck by the pot, another leaps; their legs are springs, their bodies instinctually know how to guide this brainless force, this threatening pot, a black entity that has reared up from the depths, its eight hundred blind, brutal pounds swinging across the opaque sky. And all around them, the magma of the ocean keeps up its swell.

The scene changes, I've almost stopped breathing. It's now daytime, the sea is calm and the boat surrounded by pure light, blue light, beaming from the horizon. The bow ploughs through fragments of ice.

'This was more dangerous than the weather before,' Ian says, making me jump. 'The *Cougar* lost ten crab pots that day because they got caught in the frozen seas.'

'Yes,' I say, exhaling, 'yes ...'

'And it was cold too, very cold, the whole boat was covered in frozen sea spray, pots, rails, wheelhouse, a crust of it getting thicker and thicker. The *Cougar* swollen with ice, unrecognisable.'

I catch sight of a face so flushed it looks burned, a bushy beard on which condensation or phlegm has turned to ice. The film ends with the dark waves rolling against a black background. It feels as if the whole story will start again: the men on deck, the steel monster opening its jaws to reveal seething crabs, the ocean ... But the screen's suddenly empty.

We sit in silence. Then Ian gets up to put the light back on, stretches and yawns.

'Did you like it?'

'What if I made out I was dead?' I ask him the following evening. 'You write to France, tell them I drowned.'

He frowns, he's had enough of my ideas.

'Don't you see how much pain that would cause?'

'Oh, well, a bit, of course. They'd cry, they'd think it must have been very cold when I went in, and then one fine day they'd be OK. They'd say I kind of had it coming. I'd have given them an adventurous death, and at least I'd be sorted, they could stop worrying about me. No one would ever expect me back.'

He doesn't even want to hear any more of this. He tells me I'm a coward and goes off to bed. I lie down on my mattress, laughing to myself. Maybe Immigration won't get me.

Wolf leaves, the young sea wolf. He puts a hand on my shoulder and I look away.

'I'm off to Dutch Harbor,' he says. 'I'm going to find myself a different boat. Somewhere else.'

He smiles at me kindly.

'You're on a good boat,' he adds, but then his face hardens. 'I didn't like what the skipper said when I was measuring the line, claiming my arm-span wouldn't make a fathom. He did it deliberately, making a jackass of me in front of the others. I won't forgive that. I'm a good fisherman, I have more longlining experience than him. I need to get out.'

These last words were spat out furiously through clamped jaws.

'Yes,' I reply.

He gives a short sad laugh and his eyes gaze off into the distance as if he's already left the land behind.

'Here one day, there the next,' he says more softly. 'You never know where you'll be tomorrow. Leaving doesn't matter, you know, it's what life wants for us. You always have to make a break for it. When you gotta go, you gotta go. But we'll paint the town red again next time we meet. In three months, ten months or twenty years, it's all the same. In the meantime you take care. Take care of yourself.'

One last hug. He picks up his bag and slings it across his shoulders. I watch him disappear along the road, a strange figure swallowed in the mist.

The house is sold. The lanky man is going off to fetch the *Rebel*, which is being serviced in a boatyard on the neighbouring island.

'She's the most beautiful, you'll see,' he tells me the evening before he sets out. 'I'll be back in two days. Till then you can sleep on the *Blue Beauty*. It's our owner Andy's favourite boat, he's going to run it for the cod season. I'll take you there tomorrow before I catch the ferry to Homer.'

The harbour's deserted. Ice-white birds sweep across the sky and a tug heads in through the first line of buoys. Still far away, its engine's thrum is barely audible. I have a handsome pair of boots found at the Salvation Army, old black ones, not like the real ones that are green and expensive. My footsteps resound on the wooden pontoon.

'Careful, you'll slip with the crap you've got on your feet.'

I protest and almost fall. He just manages to catch me.

'You're going to earn a whole bunch of cash, you can buy all the boots you want.'

'Oh, I just ... Just need enough to buy a good sleeping bag, some walking shoes, and have something left over to see me through to Point Barrow.'

'Point Barrow? *Now* what are you talking about?'

'I'm going to Point Barrow when the season's over.'

'What the hell do you want to do there?'

I don't answer. A young seagull on the rail of a seiner watches us walk past.

'Do you think I'll make a good fisherman?' I ask.

'We see them every day, people coming from deep in the States, they've only ever seen woods, wide-open prairies or mountains, and they give everything up to come here. Guys or girls who've been sales reps, truck drivers or farmhands. Maybe even call girls, what do I know. They all come aboard. They get treated like shit when they're green, when they don't know anything about anything, and then one day they have their own boat.'

'I'll be needing a real sailor's bag then, like the others.'

'For sure. I can picture you already, duffel bag on your shoulder, walking the docks from Kodiak to Dutch to find a boat.'

On our left is a sky-blue boat, the *Blue Beauty*. The deck's deserted and construction work is still going on: sheets of aluminium that will form the awning, with metal uprights on either side. We climb aboard, there's a smell of wet rubber and diesel. Ian throws my bag onto a bunk in a dark cubbyhole, the crew's sleeping cabin. When we come back out, I climb over the rail and Ian wants to help me step down onto the dock. I shake him off with a flick of my elbow. I'll be a real fisherman soon, I already have my bunk and I chew tobacco.

The *Rebel* comes into harbour. She really is the most beautiful, the lanky man was right. The black steel hull has a dazzling yellow stripe around it. The wheelhouse is white. I'm the first crew member to visit, after Jesse the grease-monkey who came back with her, and Simon, a young, blond-haired student – just arrived from California – who'd been looking for a crewing job along the docks in Homer. The skipper's settled himself in the deep chair in the wheelhouse, facing the multitude of dials. The semicircular row of windows gives us a view over the whole harbour.

'This is my seat from now on,' says Ian, 'but you guys will get to share it when you're on watch.'

The engine's running, it won't stop now for several weeks. I watch the harbour come to life. I've moved my stuff into the cramped space, the crew's cabin, on the first of four bunk-beds.

'First come, first served,' says the skipper who said I was welcome to sleep in his bunk, because he has his own cabin. I declined.

I've been given a blue bike, a rusty old bike that's too small for me. It has the words *FREE SPIRIT* on it. I ride across town, crimson-cheeked, in rain gear that's more orange than orange, more orange than all the real rain gear out at sea. People laugh as I go past, and I pedal from the boat to the workshop, the workshop to the boat. Rain trickles over my face and down my neck. I run across to the boat, climb down the ladder four rungs at a time, grab hold of the handrail, the grey-green water below me. The skipper's worried, he reaches out an arm – he can't help himself – but manages to withdraw it with a gulp.

'I haven't fallen yet,' I laugh, eyeballing him. 'I'm invincible.'

He looks away quickly.

'You'll die just like everyone else,' he says with a shrug.

'Yes. Right up until I die, I'm invincible.'

I get up at first light and jump down from my bunk. It's calling me: the outside, the whiff of seaweed and shells, the crows on deck, the eagles on the mast, the seagulls' cries over the smooth waters in the harbour. I make coffee for the two men, then head out and run along the docks. The streets are deserted but I'm out there meeting the new day, reacquainting myself with yesterday's world. The night concealed it, then handed it back. I return to the boat out of breath to find Jesse and Ian just stirring. The other crew members will be here soon. I drink coffee with these two, but they're so slow. My foot twitches under the table. I could weep with impatience. Waiting is painful.

The whole harbour has gone to work. The radio is on full blast on the cluttered decks, country songs mingling with Tina Turner's husky voice. We've started baiting the lines. There are constant comings and goings along the docks. We haul aboard cases of frozen squid and herring that we'll use as bait. Students who've travelled far and are hoping to find a boat come looking for a day's work.

'We're full up,' says the lanky man.

Simon the student studies us all coolly but his eyes light up with panic at the first bark of anger from the skipper. Jesús's cousin Luis will be joining us. And David, a crab fisherman who surveys us from his lofty six foot three, his great shoulders spread wide. He grins broadly to reveal regular white teeth.

We spend days on end baiting, standing at a table at the back of the deck. Jesús and I laugh about everything.

'Stop being so childish,' John says irritably.

The lion man arrives. He climbs aboard one morning accompanied by the lanky man. He hides his face in a dirty mane of hair. The skipper's proud of his man.

'This is Jude,' he says, 'an experienced longliner.'

A big drinker too perhaps, I think when he walks past me. This tired lion is on the shy side. He sets to work without a word and later succumbs to a violent coughing fit when he lights a cigarette. He spits on the ground and I catch glimpses of his face obscured by a beard. Piercing gold eyes. I avoid his tawny gaze. I'm not laughing with Jesús now but making myself small, unobtrusive. He belongs here. I don't.

Late in the evening the guys go home but Jude stays on board. There are just three of us left on deck. We need to take the tubs of baited lines to the freezer in the factory. We load the tubs into the back of the truck and tie them down securely. I step aside as soon as Jude comes over. He frowns. We drive through the evening air to the canning factory. Sitting between the two men, I look out at the sea and the straight road between bare hills. We're heading towards the open sky. The skipper changes gear with the tips of his fingers to avoid brushing me with his hand, I huddle further to the right. I can feel the lion man's thigh next to mine. My throat constricts.

23

We unload the gear. The tubs are ice-cold and heavy.

'Tough girl,' Jude says.

'Yes, not much of her but she's strong,' Ian replies.

I stand taller. We work in a chain, passing the tubs along into the freezing cold room. Our fingers stick to the metal. It's late when we drive away, and as the truck trundles through the night the hills are swallowed up by darkness. Only the sea is still there. The two men talk about putting to sea. I stay silent. I'm aware of aches all over my body, of hunger, the warmth of Jude's thigh, the smell of his tobacco, and of our damp clothes with scraps of squid still stuck to them.

We follow the coastline. A few trawlers are asleep against the dock where we usually fill up with fuel. We drive on past their dark slumbers. Up ahead the horizon is dotted with rings of reddish light pulsating in the inky sky.

'Is that the Northern Lights?' I ask.

They don't understand. I say it several times. The lion laughs quietly, a husky muted rumbling.

'She said Northern Lights!'

The skipper laughs too.

'No, it's just the sky.'

I've flushed redder than those lights whose name I'll never know. I wish this could go on forever, travelling through the darkness between the lanky man and the burned-out lion.

'Drop me at the Shelikof,' Jude says when we come into town.

He's leaving us to go off to a tavern already. Ian doesn't hold it against him.

'I think he drinks quite a lot,' he says, 'but he's the man we need.'

We go back to the boat. It's warm on board. Jesse's smoking a joint in the engine room.

Adam is a crew member on the *Blue Beauty*, moored alongside us. I hear him joking with Dave.

'Yeah, and when your hands hurt so much you can't even sleep for the three hours you've been given. And when you're on watch and you see buoys all over the place – you can rub your eyes as much as you like, those buoys just keep popping up.'

They laugh.

'Do you think I'll make it?' I ask Adam.

'Keep working the way you are and that'll do.'

But another time he warns me to watch out for danger.

'What exactly should I be worried about?'

'Everything. Lines hurtling into the water so fast they take you with them if you get a foot or an arm caught up, and the ones we haul back in that could kill you or maim you if they break. Hooks that get caught in the reel and are flung out at random, bad weather and miscalculated reefs, a crew member who falls asleep on watch, falling into the water, a wave that sweeps you away, the cold that can kill you . . .'

He stops. His washed-out eyes look sad and weary. His features are losing their shape, sagging.

'Coming on board is like being married to the boat for as long as you work on her. You don't have a life, or anything of your own no more. You have to obey the skipper. Even if he's a dick.' He sighs, then shakes his head as he goes on. 'I don't know why I came, I don't know what makes us want to suffer that much. And for what? Nothing, at the end of the day. Never enough of anything – sleep, heat, or love either, till you can't take any more, till you hate the job, and then in spite of everything you come back for more because the rest of the world feels bland, it's so boring it drives you crazy. In the end you can't get by without this, the intoxication of it, the danger, the madness – yup!' He's almost roaring now but calms himself. 'You know, there are campaigns these days to discourage young people from fishing.'

'Because they won't find work?'

'Mainly because it's dangerous.'

He looks away, stares into the distance. His thin hair flitters in a gust of wind. The corners of his mouth have a bitter, downturned twist. A dreamy gentleness softens his features as he gazes blankly ahead and adds, 'But this time it's over . . . it's really over. I have a little house on the

Kenai Peninsula, in the forest, near Seward. I should earn enough with this cod season to go back there. And to stay for good this time. I'll be there before the winter. I want to build a second house. I'm never setting foot here again. I've given enough of my life to it. Come and see me in the woods one day when you're tired,' he says, turning to look at me.

He goes back to baiting the hooks. Dave and I exchange a look.

'He always says that,' Dave says, nodding. 'Then he comes back.'

'Why does he come back?'

'All alone in the woods. Time goes slowly after a while. What Adam needs is a woman.'

'There aren't many around here.'

'No, not any more,' he laughs. 'But when he's fishing he doesn't have time to think about that. And so many of them are on their own here that it doesn't feel as bad.'

'And does he go to the bars when he's ashore?'

'He's had his fair share of drink – he quit two years ago. Alcoholics Anonymous. Like Ian, our skipper.'

'That's not much fun, then,' I murmur.

'And soon they'll all be after you, all these single men. The hunt will be on,' he winks at me. 'Except for me. I can't now. I have a girl-friend, I don't want to lose her.'

The lanky man's driving the truck and talking like an excited child. I listen and keep saying, Yes, oh yes. When he parks up facing the docks, by the B and B, we get out and head to the boat, and I just come out with, 'Let's get drunk, man,' those exact words, in English. I'm learning the language quickly. He spins round in amazement, as if he doesn't recognise me.

'Oh, I didn't mean it, I was just joking,' I gabble, shrugging.

One day he says he loves me and gives me a bit of mammoth tusk that he's had for a very long time.

'Oh, thank you,' I say.

★

We move the *Rebel* to the docks next to the factories and lug on board the tubs and stocks of frozen squid. We've filled up with water and ice. I stare wide-eyed at the mountain of provisions, dozens of boxes delivered right to the pontoon by Safeway. The guys bring their gear aboard.

'But there are only six bunks ... there are nine of us,' I say to the Skipper.

'The boat's big enough for all of us.'

I don't pursue it. He shouts the whole time at the moment.

We leave Kodiak on a Friday. Never leave on Friday, they say. But the lanky man sneers, he's not superstitious. Jesse, the mechanic, laughs too.

'It's like green boats,' he says, 'hokum.'

Still, on the dock earlier Adam warned me, 'Superstition's ridiculous, I'm OK with that, but I've seen too many green boats drift towards the shore when no one could explain why, and they hit a rock and go down to the bottom with the whole crew on board. You see, green's the colour of trees and grass, it's gonna draw you back to land. And leaving on a Friday's not good either. *We*'ll be waiting till one minute past midnight.'

The men whoop as they untie the mooring lines. My throat feels tight. Whatever happens don't get in the way. I make myself scarce and finish lining up the tubs on deck. Simon's running around with his eyes popping out of his head. He doesn't understand anything either. He barges past me, almost falls onto the deck as he labours up the metal ladder to the gangway with a rope as thick as his wrist rolled up over his shoulder. I coil up the mooring line that Dave threw down when he untied the bow. The skipper bellows. Even so I brace myself and try to drag the hawser God knows where, to the crate on the flying bridge perhaps. It's too heavy. Ian bellows again.

'I can't do it, I don't understand,' I stammer.

He softens.

'Well, tie it up behind the wheelhouse.'

I feel like laughing, or crying. We leave land at last, and I already know I'll never be the same again. The boat heads due south, hugging the coast before turning west.

The lion's gone to bed and is already asleep. Jesús goes to lie down too.

'They're right,' says Dave, appearing from the wheelhouse, 'have to sleep as much as you can, you never know what's coming next.'

But when I go down to the cabin the four bunks are taken. My sleeping bag's been dumped on the floor. John's snoring on my bunk. I go up on deck and find Simon looking out to sea. He turns a glowing, awed face towards me.

'So here I am on the ocean,' he murmurs.

'They've taken my bunk,' I say.

'I don't have one either.'

I go back below deck. I pick up my sleeping bag and kneel down in a corner of the passageway. The lion man has woken. He sits up and runs three fingers through his stiff curls. His eyes come to rest on me.

'Where am I going to sleep?' I ask feebly, clutching my sleeping bag.

He looks at me kindly.

'I don't know,' he says gently.

I get to my feet and go up to see the skipper, the lanky man sitting at his banks of dials. I still have my sleeping bag in my arms, hugging it to me.

'Where am I going to sleep? You said it was first come, first served, and I really was first, you said that was the law on boats.'

I don't say any more. He's gazing into the distance. The sky is darkening over the mountains of Ketchikan in the west.

'I don't know where you'll sleep,' he says eventually, his voice quiet. 'I did offer you my cabin, you didn't want that. But there's room on the boat. Given how little we'll be sleeping, anyway . . . Leave your sleeping bag behind my chair if you like.'

I stow it there and climb back down from the wheelhouse. Luis is lying on the bench seat in the galley. I join Simon back on deck. He offers me a cigarette and we watch the sea in silence. The wind picks up as we get further from land. The coast is already just a dark strip, growing ever smaller. The *Rebel* hits some swell and starts listing slightly. The colour drains from Simon's face. We go down to the galley and Luis makes room for us on the bench seat. It's night outside. We sit waiting under the neon light.

The guys wake up and we all have to try on our survival suits. Jude has made a meal and takes a laden plateful of pasta up to the skipper, who hasn't left the helm. They come back down together.

'Take the helm for a moment, Dave?' he asks and pours himself some coffee.

'This evening, boys, sleep,' he says, his words curt. 'You're going to need your strength. Up and out at five tomorrow.'

He turns to Jude and says, 'Dave will take the first watch. You take over two hours later. Never more than two-hour watches, there are enough of us. Jesús will be after you. Then Jesse. The others sleep. They'll get their shifts later. Wake me if there's anything at all … we're on autopilot, unless there's an incident. Stay at least 2 miles from the coast at all times. Don't forget to check over the engine room at the end of your watch, to make sure the auxiliary engine's working OK and to grease the shaft. It's likely to go on getting rougher, have a look at the deck from time to time, the tubs are well secured, but just to be on the safe side.'

'OK.'

Jude looks down and clears away the remains of the meal without another word. Jesús stands up, thanks him, and pushes up his sleeves over the small metal sink. I join him there but I don't have my sea legs yet and there's a lot of swell.

'Thanks for the meal, it was very good,' I tell Jude on my way past.

'Yup,' he replies.

John gets up too.

'Thanks, Jude.'

I help Jesús wash up.

'Whoever makes a meal always eats last, that's the rule,' he tells me quietly, 'but he doesn't do the washing-up, ever, and we always thank him. Well, normally. Sometimes you do your watch, then you make grub for everyone who's still asleep, then you go back to the helm and when you get down again no one's left you anything and you have to get straight back on deck.'

'They've taken my bunk,' I say.

'That's not good, what John did wasn't right. You need to stand up for yourself. You're very green at the moment.'

The boys have gone back to the cabin to sleep. Dave lends me his bunk and wakes me gently two hours later.

'My turn.'

I get up and almost fall over: I'm half asleep and the cabin's cluttered with clothes and boots. The engine rumbles, the boat's rolling dramatically. I totter along the passageway with my sleeping bag in my arms. The galley is still lit by its pasty neon. Luis is asleep on the bench seat and I lie down at the other end, wrapping myself in my sleeping bag, my cocoon, my lair on this screaming boat. Morning finds Luis, Simon and me sleeping huddled together on the floor of the wheelhouse, under the dispassionate eye of Jesse on watch.

We're fishing at last. Daybreak was before five. Daylight: a grey dawn, a murky leaden sky overhead. A glimmer of sunlight might just be making a pale breach in the mist. And all around us ocean as far as the eye can see. It's cold. Simon has thrown out the marker from the upper deck, then the buoy. The line unwinds as we move away from them. Dave tosses over an anchor. The first longlines slip into the water to a roar from the accelerating engine, and wheeling seagulls try to grab our bait before it disappears under the waves. I bring the tubs to Jude who ties together the ends of the lines one after the other. The wind whistles in our ears. He slams the empty tubs onto the deck and I immediately clear them away. My heart beats frantically. The men shout, making a catastrophic racket. Jude stands facing the churning waters, braced on his sturdy thighs, back arched, his whole body straining to match the urgency of the situation, jaw hard, clamped, eyes locked onto the demented beast of unspooling line, a marine monster bristling with thousands of hooks. Occasionally a hook gets caught in the gunwale and the line tautens dangerously. In a flash he grabs a pole mounted with a knife.

'Stand clear!' he yells, and cuts the gangion connecting the hook to the line.

'Last tub!' he roars to let the skipper know, and Ian always hears him despite the cacophony of men and machinery. With the bare buoy line still unwinding Dave drops an anchor and the line keeps feeding out till it comes to the last buoy and marker. The boat slows. The tension gripping us instantly falls away. A volley of laughter. I catch my breath. Jude lights a cigarette. He seems to notice us again. He says something funny to Dave who turns towards me.

'You OK?'

'Yes,' I whisper.

I haven't recovered yet. My throat constricted, I line up the tubs. I didn't understand what was going on at all. The men's shouting terrified me. Jesús is smiling broadly.

'It'll come,' he says.

While I run the hose over the deck the skipper appears.

'And now, boys, we're fishing. Go have a coffee, we're all set!'

Someone found me some boots that were knocking about on board. Real ones this time. They're very big and there's a hole in the crease at the ankle so I'm taking on water. It's cold. They've also found me rain gear – waders and a jacket – that's bigger and tougher than my clownish version.

I head up to the wheelhouse with my coffee. I meet Jesse on the way and flatten myself against the wall as he barges past me. The lanky man is leaning back nonchalantly in his captain's chair.

'Is it going OK, little sparrow?'

'Yes. When will I have my own watch like the others?'

'Have to talk to Jesse about that.'

'When?'

'Soon as you can corner him.'

★

31

The sky's dense, we're clothed in mist. The men have put out stabiliser fins on either side of the boat, like the skeletal remains of iron wings, to stop her from rolling so dramatically. The *Rebel* hovers peculiarly, an overweight bird that can't take flight, skimming the heaving waters. Heavy waves rear up, the boat wants to pitch over and for a moment hangs suspended on the crest before dropping down into the greenish trough beyond. Thin, tightly packed raindrops fall in diagonal curtains. We head back out into the cold. Without a word we put on our rain gear and rubber gloves, and buckle our belts. Ian is on edge, Dave's stopped smiling, Jesús and Luis look grey under their tans. Jesse is sharpening his knife. I make eye contact with them but they don't see me. Simon is clinging to a pile of crates, ready to jump into action as soon as the cry goes up. His eyes communicate the same fear that's knotting my stomach.

The skipper has taken up his position in the recess of the fo'c'sle, against the bulwark. With his hands on the engine control levers, he increases the throttle when he catches sight of the buoy. The boat turns, he slows her, trying to find the best course, taking into account the drift. Jude has reached out a boathook, he catches the buoy marker and hauls it on board.

'Pull!'

And everyone has to grab hold of the buoy line. It's extraordinarily taut. Ian slows further, noses forward, positions himself ahead of the longline, and the line slackens. Dave hauls it into the groove of the hydraulic reel. The men howl. The skipper yells, 'Untie the buoy and the marker! Quick!' The hydraulic engine starts turning. We catch our breath. The line comes up steadily. Ian increases our speed. Jude coils. I pass an empty tub along to him once the whole of a longline has come aboard. I quickly untie the line from the next. With the boat rolling violently, I take the full tub away. It's very heavy, weighed down with water and old bait. Jesús and Luis are cutting up squid at the stern. The roar from the engines and the swell is deafening. The wind thrums in our ears. The men fall silent. Ian's face darkens. The empty hooks coming aboard dangle forlornly. Every now and then, a small cod twitches on the end of one and slithers onto the cutting table. Jesse opens its belly with his exquisitely sharpened knife. He guts it angrily and lobs it to the end of the table, into the hatch down to the hold. Several hours like this. When the end marker finally appears, the skipper hurls down his gloves, pulls off his overalls, and leaves the bridge without uttering a word.

We hose down. Clear the deck. The boat has picked up speed with a jolt of fury. Jude lights a cigarette. Dave smiles at me.

'Not great, huh?'

We go back to baiting hooks, for a long time, a very long time, then throw the lines into the sea again, baiting others until we bring the first ones back on board, and so on, endlessly.

And then there's no day or night, simply hours trickling by, the sky darkening, darkness spreading over the ocean, lights having to be lit on the bridge. Sleeping ... Occasionally we eat. Breakfast at four in the afternoon, lunch at eleven in the evening. I gobble it down. Sausages swimming in fat, baked beans with too much sugar, claggy rice, I feel every mouthful could save my life. The men laugh.

'She can really put it away!'

We hit a bank of black cod on the third night. The sea is no calmer. Simon and I are still losing our balance, struggling to stay upright, then slamming into the corners of crates, to the exasperation of the other men. We pick ourselves up without a word, as if caught committing an offence. But we won't have time for that this evening. The first longline comes aboard and it's like a great tide of fish spilling towards us in an almost uninterrupted stream. The men whoop for joy.

'Look, Lili, dollars, all these are dollars!' cries Jesse, grasping my shoulder.

But they're not dollars, they're proper live fish ... beautiful creatures snatching at the air with their gaping mouths, thrashing wildly on the white flash of aluminium, blinded by neon lights, repeatedly battering up against this harsh world, its every contour sharp, its every sensation painful. No, not dollars, not yet.

33

We need to work fast, the table's already covered with them. I'm given a knife. Simon nudges in between John and me. Jesse runs back over, brandishing the knife he's been sharpening, carrying it blade first as the boat pitches. I catch Jude's eye: there's a flash of cold anger at the sight of this irresponsible little man, an imperceptible raise of his eyebrows. Blood spurts, the black bodies quiver and writhe.

It's late into the night. Our exhaustion has evaporated in the excitement of urgent work. Jude chops heads off still-living cod, then slices open their bellies. Simon and I gut them. They flail and squirm when we scrape out their body cavities with a spoon. It makes a rasping sound I can feel right inside my marrow. The fish are thrown into the hold at a never slackening pace. Jesse smiles savagely. Dollars, dollars ... he keeps muttering like a halfwit. John is detached, slightly disgusted. Jude works with his jaws clamped shut, his forehead resolutely tilted downward, ignoring Jesse's monologue. He's the fastest. His powerful hands slice, slash, rip. It frightens me. My eyes slide furtively from his heavy hands to his huge, impassive face. Now I'm not so frightened. My muscles are stiff, my shoulders burning. Then I just stop feeling them.

The skipper yells. Startled, I look from one man to the next, they're shouting at me, something I don't understand. Simon takes the initiative, quickly dragging away the full tub and handing an empty one to Dave who's coiling up the lines.

'You need eyes in the back of your head!'

I quash my tears. The lion glowers at me angrily, giving me a piercing look which paralyses me. Simon comes back to work next to me. I can tell he's secretly proud. He delves his spoon into a gaping belly and scrapes furiously, apparently gripped by some sort of rage. What exactly is he avenging? Or who? I keep an eye out to be sure I change the tub in good time. Simon's watching too. I move before him and push past him if he stands in my way, snatch the load from him when he's quicker than me. It's my work, my job, mine. I need to fight my corner if I want to keep my place on board.

My feet are freezing. Blood-streaked water is soaking into my sleeves. Our rain gear is covered in guts. I'm hungry. I surreptitiously swallow the pouch of roe from the fish I've just opened. Taste of the sea. It's sweet and melts on the tongue. A few strands of dirty hair have escaped from under my woollen hat, I brush them aside with the back of my sleeve. They stick to my forehead. I bring another opalescent pouch up to my mouth. Dave catches me at it.

'Lili!' he exclaims, horrified. 'Are you crazy?'

The men look up.

'She's eating this stuff!'

Grimaces of disgust. I look away, crimson under my mask of blood.

The last longline comes aboard. I totter, falling asleep on my feet. At last the anchor comes up, then the buoy and flag. Ian turns to us before going back to the wheelhouse.

'Let's do it again, boys. Send the gear back out!'

Everyone's back in position. I draw on all my strength and all my anger. I grab the tubs more vigorously, with fierce new energy. Something inside me wakes, a violent urge to stand up to this, to fight ever harder, against the cold and exhaustion, to conquer the limits of this small body. Go beyond them. The longlines spool out over the transom, against the paling sky. The last marker is thrown out. Day is about to break. The horizon is tinted with a long strip of red. Quick hose down of the deck.

'Rest,' says the skipper.

We hose each other with icy water to rinse off our rain gear. We're so tired we feel almost drunk. The men make estimates of the haul.

'Twelve thousand pounds? Fifteen?'

'You can die from eating raw fish,' Dave scolds me gently.

'I was hungry,' I protest in a feeble, apologetic voice.

'Go on, go wash your face and get some sleep,' he replies, laughing.

'She's pretty crazy but, my God, she's funny!' John jokes.

★

35

Everyone's ended up finding their own space for the night. Simon sleeps on the bench seat in the galley, Luis and Jesús share a bunk and I have the floor of the wheelhouse all to myself. Whoever's on watch steps over me to get to the helm. When I look up I can see the sky through the row of misted windows. I feel safe under the vigilant eye of the sea-watchman. They laugh and tell me I'm mad when I say I like my spot.

I wake before I need to, haul myself out of my sleeping bag and stash it in a corner. I sit on the box of survival suits, looking out at the sea and the progress we're making. Sometimes the lion man is there, staring at the slate-coloured waters with those impenetrable eyes. I don't want to disturb him. I watch the waves as we plough over them, the deep troughs, the swell rolling and unrolling all the way to the horizon. I wish he'd explain what all the levers do, what the radars mean. I daren't ask. I so hope Ian will take us on this winter, then we'll never leave the ocean again, we'll work together in the cold, the wind and the frenzied rhythm of the waves, me with these two men, the lanky man and Jude, the lion man, the great sailor. And I could watch him live and fish without ever, ever getting in his way, without ever wanting more than this shared silence, from time to time, as we look out at the advancing ocean.

It's a cold night and it's very late. Or very early. Reflections of the moon dance over the sea on the horizon, a shimmering well of gold. We bait the lines, the harsh glare of neon on our drawn features. Ian's come out of the wheelhouse. Something's bothering him. He talks under his breath to Jesse. I hear the words 'speedboat' and 'Immigration'. He leaves the deck and goes back to the helm.

I take off my gloves, throw my rain gear down in the doorway to the galley, climb the stairs four at a time and arrive in front of Ian out of breath and cheeks blazing.

'Are you worried because of me? Are the guys from Immigration going to show up?'

His face is wan under the spotlight in the wheelhouse, the folds around his mouth carved with a knife.

'There's a boat hovering around us. I can't work out who it is. Jesse and I were wondering if it's the coastguard.'

'Don't worry about it,' I breathe. 'Please don't worry on my account. If it's Immigration, I'll throw myself overboard.'

He suddenly looks alarmed.

'You can't do that, Lili, the water's way too cold — you'd die instantly.'

'Exactly. They won't get me alive. They'll never get me! They'll never send me back to France!'

Now he smiles at me, still worried, though.

'Go back on deck,' he says almost gently. 'Go back to work now. I'm sure it's not Immigration.'

No sign now of land on which we once lived. Mist still, as ever. It's dark. The sea hasn't calmed since we left Kodiak. Feet already cold in these permanently wet boots. Numb fingers struggling to do up my rain gear. Jude swallows a fistful of aspirin.

'Is your hands hurt?' I ask in awkward English.

He looks up and his eyes are surprised, faraway, briefly losing their composure and wavering. But they regain control just as quickly. The skipper yells. Jesse shirks off into the engine room. John isn't ready, he never is, he's seasick. Jesús and Luis glumly exchange a few words in Mexican. Their tanned colouring has morphed towards green. Ian pulls on his gloves agitatedly, looking like someone heading for a pounding. I watch the water spattering onto the window and stand squarely on my legs – my sea legs at last. My body sways from one to the other. With my palms against my lower back, I can feel the hardened curve of my spine matching the to and fro as we list. It no longer resists the jolts slapping the sides of the boat, but dances and plays along with them.

When Dave opens the door the wind blasts inside, and we go out on deck with him. I think of the coffee we didn't get to have. The skipper joins us, his own steaming cup in his hand. We take out knives, hooks and gaffs, unhitch the pulley from the reel, and swing the cathead over the coaming. Ian manoeuvres the *Rebel* over to the buoy that keeps disappearing into troughs. Judge grabs the boathook and pulls the marker on board. The hydraulic motor starts up. We're fishing again. The buoy line comes up. The skipper yells. Everything's just routine now.

The miraculous fishing didn't last. Dave put his hand on the line several times to check the tension. Too taut, he muttered anxiously when I caught his eye. The skipper stopped the boat and the hydraulic motor. Something was wrong. The line was heading off into the water at a diagonal. Jude leant right out over the water, peering at it furiously. Ian had that bad-day face on. Suddenly a sharp crack, shouting, swearing, the line had broken. It all happened in a flash. I didn't know what was going on, I copied the others and threw myself on the disappearing rope. We didn't catch it in time, it slipped through our fingers.

The skipper was ashen. He didn't speak. The men said nothing. Just looked away. I still didn't know what was going on, except that hundreds of feet of longline might have been lost. Ian threw his gloves down on deck, didn't bother taking off his rain gear before going to the wheelhouse. The boat accelerated with a violent lurch. We were soon at the other end of the line. The skipper reappeared with a little more colour in his cheeks. I looked at him, his eyes met mine, he gave a weak smile, a pitiful fleeting grimace. I knew things weren't good.

Jude caught hold of the marker and the buoy, cursing because he nearly missed them. We put the buoy line back into the pulley, and the hydraulic motor started up again. It didn't work for long. Two tubs later, the line broke again.

'It's fucked this time,' John said under his breath.

'If only we had time to drag the depths,' Dave replied quietly. 'This'll come out of our pockets.'

We went back to work and the skipper retreated to his cabin. Perhaps he's crying, I thought for a moment. Simon went down into the hold and handed me crates of frozen squid. Dave and Jude were talking in low voices about the incorrect angle of the line, the unusual tension on it, Ian's ineptitude manoeuvring the boat. We've lost fifteen tubs, that's going to cost us, Andy'll make us pay dearly.

'Such shit gear he dumped on us . . . all those weeks getting it up to scratch!'

'Yeah, but the skipper takes too many risks, he should have seen on the sonar that the water was too shallow.'

I sharpen my knife on the stone and hand it to Jesús. We make eye contact. He smiles helplessly, a naïve expression all his own. I smother a laugh. I've opened the crates of bait and I dive into the frozen squid, slicing them up till I have a big pile that I slide to the middle of the table. Dave has gone quiet. Jude's cigarette hangs from the corner of his mouth, the smoke drifting into his eyes and making him scowl. Luis and John are sulking. We've been baiting for hours.

'Hey, Simon, how about going to make us something to eat while we take care of this?'

An hour later we're treated to burnt rice, some sausages and three tins of sweetcorn. It's good in spite of everything. The men eat in silence and Simon stands in the corner by the cooker, flushed scarlet, waiting for us to finish before he can eat. The skipper looks up from his plate, remembers Simon exists. He sends him into the hold to cover the fish with fresh ice.

'But he hasn't eaten!' I say.

Jude glowers at me frostily, Dave looks amazed but just frowns, Jesús looks embarrassed. The others haven't even looked up.

'Shut it, Lili,' Ian snaps. 'This is part of his job too, isn't it?'

I've looked away, my face burning. I huddle at one end of the seat. A few tears prick at my eyelids. With my throat tight, I stifle a blast of nervous laughter, surprised to find a wave of anger surging through me.

The men have gone back out. Jesús and I do the washing up.

'You don't ever say anything to the skipper,' he says, laughing. 'You know you can be fired for that? The skipper's always right.'

'But Simon hadn't eaten!'

'It's for the skipper to decide, Lili, and it'll happen to you more than once if you carry on in this line of work. It doesn't kill you, you know, you just eat better the next time, that's all.'

John rushes past the galley, late as usual. He opens a drawer and grabs two Bounty bars before going out.

'Can I have one too?'

Jesús laughs again. I put the leftovers in the oven for Simon and we join the others on deck.

Bright red fish are twitching on the table. Rough bodies, razor-sharp fins, bulging horrified eyes seeming to pop from their sockets.

'Why are they sticking their tongues out, Jesús?'

'They're not, that's their stomachs.'

'Oh.'

'It's the decompression. We call them idiot fish. Because of their popping eyes and their tongues, like you say.'

Blood trickles over their brightly coloured bodies. We throw them, mouths agape, to the end of the table, and I push them down the hatch to the hold. Jesús is working next to me.

'Simon hasn't come back up,' he murmurs, nodding thoughtfully. 'I hope he's being careful.'

'About what?'

'About the idiot fish. They're dangerous. Did you see their fins? There's poison in those spines. 'Parently it's fatal if they get you in the neck.'

The skipper looks at us and Jesús stops talking. We wait for Simon. He eventually emerges from the hold, an anxious furtive look on his thin face. The wind has turned; it's almost a nice day.

We finish very late into the night. I spot Simon at the helm and go up to the wheelhouse where Jesse's explaining the dials to him at length. Knife wound to the heart: he's been given his first watch.

'And me?' I whisper. 'What about me?'

Ian's betrayed me. I hold back my tears, a fisherman doesn't cry and he told me I was a fisherman, I soon would be. He talked to me like a child, making me laugh and filling my head with dreams ... I hurry back down the stairs. The boys have gone off to sleep. Ian and Dave are talking quotas over a coffee. I interrupt them in a quavering voice that I wish was a roar.

Ian even forgets to be angry.

'What's up with you, little sparrow?'

'I'm not a sparrow and Simon's on watch.' My voice is strangled, I clutch at my own hands as I catch my breath. 'So when can I do it? You told me I could do it, that it would soon be my turn. Every morning when you're all asleep I've been training, I keep watch with whoever's at the helm. I swear I won't fall asleep!'

Dave smiles.

'Need to learn to wait, Lili,' he says.

'Jesse's the one to talk to, not us,' says Ian. 'The boat's like his baby. Go to bed, little sparrow. Go sleep, you'll get your turn.'

I don't stay any longer. If they see me cry they'll never give me a watch. I go up and hide myself away in the darkest corner of the wheelhouse. Simon has pride of place in the captain's chair. He doesn't look in my direction.

In the morning the skipper takes me to one side. He holds me by my sleeve when I try to get away.

'I've talked to Jesse. You'll take first watch this evening.'

'We're on automatic pilot ... The minute anything seems unusual, wake me or wake the skipper.'

Jesse's finally gone off to bed after an endless trickle of advice. Sitting very upright in the chair, I dunk a square of chocolate in my coffee. The sea is beautiful. Short little waves glide past the bow. Nothing shows on the radar, apart from us, a brilliant dot in the middle of concentric circles and ephemeral flashes. We're dozens of miles from any coast. Hundreds of fathoms of dark depths beneath us. A pale bird looms across the beam of white light from the stern. Its huge wings beat the air silently. It turns aimlessly, spinning slowly on its own axis. Is it asleep or am I dreaming? The radio crackles, every now and then a few words are audible. They seem to hatch out of the darkness, messages from other living beings also roaming this great desert. The skies and the sea are just one. We ease through the darkness. The men are asleep. I'm watching over them.

★

The lanky man, sitting facing out to sea, a shell vacated by the skipper he once was. He's flopped his long gangling limbs over either side of the chair. His features are pale and tired, his jaw angular and honed, his mouth half open, and his melancholy eyes far away in the distance.

'You sad?' I ask.

'Oh, Lili,' he sighs.

There's nothing else to say. The weather's whipped up again. Peggy at the met office hasn't forecast any respite: strong winds, picking up over the course of the day to a gale warning. Greenish blades topped with trails of foam are tossing the *Rebel* into swirls of spray. Drinking coffee is dangerous, cooking almost impossible. Simon has a go at burning some rice again, and even though he secures the pan handles under the rails on the stove, the water spills over and the gas goes out.

'He's going to blow the whole place up,' Jude grumbles, taking over the watch.

John's seasick and often stays on his bunk.

'He was doing fuck all anyway!' Luis complains. 'Hey, bro?'

And Jesús smiles.

Since the incident with the lost gear, Jesse's taken to looking menacingly at the lanky man.

'The dishcloth's burning,' says Dave, who's gone down with a cold. He has a temperature, he coughs and spits and never laughs any more.

Simon copes stoically with the other men's rowing. Jesús is his same old self. We always exchange a friendly look over the table, when it's cold and late.

'You're getting good,' he tells me one day. 'You're starting to understand it all. And quickly.'

The skipper only rarely picks me up on things now. The men shout a bit less, maybe. I don't have time to think about Manosque-les-Sorrow. Basically I've forgotten about it. But the urgency of everything hasn't slackened, neither has the violence of the actual fishing. Nor the blind panic that grips Simon and me, the fear of drowning in the other men's anger when all hell's let loose on deck.

The fishing's good for two days, then our luck turns again. Twice the lines get caught in rocky depths. They break at both ends. A terrible blow. Ian's lost all his arrogance. Something wavers in his eyes. The men don't say anything. Without a word, we go back to baiting on the wave-swept deck.

The skipper bellows from the wheelhouse: time to haul the gear. This time the mainline comes up without a hitch. The men relax, they risk a brief laugh that reveals how jittery they've been. Leaning out over the water with his hand on the levers, Ian stares intently at the line. Once again I dive my knife into white bellies. The smooth taut flesh resists for a moment, then gives way. The blade suddenly pierces through – blood springs up instantly, flooding the table. It runs over the deck in scarlet rivulets. We're the killers of the sea, I think to myself, ocean-going mercenaries, and we wear the colours of our crime. My face and hair cloying with blood, I slice through pale flesh. Occasionally eggs. I bite into the coral-coloured pouches. Pearls of red amber slithering into my mouth, limpid fruits for my thirst.

I don't notice the small cod slip between the steel brackets – barriers that should have kept it out. I shriek when it gets caught in the reel. My voice gets lost in the din of engines, the whistling of the wind, the roll of the waves. I shout at the top of my lungs, to no effect. Dave looks up and yells. The skipper flicks the lever off. The hydraulics stop. Jude frees the remains of the cod. I cower under the storm.

'Lili! What the fuck were you thinking? Why didn't you say anything?'

'But I did! I was screaming – no one heard.'

'No one ever hears you anyway, no one understands a word you say!'

The engine starts up again. My throat's burning, my heart beating wildly. I keep my eyes pinned on the line, ready to snap back the iron clasp if a fish gets caught in the workings. I change the tub as quickly as I can when a longline comes aboard, untie it from the next one, trundle the full load to the far end of the deck. I don't fall over any more. I get back to the cutting table without wasting a moment.

Another young cod gets through the brackets while I'm changing over a tub. It gets stuck in the pulley again and the line catches on the hook, coils round it and strains dangerously taut. Other hooks ping off and are flung to the far side of the deck. I holler, Jude hollers louder, Ian stops everything. I race to free the line, the crushed fish falls away.

'What the fuck, Lili, are you asleep?'

'I couldn't see,' I stammer, 'I was taking one of the tubs ...'

'If you can't do the work, you don't bloody belong here!' he bawls at me before putting the engine back in gear.

I look down. My eyes mist over. I grab a cod and gut it. My lower lip trembles. I bite it savagely. I'm overwhelmed by anger and rebellion. I've had enough of fish blood and these stupid men who stole my bunk. They laugh at me, they yell and then I quake. I've had enough of killing and being scared of them. I want to be free, to run along the docks again, head off to Point Barrow ...

I don't see it coming: a bright red fish lands on me and a dorsal fin bristling with spines spread like a wing embeds itself in my hand. Dave missed the hatch down to the hold. The pain is searing, punishment for my rebellion perhaps. Tears spring up for real. I take off my gloves, some spines remain planted in the root of my thumb. I pull out three that are in deep, a fourth goes right through to the other side. I drag it out with my teeth. The beautiful fish lies there gaping. Jesús waves a hand at the skipper. He points towards the galley.

'Go and disinfect the wound. I told you there was poison in the those fins,' Jesús says, looking concerned for me.

I leave the deck full of shame. My hand feels paralysed as I take off my rain gear. I lower myself onto the seat in the galley. Sit back, close my eyes. The pain comes in surges, rising up in burning waves from my palm all the way to my shoulder. My heart lurches, my eyesight

45

blurs. I sway slowly as if about to fall. The men are on deck, perhaps for many more hours, I have to get back to them. I stand up, go to rinse off the wound. My head's spinning. I'm afraid I'll collapse. So I go out onto the upper deck, passing through the wheelhouse to be sure no one sees me. The sky has cleared and a pale sun is picking out the crests of the waves. I light a cigarette, it takes many attempts. Up against the lifeboat there's less wind. I cry a bit, it almost feels good. The men are fishing. I should be with them. They're unlikely to know why I've left. Jude must be furious. Worse, he'll be contemptuous. Typical woman, he must be thinking. Of course I shouldn't pay attention to the pain. And what do I care about pain? But even so ... I'm going to die anyway, because the fish was poisonous.

The ocean stretches away to infinity. The noise from the deck reaches me up here; tubs knocking into the aluminium shelves and clanking together, shouting sometimes, in snatches. I smoke my cigarette in the sun. Will it take long to die? I sniff and blow my nose between two fingers. How sad, I think, looking at the sky and the sea, dying's such a shame. But maybe it's only natural, now that I'm so far from anywhere and so alone, so close to the Great North, their Last Frontier, and I've crossed that frontier, and found my boat and been transported ecstatically on the ocean, thinking about it night and day till I almost can't sleep on my corner of dirty floor. Seeing days and nights and dawns so beautiful I'd deny my own past, I'd sell my soul. Yes, Lili, surely you dared to cross this frontier only in order to find death, to reel in your own ending, a beautiful red ending, a fish streaming with seawater and blood that planted itself in your hand like a flaming arrow.

I remember leaving home, and crossing deserts in the bus with the greyhound on the side, the sky blue of my anorak and its clouds of down around me ... So this is what I was leaving for, this was the driving force that made me so bold: earning my own death. I can picture Manosque-les-Sorrow where, it turns out, I won't be dying and eventually found in a darkened room. I've stopped crying. I go back down to the galley. My hand has gone limp. Yet again I feel guilty when I see the men busying away on deck. I curl up into a ball in the passageway. It's warm and dark. I hug my hand to my stomach.

The skipper found me there, huddled in the shadows. I didn't hear him approach. Maybe I'd fallen asleep. He made me jump. He didn't shout, though.

'What are you doing here, Lili?'

He knelt down. There was no anger in his voice.

'I . . . I'm going back up on deck,' I said. 'I was just resting a while.'

'Does it hurt a lot?'

'Kind of.'

'Wait.'

He went into the head, rummaged in a medicine cabinet and brought me some Tylenol.

'Take this and rest some more, we've almost finished the set. We're all going to have a coffee break.'

The men came in. They didn't look furious, quite the opposite, even Jude, who smiled at me. Dave couldn't stop apologising. The skipper was back to being the lanky man. Jesús was concerned.

'You'll still have to go to the hospital when we're back ashore.'

I ended up forgetting I was supposed to die that day. I was happy among them. My hand was still very painful. The men stood up and I got to my feet along with them.

'You don't have to come out straightaway,' said Ian.

'It's fine,' I said.

And we went back on deck. I wanted to stay with them, for us to be cold, tired and hungry together. I wanted to be a real fisherman. I wanted to be with them always.

I don't want to go back. I don't want this to end. And yet when we're close to the coast, I'm surprised by the smell of the land. The snow has melted on the Old Womens Mountains. The hills are turning green. I'm faintly aware of a whiff of leaves, the suggestion of tree stumps and silt, like very distant impressions from the days when we were earthlings. When we draw nearer the coast, I'm amazed by the trilling of a bird calling to me, it stirs my heart. I'd forgotten. All I've been hearing is the hoarse mewing of seagulls, the long lament of albatrosses, their whining as they circle around the longlines. My chest swells with love, I take a great lungful of earth smells. I'm happy, and we'll be setting off again in the evening.

The men raise the stabiliser fins. The *Rebel* passes the buoy for Puffin Island. We take the hawsers out of their crates, tie the fenders to the railings. The cannery docks aren't far now. High tide. Dave, at the helm, tosses the heaving line to a worker on the dock who winds it around a cleat. Ian manoeuvres, standstill, reverse; the *Rebel* comes up to the dock side-on, I move the fenders around to protect the hull from impacts, Jude at the stern throws the hawser to the worker and he secures it to another cleat. John barges at Simon, snatches the rope from him and ties it to the dock himself. Jesús and Luis have already opened the hatches to the hold.

The skipper's left to go to the offices. A dockworker gives us a huge pipe that Luis submerges into the molten ice full of floating gutted fish.

'Yo, bro!' Jesús calls to the man. 'You can press send ...'

A sucking sound. Our cargo is slowly pumped out.

Jesús and I clean the hold. Dave dilutes chlorine powder and hands me the bucket. We scrub every inch of the place, holding our brushes at arm's length. Chlorinated scum dribbles over our faces. Our eyes sting. I laugh. Simon tosses me the hose.

'Careful, you're spraying it in our faces!'

'We're going into town, Lili, if you want a ride ...'

I've taken off my rain gear, I tuck my cigarettes and my purse into my boots, and climb the ladder four rungs at a time. I join Simon and Jude in the back of the truck – cramped between two buoys.

48

'You should go to the hospital,' the skipper tells me before taking the wheel. 'Get them to give you an injection of antibiotics.'

I lie down on the flatbed, my head resting against some rope. The air is mild. Buds have opened. With my eyes closed I inhale traces of factory smoke and the smell of trees, snatches of heavy, violent smells – almost warm after the cruel harshness at sea. I laugh and sit up to get another wave of this new air blasting into our faces. Simon is all confidence again. Jude is watching me. He looks away quickly when I catch his eye. He's huddled in the corner of the truck. It's as if his body is too cumbersome here, he doesn't know how to handle it, or what to do with it, or why. He tilts his head up, looks over the mountains, glowering. I'm frightened of him again. I look away and close my eyes.

Ian drops us by the post office. A small yellow house built on the framework of an old trailer has been parked on the stretch of waste-land in our absence – 'For Sale'. I stop – Oh, I think – then I run to catch up with the boys. Simon has a letter waiting for him, poste restante. We come back out of the post office together but Jude leaves us outside Tony's.

'Meet back here in two hours.'

He goes through the door into the bar. Simon and I walk the streets together – we're proud of ourselves, we're back from the sea. We sway as we walk, sometimes we feel dizzy and the ground seems to fall away beneath our feet. Landsick? We laugh. Then Simon goes his own way.

I head off along the port, the town is bright in the sunlight. I eat popcorn by the quay, sitting under the memorial to sailors lost at sea. A man stops beside me: Nikephoros. He has his sleeves rolled up: an anchor on his right forearm, the Southern Cross on his left. Mermaids and waves curling round it.

'Do you always eat popcorn?' he laughs. 'And did you find your-self a boat?'

'I'm on the *Rebel*. We've just unloaded. We're setting out again this evening.'

He whistles in surprise.

'The *Rebel*! You're starting out tough, don't you think?'

He takes my hands, inspects them slowly.

'A man's hands,' he says.

I laugh.

'They've always been strong, they've got even bigger.'

He runs a finger over the cracks that the salt keeps reopening.

'Take care of them, put cream on those, don't keep them like that. They get infected too quickly at sea, especially with the salt and rotten bait.'

Then he notices the swollen puncture wounds in my thumb and frowns.

'And these?'

I tell him about the red fish.

'Go to the hospital.'

I don't reply.

Luis and Jesús weren't there for the roll call. I was suddenly giddy when the men untied the mooring ropes and I felt the *Rebel* shudder towards the high seas, a rush of panic whipped through me. I took a deep breath, turned my face out to sea, and it passed. I realised I had to have faith in them, always, whatever happened. We set off. I coiled the ropes and stowed them in crates. Jude seemed relieved to be on the water again. His chest expanded. He stood taller, his chin firmer, held higher now. He was the lion man again and I lowered my eyes when he looked at me. He stared out in the distance, beyond the straits of every continent in the world. Then he spat several times and blew his nose between two fingers.

The fishing has started again. The swell throws us around, coming in great long wide blades from as far as the eye can see. Simon has taken Jesús's bunk, leaving me to my floor. I've grown used to it, it's my space on board, under the row of windows through which I can always see the sky. The men are asleep, bodies abandoned, limbs spread, in the warm bowels of the boat, the muffled thrum of the engines, the heavy damp smell of clothes that are never taken off, the acrid whiff of socks lying on the floor.

My hand is swelling. Getting redder. We fish. The men peer silently, questioningly at the water. The fish have fled. The sea seems empty and we're exhausting ourselves pointlessly. Jude has brought an old tape recorder and tied it to a steel pole. Sad soft country music lulls the interminable hours when we have to bait the hooks. The sky clears one evening. The lion man is sitting opposite me, his thigh bent against his chest, his right foot on the table to ease his lower back. He's stubbornly, patiently unravelling a longline that the sea sent back tangled with knots. A sunbeam has come to rest on his forehead, lighting his filthy mane, blazing on his already burned cheeks. Traces of salt cling to his eyelids and hang from his lashes. We're bathed in evening light, the music wafts in waves, the regular coming and going of water on the deck, draining through the hatches only to return moments later as the boat rolls, the sound of backwash, a slow sigh, the smooth rhythm of ebb and flow. An eternal music. I turn to look at the sea, burnished to copper in the last of the day's light. Perhaps we'll go on like this forever, till the end of time, on the red-lit ocean and towards the open sky, a deranged but magnificent flight across nothingness, across everythingness, heart burning, feet freezing, escorted by a cloud of shrieking seagulls, a great sailor at the bridge, his face calm, almost gentle. And somewhere still: towns, walls, mindless crowds. But not for us any more. For us, nothing more. Forging ahead through the great desert between the constantly shifting dunes and the sky.

And we bait lines, for hours and hours until the dark of night, tracing our path with foam, a short-lived wake ripping through the waves and almost immediately disappearing, leaving the great ocean virgin and blue, then black.

My hand is red and swollen. I think of the hospital I didn't want to visit. For the sake of popcorn, of wandering around town and having a beer with the boys. Jude catches me emptying the box of aspirins.

'Are you in pain?'

'A bit.'

Then on deck I screw up my face and drop a hook. Those tawny eyes are watching me.

'Show me your hand.'

He looks at the distended purple flesh.

'I've got something for infections.'

Later he takes me to his bunk, pulls a medicine kit from behind the survival suit that he uses as a pillow. He painstakingly takes out tubes and boxes in all shapes and sizes, selecting two.

'Take this, it's penicillin, and this too ... Cephalexin. It's good for all the crap you can catch at sea.'

He shows me the white scars on his gnarled fingers. Tells me about the buried hooks, knife cuts, injuries sustained fishing and at sea. I look at his hands, these hands that hurt so much they wake him in the night. I'm not proud of myself, a skinny little woman who's run away from some dusty village faraway. I hide my hand in my dirty sleeve. To be worthy of staying aboard alongside Jude I'll never complain. To earn his respect I'd rather die.

'By the way, Lili, is your hand OK?'

I've flopped my arm absent-mindedly across the table. We're eating.

'Yes,' I reply, but Ian's looking at something else.

I hoped someone would see. No one saw. Apart from Tawny Eyes, who doubles the dose of penicillin.

The wind and the cold are back with a vengeance. I'm kneeling on deck arduously unknotting a longline, my gloves long since holed, full of an icy sauce of rotten squid and brackish water. I've lowered myself so as not to fall. I'm weeping with rage and pain. The rain hides my tears. Time for a break at last.

'Go get warm, boys,' the skipper says. 'Eat. Recharge your batteries. We won't be stopping tonight. There isn't time.'

So I'm going to die, I think. I watch water spatter against the panes and crash onto the deck. The shooting pains are up to my shoulder now. I've stopped even looking at this deformed hand, the skin tight enough to burst. I finish my coffee. I have to get back to work. The guys stand up. I follow them. The fishing starts again. We work in greyness, sky and water indistinguishable. The men are sparing with their shouts, their movements mechanical and precise, their minds soon as numb as their bodies. The mist thickens till it's almost impenetrable. Darkness is closing in now. We haven't stopped. The boat continues on its course.

At three o'clock Ian calls us in.

'That'll do for today.'

'But you said—'

'Carry on by yourself if you like.'

The men don't even have the strength to laugh. One by one they disappear into the cabin to collapse exhausted on their bunks. I go back to my patch of floor space under Dave's affectionately mocking eye.

'Goodnight, little Frenchie. You're getting better and better, you know?'

'Goodnight,' I mumble.

I'm gradually losing the battle. It won't be long before something gives. I bury my head in my sleeping bag. I want to bawl like a child. I bite the wrist that's causing so much pain. I wish I could tear it off, be free of all these initiations once more, back to who I was in the early days on board. Sleep won't come, or only in chaotic snatches. I keep track of the men's various watches. A succession of them over the course of a painful half-dream state. At seven o'clock the skipper's at the helm again. We have to get back to work. I open the door, heading for the deck. Jude holds me back.

'Show me your hand – you can't go on working. You have to show it to Ian.'

'He'll send me ashore.'

I look away, staring at the tips of my boots.

'You have to talk to the skipper about it.'

'No,' I reply, shaking my head obstinately. 'He'll send me ashore.'

'If you won't talk to him about it, I will.'

They come back together. Ian's frowning.

'Why didn't you say anything for fuck's sake?'

'I thought it would get better ... Jude was giving me antibiotics.'

'She says she doesn't want to go ashore,' says Jude.

The men have gone back to work on deck. The weather's freezing, brutal. Dave has lent me his bunk and his Walkman. And I'll be back alongside them soon, they'll take care of me and my hand will get better. I've hung on in there. Jesse told me I'm 'Super Tuff', like the brand of fishing boots. They've given me a bunk ... my heart swells with gratitude.

The head is taking on water. I pull out the rags that have been stuffed into the pan, sit down on the seat and get squirted with seawater. I jump up, my backside soaked. The boat's heavy at the moment, a backwash floods in with each trough in the waves. I can see myself in the mirror under the strong white glare of the neon light. A tracery of white lines flakes round the corners of my eyes and on my cheekbones. My hand is caught in a network of buckles and knots hardened with salt, stuck together with scum and dried blood. When I run my hand through my thick mane I notice the red line. It starts on my palm and goes all the way up to my armpit. I remember hearing that you die when it reaches the heart.

I watch the birds wheeling around the bows, a wan wailing cloud. The huge rusted anchor seems to carve through the mist. Menacing rollers advance towards us. The skipper picks up the transmitter. He's trying to find a window in the radio waves to get hold of the hospital. Then he starts calling boats in our vicinity.

'Get your things ready, your sleeping bag. The bare essentials. You can pick up the rest later. The *Venturous* is going to Kodiak to unload. We'll haul the gear and head off to meet them. A stroke of luck. We've lost enough money for this season. We can't afford to go in so soon.' The lanky man is brief, curt, but he softens and adds, 'Go back to bed. It'll take a good two or three hours.'

I look down and go back to the bunk. The sea lulls me. I've lost everything. Far from the boat and the warmth of these men, I'll feel like some orphaned creature, a leaf tossed on the wind in the appalling cold outside. I can hear the men on deck. I haven't lost them yet. I contemplate hiding: it wouldn't change anything, they don't want me on board now. No one keeps an invalid fated to die in a cupboard. But maybe I'll die before then. If the red line reaches my heart before they've reeled in all the lines.

The *Venturous* isn't far away now. I've come back up to the wheel-house. Ian's at the helm with Dave standing next to him. I'm carrying my sleeping bag and my little bundle of belongings. I squish away my tears with my good hand. The skipper looks at me kindly.

'Do you have any money?'

'Yes,' I sob, 'I've got fifty dollars.'

'Here, take another fifty ... and listen to me,' he says slowly. 'If it's all OK in a couple of days you can come back. Go to the factory, talk to the people in the office, we're in radio contact with them every day. Tell them you need to get back to the *Rebel*, that you're part of the crew. They'll find you a boat that's heading back to the area.'

'Yes,' I say.

I wipe my face on a dirty sleeve. Sniff a bit.

'Where can I sleep?' I ask again, like on the first day.

'Go to the Brother Francis Shelter, or actually, no, go to the place where we worked on the lines. There's already someone sleeping there, Steve, Andy's mechanic, a good guy. You've probably already seen him there ... will you remember all that?'

'Yes, I think so.'

The two men look at me with a sad tenderness.

'We'll miss you,' says Dave.

I don't reply. I know he's lying. How could they miss someone who's failed them? He's treating me like a child. Not someone who works at sea. Sitting in a corner of the wheelhouse, like I did those first mornings on board, I stare at the ocean without saying a word. The *Venturous* is already in sight.

And I had to jump, propelled across the grey waters. The sea was rough, thick trails of foam rolled along with the waves. The big vessel came as close to the *Rebel* as possible. Leaning out in front, buffeted by the wind and smacked by spattering water, Jude held the buoys in place between the two giants, the manoeuvre made perilous by violent seas. The skipper gave me a hug, Dave a vig-orous handshake, and Jesse, who was never seen working on deck without his life jacket, put it around my chest. I turned towards them one last time, then to the lion man, his face congested from the exertion, I thought I'd never see them again, and the men threw me towards the *Venturous* as if the boat was rejecting me. There were three men leaning over the rail open-armed, ready to catch me if I slipped. I didn't slip. Moments later we were heading hard for Kodiak.

No one shouts on the *Venturous*. Brian, the skipper, is a tall man who studies me with pensive brown eyes. He gives me a cup of coffee and a cookie.

'I just made them,' he says.

'I want to go fishing again,' I say. 'Do you think they'll let me?'

He doesn't know. I mustn't worry, I need to rest for now, there'll always be other boats. But as I eat my cookie I'm thinking of the *Rebel*, sailing towards the horizon. Brian has turned his back to me, leaning over the cooker. There are pretty photos on the walls: the *Venturous* covered with ice, men breaking it; a child on a beach smiling a gap-toothed smile; a woman laughing under an umbrella. Another man has come to sit at the table, he's even taller than Brian, and fair, his blond hair tied in a red bandana.

'This is Terry, the observer,' Brian tells me. 'He works for the government, he's checking our fishing quotas.'

'You should sleep,' the man says. 'You can have my bunk if you like.'

'Aren't I too dirty?'

'No, you're not too dirty,' he laughs.

His bunk smells of aftershave. There's even a porthole. I watch dark rollers unfurl under a low sky. Every now and then someone comes in, goes back out. I keep my eyes closed for fear of reading the look on someone's face if they've come in from the deck. It must be very cold out. The people on board are kind, they've lent me a bunk and they're letting me sleep while they work. How long will it take to reach Kodiak? How many hours? How many days? Will we get there before the red line reaches my heart? My forehead's burning. They gave me coffee and a cookie.

I wake. It's night-time. The stabbing pains in my armpit are more violent now. All I can see through the porthole is darkness and the white crests of the waves which seem to be approaching very quickly. I get up and my legs wobble. The men are still fishing. The observer's standing in the passageway.

'Does the red line get to the heart quickly?' I ask him.

He smiles kindly.

'I'm a bit of a doctor,' he says. 'Let me have a look. Let's go into the shower room, there's more light.'

I follow him and he closes the door. He lifts up my countless jumpers and sweatshirts layered one on top of the other. He feels the glands in my elbow, under my armpit. His beautiful hands are soft on my skin. I tilt my head up because he's very tall. I look at him trustingly. Listen to him. He's looking after me too.

'You're not fat!' he says.

I look down at my white stomach. My ribs create a blue shadow next to the curve of my breasts. I stare at this body, bewildered, I don't remember it being so slight. He pulls my sweaters down quickly. Someone's come in. I feel ashamed and I don't know why.

We go back to the galley. A young woman is pouring herself a coffee and offers us some. I look around, see the photos and notes covering the walls again. It feels warm, like someone's house. The young woman has hung her gloves above the oven. She rubs cream over her face, then her hands. I'm amazed by her clean, neatly tied hair, the smooth skin of her cheeks, her slender white fingers. She doesn't seem frightened of anyone. Then a man from the engine room comes in carrying a bucket of black oil. He's very young and he's frowning, red eyebrows knitted in a narrow face. I huddle on the banquette. More men come through the door, the wind gusting in with them briefly. They blow into their swollen red hands. Each in turn helps himself to coffee and comes to sit at the table. A woman comes down from the wheelhouse, she exchanges a few words with the skipper, who trails a finger slowly over her cheek, her lips, then has a long stretch before going up to take over from her. She makes herself a cup of tea and comes to sit with us. The boys want to see my wound and the red line.

'She's certainly learning the ropes,' one of them says.

They all tell terrifying stories of infected wounds, limbs ripped off, faces disfigured by steel grapple hooks.

'Yours is pretty good,' someone else says.

The women nod. I flush. I'm proud of myself.

'Time to go back to shore,' says the young guy with the red eyebrows, 'we ran out of cigarettes three days ago.'

'I still have loads!'

I pull a crumpled packet from my sleeve. He smiles for the first time.

'Let's go light up on deck!'

Another man comes out with us. We're buffeted by gusts of wind under the awning. They drag deep on their cigarettes. The redhead, Jason, finishes his and lights another straightaway. He gives a long contented sigh. The other man has gone back inside. The air is icy; I think of the men's faces on the *Rebel*, the cold must be eating into them right now. Have they already forgotten me?

'I want to go back to the *Rebel*,' I tell Jason. 'Do you think they'll keep me in hospital long?'

'They might not keep you in at all, they may just give you an injection, give you a few pills, and you'll be off again tomorrow. The *Venturous* could even take you back to the *Rebel*, we're fishing in the same area. And if you have to stay ashore for a few days, you could always get on the *Milky Way*. That's my boat, the *Milky Way*, I bought it with my crabbing money last winter.'

He smiles with savage intensity as he says this.

'Twenty-eight feet, all in wood. I'll be setting out on her soon, maybe crabbing for Dungeness this summer. Brian's meant to be giving me some pots.'

His voice is staccato, his eyes bright as he stares out to sea.

'I'm like you, y' know,' he says, turning towards me. 'Not from around here. I grew up in the East, in Tennessee. Wasting my life. One day I packed my bag, said goodbye to ever'one, 'n' left. I came here cos of the grizzlies, the biggest in the world, I liked that . . . Brian took me on for crabbing. Now I don't want do anything 'cept fish.'

His eyes light up again, he gives a sort of little roar – like a lion, but a cub.

'The cold, the wind, waves in your face for days and nights . . . Fighting it! Killing fish!'

Killing fish . . . I don't reply. I'm not so sure about that. We head back in to the warmth. Some of the men have gone off to sleep. The skipper's girlfriend is eating, the observer sitting in silence and the pretty girl drinking tea. They ask me about France.

'Back home we say the Americans are just big kids,' I tell them.

Jason's eyes glower again under his translucent lashes.

'Well, the Alaskans must be the wildest kids, then!' he says, laughing as if he's about to bite someone. 'We should be arriving late into the night. I'll get you to the hospital. I'd like to take you for a few White Russians, they're so good at Tony's . . . Another time, my friend. I promise.'

We take a taxi as soon as we reach the harbour. The driver is Filipino, his black eyes shine in the darkness.

'Was the fishing good?' he asks.

The radio crackles in the background, a call for another fare. He makes a note.

'Not too bad,' Jason replies, 'we went over the 20,000-pound mark this time. This lady needs to get to the hospital. And be treated quick: she's needed on board.'

I smile in the shadows. We travel through the town with its lights, its brightly lit bars. The taxi heads into great curtains of trees. The sky goes on for miles overhead. I hug my sleeping bag between my calves, clutch my bag to me. I recognise the road to the place where we worked on the lines. The taxi slows, we turn left, there's a white wooden building on the edge of the forest, lit up by two street lamps. Jason doesn't want to let me pay.

'Goodbye, my friend,' he says to the taxi driver.

Jason leaves me in the waiting room of the small deserted hospital and a nurse comes for me straightaway.

'Here you are at last – we were getting worried.'

'When can I go back out fishing?'

They've lain me down on a table. Two nurses examine my hand and arm at length, they feel the glands in my armpit. I'm given an injection of antibiotics.

'Do you think I'll be able to leave tomorrow?'

The women smile.

'We'll see. It was high time you got here, we were really worried. Blood poisoning kills quickly, you know.'

'Yes, I know ... but how long will you keep me in?'

'Two or three days maybe,' one of them says.

'Did they really throw you overboard in a survival suit to get you from one boat to the other?' the other nurse asks.

I'm given an X-ray. A piece of tail bone is still stuck in there next to the bone in my thumb.

'We'll have to wait for the infection to go down before we take it out,' says the doctor.

I won't be drinking White Russians this evening. Jason's gone. I'm alone in a ward, between clean white sheets. A nurse sets up the drip, working slowly and gently. She straightens a pillow, tells me not to worry.

'When will I be able to leave?' I ask when she heads for the door. She turns around. She doesn't know.

'Tomorrow?'

'Maybe,' she says.

I try to get some sleep. I think of the *Rebel*, of the men asleep in her belly, of the pounding engines like a furious heart, and the men who live there, in that belly, with that heart, in the endless rocking of the waves. Of whoever is on watch. I'm cold here all alone on land. I've been ripped away from them, and now I'm suddenly far removed from that unreal time and place when we fished together. I think of the waves and their song, the long shudders of swell, the ocean and sky tipping. Everything is stable here.

★

61

It's the next day already. A doctor comes to see me. He tries to make me laugh and brings me cigarettes.

'Take the drip with you and go have a smoke outside. We need to keep you in a bit longer. You can't go back out with that in your hand.'

'I'm not much of a smoker.'

'Go have a smoke anyway, it'll do you good.'

It's a beautiful day under the black pine trees. I can make out the ocean through the trees. I light a cigarette and suddenly there's Jason climbing out of a taxi that still has its engine running. He's carrying a book and a length of rope, which he hands to me.

'Here, these are for you – to learn fishing knots. I can't chat for long, the *Venturous* is leaving soon and I'm already late.'

But he accepts a cigarette.

'We'll see each other again soon, I swear ... in the little harbour in Dog Bay, third pontoon, the *Milky Way*. Hang on in there, my friend, I'll let the guys on the *Rebel* know by radio. I'll tell them you'll soon be back.'

Jason's gone. Now there's just the empty road and the big black pine trees. I go back to my room. Seagulls through the window. I'm back in bed. Waiting.

The telephone ringtone rips through the silence of those four walls. I pick up filled with wild hope that it's the lanky man calling me from the wheelhouse.

'Hello!' I cry.

'Hello, Immigration here,' an impersonal man's voice replies. 'We've heard that you're working illegally on a fishing vessel.'

I sit bolt upright, scanning the room, then my eyes come to rest on my arm, the drip is a chain, tying me to this place.

'No, that's not true ... that's not true at all,' I manage.

The fisherman from Seattle bursts out laughing on the other end.

'You can't – you can't ever say stuff like that,' I stutter and my voice is strangulated with tears.

He apologises again and again before hanging up. I stay at the window until the sky darkens. The *Rebel* hasn't called.

They bring me a hamburger, a salad and a creamy little red cake. I cry silently over my cake. The *Rebel*'s getting further away every day. They'll never take me back. I've stopped asking the nurses questions. I've given up hope of being delivered. They just bring me meals. Drips. Cigarettes. I'm cold at night. I moan in my dreams.

Then one morning they do discharge me but I have to come back three times a day for treatment. A white plastic connector is left in the back of my hand. The fish bone is still in there. Like mothers, the nurses watch me leave.

'Will you be somewhere clean and warm? At least say you're not going to the Brother Francis Shelter?'

'Oh no, I won't go there. My skipper told me to go to the hangar where we did some work for the boat. There's a bedroom.'

And I head off into the white day. My bundle swings against my hip, I hug my sleeping bag to me. It starts to rain, fine close-knit raindrops. I hurry towards the beaten track I can see at the corner.

The misshapen, rusted shrimp cages, the punctured buoys covered in moss, the old trucks and the slowly rotting blue boat: nothing's moved. I slide open the heavy metal door. Steve isn't here. The huge hangar is damp and empty, cold enough to make you weep, but this is where the *Rebel*'s lines are kept. The men will be back. I'm surrounded by the smell of longlines and decomposing bait once more, and the harsh neon light over the dirty workshop. I walk across the hangar to the coffee machine. Turn on the radio very quietly. There's some water left in the bottom of the jerrycan. I make myself a coffee and sip it, staring out through the wide doorway. The wasteland spreads before me. The tall trees and the abandoned boat sway slowly as I watch from the rocking chair, swinging myself back and forth. It's the lanky man's chair brought over from his house, once he sold the place. He also donated his thermos, which I've filled and put on the ground. I drink my coffee from a filthy cup; the fingerprints and brownish marks must date from when we were all working here together. Through the open door the sky is unchanged, and the trees have simply turned a more intense green. My eyes drift back to the cup and its dark stains from a long distant past, and the red thermos that I used to fill every morning and leave by the bedside of a lanky man. I rock in his chair. I might still believe he'll be back, his silhouette suddenly framed by the light from the doorway in this deserted plot of land, he might say something like 'Passion's a wonderful thing', and take me back on board.

A pick-up stops by the door. I huddle into the shadows. Steve steps out and comes inside. I recognise the sweet shy smile; this was the man who came out of the bedroom that first morning, followed by the young Native American girl with her head held low. He looks surprised to find someone here. I apologise hastily, stammering a few words. We're both embarrassed.

'There are two beds in the bedroom, make yourself at home,' he says, not meeting my eye.

'I've used some of your coffee – I'll get a new packet.'

'Make yourself at home,' he says again.

He doesn't know what to do now. He looks round aimlessly, then pours himself a coffee. We watch the rain falling through the open doorway.

'The cod season will soon be over around Kodiak,' he says in a quiet voice, almost a murmur. 'The quotas have been reached.'

'So I won't be going out again? Are you sure? Is it over for me?'

His eyes finally manage to look into mine. He smiles for the first time, very kindly and gently.

'I just meant the local quotas here. Plenty of boats will keep fishing in the south-east. The *Rebel*'s highly likely to head that way, I'd be amazed if they stopped this soon.'

'Oh I hope so! I really hope so.'

I look out of the door, beyond the wasteland. Behind those trees is the sea. Travelling across the sea is my boat.

He left again. I walked across the hangar to the small windowless room, a sort of cube parked inside the vast space. The strip light flickered for a long time before coming on. I made my way through the refuse sacks cluttering the floor, bulging with clothes hastily stuffed into them. I knocked into a full ashtray and it spilled its contents on the grey carpet. In the corner a television set had been left on next to a bed, with a sleeping bag rolled up on the bare grey pillows. I put my sleeping bag on the other bed and sat down. I tried to pick up the scattered cigarette butts. The carpet was so sticky that I gave up, moving only the biggest of them. I wiped my fingers on the bottom of my jeans. I ate a crisp that was poking out of a half-empty packet on a coffee table in front of me. It was limp and slightly rancid. I sighed: Come on, it'll be OK ... Anyway, it would be too cold to sleep in one of the trucks.

I got up, switched off the TV, went out. I walked to the big Safeway where we used to have lunch. It was warm, everything was shiny, even the music, and people seemed happy and entertaining. I wandered the aisles for a long time but I had to get on, I was due back at the hospital soon. I bought cereal, coffee, milk and Mexican cookies, crackers made with flour and water – the sort Jesús likes to dip in his coffee.

The rain had stopped when I came out. The air smelt of fish, not the strong fresh smell, the live smell you get when you're fishing, but the other version, heavier and more morbid, a foul stench wafting from the canning factories and driven over town by the southerly wind. I walked to the hospital. Drip administered very quickly. I went back to the hangar to sit in the red chair, where I poured myself a bowl of cereal and balanced it on my lap. The radio trickled out its soft songs from days gone by. I gazed at the wasteland till nightfall. I waited for the *Rebel*.

And so on for days and nights. I went to sleep in the darkness of the box room. I dreamt. A man – an animal – jumped onto my back, burying its teeth in my neck, lacerating my shoulders, the crook of my armpit and the sensitive flesh of my groin with its claws. Streams of blood cascaded down. Submerging me. Steve came back very late at night. I could hear him bumping into the bags of clothes. He saved me from my nightmares as if pulling a drowning person from the waves.

'Oh, it's you,' I said, catching my breath. 'Thank you for waking me.'

He laughed softly in the dark. Perhaps he was drunk. He fell asleep quickly. The nightmares started again. I moaned. He woke and listened, but didn't dare say anything.

Steve slept in late. I was up as soon as each day dawned. I would go back to my post in the red armchair, with the full thermos by my side. Once awake, Steve stayed in that dark room for a long time. He

66

turned on the television and moved from his bed to the chair. The ashtrays were overflowing, more and more. At last he would emerge, paler than ever. He smiled wanly. Daylight poured in through the wide doorway, he blinked. He went off to work, tottering in the bright light.

I've found my bicycle in a corner of the workshop. I'm rummaging through the paint cupboard – I've already taken out pots of blue and yellow, and I just spot the red when a pick-up parks outside. I listen intently and step closer cautiously. A man unloads some longlines. Black curls loll over his bronzed forehead. A Latino's dark eyes. I come out of the shadows.

'Hello,' I say bravely.

The man hardly notices me. He drops the tubs by the hangar door, then piles them up and creates a makeshift table by putting a plank of wood across the top of them. He sets to work emptying the stinking contents of a tub onto the ground: a longline bunched into a dense mass of knots, hooks and putrefying bait.

'Did they not use squid?' I ask.

'No. Herring's cheaper. But it rots quicker.'

He unties the hooks one by one, puts them to one side, throws the bait into the empty tub. I come closer. He looks up at me irritably.

'If you're not doing anything you could help. Andy pays twenty dollars for a reconditioned longline.'

'I don't know if I should.'

'Why not?'

'My hand. I was injured. At the hospital they told me to be careful. Have to keep it clean. Otherwise it could start all over again.'

He nods towards a brackish little stream running along the edge of the abandoned field, between bits of old iron and deflated buoys.

'There's plenty of water. Everywhere. You could just rinse off your hand every now and then. The sooner we finish, the better. These longlines were left by the *Blue Beauty* last time they unloaded. Andy wants them for next time they come through.'

67

'Still, I don't think so,' I mumble.

I set to work, though. I wouldn't dare repaint the *Free Spirit* in front of this man and those dark eyes.

'Steve asleep?' he asks.

'No, no, he's at work, of course.'

'Did he come home drunk again last night?'

'I don't know.'

'He works for Andy, Steve does. Mechanic. He'll get himself fired one day.'

'Mechanic? Oh yes, I remember now. But the *Blue Beauty* and the *Rebel* are at sea.'

'There are other boats. Andy has a whole bunch of them. And you need mechanics on land too. Andy has a lot of dough. Gotta say that's just as well, seeing how many wives he's had and still has to bankroll. Six . . . and the rug rats, too.'

'It's better,' says the doctor. 'The infection's gone down. We'll be able to take that bone out soon.'

So I'll be going fishing again, I think. If the boat doesn't come back before. If they'll still have me.

I've come back to the hangar. The man's gone to have something to eat and the tubs are rotting in the sunshine. I sit down in the red chair. Swarms of flies swirl in the golden doorway, gorged with light and putrid juices. I'm fine here, I think, except at night when I'm frightened.

The tub man comes back. I don't move.

'Aren't you doing any more?'

'No,' I say. 'It's not good for my hand. I want to go fishing again.'

He shrugs. Embarrassed that he doesn't believe me, I get up and go over to him. He stays there, hunched over his work.

'Look,' I say, moving the bandage aside, 'don't you think it's better if—'

He looks exasperated.

'Stop bugging me the whole time,' he says but his face swiftly changes. He swallows hard and says, 'You stop, you did plenty already.'

I go off to fetch the blue and yellow paint and decide to take the green and red too. I take *Free Spirit* out into the sunshine and spend a long time repainting it, the frame in blue and the wheel rims spangled in the other colours. I'm careful not to paint over the name. Flies occasionally land on the fresh paint and I try to remove them, but succeed only in pulling off their wings. The man looks up. I hear him laugh for the first time. I put the wings carefully on the ground, not sure what to do with them now. I look at the man, he smiles.

'That shitty little bike looks like something at last.'

'Oh yes,' I say.

I held out my thumb towards the port. A truck braked, a huge red net in the back. A man opened the door for me. The wind blew in through the open windows and I was dazzled by the sun straight ahead of us. I let it blind me and the wind buffet me.

'Are you heading down to your boat?' I asked.

'Yes, we're getting all set. Salmon fishing should open in the next three weeks.'

'Do you need anyone?'

He smiled.

'Maybe someone to watch the children. My wife's coming with me.'

'I don't need work, anyway,' I was quick to reply, 'I'm heading back out with my skipper.'

'You fishing herring?'

'Black cod. Well, I was ...'

I showed him my hand. He understood.

'That can't have been pretty.'

'Nope,' I said. 'And I didn't say a thing. I wouldn't have said anything, anyway, because I wanted to stay on board.'

'But you'll be able to come to our annual festival at least, the crab festival.'

'I may be leaving again before then.'

'I'd be surprised. The festival's tomorrow.'

He left me outside the B and B. I held my head high and walked very quickly past the huge windows. I stopped at the small liquor store for some popcorn, then headed to the factories, passing crab pots and old gill nets. Sheets of aluminium had been left here and there, and blue tarpaulins that snapped in the wind. Ahead, the refrigerated containers stood waiting, lined up one against the other, stacked like a child's building blocks amid the constant hum of generators. As soon as I was past the tall facades of the first factories, I was at the docks. Longliners moored up here seemed to be sleeping. The decks were deserted. I recognised the *Topaz* and the *Midnight Sun*. The waves were topped with foaming crests. The *Mar Del Norte* was leaving, just drawing level with Dead Man's Cape. It looked to be heading south-east.

I sat down under a crane and gazed at the horizon for a long time, thinking that somewhere behind this blue, and in a still deeper, noisier and more agitated blue, there was a black boat embellished with a fine strip of yellow, ploughing through the waters. That I'd been granted the greatest happiness, the most wonderful feverish activity, the hardest work. That we'd shared so much in among the shouting and my fear, we'd shared because we were nothing without each other. I'd been given a boat so that I could give myself to her. I was part of that journey and I'd been cast aside along the way. I'd come back to a world of nothing; a world where everything is shared out and exhausted pointlessly.

I thought of the men working right now, of Jude, Jesús, Dave and Luis, Simon, the lanky man and the others, still working, always working. They were really alive, and they felt alive every moment. They were living a magnificent life, battling hand-to-hand with exhaustion, with their own tiredness and the violence of what was going on outside. And they stood up to it, they overcame their weariness until the slow hour when you're carving through the darkened sky towards perhaps some rest at last for some, but further effort for whoever was on watch, further struggle, against sleep, against eyes closing of their own accord, against the half dreams that fill the cramped space in the wheelhouse, whoever was alone in carrying all those abandoned bodies on board, in a one-to-one with the ocean and its moods, braving the sky and the demented birds spiralling in the white glow around the prow, carried by the roar of the engines, the never-ending swell of the waves and an awareness of every single person asleep in the world at that moment. As if he was the only person awake in the whole universe, a night watchman who cannot flag, his earthly loves turned to scalding pebbles that he cherishes deep inside him and that glow in the dark of night.

They were in the real world. And here I was in port, washed-up, in this day-to-day nothingness punctuated by rules, day, night. Time held captive, the hours parcelled out in a fixed order. Eating, sleeping, washing. Working. And what to wear? And what for, anyway? Using a handkerchief. Women: their hair domesticated around smooth pink faces. Tears came to my eyes. I blew my nose with my fingers. I looked out to sea again and sat for a long time. I was waiting for the *Rebel*. The horizon was still empty. So I stood up and walked back to town. Some men were unrolling a trawl net on the huge embankment along the docks. They waved to me. I waved back. The *Islander* was offloading. Dark-haired workmen busied themselves outside the Alaskan Seafood canning factory. A forklift coming up behind me made me jump. It gave a peremptory beep-beep and I stepped aside. I went back along Cannery Row, the dank road between the factories and piles of pots. The combined smells of ammonia and fish prickled my nose. The motor for the refrigerated containers was still humming as I passed. I walked, and walked some more.

Stands were being erected outside the harbour master's offices. I looked away, not wanting to see preparations for their festival – my own festival was out to sea and it was over, anyway. I was crossing Dog Bay Bridge when a car stopped. A compact woman with dark hair opened the door.

'Are you going far?'
'Just to the hospital.'

'Get in then. I'll drop you there. I'm going to Monashka Bay.'

She was so tiny I could have believed it was a child driving, but there were those fine lines around her eyes, the strong oblique grooves framing her mouth.

'Did you get hurt?'

'Yes.'

I moved aside the bandage and showed her the wound.

'Blood poisoning. A fish, right?'

'Yes.'

'That happens.'

'Do you think the cod season will end soon?'

'I couldn't say. I don't have time to follow all that too closely any more. When I was a skipper I'd have known straightaway.'

'Oh … you were a skipper?' I asked, eyeing the delicate wrists, the slender manicured hands holding the steering wheel. 'So a woman can run a boat?'

'I stopped when I was pregnant. I still have the boat but someone else skippers her for me.'

'And how do you get there?'

'Where? Get to be a skipper? You work. I started out as a deckhand, like you. You must know this – it's not the size of your muscles that matters. What matters is holding out, looking, watching, remembering, having some common sense. Never giving up. Never getting upset when the men yell. You can do anything. Don't forget that. Don't ever give in.'

'They're always shouting on the *Rebel*,' I said, 'and I was terrified, but I'd give anything to go out with them again.'

'You're green, that's how it works. We've all been through it. That's how you'll earn, first, their respect and then, more importantly, your own. You can hold your head high because you know you've really given your all.'

Her face hardened, her voice grew a fraction quieter and she hesitated briefly before saying, 'And sometimes it turns out you have much more to give than you thought possible.'

She paused, hesitated again.

72

'I had another boat,' she went on, 'ten years ago, or nearly. I was skippering it. We were crabbing. Shit weather. Fire in the engine room one night ... My guy was working with me. The boat didn't hold out long. The coastguard fished almost all of us out, twelve hours later. We'd drifted for miles in our survival suits. But him, he was never found.'

The wind had picked up. Steve came in late. Like every night. Like every night he tripped on the bags of clothes, bumped into the table. A cup rolled onto the carpet.

'You asleep?' he whispered.

'Yes. No. I'm still having nightmares, it's never going to stop.'

He sat down on my bed. With his elbows resting on his knees he rubbed his hands over his face, palms wide open, fingers spread as if wanting to cover his eyes. Then he dropped his hands and peered into the darkness.

'So are you going fishing again?' he asked.

'Oh, I hope so, I really, really hope so.'

'It'll be lonesome when you're gone. I'll be on my own, like before. Sometimes I go to Brother Francis's shelter, when I can't take it here any more, or I want a hot meal with people around, or I've run out of money. Other times, if I'm feeling rich, I spend a night in a motel, the Star. I order pizza and watch TV. It's still boring but it makes a change. Friends come by from time to time. But otherwise I like it here, I'm chilled.'

'Yes,' I said. 'It's not bad really. I wanted to sleep in one of the rusted trucks on the wasteland because I find it kind of claustrophobic here. But it would have been too cold. And it wouldn't have been polite to you.'

He laughed quietly. We talked in hushed tones as if not wanting to wake the silent building. I extricated myself from my sleeping bag and sat next to him, then reached for a cigarette from the table. He took out his lighter. The flame lit up the curve of his cheek, the lozenge of shadow over his eyelids.

73

'Thank you. Have one.'

'I smoke too much, you know,' he said but lit one anyway. 'And drink too much.'

'What will happen to me if the boat doesn't come back?'

'You'll find another. It's nearly salmon season.'

'But it's the *Rebel* I'm waiting for. It's with the guys on board the *Rebel* that I want to fish again.'

'The season's ending, they'll be leaving anyway.'

'That's true. Well, I'll go to Point Barrow, then.'

'What the hell do you want to do in Point Barrow?'

'It's the edge. There's nothing beyond it. Just the Arctic sea and ice fields. And the midnight sun. I'd really like to go there. To sit on the edge, right at the top of the world. I always imagine I'll dangle my legs over the void ... I'll eat an ice cream or some popcorn. Smoke a cigarette. And I'll know I can't go any further because it's the end of the earth.'

'And then?'

'Then I'll jump. Or maybe I'll come south again and fish.'

He laughed softly, 'Your idea's kind of crazy.'

We sat in silence. Steve stared at the floor. The wind outside whistled through the corrugated-iron roof and made the tarpaulins flap. I thought of the icy limpid darkness, the black boat which must have been pitching terribly under the vast sky as it followed its course, the men tossed about on deck, while the two of us whispered in that dark room, a dirty little box hidden in a bigger box, in the middle of a wasteland, the abandoned boat on its blocks acting as our night watchman among the sleeping ghosts of broken down trucks.

'It must be pretty lively out at sea,' I murmured.

'Yep. Pretty much.'

'How about you? Do you always stay ashore?'

He gave an embarrassed laugh. 'I get seasick, you know ... I'm more of a landlubber. You don't have to be a fisherman to love this place.'

'Where are you from?'

'Minnesota. Nearly two years since I came here.'

'How old are you?'

'Twenty-six. I didn't leave home till I was twenty-four. Sometimes a trip to Chicago, and that was all. Out in the country, right. My parents had – well, they have – a ranch. I've always lived with horses. That was good' – his eyes lit up in the darkness. 'I'm good at rodeos. There's always competitions where I come from. I won a lot.'

'Why did you leave, then?'

'I had – well, I have – four sisters. I was kind of alone out there, looking out across the great prairie.' He gave a little laugh. 'I had to go, you see. My future was right there in front of me, no questions, no surprises. It was just like the horizon, flat and even as that prairie stretching in every direction. I'd take over the ranch, as far as my parents were concerned that was a done deal, and my sisters too, they'd get married and go live in town. Basically, it suited everyone. So I left.'

'But why Alaska?'

'I wanted to become a man. There was no place else to go. Anywhere else I'd have been lost, it would always have been too close, more of the same. I'd have missed the ranch ... I came straight to Kodiak. And I swore I'd never set foot back there again. Ever. They don't get it, at home. They think I'll come home some day. They write me sometimes. For the first time in my life they may be worried about me' – he gave a sad little gulp – 'but that doesn't really change anything. Anything,' he said again in a whisper.

'I'm here now,' he said more brightly. 'I've learned how boats work, I already did a good job with my dad's machines, I'm a good mechanic. Andy's pleased with me ... he's demanding, Andy is, not easy to get along with, but he works hard and he respects people who work. He's kind of like my dad.'

He fell silent. Lit another cigarette.

'Sometimes I go watch the sunrise. We could go together if you like. It's in a few hours – that gives us time to get some sleep. I often get to see roe deer.'

We drove to the end of the road, some ten miles further north. The gravel track ended abruptly by a wood. I climbed out of the truck, amazed; I'd forgotten there was a world beyond the port. We walked under the trees, not talking much. Then we went along the coastline. A doe darted away ahead of us. And right after that the sun broke through the water.

We went into town for breakfast. The young waitress serving sugar and porcelain at Fox's recognised me. She gave me the same hostile look as when I came here with Wolf the day he was leaving for Dutch Harbor. She sure must be getting laid a lot, she seemed to be thinking.

Steve left me there to go to work.

'I'll get in earlier than usual this morning,' he said happily. 'I'll be there before everyone else. We don't have much to do right now, all the boats are out. Shitty little repairs, keeping ourselves busy basically.'

He turned away and pointed to the house over the road.

'Hey, you see that, that's the shelter, the Brother Francis Shelter.'

Wind, the ever-present wind. I walked down Shelikof Street; eagles glided over the harbour, the wind whistled through the masts. Wooden houses made splashes of bright colour against the increasingly green mountainside. I ate salmonberries growing along the embankment. They weren't ripe and the dust crunched between my teeth. Back in the harbour, boats danced, tugging furiously at their moorings as if wanting to break free and head out to the high seas, which must have been very rough. Even just beyond the harbour the waves were crested with white horses, indicating stormy weather at sea.

The stands for the festival were now all set up. Women stood laughing in a group, their hair billowing in every direction in the wind. I crossed the street, the doctor's surgery was just opening.

They made an incision in my thumb and the fish bone came out of its own accord. I kept it like a precious treasure, a big needle that looked as if it was made of glass. They told me it could have killed me.

'Next appointment in five days to take out the stitches. Keep the hand clean and dry.'

I was good to go fishing again.

I almost ran back to the hangar. I packed my things: one bag and a refuse sack for my sleeping bag and rain gear. My boots were on my feet. I poured myself one last coffee, the red thermos, the crimson chair. And I left. Ran all the way to the port. I returned to the lookout point I'd chosen the previous day, on the quay by the Western Alaska canning factory. I waited on the dock, staring out to sea, by my feet the refuse sack punctured by my Victorinox knife. A pick-up braked behind me, and a man climbed out and slammed the door violently. He was heading for the office in a big hurry when he noticed me.

'Do you want to go fishing, girl?'

'Er ...' I mumbled, hesitating, even though I was ready.

I didn't go with him – it was my boat that I wanted. I waited a long time for it again. In the end I got up and walked into town.

I'm drifting around the crab festival. Weighed down by my bags. I eat a turkey thigh at the coastguards' barbecue. Mothers stand around eating candyfloss while their children play in the dust, behind the chubby pink thighs of a teenage girl who laughs very loudly on the arm of a spotty-faced boy. A man on a bench opposite is overheating. He's just finished his styrofoam tray of fish and chips. He mops his flushed forehead, the palest eyes peeping from under his half-closed eyelids. He looks at the festivities around him, lingers on the girl's legs, her too-tight shorts, moves on swiftly, turns to me. He finishes his plastic cup of beer and smiles at me.

'Boring, isn't it?' he says in a gravelly voice.

'Yes,' I agree. 'It's a nice festival, but very boring.'

I leave my bags at the taxi office and we walk together to his boat. He reminds me of the fisherman from Seattle. Like him he's jovial and good-natured. He's just back from herring fishing in Togiak. Country music wafts from an old tape deck. We have a beer. He cuts up a fresh pineapple and pops some popcorn. He claps his big hands in time to songs that bring tears to his eyes.

'This is the most beautiful one, listen. *Mother ocean, oh mother ocean ...*'

He sings along, out of key. He has a child's eyes in a bright red face.

'The ocean's my mother,' he says. 'That's where I was born and that's where I'll die. That's where I'll go find my Valhalla when my time is up.'

He cries a little, sniffs behind his fingers. To break the mood he cracks open two more beers and hands one to me.

'So I did well this season but only because I'm careful and patient,' he tells me between two slugs of beer. 'I know where to find the fish. Maybe I'll have my own boat soon, seeing I don't drink like I used to.'

He's put 'Mother Ocean' on again and can't hold back his tears any longer. I look round the cabin, the two bunks covered with patchwork quilts, the enamel coffee pot on the stove, the varnished wooden wheel, the compass in its copper case.

'This boat's beautiful,' I say.

The man's strong shoulders are outlined against a square of sky, and the pearly orange of a fading sun that looks as if it's covered with foam as the clouds roll over it in heavy waves. Evening is approaching, ten o'clock maybe, and the colours grow more tender. It won't be long now before the sun tips behind Pillar Mountain. I suddenly need to get out, walk in the daylight before it dwindles to nothing. I drain my beer almost in one gulp and take a deep breath.

'I'll be going.'

He's sorry to see me leave.

'If you need somewhere warm to sleep' – he gestures towards one of the bunks – 'if you're ever in the shit, come find me. And be careful with the people you meet, you can get the worst kind of trash here, all the people who've chosen the Last Frontier because it's as crazy as what they have inside their heads. I'm Mattis, your friend, and you, you're a free spirit.'

That's the name of my bicycle, I think. And I say, 'Thank you, thank you so much,' and I look a little longer at his kind moon face, his eyes with a dried tear in the corner of one eyelid.

'Goodbye, Mattis.'

I've picked up my bags and I'm running under that sky. The sun has melted behind Pillar Mountain. The crab festival is still going on in the distance. Grey smoke rises from the coastguards' stand, spiralling, turning towards the sea and dissolving between the masts. The happy crowds are still eating hot dogs, turkey and crab. The girls' pink thighs have turned red. Alone on a bench facing the harbour, a man sits drinking from a bottle. His straight black hair falls over his shoulders. His dark eyes follow me briefly, then screw up further.

'Hey! Come have a drink,' he calls, waving the bottle of schnapps.

'Thanks,' I cry into the wind, 'but I don't like schnapps!'

I walk on to the hunting and fishing shop with its knives and guns in the window. In a photo pinned to the wall a colossal grizzly bear towers on its hind legs, jaws agape. One day I'll have a Winchester, for sure. I reach the arcade. The doors to all the bars stand wide open. I catch sight of men slumped on counters, dartboards, red snooker tables in back rooms. Bursts of conversation drift out to me, cries, glasses clinking, music ... I hurry past, afraid they'll see me. I reach the square, a small plot of trees and grass between two bars, the Breaker and the Ship. There are four benches arranged facing each other, and a few Native Americans are sitting here. Drinking vodka. An ageless woman drags on a joint. A fat man next to her calls out to me.

'Hey, you, I know you! You worked with Jude, right? My friend Jude, big Jude.'

He emphasises the word 'big'.

'What the hell are you doing here? Did you leave the *Rebel*? And these bags? Are you living on the street or did you just come ashore?'

'I was injured.'

'I don't understand a word of your frickin' accent. Come sit with us!'

I hesitate, he pats his huge thighs, sways from left to right, a big smile on that radiant face of his.

'We won't hurt you!' he proclaims in his loud voice. 'Don't tell me you're scared of the bums hanging around the square?'

'Oh no, I'm not scared.'

I sit down. He shakes my hand in his huge hot fist, it's slightly clammy and so soft and deep I don't know whether I'll ever get mine back out of there.

'I'm Murphy. They call me Big Murphy. And she's Susan. She's tired this evening, not sure she even knows you're here, but normally she's a really good woman.'

'I'm Lili.'

'So you left my friend Jude out at sea? Are you always this red?' he laughs, pinching one of my cheeks.

'I was evacuated off the *Rebel* for a reason, but it's healing now. I'll go join them again the minute they're back in town.'

I unpeel the dressing and show him my swollen thumb, the new incision and the black stitches coloured by disinfectant.

'Oh shit,' he cries, 'looks to me like your season's fucked.'

'You think so?' I ask, looking at him anxiously.

On the next bench a Native whose face is slashed with old scars slumps slowly until he topples over into a mass of red and yellow flowers.

'Oh,' the little woman exclaims.

Big Murphy puts a hefty arm around my shoulders.

'Come on, you're not gonna cry, of course you'll go back out on the *Rebel*. Even if you don't finish the cod season with them, they'll sure as hell keep you on for the halibut opening.'

His arm pulls me close to him and hugs me kindly. I relax against his broad chest. The little woman is about to fall, her head has drooped against the other side of this mountain-man. The man on the ground snores and his companions finish the bottle.

We hear shouting from the Breaker.

'It's nothing,' Murphy says gently, 'a fight. It must be Chris, he's stuffed a bunch of it up his nostrils again. He shoulda shared it out, woulda done him less harm.'

I make my way back along the road past the shipyard. Boats wait, shored up on blocks. A trawler passes on the horizon. The soft sound of the sea drawing back down the strand reaches me. Waves made iridescent by the last glimmers of daylight come up to lick the black pebbles on the beach. I go under Dog Bay Bridge. The deafening roar of a truck is amplified overhead, dwindling until it expires far in the distance. I walk past a stretch of wasteland with piles of old crab pots and gill nets; I pass the white wooden Orthodox Church with its turquoise dome. A raging storm is painted on the wall of a large stark building, opposite the Salvation Army, on the beach where three children are still fishing. A pick-up stops next to me: it's Steve, heading into town.

'I'm going for a milkshake, get in, I'll take you home after.'

I climb in and he sets off again with a squeal of tyres. I turn to face the wide-open window and close my eyes. The wind buffeting me smells of seaweed. Steve smiles as he accelerates and I can just picture him on the wide prairie, riding into an open sky.

He picks up milkshakes from a drive-through McDonald's.

'It's like a movie,' I say.

'Be my guest,' he replies solemnly.

We head home in the gathering darkness and chill night air, and each sugary mouthful makes us shiver. We sit in silence as the white pick-up races along the road between the trees that seem to open like curtains as we pass. Steve swerves to avoid ruts, the tyres crunching on the gravel. A pothole he doesn't see shakes us up violently, and I laugh. I turn to him and see a shy smile hovering over his smooth features, a delighted, incredulous expression, maybe he's amazed to have caused such amusement.

'Come to the bar with me,' he says.

But I'm tired. He leaves me at the hangar and sets out again alone. I go back to the red chair. The deserted workshop is lit up by neon strips. Darkness outside. Limpid. I look at my hand. In five days, perhaps. But where is the *Rebel*?

Steve woke me. I sat up in bed.

'Is it late?'

'Early more like, go back to sleep.'

But he sat down on the end of my bed. Like the day before, he put his forehead in his hands and stared into the darkness. I climbed out from my sleeping bag and took a cigarette, which he lit. The flame illuminated his sad face.

'Was it fun?' I asked.

'The usual.'

The wind whistled under the roof. He took a cigarette.

'So you'll be going fishing again now they've taken that piece of crap out.'

'I think it's fucked up for me,' I sighed, a wave of sad anger bringing tears to my eyes.

'You'll find another boat OK ... Andy will take you on for the salmon. Maybe even tendering, that's a cushy job, and you'd be at sea the whole summer.'

'I'm not interested in cushy jobs. And the end of the summer will be too late to go to Point Barrow: I wouldn't see the midnight sun. The sea starts freezing over. And it'll be too cold to sleep out of doors.'

He laughed sadly.

'You sure are stubborn. Maybe there's someone on the *Rebel* you want to go back for. The skipper, or Dave.'

'No, no. Besides, they have wives.'

'I'll end up all on my own. Like before.'

'You won't notice the difference really, we haven't talked much.'

'Yes, but you've been here. Deep down we're kind of the same, you and me.'

He looked down and sighed. A stronger gust of wind blew something over outside. I thought of that deserted wasteland under the moon again, the huge clouds unfurling across the sky like silent waves, the opposite of an ocean, which rumbles and roars, or of the wind, which howls. I thought of the ocean and the wind heading into the night, perhaps as far as the Bering Straits or even further, never ending; I thought of the boats out there now in that icy velvetiness, and of us, shut away behind these impenetrable walls like two stray animals.

I moaned in my sleep, still tormented by dreams. Steve snored softly. He went out to watch the sunrise but I didn't hear him go. Then there was someone here, sitting down on my bed. I opened my eyes, recognised the lanky man. I sat bolt upright. You! I threw myself at him, clinging on with all my strength.

'Can I come with you? Will you take me back on the boat?'

Even though he'd washed, he smelt of the sea and bait and wet rain gear under the soap and aftershave.

'Yes,' he said, laughing. 'Come.'

I rolled up my sleeping bag and was ready in a flash. I grabbed my bag from the floor.

And we left. I didn't think to leave a note for Steve, I didn't go back to the red chair. We drove to Safeway. He was talkative and I couldn't speak, my heart beating, afraid he would leave me ashore if it occurred to him to look at my hand.

We bought muffins for the men and sat down for a coffee. It was very early.

'We arrived at 4 a.m .... I left the guys unloading. The fishing was OK and we didn't lose any gear.'

I recognised this over-excited kid.

'How about your hand? Did they take good care of it? I called the hospital from time to time, they kept me up to date. Let's have a look ...'

I hesitated to show it to him.

'They told me it was fine, I can go fishing again.'

'Yeah ... it's still pretty ugly.'

'I just need enough clean, dry gloves.'

I scanned his face, his impassioned exhausted features.

'I've done a lot of thinking,' he said. 'We need to straighten out your situation. Immigration won't do you any favours ... Still, that's not gonna stop us in the meantime: you're coming with us for the halibut.'

I exhaled. My heart was pounding. I could have cried.

'Did Steve behave himself with you?' he asked.

'Steve's a good guy. We got along well.'

Ian frowned, his mouth hardened.

'What I mean is he behaved himself, yes. And so did I.'

His face relaxed.

'John's leaving the boat,' he told me. 'But we'll have an observer for this last trip.'

'So will I still be sleeping on the floor?'

He smiled.

'No, you've earned your bunk.'

He filled our cups from the urn of coffee.

'You know, on the *Venturous* there was an observer who was kind of a doctor ...'

But he didn't hear me, he was already on his feet and I had to run to keep up with those long thin legs.

'Time to go,' he said. 'We have a lot on our plate.'

We're leaving. It's a grey dawn. Windy, always windy.

The cold damp air whips through our blood. I'm alive. The skipper parks outside a long oval-shaped building, a vintage submarine, perhaps, with its metal walls and rusted portholes, washed up here one wild night, one stormy foggy winter.

'Where's this from?' I ask.

But he's already heading for the office.

'Wait for me in the refectory – go have a coffee.'

I wade through muddy ruts. I forgot my holey boots in the truck and my feet are soaking already. I tip my head back and feel the rain on my face, open my mouth to get a taste of it. A flock of seagulls circles over the dirty buildings, under a leaden sky. A group of Filipinos walk past me, the women's laughter mingling with the lilting tones of their voices. I open the door to the seating area. A smell of ammonia wafts down from the corridor. The men inside fall silent. I walk self-consciously across the room under the full weight of their curiosity. The neon glare is grim on their dark faces. I pour myself a coffee from a large thermos and sit in the corner by the cigarette machine. Conversations pick up again. I wait for my skipper ... the room empties. I'm pouring myself another coffee when the door swings open abruptly.

'OK, little sparrow, you coming?'

And I run after him again. My coffee spills left and right, I gulp it down, scalding my throat. I don't know what to do with the paper cup so I crush it in my hand and ram it in my pocket. A clerk almost bumps into me as I run. Ahead of us, the docks. The *Rebel*'s mast, shrouds and Furuno antenna emerging from the fog.

'I've brought you the sparrow,' the skipper calls out.

I jump down the metal rungs four at a time, my feet sometimes finding only thin air, and I steady myself with my arms. At last the tips of my feet feel the rail. And I jump aboard.

The buoy marking the channel glistens in the mist. The town shrinks further into the distance as the boat picks up speed. It's night-time. The skipper shouts an order and Jude replies from the bows with another hoarse yell. Dave has thrown me the stern line, Simon's taking care of the breast line. I've cleared the decks of longlines and lash them down along the sides. I coil up the ropes and attach them securely. After passing the coastguards' base, the boat turns towards the open sea. We leave the land behind and the wind picks up.

We bait hooks until deep into the night. The men are quiet. Waves surge up onto the decks to die.

'We missed you,' Dave says.

'So how was your little vacation?' asks Simon.

Jude cinches my waist when I bend over to pick up the fid. John isn't on board – you don't even notice, the guys say. Late into the night the skipper calls us in at last, and we head inside, cheeks burning.

'Holy shit, that smells good ... that smells like man-food!' Ian announces as he comes down from the wheelhouse.

He barges past Simon at the stove, helps himself to a huge plate of spaghetti and three ladlefuls of sauce swimming with hunks of meat. He comes to sit at the table and still refuses to notice Simon who's standing waiting. Dave squishes up next to me and Simon slips in at the end of the table.

'We missed you,' Dave says again. 'We really thought you'd taken another boat or been kidnapped by a handsome fisherman.'

The talking stops. We're devouring our food.

'Fuck!' Jesse exclaims suddenly. 'We forgot to fill up with water.'

Ian's face darkens.

'Well, we'll make do with what we have,' he says quickly and his voice has a hard edge to it as he adds, 'You get that, guys? Not a single drop wasted from now on. Clean the dishes with paper towels and wash cooking pots with seawater. And brushing your teeth can wait till Kodiak. We keep water for coffee and food.'

'I brought a jerrycan of water this morning,' says Dave. 'Ten gallons. I filled it at the tap on the docks. It's not meant to be drinking water but once it's boiled it should be fine.'

The newly arrived observer, a blond-haired man with a chubby face, glances at him in surprise. He doesn't dare to comment and stays huddled in his corner.

'What matters is we remembered gas oil,' I say with great conviction, taking a huge mouthful.

The skipper glowers at me. I drop my face towards my plate.

The men have gone to bed and Dave is on first watch. I go out on deck: the wind makes the cables clack, and the sea crashes onto the decks. The smell of the open sea. Inhaling the air like a horse, until my head spins, my body rigid with cold. The swell is inside me. I've slipped back into its cadences, its rhythm of deep surges transferred from the sea to the boat, from the boat to me. They travel up my legs, roll through the small of my back. Perhaps this is love. Being the horse and the rider. We'll be fishing again tomorrow. Tomorrow ... In a few hours the shouting, the fear in my belly, the line hurtling into the water, the noise, the waves and the fury of it all, a sort of whirlwind in which this taut body will no longer be its own, but a mechanism in flesh and blood driven only by the need to cope, hectic heart-rate, icy sea spray, face flayed by the wind, the final anchor on the mainline a longed-for deliverance. And fish blood will fall in streams. Somewhere right now those motionless old trucks still wait, the blue boat still rots on its blocks. They fall deeper into their mineral sleep, already dead, frozen forever in that bleak wasteland. And Steve within those walls, inside other walls, Steve's life sheltering amid a random collection of objects, between a pile of dirty washing, a television, the red chair, a thermos ... Is he back from the bar, did he bump into the refuse bags? Is he asleep?

But not us. Never again for us. We've left behind the fixed contours of that world. And at last we'll be back to the blazing splendour of this life. We are part of a breath that never ends. The mouth of the world has closed over us. And we'll give our strength, perhaps until we drop down dead. For us the exquisite pleasure of exhaustion.

My skipper's looking out to sea, daydreaming. His pale eyes have the same bright flash of grey. He lets his long, long arms rest lifeless on his parted thighs. His wide, soft mouth – almost a woman's mouth – is half open. I don't like creeping up on him like this so I cough. He turns, runs his fingers over his tall forehead and gives a tired smile.

'You have your own bunk this time, huh?'

'Yes, the same one as before.'

'The same as before?'

'Well, the one that was meant to be mine.'

He laughs.

'You see, everything comes around eventually. Now you'll have your own proper watches like Dave and Jude. There aren't enough of us to save that for the old hands. Is that OK?'

'Oh yes.'

'I thought so ... This is our last cod trip. We'll need a good week to get ready for the start of the halibut season. They're saying it'll be the 25th. It's already the 7th.'

'So will I be coming?' I look at him intently.

'Of course. It's a twenty-four-hour window, but that's twenty-four hours with no breaks. We'll have to pull out all the stops. We can't waste a minute to rest or whatever. It can be very, very lucrative if you find the fish ... And you'll see how beautiful halibut are. Huge too, sometimes. They can be over four hundred pounds. If they're less than three feet we're not allowed to take them, have to throw them back.'

'Will I be strong enough?'

'Not to get them out the water, well, I don't think so,' he says, laughing. 'But what with baiting, coiling, gutting fish, there'll be plenty to do, believe me, work for everyone, enough to drop dead with exhaustion at the end of those twenty-four hours, don't you worry.'

We're back to work and it's tougher than ever. The boys have heard that the *Blue Beauty* is kicking ass. But it will be a bad season for us. We've lost too many lines and the miraculous fishing of the early days never resumes. The shoals of black cod have snuck off elsewhere, and although the fishing isn't poor, it's never more than very average. Short of a miracle, we'll have little to show for our efforts.

But right now the skipper wakes us every morning with his yelling. We have to jump into our damp rain gear, I have to go back to my still-soaking boots. No time for a coffee, the wind whips our faces and the white sky dazzles our eyes. We don't even have time to realise that we're back out in the cold and the action – we shift from brutish sleep to a blind half-sleep. Our swollen hands are difficult to straighten, these arms and wrists need waking, forcing back to life. Our movements are mechanical, nothing matters now except the line winding back in, we must watch it and relieve it of its catch. Fishing, no respite.

Jude gulps down a fistful of aspirin every morning. For me the fever returns in the evenings. My sleep is haunted by the ocean. I'm in the swell. I turn over on my bunk and it's the current changing and I must follow it. A shiver runs through me and it's the wind buffeting me, I clutch hold of a damp piece of clothing rolled into a ball on my bunk, and it's a fish getting away, I struggle and call out: I'm trapped in it! Trapped it in! I'm rolled around inside a black wave.

'Shut it, Lili,' one of the men mutters. 'It's just a dream.'

The hooks file past. They launch themselves into the air when we put the lines out amid a deployment of pale shrieking birds. The mainline is our Ariadne's thread, our one obsession. We fish. Hours go by, we're no longer even aware of time. All that matters are the lines that need baiting, throwing back into the sea, hauling on board again … The fish that we gut, the ice that needs breaking up with a pick, as we kneel in the hold and the boat's listing tumbles us into the slimy water, against the turbulent tide of fish rolling around.

The cut in my thumb has scarred over. The purple colour of the joint is now edged with orange. I've pulled the stitches out with my teeth. The weather's sullen. The sea toys with us. We bump into the walls whenever we're in the cramped space of the galley.

Up on deck the boys are baiting lines. The lanky guy's in the wheelhouse. Jesse's working on the engines, I think. I bring out coffees and chocolate bars. The men pull off their gloves, Jude takes out a cigarette, and Simon grabs a cassette.

'May I?'

'Sure,' Jude replies in his deep voice.

He lights a cigarette, which makes him cough and spit. He blows his nose with his fingers.

'You'll end up killing yourself with your shitty tobacco,' Dave says, nodding.

Jude shrugs.

'What's killing me right now is imagining a woman and a shoot of heroin.'

'You'll never change,' Dave laughs.

Bob Seger has started up again on the tape deck with *The Fire Inside*.

'And a good bellyful of whisky with my coffee … that wouldn't do any harm,' Jude continues.

'Or a brandy,' Simon adds.

'For me it would be breakfast,' I say.

'She only ever thinks about food,' Dave says, laughing. 'But it's true it's nearly three o'clock. 'S about time.'

The observer was cold and has gone in.

'I think he's expecting breakfast too,' mutters Simon.

We've finished our coffee. I stub out my cigarette and put my gloves back on.

'There's no bait left. Who's going to get some?'

'I'll go.'

I slip behind Simon, crouch down, turn the metal handle and haul the heavy steel panel aside.

'I would have helped you,' says Simon.

I shrug and jump down into the hold where we keep the squid. The piles of ice have solidified, the boxes are held fast. I call out for someone to hand me a pick. Hunkered down on the icy floor, slipping and tipping from left to right, I battle to free the frozen boxes. My fingers stiffen. It hurts. I'm swept up in a wave of mounting amusement, unstoppable laughter, intoxicated by these frozen depths perhaps. I lift the boxes free and hand them up at arm's length.

'Hey, Simon! This is heavy!'

'Coming, sweetheart!'

I heave myself out of the hold. Jude offers an arm.

'What the hell was so funny in that black hole?'

I laugh again. I take off my gloves and blow on my freezing fingers. I find a hunk of waterlogged chocolate up my sleeve. Then head off to help Simon cut up the squid.

We've brought three successive sets back on board. Dave has gone down to ice the fish, Simon's at the stove, Jude and I are cleaning the decks. He works away in silence, the hood of his sweatshirt down, the neckline slashed with a knife. I still daren't look up and meet his eyes when we're on board, because he's the fisherman. For me he's the only one. He knows everything, Jude does. His strength isn't about the breadth of his shoulders or the size of his hands, it's in his words, the echo of his voice when it's lost on the waves and the wind, as he stands, nostrils flaring, alone in private conversation with the sea, sounding the waters as if reading something there – or nothing, perhaps he sees nothing there but a great desert stretching endlessly beneath the whinnying cries of gulls that rise off the sea in gusts like wind-horses.

Lunch at last. It's after midnight. I came inside when Simon was just finishing setting the table. The rice was waiting on the stove. The sausages and the tin of beans were warming, securely attached to the metal edges. Jesse went back up to the wheelhouse, plate in one hand, a Coke in the other. Ian was already sitting at the table. Jude was finishing his cigarette on deck. Dave was ahead of me. We wiped our hands on our dirty shapeless sweatpants, spattered with reddened water. We helped ourselves from the stove and sat down.

'Shut the fucking door, we're freezing our balls off!' the skipper yelled when Jude came in, taking his time about it, turning back to spit through the doorway. He pulled the door to without a word, an awkward half-smile on his lips.

He still has his eyes down now. The lion man always grows smaller indoors. He seems to be out of his depth in neon light, it flattens his features in a face scorched more by alcohol than the wind at sea. And much as he frightens me on deck, I'm all the more terrified when he turns back into this wounded man.

We eat in silence. The lanky man seems strung out. He's wolfed down half his plateful, pushes the rest aside in disgust.

'Please don't bother switching up the menu,' he says aggressively to Simon.

Dave makes a comment that only Jude hears. They laugh. Simon's nose is almost touching his rice.

'Well, I think it's very good,' I say.

'She'd eat anything. By the way, it's a while since I've seen you eat that fish gut crap of yours.'

'I saw her do it earlier,' says Jude.

He sneaks a glance in my direction which makes me burrow into the floor.

Ian looks at us in exasperation and gets up without a word. He disappears to the heads and the other men get up in turn: Dave stretches his great athlete's body, Simon goes out to smoke, Jude disappears into the cabin. I do the washing-up.

Jude has reappeared, he has his arms clasped around him.

'I'm cold,' he whispers and squats down only inches away from me, pressed up against the vent that blows hot air from the engine room. Dave has sat back down and is drinking a coffee. The skipper's taking his time. I look away. The lion man is reduced to just

Jude huddled up in an old woollen sweater, a shapeless faded blue thing.

'Nice sweater,' I say.

'A girlfriend made it for me a long, long time ago.'

His expression isn't fearsome now but gentle, almost shy. He gives the beginnings of a smile. What can the great sailor be smiling about? I think that right now he doesn't want to be a legend of a man, that he's tired and his hands hurt, he's cold, and doesn't even have any whisky or women or heroin. He just wants to withdraw to the warm breath exhaled by that vent.

The skipper emerges from the heads and tells us who's on which watch. One by one we disappear into the cabin and its hot stale air. Wrapped in our sleeping bags and propped against our dirty, still-damp clothes, we sink into our bunks, faces turned to the shadows, arms thrown back, bodies stretched out. And having strained, coerced, forced and injured these bodies, we release them at last to the sound of the engines and the endless rocking of the swell. And just as we gave ourselves over to the effort, we now surrender to sleep.

I fall asleep with my eyes turned in Jude's direction. I can make out his slumbering form occasionally wracked by bouts of coughing, the form that houses those yellow eyes, the breast that harbours strange violence, the breath shot through with alcohol and ocean winds. Hidden by the darkness is his face, the burned face that I no longer fear. No one can make out where I'm looking in the shadows. The swell lulls me and I roll in its embrace. If the lanky man will allow, this could go on forever, motoring over the black waters, the Bering Sea. Me giving my strength till I'm dead to my previous life, or till I'm dead, full stop. Till wear and tear and exhaustion have polished me down to a crystal, leaving nothing but the sea in me, beneath me, around me, and the lion man in flesh and blood confronting the waves, standing square on deck, his filthy mane buffeted by the wind that makes the shrouds clack, the crazed wails of seagulls spiralling, spinning and diving, a hoarse tormented sound amplified and then smothered by the wind.

'Your turn … Aren't you the lucky one?' Dave wakes me by shaking me gently.

'Yes.' I sit up straightaway and, still asleep, I whisper, 'Aren't I the lucky one, aren't I the lucky one …'

'Simon's up next,' Dave says before climbing into his bunk.

'Yes, yes.'

I stumble over piles of clothes, socks, boots. I don't bother to put mine back on – they're soaking anyway. I head for the wheelhouse in a daze, bumping into walls. Got to get there. I'm still half asleep. I gather my wits as I contemplate the screens: a dot of light represents a boat far behind us. It's a dark night, the sky will start brightening from three o'clock. Simon will have the glow of dawn, a red stripe on the horizon intensifying to strong fire then turning orange. I rub my face briskly, pinch my eyelids, which keep closing. The pressure from my fingers weakens. I stand up, leaning on the map table, and watch the bows break through each wave, which then crashes onto the streaming anchor. The supple shifting expanse has no beginning or end. We may or may not be making progress through space, through the black velvet of night. Sky and sea are as one, as one and tipped upside down perhaps, to confuse me all the more, and the foam glistening along the sides of the boat is just the Milky Way … But I'm falling asleep again. I rub my eyes and hop from one foot to the other. I take a nautical chart from behind the chair and a magazine slips out. I bend over to pick it up: now there's a girl lying on the floor of the wheelhouse with her thighs open. Well, well, a girlfriend for whoever's on watch. I respectfully stow the magazine back in its place and put away the map. The observer's sleeping like a baby in the corner by the stairs. The dot of light on the radar screen is further away now, the coast is hardly visible any longer.

I've come down into the engine room – deafening sound when I opened the door because the auxiliary is running. No water in the bilge. I pick up the grease gun (they described this procedure for me three times) and pump five good squirts onto the greaser for the propeller shaft. I cast an eye over the decks on my way back up:

nothing's moved, the tubs are stacked securely. I pour myself a coffee, too weak but still bitter, then make a long arm for the drawer to take a chocolate bar. When I get back to the wheelhouse I feel better, the icy wind has done me good. The observer has turned over in his sleep. All I can see now is his back, a tuft of blond hair, and a foot sticking out from under his sleeping bag. I settle into the deep chair – it's too comfortable a seat for keeping watch. Quick look at the GPS: all dark, nothing there now but the central dot, us, and the occasional faint glitter of light. A mouthful of scalding coffee, a bite of chocolate. The men are asleep, the boat's ploughing forwards, the whole world can sleep – I'm keeping watch. Are they all asleep in Kodiak too? Is there a bar still open? Men yelling at each other as they keel over onto the bar, old Native women watching them dispassionately, waggling their heads, cigarettes held in the tips of their heavily lined fingers and brought to their lips with a slow, elegant gesture, perhaps they're drunk as they slump slowly over the wooden bar ... It's not dark yet in Point Barrow. The sun climbs back up into the sky long before it touches the horizon. It's daytime in France now. From here I can love them with nothing to fear. I talk to them, so quietly that even the observer can't hear. He's asleep anyway. The boat carves through the black ocean. The horizon's growing lighter already, a thin trace of blood spreading, Simon's turn ...

'Time to pull up the gear, guys! Move your asses, let's go.'

I'm first out. The skipper's already in position, one hand on the outside control lever. The boys put on their rain gear. I've taken Jude's spot against the bulwark, to the right of the skipper. The buoy and its marker are drawing near. This time it'll be me who catches hold of them. Leaning out over the churning water, reaching the pole at arm's length, I'm going to hook seamlessly onto the buoy line. I lean out as far as I can. Below me, slabs of water smack furiously into the hull. They explode against its steel surface with a dull thud. The skipper eases us towards the buoy. I lean further. If Jude doesn't show up

I really am going to have to grab this line. A blast of cold water slaps me full in the face. I choke briefly, my face streaming with water.

'Get the hell out of there, Lili! It's not your place.'

The lanky man is looking right at me. Jude appears. I see him reach to brush me aside, and I scuttle out of the way. They all laugh.

'You're soaked now, that was clever,' says Dave.

'No, it's fine.'

And I go back to my place by the cutting table. I envy Jude his post, working over the waves.

The wind drops, the sky breaks open and a pale sun appears. Jesse is first to spot the jet of water through the mist. He drops what he's doing, points. The skipper stops the hydraulic hoist. Everyone will have time to admire the dark shape that goes on and on surging out of the water, half its body rising as if in slow motion, with infinite majesty and grace. The men's eyes light up with the same wonder every time we see the queen of the oceans.

'Fuck me, she's a beauty,' Ian says dreamily before restarting the engine.

Later we come across a sea otter floating on its back, holding a fish between its front paws and eating it comically. Dave tugs at my sleeve and I burst out laughing. The animal turns its alert eyes to us but doesn't stop eating.

'Look at that bastard eating our fish!' roars the skipper.

Two black fins break the surface of the water: a pair of orcas. The sea otter dives. Now all that's left is the solitary cormorant watching us in the distance and a plaintive wake of seagulls in a mackerel sky.

All the while the observer counts, weighs and measures our catches. Dark cod with an iridescent sheen, green and black rock fish with flashes of gold, red fish with bulging eyes, young halibut that have to be thrown back even though they're dead. This man lives in our midst, utterly silent since we left Kodiak. We barely even know he's here. We might sometimes remember him at night, when we step over his sleeping form on the floor of the wheelhouse.

'Not too bad sleeping there, is it?' I say one day as he gets up.

He gives a slight smile. He's very shy.

'Yeah, fine.'

'That used to be my spot,' I tell him proudly.

Simon's lost weight. He's grown tougher, his expression more confident. The men treat him almost as an equal. But mostly they just don't see him. If he'd learned to swear and spit and blow his nose with his fingers it might have been different. He clings to his student vernacular, hiding his private disasters behind formulaic expressions. Jude raises a surprised eyebrow, Dave smiles to himself, Jesse completely ignores him. He's losing face all over again so I pay him some attention. But it's the men's recognition he wants, not the greenhorn's, especially as she's a woman: it's his turn now to show me only indifference tinged with scorn. We're wary of each other, each defending our position on board. I hold my head no higher than he does, though, when the shouting starts up. And there's constant yelling once we're fishing. His fear produces a servile sort of eagerness. I'm no more impressive myself.

'Why are you here?' I ask him one night.

We've finished early, it's two o'clock. The sea's calm and we're smoking a last cigarette. Purple bags under his eyes make him look feverish, deepening the gaunt shadows in his thin face tensed against the cold. Crouching down on his heels, he shivers slightly as he brings the cigarette to his lips.

'I wanted to be on the ocean,' he says, looking out at the water. 'I was lying in hospital, car crash, stupid situation, coming back from a party one Saturday evening, we'd had quite a lot to drink. It suddenly hit me. Wanting to go to Alaska, the Last Frontier ... wanting to go away to sea. Leave everything behind. That suffocating life.' He smiles to himself in the dark as he admits, 'I did go back to college, though. No one would have got it if I'd disappeared just like that. I owed – I still owe quite a lot of money for the accident. So I said I was going up to Alaska to work for the vacation.'

'You won't be making a fortune this trip.'

He gives a disillusioned smirk, a blood vessel twitching in the corner of his eyelid makes him blink for a moment.

'No. But what mattered was doing it, coming here on my own and finding a boat.'

I look at him, amazed.

'And do you like it?'

'Oh yes,' he says.

'But you can't exactly say the men are nice to you. The skipper yells at you the whole time.'

He shrugs.

'Do you think they're any nicer with you?' he asks. 'At first I couldn't believe they'd give work like this to a girl who'd never done the job before, who'd come straight from her hickburg corner of countryside and wasn't even legal. I thought Ian definitely had other reasons for taking you on ... I can tell you I wasn't the only one who thought that.'

In the darkness I flush with anger and shame.

'And now, do you get it?'

'Yup. The fact you slept on the floor from the first night, I thought that was fair.'

'But it was totally unfair!' I say indignantly. 'Boat law says first come first served. I started working three weeks before you did, with Jude and Dave. I didn't have a single day off, and it was unpaid of course, not a cent. I came on board before any of you did, except Ian and Jesús. I had a right to my own bunk!'

'Don't get mad,' he says. 'Maybe they treat us like that on purpose, to see what kind of guts we have. You were kind of lucky in the end, with your infection thing. It's like they respect you more now.'

'I never complained. Never said anything. It was Jude who—'

'Yeah, big awesome Jude who went off and told the skipper he had to stop little missy cos she's never going to say it for herself ... We could have been in the shit because of you.'

'If I'd said anything sooner you'd have said I was being a girl, and I was complaining because I was a woman.'

'Yeah,' he said. 'Anyway, it's not a woman's place on board a boat. You're messing up your hands and your skin, you're exhausting yourself, and men can't help wondering about you.'

'About my ass, you mean? You exhaust yourselves and destroy your hands – I don't see why I have no right to do the same.'

'Don't you have a husband?'

'No.'

'Well, you'll soon find one here.'

'I didn't come all this way just to end up in someone's bed.'

'I don't see any harm in that,' he mutters.

Our cigarettes are long finished. The cold is more raw by the minute. A crescent moon has entangled itself in the shrouds. The door to the galley clatters open and Ian peers into the darkness.

'Hey, Simon, for God's sake! What the hell are you doing? You putting the world to rights? Do you think I'm doing your fucking watch for you?'

'Looks like I have to go,' Simon says.

'So, Ian, is it true that a woman has no place on board a boat?'

'Who told you that shit?'

'Simon ... Well, we were talking the other night. It came up in conversation.'

The lanky man shakes his head.

'Listen to what real fishermen have to say next time, not some kid who's never been out of school.'

'A woman picked me up hitchhiking in Kodiak. She was a skipper and told me I could be.'

'Women are tireless. And they can often be more patient than men. Men like to get stuff done, they want everything right away, they'll bust a gut getting stuck into things, they like using brute strength, the harder it is the more of a hard-on it gives them.'

'Dave and Jude aren't brutes,' I protest. 'And I like it tough too.'

'That's not what I meant,' he laughs. 'A woman fishing will tire herself out just like a man, but she has to find a different way to go about doing something men can do with just brawn and no brains, she has to turn it around, use her brain more. When a man's burned out and exhausted she can still keep going a long time, and most importantly she can still think. She has to. And I can tell you I've know women, itty bitty little women, heading up a whole crew of big tough guys, crab fishermen and rod fishermen. Not one answered back. First of all because the women were good at it, shit-hot skippers, and my God were they respected. The loads they'd bring back ... Guys would fight to work on boats like that.'

'So why are some people against it?'

'The men who don't want women on board – not little guys like Simon who's just repeating what others have said, but real men – maybe afraid they'll have their boats taken, that women want to run the show, change everything, organise everything – their own way – and rumble their shit.'

'Their shit?'

'Well, yes, all their talk of power, their tempers and grudges, the scores they're always settling with other men, all that crap that has no place on a boat. Get the picture? The shit that would be stirred if men were criticised in the heat of action, when they're fighting something out, for example, or being macho pricks for yelling at someone ... and the sex-related issues there'd be if there were as many women as men. There's no room for sex on a boat. That happens before or afterward. You're the only woman here and we all respect you. There are two of them on the *Blue Beauty*. And they're good, too ... For Andy to have chosen them over guys ...'

I chew nervously at the skin around my fingernails.

'Don't eat your fingers, they're dirty. Don't make that face either. It's just a generalisation. What men are afraid of is ball-breakers. Women who want to rule the roost on the grounds that they've been treated like shit for centuries. We leave our houses to women like that, they can leave us our boats. But the ones who like fishing, who fit in with life at sea and are prepared to prove themselves like the youngest little greenhorn, there's no problem with them. It'll always be harder because they have to prove themselves more.' Ian gives a long yawn. 'You're getting me talking, Lili, like this is really the time and the place, after a day like that.'

'So no one's pissed that I'm here, then?'

'Even if they were, you'd tell them to take a hike. Do your work, do it well, and learn to yell like them. Until you know how to tell them to fuck off they'll walk all over you. Anyway, if you were pissing them off they'd be sure to let you know. They had no trouble making you sleep on the floor. And they don't have a problem balling you out if you don't do what they want.'

'I don't fuck up too much, do I?'

He laughs.

'Now you're pissing *me* off, Lili,' he sighs. How about you go get me a coffee?'

'We've dropped anchor for the night – you just have to make sure we don't drag anchor. Check the Loran from time to time. I've marked our position on here. The anchor chain needs to stay at an angle of about forty-five degrees. Don't judge it by the water, the tide's strong, you'll keep thinking we're drifting if you look at the ocean. Go by the coast instead, but mostly use the radar, because we're likely to turn around on the spot. There shouldn't be any problems, the seabed's very rocky, we're securely anchored. There you are, enjoy, Simon's on next. If there's any problem—'

'Yes, I know, I should wake you, or Ian or Jesse.'

So here I am alone again in the vastness of the night. The boat tugs at its chain like a tethered animal but the anchor's well embedded. The engine idles slowly. Waves slide over the front of the bow. I think of the cod we've killed today. It must be wonderful to be a fish right now, naked in the swell, caught up in the rising tide. The observer makes a strange moaning sound in his sleep, a sort of yelp. He sits up. No, he's gone back to sleep. I look at the coast to my right: it's disappeared. I panic for a moment. The water's scudding past us too quickly. Has the boat broken loose? I peer at the Loran, we haven't moved. I look around, the coast is on the left now. I can breathe: we've just done a one-eighty.

My eyes drift over the floor and I catch sight of a gangion. When I bend over to pick it up I come face-to-face with a small cupboard.

I open it: it's stuffed with old pairs of gloves. I push them back and feel something hard with my hand – a half-full flask of Canadian Whisky. I bury it back under the gloves. Jude. I think of the swigs he takes every night, looking out to sea, maybe drinking it with his horrible coffee, just a tiny tot of the amber liquid. I notice the horizon growing lighter. And suddenly I find myself thinking about crickets ... in summer in France. Strange to think it's summer in France, the smell of earth scorched by the sun all day, the sound of a river, the brambles and dry grasses along its banks ... There was a river where I used to go and sleep in summer, the soft chirrup of crickets in the warm night air.

My eyes open wide in the shadows. The muted sound of the engine. The men's breathing. I turn to look at Jude asleep. He's moved. The soft light from the passageway has glided over his face. His hand between his heavy thighs. He must be dreaming about women and heroin. And whisky.

My skipper's looking out to sea, daydreaming again. He has told me people reveal themselves on board a boat. He must be so sad, I think as I watch him.

'So, Lili, not finding the season too hard?' he asks, turning round.

'Oh no.'

He smiles.

'I knew you'd like it. I've seen enough greenhorns to recognise the one's who'll get hooked.'

'Am I up to it?'

'Sure ...'

'Are you going then, crabbing in the Bering Sea?'

'Maybe. Have to go down to Oklahoma first. See my kids. My wife.'

'You don't see them often.'

'Not very. I did spend the winter there, though. They're growing. They're beautiful.'

'Your wife must miss you.'

He gives a sad smile.

'Maybe. I gave her a tough time, behaved like an asshole. In the days when I came home blind drunk every night.'

'But you don't drink now. And you're a handsome man.'

His face brightens briefly, he looks embarrassed.

'If you say so.'

I move closer to the window, look out to sea.

'Will you take me on if you do it, this winter season? I'll work as hard as I can. I'll give everything.'

I turn around. His eyes are wavering, then he looks away.

'Your goddamn accent ... it does something to me. But yes, I'll take you on.'

'Will there be lots of us?'

'Same. Six or seven.'

'Will you take the same crew?'

'Jesse'll probably come. Dave already has a job somewhere else. Simon's going back to college – and I don't want him anyway. Jude, yes, if he's still OK.'

'I'd be glad if he came. I'd like to go fishing again with you and Jude.'

He frowns.

'Why Jude?'

'He works like a lion. And he's good. He never says anything, doesn't get involved with anyone. When it's done he goes to sleep. And he always brings us a coffee when we're working on deck and he goes to get one for himself.'

'Yes, Jude really is someone. Without him and Dave ...'

'The greenhorns weren't going to fill the hold, that's for sure,' I admit.

'Come on, you two worked well. But if you want to keep fishing, Lili, you can't stay illegal. Immigration will get you sooner or later.'

'Yes, but what can I do?'

'Get married.'

'I don't want a husband.'

We're going back to shore. We'll be able to shower at last. And brush our teeth. Dave grins at the thought of his girlfriend.

'And maybe we'll make a trip to Hawaii after the halibut season, if the fishing's good.' He looks at me a little sheepishly and adds, 'I mean, that's not really my thing, the beach and all that shit, but she gets kind of bored in Kodiak and she's been dreaming of Hawaii the longest time.'

Jude's dreaming of bars, the whisky he'll down as soon as he's ashore, and the next day and the next. Simon doesn't say anything. A Scandinavian beer perhaps. Jesse can't stop talking about the giant pizza he'll order the moment the *Rebel* touches the quay.

'De-ca-dent,' he keeps saying excitedly. 'A decadent pizza with a six-pack of beer.'

The skipper looks worried. He just says it's high time he called Oklahoma.

'How about you, Lili? Will it be ice cream or popcorn?'

I'd really like to get drunk too, go and paint the town bright red, with or without Wolf, and finally taste these White Russians that Jason's told me so much about.

Ian wakes us at dawn on the last morning. The thought of going back hasn't put him in the best of moods.

'Get up in there!' he bawls. 'Don't go thinking you're on vacation already!'

We're instantly on our feet. We pull on sweatpants over our long johns, then socks and boots. The daily aspirin as we pass the medicine cabinet. Jude hands me the box wordlessly. I look away and stand aside. He passes me apparently without even seeing me. Ian's still yelling in the galley, his features carved with a knife.

'Move your asses, guys! We need to polish the boat, she has to be spotless when we get into harbour. Can't show up looking like this. You, Simon, take care of the galley. Scour the oven with wire wool, it needs to shine like new. Put oil over it. Same with the floor. You, Dave, the walls. Wash them down and put linseed oil on the woodwork. Bleach for the fridge. Get all your crap off the seat and the shelves. Scrub the stairs to the wheelhouse with wire wool also, get the heads spotless. Jude, you can do the decks with Lili. Scrub them with brushes. The whole lot. I don't want anything left lying around, not the tiniest scrap of squid or guts, not one hook or gangion. Dig out the fish guts from every corner. The boat needs to look like new. I want to give them a real eyeful when we come in.'

Jude nods.

'Sure,' he says and goes outside.

I follow him. Fine dense rain, mist all around. A damp chill worms its way right into my heart. This is so sad, the end of a season, the boat going back and everything dying after the show. We put on our rain gear. Jude grabs a scrubbing brush, throws me one too. Icy water streams over the deck when he turns on the pump. I step aside too late, the powerful jet pours over my boots. My feet are soaked and I feel like crying. We haven't been allowed coffee and I'm alone on deck with a grumpy Jude. And this evening we're going ashore.

He fills a bucket with water and chlorine, he's already scrubbing the standing shelter. I do the same, at a safe distance. Guts, dried blood and old bait cling to every inch of it, you have to scrub long and hard to shift them. At the stern the deck is worse: along the gutter and in every corner I find scraps of whitish flesh, bits of putrefying squid. Jude works quickly, scrubbing tirelessly. I bite my lip and put my back into it. It had to come to an end some day. I'm already feeling warmer. Jude stops but I keep going, frowning intently. I'm afraid of his contempt if I stop too.

His deep, slow voice: 'Take a break, you want a cigarette?'

I look up, hesitant.

'Yes,' I mumble eventually, 'please.'

He gives me the packet and I stop to catch my breath. My cheeks are blazing.

'Light it yourself. It's windy,' he says, handing me his lighter.

'Yes. Thank you.'

'Sure,' he replies with an amused smile. 'You're red ... I haven't seen that very often.'

'Yes, I know,' I say in a strangulated voice, then pick up my brush with a, 'Well, I'll be getting back to it.'

He spits and blows his nose. I attack the flying bridge, putting all my weight into it. Jude rinses down the decks with great streams of water from the hose. Icy droplets sting my face. I have stomach cramps. My neck and shoulders are screaming. I think of the skipper drinking coffee, slumped in his captain's chair. Well, this evening, I'll be having beer.

'That's enough,' Jude says eventually. 'Let's see how they're doing. It may be coffee time too.'

The land draws closer. We're out on deck, dirty and happy, a coffee in our hands. I feel thin, my stomach's empty, my body hollowed out. I look at the decks and I'm proud of us.

'Lili!' Dave calls. 'There's someone here for you.'

The *Rebel* is moored at the docks and I'm coiling a rope. I turn round: a thin fair guy is standing on the quay, looking tiny between the white plastic containers and the orange crane. His red hair stirs in the wind – Jason. He heard from the factory that we were coming in this evening. He came to wait for me to go and drink White Russians.

'I have stuff to do ... Later!' I cry down from the deck.

'Tony's?'

'Yes, Tony's!'

The boat's unloaded, the hold clean, and we're sitting on deck eating pizza. We all shower in the factory's changing rooms. I put on clean clothes and my untied hair shines and floats on the wind. Jude looks at me amazed and with a new kind of respect but looks away when I catch his eye. I'm not afraid of him now: he's not the master on board this evening. The *Rebel* goes back to her mooring in the harbour. Eager to get away, we swiftly tie her up to the pontoon and plug in the electric cable.

'Watch out for hangovers, guys ... I want you all up at six o'clock tomorrow morning.'

The boys are far away already. I run to catch up, then turn round: the skipper's stayed aboard, tall, lankier than ever, framed in the doorway. I retrace my steps.

'I guess you can't come with us?' I say.

He's lit a cigarette. Sketches a smile, only just, then the corners of his mouth drop again, his lower lip heavy.

'Go with them, can't you see you're getting left behind? Go to the bar, go on, have a good time.'

They've already disappeared round the corner ... I'm off again, running, jumping over ruts, my hair flying like a wake in the wind. I catch up with them along the docks, out of breath. Dave has stopped at the phone booth to call his girlfriend. Simon's gone to meet up with his gang in Gibson Cove, students from the lower forty-eight, in the bare wind-battered inlet, in an improvised encampment of tents and tarpaulins. Jude didn't wait for anyone. Dave and I walk over to Tony's and find the place full. The crew of the *Venturous* are drinking at the bar. Jason was watching the door and waves to me.

'Hey, my friend!' he cries. 'Welcome aboard!'

His eyes roll like marbles under his bushy eyebrows. Dave nudges me towards the crew.

'I think I can leave you, you're in good hands. I have to go, my beauty's waiting for me and I can't wait to see her. Get someone to walk you back when you're done. Stay away from trouble, girl.'

I dive into the fray. Jason's found me a stool, and a scrawny waitress with dilated pupils in a ghost-white face serves me a milky brown drink in a wide glass. White Russians are strong and sweet. The alcohol goes to my head very quickly and it's a searing pleasure, honey in my aching body. Men clink glasses all around. Everyone's just back from sea.

I pay my round.

'A rum for me, I'm a pirate!' Jason bellows.

I decide to stay Russian, and opt for vodka. I look at the faces around me, and don't spot anyone I know. Steve must be at the B and B. Jude at the Ship, the gloomy old bar with the Native women in the shadows and the fat nudes on the walls.

I don't stay late. It's too clean at Tony's and the boys are all crazy young dogs. I think of the blue darkness and suddenly miss the boat. I wish I was on deck, alone, rocked by the waters of the port, sniffing the air, looking at the reflections of the town's glowing red lights. I abandon Jason and make my way through the crowds to the door. Outside the air is pure, the roads deserted. Taxis wait for rides by the harbourmaster's office. I take a road that cuts through town and see the sea at the far end, rippling black in the light of the lamps along the quay. I run towards it, there's a light breeze. A bird flies off with what seems like a deafening beating of wings.

I slow down and then remember the *Free Spirit*, which I left behind the B and B during the crab festival. I hurry along the quay enjoying the good silty smell of the night air. I cross the street, sneak behind the bar and search through the dark recesses between the building and a bank of earth. But there's only a torn gill net, empty bottles, a hunk of rusted iron. A punctured buoy gleams pitifully through the brambles. The *Free Spirit* has gone. I give a wistful sigh. A burst of voices as two drunken men come out of the bar and I slink into the shadows behind a pile of pallets. When they've moved away I emerge from my hiding place and cross the street back to the dock. Low tide. I cling to the handrail on the wet footbridge that slopes down to the pontoons. They say drunken sailors fall into the water on their way back to their boats and that's when they drown. I lean over for a moment: the water's black, hardly moving. I spit, just to see, and my spit falls with a soft plop. I hear someone coming and scarper back to the *Rebel*.

The lanky man is on deck. I can see the incandescent tip of his cigarette moving in the darkness, coming up to his lips, growing brighter and more intense, then dimming when his arms drops back down. A red palpitating thing like a heart in the night. He's looking towards the town. I jump on board.

'Hello, skipper,' I say softly.

He turns. A mask-like face buried in shadow.

'Is that you, Lili? Already?'

I laugh quietly.

'Yes, my bike ... well, it doesn't matter.'

'Did you have a good time? Were you with the guys?'

'Yes, no, I met up with the crew of the *Venturous*. We drank White Russians. Then I got bored.'

He hands me a cigarette and comes closer to light it.

'Thanks, Ian.'

The harbour is quiet – life happens in the bars at this time of night. We can hear boats tugging at their moorings, buoys rubbing back and forth, trapped between the hulls and the pontoon, the water lapping at hulls. I sit down on the panel over the hold and he sits next to me.

'What did you do?' I ask.

'We went for something to eat at the Mexican restaurant, Jesse and me. Then he went off drinking, so I came back.'

'Aren't you bored?'

'I've stopped drinking. Not gonna get back into that shit just cos I'm bored.'

'You're right. It's not even any fun in the bars. It's good at first, but it doesn't last.'

'It's OK, you know,' he says.

He's not fooled so I stop talking.

'Gonna have to work like crazy,' he says. 'Only a week till the opening. Tomorrow morning we'll begin cleaning tubs, any lines that are too knotted we'll put to one side, no time to lose. Have to take the old bait off the others, change any damaged gangions, replace missing hooks. And get back to baiting straightaway.'

Jude and Simon came back late in the night, I didn't even hear them. I wake at five with a feeling of urgency. It called to me through my dreams: a morning in harbour. Jude snores terribly, coughing in his sleep every now and then, paroxysms of hoarse coughing, almost choking him. Simon sleeps with a sort of application. Dave isn't back. In the half-light I grab my clothes, feeling for my socks among the men's things, and take a few coins from under my pillow. I slip out without a sound. The light in the galley smacks me in the face. I throw my clothes on, shapeless trousers over my long johns, sweatshirts and sweaters, my boots. I fill the coffee maker with water and turn it on, then leave. Alone and free on the docks. A boat moves away from the quayside as I walk through the morning air. Breathing in the water, its smell of seaweed and salt, the undertow of sludge and diesel, so thick they stick in my throat. The wind has dropped and there's barely a ripple on the water. The wail of the ferry cuts across the harbour briefly. An occasional pick-up drives past. Men sleep it all off, nestled in bunks or in the fresh feel of clean sheets in a motel, at the Brother Francis Shelter, on a bench . . .

I walk. Seagulls sweeping slowly across the sky, eagles motionless on masts. Birds seem to be the only ones to have survived the night. The sun appears and with it Pillar Mountain, tearing its way out of the mist. The taxi office is already open and I stop off at the washbasins in the harbourmaster's building. I jam the door shut with a foot and wash myself with my scarf. My hip bones are like white fins on either side of my stomach, my buttocks as hard as polished wood. The comb gets stuck in my hair, I grit my teeth and pull, dragging a clump out with it. I give up on the comb and finish tidying my hair with my fingers. When I come back out an eagle and two crows are fighting over a dead fish on the deserted quay. The air feels good in my throat after last night's cigarettes. I walk past Tony's, the liquor store, a truck unloading at a supermarket and a tired man swaying against the morning sky. He abandons his attempts to go anywhere and collapses onto a bench. His face hidden by dirty black hair, he stares at his muddy shoes in a daze. I walk across the deserted square, avoiding ruts. The wings I've grown and the feeling of splendour evaporate when I walk into Bakery Hall, swapping the daylight for neon light. Smell of freshly ground coffee. A plump redheaded girl is just finishing arranging her display of cakes. She glances quickly in my direction.

'Just a minute please,' she says in her high-pitched voice.

I shrink back. My disproportionately large man's hands suddenly weigh down my arms. She turns her green, woman's eyes on me.

'I'm all yours now.'

'Oh, I'd just like a coffee,' I reply, my voice reduced to a whisper.

A young fisherman in green boots comes in, his lightweight trousers a second skin over his vigorous thighs. He lopes up to the counter, tall smooth forehead under dishevelled hair. Every muscle in his legs ripples under the sheath of cotton. The young redhead has turned, her face lighting up. She works her eyes, there's something more rounded about her every move and the tone of her voice. I go and sit down opposite the door, their conversation reaching me only in distant snatches. It's white outside.

The docks are already coming back to life when I return to the boat. I was worried I'd be late but the boys are still asleep. Dave is on deck. Planting his hands in the small of his back, he stretches his long supple limbs.

'You look happy, Dave!'

'I am happy,' he laughs. 'Are you only just back from last night?'

'No. A little coffee ashore, that's all. I got back early last night.'

'You abandoned the handsome Jason?'

Now it's my turn to laugh.

'I don't give a damn about Jason.'

Dave disappears into the cabin and I hear him rousing Jude.

'Hey, brother! The party's over,' he says almost gently. 'Those rotting tubs are waiting for you.'

Simon has emerged from his bunk. Dave comes and sits in the galley where I've put four mugs on the table. Jude appears, pole-axed by the early-morning call. He heads for the sink like a sleepwalker and splashes some water over his blotchy swollen face. He pours himself a coffee, blank stupor in his unfocused eyes.

At the bottom of the footbridge two men are fighting over a trolley to load their crates of bait. We're hard at work at the back of the deck, on the long aluminium table laden with stinking tubs. The *Rebel* is moored stern-to and we can see people go past when we look up. Our fingers are marinating in a briny liquid. The bait is beginning to rot and when we take it off the hooks, it's just a stretchy viscous slime that sticks to our holey gloves. Guys walk past, duffel bags slung over their shoulders. Others have rammed all their stuff into refuse sacks.

'Need anyone on board?'

'Full up!'

Smooth-skinned students go from boat to boat offering their services, hoping to find a place.

'Need any help baiting?'

'Have to see the skipper about that. But he's out right now.'

And off they go to try their luck elsewhere. Murphy, the mountain of a man from the park, appears from the end of the quay, swinging his bulky hips. He stops by each boat, jokes with the boys, laughs loudly, rolls his way heavily to the next.

'Lili!' he cries when he reaches us. 'So you made it back to your boat! Suddenly you weren't around ... How's your hand?'

Jude is working opposite me. He looks up for a moment, glances at me, surprised. His right eyebrow arches. He turns towards the dock.

'Hi, Murphy,' he drawls. 'How are you? I get the feeling you're looking for work.'

'Hello, brother, no fucking way do I want to do this opening, think I'll make a few bucks on gear work.'

'Come back later if you don't find anything, the skipper shouldn't be long.'

'Where is your skipper?'

'He must be nitpicking somewhere in town.'

Murphy shifts his great bulk from one leg to the other.

'I'll keep looking for a while,' he says. 'If that doesn't work out I'll take a walk around the square. Come by and see us when you have the time. We may have a little something to drink.'

'So you're back on it?' Jude asks.

'Some days, yes. OK then, I'm out of here. Hang on in there, Lili!' he says, turning to me. 'Take care, Jude. I remember how sad she was to leave the *Rebel*. She cried on my shoulder.'

'Sure,' Jude replies in that unreadable way of his.

Murphy walks off to the next boat.

'How do you know him?' Jude asks, scowling.

'From the square.'

'What the hell were you doing in the square?'

'It was the crab festival. When I was waiting for you all after I was in hospital. We chatted one time.'

'Hmm,' he says.

He looks down at the longline, goes back to splicing a broken line. He lights a Camel, spits on the deck. He's far away again.

Simon tips a tub full of old bait over the rail.

'Enjoy your meal, crabs!' says Dave. 'Maybe it's our lunchtime too.'

Adam who crews for the *Blue Beauty* comes by in the afternoon. Ringed with grey, his eyes look paler still, hunkering down in their sockets like wild animals on the lookout. The withered skin of his eyelids quivers constantly. Deep wrinkles run across his forehead and carve into his haggard cheeks, from the edge of his nostrils to the corners of his embittered mouth. His face frightens me but Dave slaps his shoulder and laughs.

''Parently you filled the boat right up? Congratulations, old man ... From the look of you, you must be glad to be getting some sleep.'

'It's all I'm doing right now. Ten hours in total, that's all the sleep we got the first week. I only get up to grab something to eat at Fox's, then I go back to bed. I'm too old now to fish for Andy ... he'd have killed us on the job if he could, the bastard, the son of a bitch. I don't even know how he holds out himself, he didn't get any more sleep than the rest of us, less probably. It must be the thought of the dough that makes him so driven. But I've earned enough.'

'So you're not doing the halibut opening with him?'

'I'm done working with him,' Adam says. 'Ron, the guy I keep the *Anna* for, is letting me take her out for this season. Nice boat, stands up to the sea well, thirty-two feet. I'll do the halibut and then I'm out of here, back to my forests.'

'How much cod did you catch?'

'Hundred and twenty thousand pounds on the nose. How about you?'

'Ninety thousand tops.'

'I heard you lost some gear?'

'Thirty tubs,' Dave mutters.

Adam gives a long slow whistle.

'Fuck! How'd that happen?'

'Caught on the seabed. Strong current. The lines drifted.'

'Could Ian have avoided it?'

'Yeah ... maybe. He's really pissed because Andy gave us shit gear.'

'Well, yeah, compared to ours.'

'What makes him even crazier is we have to replace it with new.'

'Andy's not the type to do anyone a favour,' Adam says wryly.

'I don't know many owners who'd do favours for the skippers they take on.'

'Yeah, right.'

Dave drifts away and Adam turns to me.

'So how's that hand?'

'It's OK. I pulled the stitches out with my teeth,' I tell him, laughing. I take off my glove and show him my dirty hand. He grimaces, his face looking even more tormented than usual.

'It's really not pretty,' he says, then drops his voice to add, 'I was looking for you last night. I need one more person on the *Anna*. There are three of us. Four would be better.'

'That's kind of you, Adam, but I'm on the *Rebel*.'

'With me you'd be properly paid, I don't yell, you'd be respected and you wouldn't sleep on a gross corner of floorspace.'

'I have my own bunk now.'

He shrugs his shoulders and looks away. He's tired – he looks ready to weep he's so exhausted. He should go back to bed.

'I found myself a room at the bunkhouse, the long grey building beyond the orthodox church, just before the boatyard. Fifty bucks a week. It's just a room but I have a hotplate and there are showers, as much hot water as you want. Come see me. You haven't stopped since April. Need to rest too. They'll wear you down and use you up.'

Adam says all this quietly but Jude looks up from time to time and eyes us irritably. He spits more loudly than ever, blows his nose angrily. A gob of spit spatters on deck right next to us. Simon barges past me with a tub full of rotting bait: Sorry! Dave comes out of the galley with a steaming cup in his hands.

'Fresh coffee for anyone who wants it!' he calls.

'Maybe I'll come by one of these days if I have time,' I tell Adam.

I get straight back to work. Jude raises a scolding eyebrow at me.

Ian reappears and hardly even casts his glowering eyes over us before disappearing into the wheelhouse. Andy follows close behind him, taking no more notice of us. His inscrutable face shows very little sign of exhaustion. Dave and Jude glance at each other. We can hear raised voices. Adam nods, Simon smiles, Jude looks unperturbed.

'Oh my,' says Dave. 'Looks like there's a problem.'

'Get the feeling you won't be seeing much dough, guys,' Adam murmurs.

Jude spits overboard.

'I've been killing myself working for more than a year to earn nothing, or maybe just a few cents,' he says. 'It would have been too good to be true if my luck had changed.'

His rugged face softens, he pulls off his gloves, puts one foot up on the table and leans his whole body against the thigh of his bent leg. He lights a cigarette and watches the smoke rise, a resigned smile just curling the corners of his mouth.

'Might as well take a break seeing as whatever we do we're not being paid.'

'The game's not over,' says Adam. 'There's still the twenty-four-hour window.'

Jude shrugs and looks off into the distance, beyond the entrance to the harbour.

'Mmyeah. Looks like the price of halibut's going up a bit.'

'Lili doesn't give a damn,' says Dave, smiling at me over the table. 'She won't be paid but she's happy.'

'Well, not exactly. I won't even be able to go to Point Barrow.'

The boys turn to look at me.

'She's at it again,' says Dave.

'You're crazy,' says Jude.

I don't say any more because the boys think I'm a dope and maybe they're right. We can hear the radio on the neighbouring boat: the Kinks, something about going away to sea in summer.

Jude has gone over to the other side of the deck for a pee. Simon glances at me over the longlines to see whether I'm embarrassed.

'In my country, men piss wherever they like,' I say. 'What the hell should I care?'

In the end Jude's the one who's shocked. He tips a tub overboard, emptying out the dregs of old bait. Then goes off for his pee. Inside.

'The sea lion must be turning,' says Adam.

'Andy's asking for you,' says Dave.

'Me?'

I jump to my feet, immediately thinking of Immigration ... Or does he not want me on board any more? I remove my gloves and slip behind Simon. The man standing imposingly in front of the fo'c'sle watches me approach, his square shoulders broad across the doorframe, a taunting self-assurance about him. I stand in front of him, flushed scarlet.

'Yes?' I manage in a strangulated voice.

He senses my fear and I see him smile for the first time.

'I owe you some money,' he says in a clipped voice, and hands me a cheque.

'Me?'

'Your gear work with Diego for the Blue Beauty.'

He's already gone back into the galley. I look down at the cheque in my filthy hands, then take off my rain gear and try to join him.

He's talking with the lanky man, a tense exchange. I hang back, parked in the corner by the oven.

'What the hell are you doing there, Lili? Isn't there enough to do on deck so you have to come and hang around here?'

'It's just I wanted to talk to Andy,' I say feebly.

Andy turns to look at me, the pale steely eyes as piercing as ever.

'What is it?'

'The cheque, it's way too much ... I didn't do that many tubs.'

A glimmer of amusement comes into those cold eyes. He smiles for the second time.

'You've earned that money. Go back to work.'

The men have been waiting for my return.

'So, are you fired?' Dave asks, laughing.

'Not yet. He just gave me some money. I told him it was too much but he didn't believe me.'

They've all turned to look at me, their faces stunned.

'How come you've been paid already?' Simon asks suspiciously.

'The damaged longlines that I overhauled for the *Blue Beauty* when I was ashore.'

This reassures them.

'Still,' Simon mutters.

'You must never, do you hear me, never refuse what Andy gives you. It's rare enough as it is. Pocket it right away,' Adam tells me with a note of reproach.

Andy leaves and Adam heads off too. Ian stops our work when the sky shifts to mauve and the decks of neighbouring boats have been deserted for a long time. Dave is in the biggest hurry to shake off his rain gear. Simon's gone off to meet up with his students. I leave the boat. Ahead of me on the road, Jude is walking into town. He moves slowly, his shoulders heavy, above him the summer sky with the full weight of its emptiness and wind. I'm about to overtake him, but I slow down. I wish I could vanish. The piercing cry of a seagull seems to laugh at us. Don't let him see me, don't let him know I've seen him, this tired man walking in the evening light. An eagle still glides overhead. Jude turns at the corner of the quay, walks past the toilets and the harbour master's office, now very close to the Mecca, another twenty paces and he'll be at the Ship. The Breaker or Tony's will take him a good thirty. He treads slowly, he knows they'll all wait for him.

Noon. Three boats along from the *Rebel*, on the other side of the pontoon, men are repainting a wooden seiner. Its hull will be red and green, the cabin yellow.

'Hey, Cody!' a big strong guy on board the boat calls.

A tall gangling man turns around, he has a haunted face and blond hair plaited like a Native. Nikephoros is sitting on the hatch cover. He waves as I walk past. On the next deck a man is baiting by himself. An empty bottle of beer has been forgotten in a corner, on an iron ledge eroded by rust. What was once white paint flakes across wide stretches greyed by time and the rain. Half the name has disappeared: *Destiny*, I manage to make out.

'Hello,' I say to the man.

Behind him are piles of full tubs and uncoiled ropes scattered about, a plastic bucket full of green stagnating water, greasy rags and crumpled Coke cans.

'Hi,' the man replies.

Working quickly, he reaches mechanically for a hook in the left-hand tub, attaches a piece of salted herring and drops it into the right-hand tub, arranging the line in regular little coils, each overlapping slightly with the last, the hooks laid absolutely flat. His eyes are focused on his work. Bags under his eyes, a tired heavy face, shoulders slumping slightly. He looks like his boat, they're as worn as each other. The radio's playing the same song from a few days ago: the Kinks' 'Sunny Afternoon'.

'Your boat's beautiful,' I say, blinking in the sunlight.

'And she does well at sea,' the man replies, 'but she needs a good coat of paint, and quite a bit of work too … don't have the money for it.'

Take me, take me to sail away … says the song. I look at the boat's strong broad hull.

119

'Yes,' I say, 'but still she's beautiful. Are you off fishing halibut?'

'Yeah, but on another boat. This one's not up to it. One day maybe. Then I'll need a crewmember. I'll take you fishing if you really like my *Destiny*.'

'Oh yes,' I say.

I listen to the end of the song, the lyrics rising up and drifting out to sea. My face is bathed in sunlight, and so is the man's. The song ends and something snaps.

'I better go. Bye,' I say.

He gives a little tilt of his head.

Jude was drinking a coffee on the rear deck. I can feel him watching me as I straddle the rail onto the *Rebel*. Those yellow eyes have an icy sparkle, it could be anger. He turns and spits, his face swallowed up in the shadow of his hood. I look away.

Some evenings Jason stops by the boat and finds us still working when everyone else has long since finished.

'Hey, Lili, still at work? I was coming to get you for an ice cream, some popcorn or a few White Russians.'

'Another time, Jason, we haven't finished.'

He turns back, disappointed. He looks very young, walking away like that between the resting boats along the deserted pontoon, and climbing the footbridge back up to the dock. Above him the whole of the sky. The black footbridge and the sky. It looks as if he's climbing the sky.

'There goes your boyfriend,' Dave teases.

The skipper joins in, 'Oh, Jason comes calling again.'

Night is closing in. The sky has turned a sulphurous colour. Wind is forecast for 26 June.

'Same as usual,' says Adam. 'That's what we get for the halibut opening every year, gale warnings and boats going under.'

We're leaving tomorrow. We've filled up with diesel and water. We'll be at sea for two days before the fishing starts. Jason has stopped by the *Rebel* again this evening, and yet again he's leaving alone. Jude spits over the rail.

'Finish the tub you're on and you can go,' says the skipper.

Jude turns to me, flicking his chin in Jason's direction as he climbs into the orange sky.

'Is he your boyfriend?'

He says it quietly, his eyes fierce.

We motor through the narrow neck of the harbour and past the first buoys. It's so beautiful in among all this mewing of gulls. The sun was almost warm in the port, but as soon as we leave the shelter of the jetty the wind gives us goose pimples, makes the hairs stand up on our bare arms, blows our hair over our eyes, and intoxicates me with its smell of seaweed, its powerful acrid fragrance like the call of the open sea. The cascading laughter of the crazed seagulls rises to a crescendo. We pass the white reservoirs of the fuel docks. The men are busy sweeping the foredeck. Simon and I are baiting with three students Ian has taken on for the day. We soon reach the canning factory and the boat slows. The skipper manoeuvres skilfully to wriggle between the *Midnight Sun* and the *Topaz*. The boys tie up the *Rebel* to wooden pillars surrounded by dirty foam. A Mexican dockworker calls out to us from the quay and propels the huge plastic tube in our direction. Dave has put on his rain gear and jumps into the hold. Jude angles the tube towards Dave, who grabs it.

'OK,' he shouts, and the tube spews out several tonnes of crushed ice, which Dave carefully directs to each corner of the hold. He looks as if he's been caught in a snowstorm.

We load the provisions that Safeway has delivered onto the pontoon and Simon gulps when he sees the delivery note. Dave is delighted with the pile of longlines ready to be dropped into the water.

A middle-aged man comes aboard and dumps his bag on deck.

'Hi, guys. I'm Joey, the new deckhand for the opening.'

He goes into the cabin to put his bag away. Jude's gone to get cigarettes, the skipper's probably on the phone to Oklahoma and Jesse's smoking a joint in the engine room. I loiter on deck, not knowing what to do with my hands.

'I hope we're going to fill the hold. Hope we'll get them, the bastards,' says Dave.

'I hope there won't be too much yelling,' I reply.

He laughs.

Jude is back and the skipper jumps aboard moments later.

'We're off, guys,' he says. 'Cut it loose!'

Nine o'clock in the evening. The town slips into the distance. The sun bathes the deck in light, pouring gold over the furthest limit of the sky, the green mountain and the white sand of the beaches far to the south.

'One day I'll go there,' I think out loud. 'With just a small bag and my sleeping bag. After fishing, after Point Barrow, I'll go there.'

'It would be best if you took a gun too. For the bears.'

Joey is standing next to me, smiling kindly. I look at him, a stocky man with his head hunched between his shoulders as if to gather his strength, black eyes deep set in their sockets, nesting between slanting eyelids and tired bags.

'Grizzly females with cubs are dangerous in summer. One time I was hunting roe deer . . .' He falls silent, then starts up again, 'I'm from the island, from Akhiok, a village in the south, I know those mountains like the back of my hand. It'd be dangerous headin' out on your own, especially if you've never done it before. I could come with you, if you like. I could show you how and – most important – where to aim. When a bear comes at you, there's no room for mistakes. If you aim for the head you can be sure you're gonna die.'

'Aha,' I say.

'Not too hard, then, your first cod season?'

'They say crab fishing's the hardest.'

'Yup. One year I lost seven members of my family. All on different boats. Bering Sea.'

'I may be going there this winter. The skipper's taking me if he does the season,' I say under my breath.

Joey doesn't say anything for a while. He's still staring over the waves.

'I hope you don't,' he whispers. 'Wouldn't wish that hell on anyone.'

'Others do it OK. Women too. Why not me?'

'Cos you're small, you know nothing about it, and you don't have to do it. I hope your asshole of a skipper doesn't come back from Oklahoma. He can go to hell!'

'Seems you don't like him much.'

'He's an idiot. He doesn't know what he's doing, or what he's saying.'

The boys are drinking coffee in the galley.

'What were you doing coming here?' Joey asks, handing me a cigarette.

'I dunno. I just left. Well, yes I do know, of course I know … I knew this much for sure, at least: it would be different here. I thought it would be clean on the ocean.'

The *Rebel* has passed Buskin River and Womens Bay, a seagull spirals giddily in the light.

'Maybe I also wanted to fight for something powerful and beautiful,' I add, watching the bird. 'Risking my life, sure, but at least I'd find it first. And I'd always wanted to go to the ends of the earth, finding the edge, the place where it stops.'

'And then?'

'Then when I'm at the edge, I'll jump.'

'And then?'

'Then I'll fly away.'

'You'll never fly away, you'll die.'

'I'll die?'

'That's exactly what can happen to you here, and quicker than you think. This isn't an easy place.'

I look at the coast and its gradually softening contours, the golden ocean. I heave a sigh.

'I have a guitar,' he says in a soft, almost lilting voice. 'I play in bars when I've had too much to drink. I also work with wood and

leather. I tan it the old-fashioned way . . . I've made my own leather
tunic. I wear it sometimes when I'm drunk, when I sing in bars
with my guitar. They think I'm a crazy Indian. A dirty back Injun,'
he adds.

We hear Ian's voice from the wheelhouse. He's shouting. The boys
come back out on deck, we set up the tubs again and go back to work.
The sea's already rough when we pass Chiniak Cape. It just keeps
getting wilder. As far as the eye can see, the waves are topped with
white horses.

Jude stares at the ocean, his eyes twinkling with gold under his
bushy brows. Two days he's been sober. His features have the strong
contours of a great sailor once again. The *Rebel*'s engine idles slowly,
and we bait hooks on the rear deck, rocked by the regular to and fro
of the water. A strong wind scours our faces. The sound of the waves
sweeping over the deck is never-ending.

'How about we fill the boat right up, hey? That should be around
fifty thousand pounds.'

'With the little second hold we should be close to a hundred thousand! At ninety or a *hundred* per pound.'

'The price isn't set yet, it could be way more. At the canneries they
said . . .'

Simon joins in with them. He's gained in assurance since Ian kept
him on for this last fishing trip.

'What are you paid, Simon? Half share?'

'Yeah, half share.'

'And me?' I ask, turning to look at him.

'You? Probably the same as me, have to ask the skipper.'

'You sure they won't give me a quarter share?'

Simon pushes out his lower lip to show he doesn't know.

'Don't think so. Is that even a thing?'

Of course it's a thing, I think privately.

'Hey, Simon, do we get to have rice this evening?'

'I got some cans of beef stew to make things quicker.'

'Cans? Of beef stew, really? I'm disappointed, Simon. I'd prefer
your burnt rice.'

Simon gives a tight-lipped sigh. I turn to look at the coast. A blue boat has dropped anchor in the bay.

'We have neighbours,' I say.

'That's Adam. Don't you recognise the *Anna*?'

I drop my fid and wave expansively from left to right. A tiny figure replies. The sky clouds over, their boat disappears into the fog and we're treated to a downpour.

The boat is listing hard. A stronger wave slams me into a metal crosstie and I lose my balance because of the tub I'm taking to put away. I lean on the bar to try to pull myself upright again, but get dragged by the tub. My whole torso is twisted in two with a sharp snapping sound. I grimace and try to stifle my tears but they still spill over my cheeks. Jude and Dave have watched the scene and remain expressionless but I think I can see a hint of criticism: I just don't belong here if I don't have my sea legs. I pick myself up and Simon asks if I'm OK. I shrug, but not too much because it hurts.

'I must have broken a fucking rib.'

'A rib? Broken? How do you know?'

'I can just tell.'

Nearly time for the signal to be given. Almost noon. All of us at our posts. Ian at the helm, glued to the radio and its steady countdown. Simon up on the flying bridge, ready to toss the buoys and markers overboard. Dave braced against the bulwark. On his outstretched arm, poised at the ready, are the first coils of the buoy line ready to follow the marker into the water. The anchor is within reach. I've finished helping Jude ballast the first tubs and tie them together. I hover behind Dave, ready to hand him the rest of the buoy rope. We've stopped talking. I nervously grip the small red knife that hangs from my belt. Fear ties my stomach in knots.

A sudden bellow from the wheelhouse: 'Let it go!'

We're off. Simon lobs the buoy, Dave drops anchor and throws the loops of buoy line after it, I pass the next coils to him and watch them drop down into the waves. Then the first longline: we're fishing again. A bevy of seagulls deploys overhead. We drop three sets of lines in quick succession. A fourth in a different location, the lines spooling off the boat to whoops of joy from Dave and Jesse.

Ian calls us inside.

'Build up your strength, it's gonna be tough.'

We help ourselves to snacks, confident we're in luck. As on the previous trip I go up to the wheelhouse to see the lanky man, who's paler and more emaciated than ever.

'Here we are again,' he says. 'It's been a long time. Too much to do ashore. I was going crazy. And then you like doing your rounds of the bars in the evening.'

'Not always bars. I also like strolling through Baranof Park and eating McDonald's ice creams and wandering around town.'

He smiles, still gazing into the distance.

'Things aren't good with my wife. We're splitting up. She wants a divorce. Maybe it's better that way. I have two beautiful children. A boy of eleven and a nine-year-old girl.'

I daren't say anything. We watch the sea exploding around us.

'It's gonna be rough, huh?'

'Yup,' he agrees. 'By midnight we'll be right in the middle of it.'

'Why's it always rough for the halibut season?'

'How do you expect me to know? You talk a lot of shit too. I'm not on speaking terms with the old man upstairs who decides this stuff.'

'Yes, of course, it was dumb of me,' I mumble. 'Will I be gutting the halibut too?'

'Have to ask the guys. It may well be you who coils the lines. Or Simon. Either way, you'll be plenty busy.'

'I hope I'll learn to gut them. The men keep saying they're the best and the fastest. See if I can prove unbeatable too. And it would be useful on my next boat.'

'I have a beautiful little girl,' the skipper says again. 'I could ask to have custody. Her mom would be OK with that if I found a good nanny. Would you like to come fishing with me? In Hawaii?'

'No, not Hawaii. Alaska.'

At midnight we set the last tubs. The first lines have been hauled back on board but the fish are scarce, the shoals are somewhere else. A few solitary halibut are torn from the water's clutches. They land on deck, pulled up by Jude's gaff, thrashing the night air with their great tails. Some are bigger than me, smooth flat giants that twitch spasmodically. From their dark faces two round eyes stare at us in amazement. The underside is white and blind. Jude unhooks the youngest of them and throws them back. They're mostly just corpses drifting away, tossed by the waves before slowly sinking from view. They seem to eclipse themselves, swallowed up by the black water.

Cod struggle on their hooks, glistening green and gold, also crimson rock fish, jellyfish and huge starfish.

'Keep the cod and the rock fish!'

Simon coils the longlines, sitting on a tub under the pulley. Jude leans out over the rail, studying the incoming lines. He gaffs halibut as soon as they emerge from the waves, arching his back as he strains, jaw clamped, face streaming. He heaves them on board, detaches them with a quick twist of the hook. Joey, Dave and Jesse slit their throats and gut them. I scrape out their opened body cavities, wash off their blood. I take away tubs and put out new ones as Simon fills them with lines relieved of their catches. A searing pain shoots through me when I bend to pick up each full tub, and I have to lug it to the far end of the deck, staggering in the violent swell. Guts, shreds of bait and semi-vegetable creatures swill back and forth across the decks.

But the fishing is bad. As soon as the lines are back on board we have to bait them again. The sea tosses us around. Our feet are frozen. We stand on the rear deck and work in silence, our necks hunched between our shoulders, our arms pinned to our sides. We move like automatons. Our backs curve and straighten in time to the swell. The slow, hoarse repetitive sound of the waves ... I fall asleep briefly but still keep baiting. I dream of fish and the midnight sun. I'm woken by Dave laughing at me.

'You're asleep, Lili!'

I pull myself together.

'I was dreaming ... but I'm still working!'

Facing me, Jude. He hands me a cigarette. An almost gentle smile hovers over his face, which is red with cold, his chapped lips behind the bushy beard with a frozen gob of mucus trapped in it. Ian has joined us, time is short.

'The black cod season's over but we're starting to get quite a few of them,' Dave says anxiously. 'I know we're allowed to take—'

'Chill,' says Ian. 'We're well within the quota. We can still take plenty more.'

'I'm not so sure,' Dave says quietly. 'I'd say we already have too much.'

Jude has disappeared into the galley. He comes back and passes me a mug of coffee.

We have about thirty tubs ready to go back into the water.

'That's enough,' says Ian. 'Clear the decks for me. Get the next set ready. Send this lot out and bring the last lot in.'

Two in the morning. Our luck turns and the halibut appear.

'Stop!' Simon wails. 'I'm hooked!'

The skipper is slow to stop the line. He looks exasperated. 'What now?'

Simon quickly extricates the hook buried in his glove. He's bleeding a little. He's very frightened. Ian sets the engine going again. Simon grabs hold of the line, looking panicked.

'If that's what he calls being hooked,' sniggers Jesse.

Jude says a few words in reply, in the same tone of voice. Dave smiles. I swap over the tubs and try to smile at Simon but he doesn't notice. My rib hurts. Joey has taken Jude's place: leaning over the stormy black water, he heaves out the magnificent giants, their fleshy lips parted, their wide mouths distended by the weight of their great bodies arching, flapping and twisting in furious spasms, while the hook burrows deeper with their every jerking move. The fish fall onto the deck, into blood-streaked water, foam and guts. Joey doesn't bother sparing the younger fish. He goes ahead and harpoons their bodies so it's easier for him to unhook them with the other hand. Their mouths are torn before they're thrown back into the waves.

The others gasp for oxygen on deck. The boys manhandle the largest one of them all onto the table. The colossus struggles and bucks. Puffing and panting, the men manage to lay it flat on the table. Still it struggles, its flailing tail splattering us with blood. Then the men drive a knife into its throat. Slicing the membrane around its gills, they swiftly arc the blade round to the other membrane over the entrails, then grab the lot and tear out guts and gills all in one go. They toss them into the sea, and slide the still-twitching belly towards me. All that's left are two balls right in the depths of the abdomen, I have to remove these along with a whitish skin. Once again my face is covered in blood and foaming mucus. When he sees me, Jesse says something and laughs. Jude looks up. He shrugs with what I interpret as contempt. My rib hurts. I'm cold. I want to go back to Kodiak. I'm horrified by Joey: he was gentle yesterday, talking about animals and forests, wistfully calling himself the 'Indian negro', but he's barbaric now. We have to kill the fish as quickly as possible. Time is money, the fish dollars, and when a starfish turns up − bigger than both my hands together − when it falls limply onto the worktable still attached to and sucking avidly on the hook, he hurls it against a steel upright.

Occasionally small rock fish are crushed in the pulley or shredded by the metal guards on either side of the line. Any that come within my reach, I furtively throw back into the sea, a pointless gesture that I try to hide from the others, my men, my nearest and dearest, long-distance killers − mercenaries, barbarians who frighten me, turned into animals as they disembowel fish in this vast butchery amid the roar of the engine and the fury of the sea. Then I just don't have the time or the strength. I'm frightened of those yellow eyes, of the skipper who's bound to yell, of the men, these broad powerful men who sink their knives into those white bellies with such dexterity.

Dave asks me for the sharpening stone.

'The tub's nearly full,' I say.

'You have to do what I ask!' he shrieks.

I stare at him in disbelief, fear, indignation. I hate you, I think, oh how I hate you! I have a soul-destroying feeling that he has double-crossed me. He, Dave, is a man like all the others, a man who gives orders and expects to be instantly obeyed, one of the men who stole my bunk and let me sleep under his feet when he was on watch; one of the men who hasn't taught me how to gut halibut, who yells and I shake with fear, who utters one word of comfort and I love him blindly. Who may not even pay me a half share. I bring him the stone and hand it to him with lowered eyes.

'Thank you, Lili,' he says as if forgiving me.

'Lili, fish in the reel! What the fuck are you doing?' bellows the skipper.

I gut the red rock fish then push them to my left, where they slither into the hold. A halibut's heart on the table palpitates under the neon light. Will it go on beating long if I throw it out with the guts and blood? Perhaps I should return it to the sea. Will this new day never dawn, for the love of God? The tension used to destroy me, now it numbs me. Jude takes Joey's place and Joey comes to sit next to me. On the line I can make out the knot marking the end of a longline. I grab an empty tub, change it over for the full one and untie the sheet bend knot. Fish jaws have stayed attached to the hooks in the tub. I pick up the tub but Joey takes it from me.

'It's too heavy for you.'

I look up, surprised. But then I get it. I take the tub back from him, shaking my head.

Day does break, though, eventually. Only nine hours to go. On the stroke of noon we need to have reeled in the final marker. We bring in the last set at hellish speed, fish are thrown pell-mell onto the decks, now awash with blood. The men keep on gutting surrounded by a slew of crushed starfish and pop-eyed idiot fish and the stench of guts. I try to wrestle one of the giants onto the table. It's very big and heavy. It struggles fiercely and I slip to the ground with it. I don't let go but I could weep with rage at the pain in my rib. The two of us wallow in guts. My first hand-to-hand combat with a halibut, an embrace in blood and foam. I grip it with all my strength and hold it tighter. It's weakening. The men have bled it, it will soon be dead. It's already barely quivering. I slip one hand inside its gills but it closes them and my hand gets injured through my gloves. I manage to lay the fish down on the table. It's stopped moving. It's very smooth, the most beautiful fish I've ever seen. I pick up a knife, I stab it into the gills and copy what I've seen the men do.

I've gutted my first halibut. I wash out the inside of the white body cavity. Its severed heart has spilled onto the table, still beating. I hesitate. I take this heart that can't make up its mind to die and swallow it. Warm inside me, that solitary heart.

Ian barges into me.

'Get out of here and bring the halibut over to me!'

Jude looks up and gives me a frosty stare. Tears spring under my eyelids. I wipe my nose with my fingers. Joey the killer isn't far away. I meet his eye and cling to this exchange.

'Nearly done, Lili,' he smiles. 'Hang on.'

We finish putting the last fish in the hold. Jude and I gut the remaining cod. I use a broom to sweep the detritus into the hatches. The skipper grabs the hose and directs a violent jet of water at the decks. I'm in his way. He sprays me without even noticing. His face is exhausted.

'Maybe eighteen thousand . . .'

'Way more! At least twenty-five thousand.'

'I'd lay money on twenty thousand-ish.'

We're eating the omelette and baked beans Simon cooked for us while we cleaned the decks. I haven't washed my face. The skipper allocates the watches. I finish my coffee without looking at anyone, then get up and go to the cabin. I pull off my boots, go back to put them in front of the warm air vent. My bunk. I lie down with my back to the rest of the boat and curl up tight. I'm a killer like the rest of them, I've gutted my first halibut. I even ate its still-beating heart. I'm the killer now. Salt burns my face, blood has hardened in my hair, sticking it together. I fall asleep in this outlandish helmet, cheeks smarting and a trickle of dried blood in the corner of my mouth.

Simon wakes me. Nine o'clock in the evening. I'm in a deep, animal sleep. He has to shake me for a long time. My brain a complete blank. I have to trawl for several long seconds to remember my name and where I am and why. I sit up. The pain in my side reminds me about my rib, my huge numbed hands, my battered body. As I cross the galley I put the coffee back on and grab a chocolate bar from the drawer. I glance out at the deck through the door window. The lines are neatly tied up. A tub slides from left to right across the deck and the sea flows in through the scuppers, washing away the colours of the night. The hoist and the reel, even though securely fastened, keep up their constant rhythmic creaking which grows frenetic every time the boat takes a wave. Have other boats gone down in the last twenty-four hours? The evening sun breaks through the clouds, bounces off a knife blade and blinds me. I scratch my cheek. The corners of my lips are tight and sore.

'So that's what you call a French kiss?' Dave said earlier. 'You're scary!' And they all laughed about the blood around my mouth. Not me.

I climb the stairs to the wheelhouse. Joey is ensconced in front of the dials. Up ahead, the sun. A cormorant has settled on the bow.

'I'll hand over straightaway,' he says. 'I've adjusted the visibility. Simon doesn't know a thing about it.'

'I don't know anything about it either. But we can still do our watches. We don't go to sleep, you know.'

'I know ... sometimes the greenhorns are the best, they just don't have the experience, and that takes time. They need someone to explain things to them. I'll show you, it's easy.'

I listen. Try to understand. How can the Joey from last night also be this kind patient man whose gaze travels over the white horses. In the end I give up, I'm too tired.

'How's your rib?' Joey asks. 'Simon said you broke a rib?'

'Maybe. It happens to me sometimes. But maybe not. It made a noise like it broke. It'll be better in a couple of weeks. You can't tell the others. No one will want me on any boat if I keep hurting myself.'

'Need to take care of yourself,' he says quietly, nodding his head. ''S'not a good idea to hide pain. I wouldn't normally say this but I didn't enjoy watching you last night. You were almost in tears carrying the tubs, but you wouldn't tell anyone. You know, women on boats ... I've always been against it. But I've never fished with one before. It's a man's world, man's work – and plus we can't even piss overboard in peace, always have to check they can't see you. But then women like you, who work like guys, twenty-four hours with no complaints, well, I wouldn't mind having one of them on my boat.'

We'll reach Kodiak in the middle of the night. I'll hear the change in engine tone, Dave and Jude getting up, the skipper's shouts, then the engine slowing until it's almost stopped, only to rev louder while the boat's manoeuvred.

'Stay in bed,' Dave will say when he sees me sit up in my bunk, ready to go back on deck.

Then everything will be calm. Silence. Just the lightest rocking. I'll know that in a few hours I'll leave the men to their deep sleep and head off into the morning, free again.

I'm still dreaming of fishing when I wake, of grappling with halibut to get my knife into them, and lines that fall into the sea and escape our clutches. I wake fully in the dazzling air on deck, right on time to hear the ferry's call. I run up the wet wood of the pontoon towards the mountain. I still haven't cleaned my face of its barbaric daubing, its scarlet smears, the battle scars of my first halibut hunt, so I wash at the tap on the dock. A burning pain flashes through me when I squat down. The water gushes out and streams over my arms. I stand up and arch my back, wiping myself with the least dirty corner of my sweatshirt. In front of me is the brightly coloured *Kayodie*. A few empty beer cans roll across her deck. I run on up to the dock and sit on a bench looking out across the sleeping waters. Every now and then a boat comes in through the narrow mouth of the harbour. They're not all back yet. The *Mar Del Norte* is past the buoy. She looks heavy and makes slow progress.

I meet up with Jason at the bar. The dark rooms have been full since midday: raucous men getting drunk, their scratched hands resting on the wooden counters. Swollen fingers fiddle with a glass or a cigarette, knead a ball of tobacco before slipping it under a lip. They're all describing the same thing, how well they did and how they filled the hold. The queue outside the factory is so long you have to register to unload. They estimate, reckon, buy another round. There's talk of a boat that sank because there were too many fish – the hold was full, the decks covered in halibut, still more coming aboard. At five in the morning the coastguard received a frantic Mayday call. By the time they got there the boat had sunk and the scattered crew were floating in survival suits. Fuckwit coastguards, a stupid skipper ... everyone pokes fun.

We drink tequilas to our boats. Jason gives a feverish account of his night, daybreak in a storm of swell and blood. He talks quickly, his words colliding with each other, his eyes fiery under his bushy orange eyebrows, staring into the distance, perhaps into the reddest corner of the bar behind the snooker tables. We order White Russians again, then rum for him, the buccaneer, and vodka for me. I end up drunk and head home to the boat in the dead of night, trying to walk straight. Mustn't fall in the water. Bound to make me sick with all the rotten bait that's been thrown in there. No one on the boat. I make myself a sandwich and some very strong coffee. I drink the whole pot. Outside other people are laughing, having a good time. I'm not tired now so I go back out and this time I can walk straight. I need to paint the town red again. Now I'm a real fisherman.

We're back to work. The lines need cleaning, mending and putting away till next season. Bait has melted on the hook, rotting a little more with each passing day, slithering and falling apart in our hands. At night I dream of a dirty grey ocean; the wind blows and we blunder into great viscous walls of water the same greenish colour as the rotten bait, we fall into a stinking slop. It's spread over the whole boat.

We slip on it just as we fell on halibut blood. Now it's not a handsome scarlet that smears our cheeks and blazes on our foreheads, but a besieging rising tide of unwholesome gelatinous gloop, the remains of squid that died for nothing.

Jude comes back drunk. I hear him crash into things in the galley, move plates and cutlery, open the fridge. Things fall. He does too, more than once. He swears under his breath. Later he comes and collapses on his bunk. He coughs. The paroxysms sound like animal cries, strange yelps that wake me with a start. I'm afraid he'll die in the night, strangled by his own hoarse howling.

He's always last to get up. Dave or Simon usually wake him, but one day the lanky man asks me to do it.

I stare at him in amazement, shaking my head.

'Not me,' I mutter.

I escape onto the deck and get on with my work. Jude eventually joins us, his red eyes evasive, his face still creased from his pillow. He lights a cigarette, coughs.

'Y'need to stop, old man, or you won't be goin' far,' Dave tries to joke.

'I'll stop the day I die,' Jude glowers.

'Well, it won't be long then, hey, Lili?'

Ian rushes past us.

'We're unloading in four days, guys!' he hollers. 'The factory's finally given us a date. We'll know how much we've earned ... The price has gone up a few cents, not as much as I hoped. Those bastard sons of bitches will rip us off every time.'

'By the way, did you find out about the cod quota?'

'Why the hell are you breaking my balls about that? I already told you we were well within the figures.'

The skipper leaves and Jude and Dave whisper together: the fish will have been in the hold a whole week ... Don't try telling me the ice will hold out that long ... It must be starting to marinate in its own juices. You won't find me eating it, anyway ...

Simon and I don't say a thing.

★

Murphy's waiting on a bench in the square, a small grey-haired man beside him.

'Come sit with us for a while, Lili, we're bored ... Work going OK?'

'No,' I say.

Music blares at us from a nearby bar when the door opens as some guys go in. I think I recognise Jason.

'I'd like to introduce my friend Stephen,' Murphy says. 'A great scientist.'

'Physicist,' corrects the little man.

I sit on the end of the bench with them. The wind has turned and the stench from the canneries has blown away offshore. The smell of trees and leaves is back, the smell of flowers from the red and yellow flowerbed.

I eat ice cream and drink beer. White Russians, tequilas and vodkas too. We've been working from early in the morning till late at night, when the docks have been empty for a while now. It's summer.

'In Alaska we have the biggest vegetables in the world,' says Dave. 'Specially in the north when there's virtually constant daylight till mid-August.'

'I must go to Point Barrow while it's light,' I tell him.

The skipper's not in good spirits. Simon's preoccupied with the studies he's to resume shortly. He'd like to leave as soon as we've offloaded the fish, but Ian has refused.

'You have to come with us and drag the waters to try to find the lost lines. Fishing's not really over till we've made an attempt. And any-way, if they're lost you have to pay your share of compensation too.'

Jason drops by the boat every evening and invites me on expeditions to bars, to wander round the streets, walk along the docks or sit on a bench. We set off surrounded by the sound of the wind in the masts, by seagulls flying overhead, the smell of silt and of popcorn as we pass the cinema – I buy a tub – or the stench of rotten fish just by the land-ing stage for the ferry when the wind blows from the south-east.

'Would you like to come for a drink and some popcorn when you're done?' he says if I'm still working, and heads off to wait for me somewhere, at Tony's or the Ship, or on a bench outside the B and B. He tries his hand at the harmonica he's had only three days, his eyes wistfully distant, his lips slack. Sometimes a guy sits down next to him. He has a thick beard, long yellow hair held back by a cap in the bright colours of some hockey team, and a pipe he carved from a branch. He cycles all over town on his resplendent mountain bike. And plays the flute.

Big Murphy drops by the boat again and chats to Jude for a while. He looks at me and laughs about my red cheeks. Jude studies me uncharitably for a long time and spits overboard.

'I didn't do the opening,' says Murphy. "M resting up. In the daytime I hang out around the harbour, find some gear work, just pocket money. Then I go to the square, meet up with buddies. We watch people go by. It's nice. In the evenings the shelter and something to eat ... what else could anyone want?'

Jude replies in monosyllables. The guys on the multicoloured boat have turned their music right up. We hear the sound of ring-pulls on beer cans.

'Makes you thirsty,' Jude mutters to himself.

'I'm taking you somewhere you've never been,' Jason tells me the next day. 'It's in Kodiak and no one ever thinks to go there, but it's so beautiful it takes your breath away. You're the first person I've shown it to, but first you have to swear you won't tell anyone about it.'

I swear and we set off, stopping to buy cigarettes at the supermarket. We head out of town, walking at a good pace. We come to Tagura Road, then the boatyard, and I pick salmonberries on the edges of a ditch. Jason collects a whole handful for me. We end up under the bridge that links Kodiak's Long Island to the town and the small mooring harbour in Dog Bay. Jason stops and looks up.

'This is it.'

I look at him, confused.

'Come!'

He clambers up the grassy bank, clings to the rock face and pulls himself up to the first steel girder. I follow him onto the framework that supports the bridge. He treads along a narrow walkway, with a grille underfoot through which we can see the sky. I walk behind him and we both grip the handrails on either side. My stomach ties itself in knots that pull tighter as we climb higher and the void beneath our feet grows. We're now over the road that runs alongside the inlet, soon we're over the water. Underneath us mewing seagulls glide and nosedive, overhead the rumble of cars amplifies as they roll past. The wind blows violently and seems to be getting stronger and stronger. I follow Jason, staring at my feet and the empty space below, my jaws clamped, so tense they're painful. When we reach the middle he stops and gestures for me to sit down. Our legs dangle in thin air and far below the dark water looks forbiddingly dense. It shifts slowly, coming and going in regular undulations as if breathing, its vast inhalations coming from the belly of the sea.

'Sometimes, late in the evening,' Jason says, shouting to make himself heard, 'I come here on my way back to the boat. Last night included.'

He takes out his harmonica and plays a rambling melody that gets carried away on the wind. I hand him a cigarette and we smoke in silence. My heart is delirious with vertigo and wonder.

On the return trip I feel as if I'm coming back from very far away. I was with Jason the Hobbit, walking through the air above the birds. The wind wanted to carry us off. Jason leaves me by the statue of the sailor lost at sea, and I walk along the quay to the *Rebel*. Night has fallen over the harbour. I think of the others who stayed behind, their feet glued to the ground in a square-shaped world, lugging around their human weight. I feel bad for them. I wish I could tell them that I'm just back from above where the seagulls fly – I'd even like to tell the greatest of sailors. But Jason made me swear. I won't say anything.

★

The boats around us finish one after the other and their crews head off to bars or to Hawaii. They get ready for salmon fishing or buckle their bags for Juneau, Bristol Bay and Dutch. But not us. Our cargo of halibut is still waiting in the hold, and the longlines just keep on rotting on deck.

'I don't have any dough left,' says Jude. 'The skipper's starting to get pissy when I ask for an advance. Maybe he's scared that I'll end up owing him.'

'That's what happens if you ask for more every day. I'm broke too, but I don't think he'll pay us separately for cod and halibut. And right now, my friend, till we've unloaded ...'

'Hey, Lili,' says Joey, 'you know there's talk of you staying on the *Rebel* for the salmon season? Andy was talking about it this morning with Aaron, the next skipper. I'm in the crew too.'

'Very cushy!' Dave exclaims. 'Look at you tendering! You sure are lucky. Paid by the day, nothing kept back for food and fuel – net gains, basically. Hundred or hundred fifty dollars a day to unload the seiners. You're selling them ice creams, talking to nice guys. You take a nap while you wait for boats, then at the end of the day you pump out their fish. In the middle of the night you head off to meet a boat like the *Alaskan Spirit* or the *Guardian*, I don't know if you've seen them yet, huge great ships, absolute beauties ... I had a good crab season on one of them – and they take the fish off you.'

'Oh, right,' I say.

I think of the midnight sun, think of sitting on the edge of the world, swinging my legs over an intense blue Arctic emptiness, eating an ice cream and smoking a cigarette as I watch that incandescent sphere circle around the sky, skimming the horizon but never dipping below it.

'A trip to Abercrombie with a six-pack of beers, now that would be nice.'

'Yeah, if you can afford the beers.'

'Abercrombie?'

'Oh, Lili, don't you know Abercrombie? You gotta see it some day. The sunrises you get from those cliffs!'

'Maybe I do know it then ... But it's a bit late now for the sunrise.'

'Uh-huh ... We'd still have the beer.'

A cloying bit of bait has stuck between my fingers. Out of nowhere I remember the cheque Andy gave me.

'If I bring you cash to pay for the beer, will we go to Abercrombie?' The boys don't hear me.

'I'm off to rob the bank,' I say, taking off my gloves. 'I'll be back.'

I run along the docks, clutching the cheque in my dirty hand. The guys on the colourful boat call out to me and I wave in reply. I go under the arches and hear a raucous din coming from Tony's as a man emerges from the bar – it's Adam, from the *Blue Beauty*.

'Hi!' I say.

'Come have a coffee, Lili, I'll buy you one.'

'I was just going to the bank to cash a cheque. But I'm not sure they'll accept it if I don't have the skipper with me.'

'They'll take it in the bar here. I know the manageress well.'

'Shut the door behind you!'

The roar of men's voices deadens. Susie opens her safe and hands me two banknotes with a big smile.

'You're lucky, I have some cash today.'

I go back to Adam at the bar.

'This is at least my fifth coffee,' he says.

'You'll have a heart attack, Adam.'

'Need to dig ourselves out of our pits. So, when will you come see me?'

'When we've finished work,' I tell him.

My legs jig impatiently under the counter. The boys will think I've run off with the stash.

'Well, what the hell are you doing here if you're meant to be working?'

'I had to run an errand for the boys. They needed cash.'

'Is that for more beer?'

'Yes,' I laugh, feeling slightly guilty.

'Those guys all have an alcohol problem.'

I look into Adam's face. He's staring at the room rather miserably.

'Will your second house take a long time to build?' I ask gently.

'Oh, a while,' he replies in a half-whisper.

Without a smile.

The four of us have climbed into Dave's truck. Simon and I are squished into the back on the tiny bench seat behind the fold-down seats – cramped little spaces for the half-share earners. The others settle their big square men's frames onto the front seats. We're heading for the big Safeway liquor store.

We open beers in the truck. I'm thirsty and it's a beautiful day with the wind blasting in through the open windows. Up ahead the potholed road tapers away into the woods. Some ten miles later we come to the end of the road and a large entrance with the name Abercrombie carved over it. Dave parks the truck, which looks very red against the black pine trees. We walk to the cliffs, wishing we didn't have to climb up and that we were already collapsed on the grass, knocking back beers. But Dave guides us until we're poised between rock and sky, looking out over the glinting ocean and its great slow inhalations. Birds fly by, carried by thermals rising off the rocks. Their harsh cries mingle with the crash of waves throwing themselves against the wall-like cliff.

Propped between two rocks, Jude opens his bottle of rum. Simon is sitting further off, out of the way. I can't decide where to settle. Dave has positioned himself facing out to sea, his head tipped back and his hands pushing into the small of his back as if feeling its supple arch out of habit. He's laughing.

'Why are you laughing, Dave?'

'That kayak over there,' Dave says, turning round. 'To the right of the rock, can you see? The guy doesn't know how to handle it. He'll still be there tomorrow. I have a kayak myself. Sometimes me and my girlfriend ... Hey, wait a minute, we're gonna have a drink too.'

So I sit down next to him. I like his kayaking stories.

'I used to go kayaking as a kid,' Jude says. 'My brother and I would go off into the woods and we'd be gone for days. It drove my mother crazy. We had our own kayak, a decrepit old thing that nearly drowned us several times.'

Jude's voice is very quiet, we have to strain our ears to hear him what with the fulmars' cries and the boom of waves. He takes another gulp of rum, his eyes already reddened, his face congested. The light accentuates the blood vessels in his eyelids. His shoulders have stooped, too heavy for him once more. I look away. He's fallen silent and is gazing into the distance. Simon's describing something but I've stopped listening. I study the horizon, which is lighting up with red. The rich copper colours of evening drop down onto the ocean. I think about Point Barrow.

One evening we'd all met up at the Mecca Lounge. Jason joined us and solemnly asked me to be his sailor for the Dungeness season. Dave squeezed my shoulder affectionately. A band was setting up their sound system.

Jude sat drinking in the darkest corner by the bar and I went over to him – in the shadows of a bar I found him less frightening. The ground swayed as I walked across the room. Some men laughed at me and I laughed with them. They stood me a drink and I told them proudly I was here to fish. They were coastguards, and said they hoped I stayed safe and sound. I'd stopped worrying about immigration controls.

The band started to play. The girl singer was wearing leather, a short black skirt moulded to her thighs. I felt like dancing and drinking through till morning. I swayed at the counter, the rhythm of the waves still rocking through my back.

'We could dance,' I said to Jude. 'Do you like dancing?'

He looked at me with complete disbelief. Then he gave a short laugh – Jude laughed – and said, 'Oh . . . in my younger days.'

'You're not old.'

He smiled awkwardly. I'd embarrassed him.

'I'm thirty-six,' he murmured.

'Well, there you are.'

'But I've stopped dancing.'

'I'm silly, you must think I'm so dumb jigging about like that for no reason.'

He laughed again.

'It's not dumb. Pretty sure I liked it at one time. But nowadays when I'm in a bar, it's to drink. That's what they're for, wouldn't you say?'

'Yes,' I agreed, taking out a cigarette.

He lit it.

'Thank you. Where are you from?'

'Pennsylvania. Not far from New York.'

'That's right over the other side of the United States.'

'I've been to all of them. All the states.'

'So you haven't always fished?'

'Eight years I've been in Alaska. Before, I worked as a logger. Mainly. My dad and I would head off on road trips. We travelled together a long time. We'd find work along the way, construction, a bit of everything, mainly lumber-jacking. We weren't rich but we often earned enough for a motel room, the bars, girls from time to time ... yeah, we had a good time. We did it for years, going from one state to another, one bar to another, one motel room to another.'

'And Alaska?' I asked. 'How did you end up here?'

'We went our separate ways and my father found a job near Seward. A construction site in the woods. He told me to go join him. I found work on a boat. Haven't stopped since.'

'So you don't really have a home then?'

He laughed, mirthlessly this time, an indifferent laugh.

'No. I have the boat when I'm on one. A motel, sometimes, when I'm ashore. Bars. Don't you think that's enough?'

He fell silent and sat slumped on his stool, staring dead ahead, at the waitress, the rows of bottles, the darkness of the bar, apparently no longer aware of me. He lit another cigarette, coughed, his body wracked with a paroxysm that left him red-faced, short of breath and teary-eyed. For a moment he was the great sailor again, broadening his shoulders, expanding his chest and swaying his powerful back to the rhythm of the waves. Then he hunched in on himself. He took his glass, downed it in one and ordered another.

'We thought we'd lost you,' said Dave when I went back to sit at the bar with them, then he resumed his conversation with Jason, who was getting heated about fishing quotas. I felt like going home to the boat, being back on deck in the blue night air. I didn't feel like laughing any more. The cigarettes I'd smoked had left a bitter taste in my mouth. I scanned the whole bar: they were all just so much drunk meat. And me too. I'd missed the evening steadily rolling in over the harbour water, the slow imperceptible arrival of darkness.

'I'm going back,' I said, looking over towards Jude.

I was hoping he'd turn round but he'd forgotten me. He was just drinking. I felt so stupid. For a moment the world seemed like a desert: going home alone to a boat, going to bed only to start all over again tomorrow, and keeping going – it all seemed beyond me. But what else could I do? I gathered up my change from the bar and slid my cigarettes into my boot. Then someone behind me grabbed hold of my shoulders and pulled on them as if trying to tip me backwards.

The lanky man.

'You?' I cried, laughing out loud. 'What the hell are you doing here?'

'I was thirsty. Have a drink, it's on me,' he said laughing, perhaps proud to be giving us such a surprise. He looked happy, as if he'd come home from miles away, after a long absence, thirsty and ten years younger. Dave gasped in amazement, Jude turned round and gave the beginnings of a smile and Simon raised his glass in Ian's direction. We were all glad to have him with us at last. AA was forgotten, along with the respectful silence behind the taunts when he came back from meetings. We all offered him drinks, one after another. We genuinely wanted to do something for him to thank him for the pleasure of having him there.

I forgot that I wanted to go back. Jude's presence stopped enticing or sickening or upsetting me. Everything felt straightforward again.

Now it was all about laughing and drinking and succumbing to the fun of it with Ian exultant, yelling and drinking, letting himself go as he had in his happier younger days.

Someone tapped me on the shoulder with a 'Hey, Lili!' and I didn't have time to turn round before Ian leapt up, fists balled.

'Get your filthy hands off her,' he barked. 'Leave her the hell alone. Can't you see she's with her crew? Maybe I need to help you understand?'

'But this is Mattis,' I cried. 'Stop it, he's a friend!'

Mattis, who'd once invited me onto his boat for burnt popcorn and beer, who'd cried when he listened to 'Mother Ocean'. Mattis stood stock-still for a moment, his mouth half open and still trying to smile, stammering a few words, his big face looking surprised and hurt, as if the tears were still there in his eyes, ready to spring up. The skipper kept bearing down on him threateningly. Mattis shrank away and melted into the groups of drinkers.

'But that was Mattis. Why did you do that?'

'To hell with Mattis and any son of a bitch who tries to touch you while I'm in this bar with you. Go on, finish your glass, I'm thirsty. Same again!' he hollered to the waitress. 'Gin and tonic with a Rainier!'

I drained my beer and reached out my glass for the next one. The bar was starting to pitch and I began seeing my glass double. I wanted to leave.

'You're too drunk. You'll fall in the water. Wait a while, we'll go back together.'

'No, 'm going now. I'll be careful. I won't fall.'

'Wait for us. They'll be closing soon, anyway. And you can't be sure. All alone at this time of night, all those hooched-up guys in the street. No telling what they could do.'

'I'm off. I always go home to the boat alone, and pretty drunk sometimes. Never had a problem.'

'I'll take you back.'

I left the scrum. The wind had dropped and I shivered in the clear cold air, but it felt good. I stood at the top of the steps outside the

Mecca while the skipper said his goodbyes. Lights were reflected as pillars of gold on the black waters in the harbour, with barely a ripple of waves. The shadow of the mountain stood out against the sky, in the distance Barometer Mountain was still snow-capped.

'I'm not all that drunk,' I said. 'The cold air's doing me good. You should stay.'

He gave me a playful shove and I fell headlong down the steps. It was a long way down.

'Lili!' he cried. 'I'm so sorry, Lili.'

He hurried down and knelt to pick up the crumpled sparrow on the road. I was laughing so hard I couldn't get up straightaway.

'Fucking rib!' I managed to say.

We went back to the boat between the shifting reflections on the water and the motionless sky; the one dark shot silk, the other a midnight-blue diamond.

'You see, you can fall over just like that, people drown at this time of night the whole time when they're tanked,' he said seriously. 'You lose your balance and you die. It's a good thing I did bring you back.'

The sliding pontoon rocked slightly. Our footsteps thudded quietly on the wet wood. I watched the water with respectful fear.

'Not me, though,' I said. 'I can swim. If I fell in I'd swim ashore.'

'No, you'd die. And you never know. If you came across some asshole ...'

'There's no one around now.'

'That doesn't matter. That's just the point. Someone could take advantage of that.'

We heard the sound of an engine, the *Arnie* leaving.

'I won't push you again, I promise. You didn't hurt yourself, did you?'

'No, no, and it made us laugh!'

'They'll think I pushed you deliberately, at the Mecca. I'm not happy about that,' he said, frowning.

'You'll just have to go back and say it's not true.'

'Think so.'

147

'Why did you join us at the bar this evening?'

'I wanted to, that's all. I have every right if I want to, don't I? I'm not married to AA ... Do you think that's dumb?'

'No. I didn't like it when we left you alone on the boat every evening. But why *do* we drink?'

'Because we're dumb.'

'Yes but why?'

'You're exhausting, Lili, you make me want to drink some more.'

The light in the galley was still on and the white neon blinded us as we stepped onto the boat.

'We didn't even eat,' I sighed. 'Never mind. Tomorrow.'

He laughed at me and we caught each other's eye, standing facing each other. The fishing was over, we'd worked hard together. He had played his part as skipper, shouting when he needed to. I had been true to mine, the greenhorn who complied with the rules of the boat. He reached out an arm to stop me walking away. I ventured my hand towards his face, brushed my fingers over his cheek. He touched my lips briefly with his but I stepped away.

'I'm off to sleep,' I said.

He went back out and I went to bed. I laughed until everything started to spin, the giddiness corkscrewing in my stomach. Sleep hit me like a mallet.

The owner's yells wake us. We sit up, foggy heads pounding furiously. Wordlessly, we get out of bed, bumping into each other in the narrow confines of the cabin. We hunt for socks, jog pants and sweatshirts, feeling guilty, like bad soldiers caught sleeping when they should be leaving for the front. Someone puts the coffee on to heat straightaway and we go out on deck, mugs in hand. Andy must have gone to wake Ian. Jude lights a cigarette and noisily spits out the night before. I keep my distance. Simon complains he has a migraine.

'You're paying for your night out,' says Dave.

He goes to pee at the end of the deck, then gives a long modulated yawn as he rubs his eyes. I help Simon move the tubs onto the table and we set to work with some difficulty. The silence is punctuated by Jude's throaty coughing, spitting and stifled swearing.

'He's crazy, waking us like that,' I say. 'The boat *is* our home, after all.'

'Yes, but it's his boat,' Dave says with a shrug. 'He can do what he likes. And he can't wait for us to finish so he can have it back. Need to get everything ready for the tendering season.'

I don't care about Andy, my stomach hurts.

'I'm hungry,' I say. 'I'm running on empty.'

When the skipper appears I blush and bury my nose in the tub, concentrating on a splice.

'Hi, guys,' he booms. 'Feeling good this morning? I have a bitch of a headache, a hangover you wouldn't believe.'

He talks loudly, addressing whoever's prepared to listen. His voice must be carrying to the far end of the docks, but he's in a good mood.

'How about you, Lili? Feeling better than last night?'

My cheeks are blazing, my trembling hand struggles with a strand of line that I'm trying to slip into the splice. When I look up I can see he's laughing.

'Oh my, Lili – quite something.'

The guys have turned to look at me.

'You wouldn't know it but when I brought her back last night ...'

Dave's already grinning, baring all his white teeth. The yellow eyes come to rest on me. Simon waits.

'Well, I was drunk!' I say helplessly.

'I wanted to kiss her.'

'And? What? Did you nearly get lucky? Did you actually?' Dave asks gleefully.

'I wanted to kiss her. She doesn't look it now but she's a hell of a tigress – the slap she gave me!'

I can breathe. The lanky man smiles at me, teasingly. I smile back. Dave bursts out laughing.

'Our little Frenchie,' he says.

Jude looks at me with surprise and respect. Simon doesn't give a damn.

The skipper goes off to call Oklahoma. Will he tell his wife everything? His broken promise to AA, the drunkenness and then the kiss? Well, kiss …

The radio's blaring on the next boat as we get on with our work. Andy reappears, accompanied by a short pudgy man. He has very blue, very round eyes, set far apart in a moon face, half hidden under a felt hat.

'Hi, Ronnie,' says Dave. ''Parently you're taking the boat again?'

The little man nods his round head. 'I'm Aaron,' he says, proffering his hand to me. His cheeks have gone a little pink and he smiles sweetly. 'Would you like to work with me for the tendering season?'

The deal is done. Aaron leaves with his small footsteps and his forget-me-not eyes under black felt … I won't be going to Point Barrow just yet.

Nearly midday. Nearly food time, I think. Jude coughs, Dave yawns, the hangovers are wearing off.

'We're looking in pretty good shape to hand this over,' says Simon.

'Not me,' says Dave. 'My girlfriend's coming over this evening.'

Jude doesn't say anything.

'I'm hungry,' I sigh.

The skipper's back, more wired than ever. He's just bumped into Andy at the bank, and Andy asked how he was.

'Terrible!' Ian exclaimed across the whole bank. 'I got fucking drunk last night!'

People pretended not to hear, Andy shuddered but said nothing. Another veteran of AA, was Andy. The lanky man's still happy, though. He tells us he stopped at the Westmark, the hotel that runs a bar up above the port. Judging by the twinkle in his eyes, he must have had a few gin and tonics. He won't stop talking now and wants to help us clean the lines, so we make room for him at the table. He goes back over his disappointing experience with Lili-the-wildcat. The men are tiring of the story, but he keeps going and now the tone has changed.

'I guess you want someone richer?' he asks me, looking me in the eye. 'Richer and stronger?'

I shrug and – muttering an angry 'Yeah, that's right' – I throw my gloves onto the table and go to get a coffee. He comes and takes me to one side in the galley.

'Lili, I've been thinking, we could get married if you want.'

This is the lanky man talking to me, a pallid adolescent with a weather-beaten face. His eyes wait for an answer, shining so brightly they look wet. I look at him. What the hell have I done now? I think.

'I don't want to get married. You have a wife and kids. You're going home to Oklahoma. And I'm going to Point Barrow.'

Jude walks in at this point.

'Can I come through?' he asks, looking at the two of us suspiciously.

I go back out on deck, my coffee forgotten. The sun is dazzling but I feel very low. The men have resumed attempts to estimate our haul of halibut but we'll know soon enough: we'll be unloading this evening.

'How's this evening going to work?' asks Simon.

'Jude, Joey and I will take care of everything,' says Dave. 'It's our job. You just need to clean out the hold when it's empty, disinfect it and scrub all the corners. But the bulk of the work is our problem.'

Simon lowers his head. We catch each other's eye.

'We're just greenhorns,' I tell him.

He smiles, a hint of bitterness in the corners of his mouth.

'Yeah . . . . Just greenhorns, half shares.'

Mattis comes by in the afternoon when we're all busy working. He's drunk and sways from left to right along the pontoon.

'Where the hell is your fucking son-of-a-bitch skipper?' he yells at Jude, who's closest to him. 'Go get him for me! If he dares come up, we'll see who's stronger.'

The skipper is here and he's heard every word. He emerges from his shadowy corner and cranes his neck towards the dock.

'You looking for me?'

'You motherfucker, talking to me the way you did yesterday – *and* in front of the others too. You ever do a thing like that again and I'll redesign your pretty little pain-in-the-ass nitpicking face.'

He's still shouting as he storms off along the pontoon, stumbling in every direction.

Jude's jaw has hardened.

'Sounds like he was threatening you,' he says. 'I wouldn't let him do that if it were me.'

'He's right,' says Jesse. 'That animal can't treat you like that.'

'I'll go find him,' says Ian, 'the bastard can apologise to me.'

He throws his gloves onto the deck, climbs over the bulwark and jumps onto the quay. Little Jesse scampers behind him, trying to keep up with his long thin legs. Simon laughs, Dave says nothing.

'I hope they won't throw him in the harbour,' I whisper to Dave. 'Mattis didn't do anything, and he was kind of right, anyway.'

'Yeah,' Dave agrees glumly, 'dumbass situation, goddamn stupid men's problem. But don't worry about it, they won't chuck him in the water, not in broad daylight, too many people around.'

Five minutes later our two men are back and they're smiling. I don't dare to ask if they killed him. Jesse goes back to his bunk for a snooze.

'I've done enough work for today,' Ian announces. 'I'm outta here. We're unloading at midnight, guys. The boat needs to be at the cannery at eleven. Be here at nine.'

Dave heads off too, he has a meeting about a job, and Simon goes back to bed. Jude and I are left alone with our tubs. We keep working without saying a word. Joey shows up, accompanied by another man.

'You still working? *We* finished ages ago!' the man says. 'I hope you at least lined your pockets …'

Jude doesn't reply. The guy is wearing new clothes. He takes a wad of banknotes from his pocket and waves it in front of us for a moment, an encouraging look on his freshly shaven face. He looks me up and down.

'A chick.'

He proffers a hand, which I crush in mine.

'And tough with it! OK, come on, I'll buy you a drink at Tony's. I'm getting smashed this evening.'

Jude drops his gloves onto the table.

'It won't do any harm.'

I watch them leave.

'Aren't you coming?' Joey asks, turning round.

'Can I?'

'Sure! If that asshole said he'd buy us a drink, that goes for you too.'

They walk ahead and we follow. In the distance I spot Mattis beside the *Kayodie*, a little more drunk, perhaps, and waving to me expansively. I feel relieved: they didn't throw him into the harbour. I reply with a far-off little wave, no desire to start all that again. And I don't want to miss the round.

Unbelievable chaos in the bar. End of season. The men are all beside themselves. They've been ashore too long: having regained their strength since the last fishing expedition, they don't know what to do with it. It's not Jimmy Bennett crying on the jukebox this evening, but the Doors and AC/DC wailing. Joey was a little drunk when he turned up at the *Rebel*, he's finishing the job at the bar now, the grim set of his forehead obstinately lowered over a Bud whose label he's slowly tearing off. I concentrate on drinking my beer, not even given time to finish one before I'm handed another, but I'm getting bored. The waitress puts a whisky in front of me – someone's bought it for me. I have to drink it. A guy next to me strikes up conversation but we can't hear each other and he gives up. On my other side Joey confides his resentments to me: an Injun negro ... just a dirty Indian negro ... an impenetrable rant. He drinks with savage intensity as he ploughs on with his monologue. He gets angry when the waitress doesn't come over straightaway. I could see that if he didn't have to go back to the boat to unload this evening, he'd keep going till he dropped, he'd just keep on being a 'dirty Indian negro', full of rage and rebellion. And confusion.

I look at the clock on the wall and get up.

'Thank you,' I say to the man who invited us.

Joey wants me to stay. He's just ordered a beer.

'No, Joey, have to be at the boat at nine. I'm going.'

His face drops back towards the counter top, and he's still muttering, Indian negro . . .

I'm about to leave when Jude calls me back.

'Wait. I'll come with you. Otherwise I'll never leave.'

He has trouble getting to his feet, sways slightly. I wait for him and watch him struggle to get to the door.

Outside, daylight. I have a bitter taste of tobacco and beer in my mouth. Jude spits for the both of us and almost falls over. I reach out an arm and help him right himself. His face is very red, he's aged a lot in the space of a few drinks. I don't dare to look at him now, I'm frightened of his eyes, staring and almost dazed, of his slack half-open lips, his heavy features, his burned-looking skin scored with endless fine lines and purplish blood vessels.

'Come on, then,' I say. I walk slowly and take his arm to cross the street. He lets me lead him like a sleepy child. We walk along the quay, with me still holding his arm. The sun will soon disappear behind the mountain. When we reach the white wooden bench Jude wants to sit down.

'Let's have a smoke,' he says.

We sit looking out over the flotilla and he lights a cigarette.

'Could you give me one please? I have none left.'

He opens an astonished eye, as if only just realising I'm there.

'Then you give me a kiss.'

'No.'

'Uh-huh.'

I hesitate for a moment, touch his lips with mine very briefly.

'Better than that.'

I do it again. He holds my head to him with a heavy hand. And kisses me. His mouth tastes of whisky and tobacco. I pull away and he slumps back onto the bench, his eyes closed, breathing deeply. I don't dare remind him about the cigarette. Over there, bobbing on the clear water in the harbour, the *Rebel*'s impressive hull – black picked out with a line of yellow. They'll be waiting for us on board.

Jude opens his eyes and tries to sit up.

'Let's go to the motel,' he says softly.

I look at him, at his eyelids closing in spite of himself, his head lolling onto his chest.

'Gotta get back to the boat, Jude. We'll be moving her soon.'

'Let's go to the motel,' he says again in a slow drone of a voice. I don't think he can hear me.

'You can do what you like. I'm going back to the *Rebel*.'

'Wait. First tell me ... are you a woman?'

It feels almost as if I've been pinched. I stare at him for a moment, not understanding.

'What makes you say that? I don't look like a man. I don't have hair on my face, or muscles like you. The others have never said that ... they know perfectly well ... and anyway I have this tiny voice. That no one can hear.'

'I dunno – can't even tell if you have breasts. At least, I've never seen them. You could easily be a very young guy.'

I look up at the sky, the dirty embankment cluttered with crumpled beer cans, a stranded vodka bottle right under our noses.

'Answer me, are you really a woman?'

'I think so,' I murmur. 'At least it says "Female" on my passport.'

'Let's go to the motel, then I'll know.'

'Do what you like, Jude,' I say again. 'I'm going to the *Rebel*.'

'We could go to the motel first, and then—'

'I'm tired. We're going to be late. See you later.'

'Wait. I'll come with you,' he manages through flabby lips. 'We'll go back to the boat, you'll lie down on my bunk, and I'll lie on top of you ...'

I stand up, take a few steps and turn round. He hasn't moved so I go back over to him and take his arm.

'Come on, we'll be late, there'll be trouble.'

I keep hold of his arm all the way to the pontoon. We go down the footbridge very slowly, someone walks past and smiles at us; my own face stays serious, focused. I let go of Jude's arm, the *Rebel* is only a few yards away. Two guys step off the *Arnie*, the old tugboat that leaves port every night and returns at dawn. Jude stops, stands squarely on his unsteady legs and blocks the way. His eyes glitter and he has trouble enunciating his words.

'Hey, you two,' he says in an incoherent growl. 'Where's your fucking skipper, the goddamned son of a bitch who took the *Arnie* when she was going to be given to me?'

The men laugh.

'Must be in town, where you've just come from, we'll let him know.'

Jude grabs his penis through the thin cotton of his trousers.

'You can tell him I say "suck my dick!"'

I'm back on the boat. The men are in the galley, busy making sandwiches for themselves. The skipper isn't back yet.

'There you are!' Dave says, smiling at me. 'Not too drunk? And Jude?'

I nod towards the deck.

'I don't think he'll be long.'

We hear a dull thud from outside, then swearing and a tub rolling on the deck.

'That must be him.'

We find him unconscious, collapsed between the glory hole and a pile of tubs. Dave shakes him.

'Hey, old man, wake up, you can sleep it off afterward. We're unloading this evening.'

'A coffee?' I suggest. 'Do you want a coffee?'

He's opened his eyes, seems to be nodding. I hurry into the galley, heat the coffee in the microwave and come back out on deck with a steaming cup.

'Wake up,' Dave cries. 'You're gonna drink this and get on your feet before the skipper gets here.'

Jude has closed his eyes again, no way of waking him now from this semi-comatose state.

Ian appears suddenly. I turn round, still holding the coffee in my hand, not sure what to do with it.

'He fell,' says Dave.

We all go quiet. The lanky man blenches, and he too says nothing for a while. His longliner, his hardworking trustworthy right-hand man, is sprawled on the deck. Jude opens his eyes, his wandering gaze focuses, his pupils dilate and a horrified look fills them. He tries to sit up. He and Ian stare right at each other: Jude is full of panic and shame, Ian in a state of complete consternation. Perhaps in other circumstances Ian would have patted him on the shoulder, but right now he has to be the skipper. He yells half-heartedly, sending Jude to sleep it off on his bunk. Jude gets up and, head hunched between his shoulders, back stooped, he makes his way to the cabin, hardly staggering at all.

Ian turns to me with a dejected smile.

'You see, alcohol ...' His words tail off. 'Still, we'll manage OK, won't we?'

Ian went up to the wheelhouse without a word and sat looking at the harbour. We waited for two hours. Jude still didn't get up. So Ian took the controls and we untied the boat. It was midnight when we left the quay and neither Dave nor Simon had succeeded in waking Jude. Joey was drunk but he could stand up. Dave looked at Simon and me.

'Sorry, guys,' he said. 'We're going to need your help ... You're going to go into the hold and pass us the halibut one by one, because the hatch is too small to get the cannery brailers in. Joey and I will take care of the rest up on deck.'

It was cold. We tied up to the wooden posts – the only boat there, we must have been the very last to unload. The skipper stepped up onto the quayside. We put on our rain gear and cleared the decks, then Simon and I jumped down into the hold. The ice had melted. Slipping on fish underfoot, we waded through the cold, blood-streaked water, which immediately started filling our boots. My rib reminded me it was there when I coughed. I looked at Simon: tonnes and tonnes of fish we would have to lift up at arm's length. He didn't look particularly confident either. In the end we just smiled at each other. There was nothing else we could do.

One of the factory workers lobbed us a sturdy square net that Dave and Joey spread out on deck. We sent up the black cod and they threw them into the net. When the pile was big enough, the purse line came down and the boys passed it through the ring in each corner of the net, then stood aside while it was hoisted onto the factory's wharf and weighed. After the black cod came grey cod, then rock fish, the poor 'idiot fish' with their bulging eyes. Their tongues still hadn't shrunk back to size despite their long stay in the hold.

A brief pause. Joey handed each of us a lighted cigarette. I slipped on the halibut as I tried to take mine, and fell flat on my face. We laughed feebly. I wasn't sure whether to laugh or cry. It didn't matter really, there wasn't much difference. Dave asked the others to pass us sweet, ice-cold Cokes. He was chatting to a factory worker and his face darkened.

'Bad news,' he said.

'What is it?' Simon asked.

'We've broken the law for sure, the black cod quota is four per cent of the halibut catch. One thousand two hundred and eighty pounds of black cod, so if we have nineteen thousand pounds of halibut we're up for a fine.'

'What then?' Simon asked.

'What then is you might not even earn enough to get drunk at Tony's. Come on, time for the halibut, you can send them up. Be careful not to hook them through the body, always the head, OK? We don't want to be penalised for damaged halibut as well.'

The water was seeping into our rain gear. It ran down our arms from our wrists, trickling right into our armpits. Soon we were soaked. We harpooned the huge fish and, slipping the whole time, we had to throw all our weight into freeing them from the shifting mass. Dave and Joey leant in over us as far as they could to grab hold of the gaff and pull the halibut up on deck.

'Your rib's hurting, right?'

'A little.'

I grimaced a smile, tears in my eyes and bloodstained slime all over my face. Simon was growing up: under his streaming wet hair, his hollow ashen features had taken on stronger contours. He upbraided Joey, his senior by almost twenty years, when the latter, still too drunk for the work, almost injured him by lobbing a gaff hook back down. I looked at him in amazement: he'd soon be a man, ready to dish out to others what these guys had made him endure.

We'd been in the hold several hours and the level was going down slowly. When I was truly frozen through I remembered Jude asleep, and my anger gave me new strength. At one point, when I reached up my gaff with a halibut on it to Dave, I caught sight of the skipper watching us from the dock. He was laughing at this pair of novices dripping with scum and dirty water, their hair plastered to their foreheads in stiffened clumps. He shouted something and the factory workers laughed along with him. I clenched my teeth. Smiled. Fucking rib, I thought, asshole skipper. I was impervious to their scorn once more.

The night sky was paling overhead now and Ian had gone to bed. We'd taken over twenty thousand pounds out of the hold and it was dawn. The last fish, the largest, were lifted with the help of the hoist, block and tackle. Then Dave handed down the ladder for us to get back on deck. Simon and I looked at each other and smiled: the work was done. All that was left now was cleaning out the hold.

'I'll take care of that,' said Dave, 'you go warm up.'

Day broke very quickly. Joey woke the skipper and we untied the mooring ropes. I'd stopped coughing, but the air was harsh and raw. A glacial wind picked up when the boat started to move away. In the distance the harbour was still asleep and the water was motionless in its iridescent embrace. Two seiners headed towards us, suspended between the sky and the sea. Their slender masts stood out from the misty waters, black against the silk of dawn.

When the *Rebel* was moored up again Simon handed me a cigarette. He had dark bags under sparkling eyes. Dave came over, his face serious, and shook both our hands.

'You did a good job, guys. Thank you.'

The only people left on deck were Simon, me and Joey, who was slicing fillets from the fish put to one side. We were hungry.

'How about some food?'

I was alone with the birds and the pungent smell of the catch. I went inside and took my sleeping bag from the cabin. The air in there was stifling, a smell of sweat, damp clothes drying on bodies, and the acrid stench of boots and socks all mingling with a lingering reek of alcohol. Jude was breathing heavily. I didn't want to listen to him choking and yelping in his sleep. The light from the sky dazzled me when I went up to the wheelhouse. Like in the early days, I found my spot on the damp floor. My helmet of salt water had dried. I fell asleep instantly with my forehead resting on my dirty boots, feeling the soft burn from the mask of mucus and blood flaking on my face. The sun was rising higher, making spots of golden bronze light dance behind my eyelids.

I slept for two hours. When I sat up, every inch of my body hurt. Not a sound on board. The men were asleep. There was still time to sneak off through the streets. I rolled up my sleeping bag in a corner and went down into the galley. Joey's knife was abandoned on the table, a smear of blood had dried on its blade. I hastily washed my face under the tap and untangled the worst of my hair with my fingers. I was about to go out but someone was standing in the shadows in the passageway. It was Jude. I turned my head away.

'I'm going for a coffee ashore,' I snapped.

He didn't dare look me in the eye.

'Good morning,' I added, softening.

He didn't reply and I headed for the door.

'Can I come?'

'If you want,' I said quietly.

The docks were deserted and we walked in silence till he asked, 'Could you really not wake me yesterday?'

'We did everything we could. You didn't even want a coffee. And to be honest, coffee wouldn't have much effect. Even at midnight Dave and Simon couldn't get you to move. And they sure did try.'

A pause. Jude kept his head lowered. We reached the harbour master's offices, where three crows were squabbling over a scrap on the refuse container.

'The skipper must have gone crazy. What did he say?'

'Not much. He sent you to bed. Everyone could tell you weren't up to it.'

'Yeah and now you're gonna tell me he gave me a friendly pat on the shoulder.'

'He didn't yell. No, he pulled a funny face and said something to me about "you see, alcohol", then went up to the wheelhouse.'

We were close to the bench where we'd stopped the day before. I blushed but he seemed to have forgotten everything. So did he still think I wasn't a woman, then? I pulled back my shoulders to make my chest stick out, not that it could be seen anyway.

'How did you manage?'

'Just fine. Simon and I went into the hold. We passed the fish to Dave and Joey. I'm sure it took longer than if you'd been there but nobody yelled and there were no other boats waiting.'

He walked with his head drooped, I could feel his shame. The sun was rising over the harbour as we passed the bars and walked along the arcade. I was no longer afraid of him.

'It won't happen again,' he said in a muted voice. 'Ever.'

We drank our coffee in the sun, at the tiny coffee shop's only table. He bought it for me like a man on a date with a woman. We drank it too quickly, burning our throats, because we couldn't think of anything else to say. Each paralysed by the other's embarrassment. We were like two stupid, bright red idiot fish. Big Murphy put us at ease again when he appeared, swinging his colossal body from side to side. The Brother Francis Shelter was unleashing its family onto the town so Murphy was heading out into the new day. When he saw us from the end of the street his face lit up. He looked at us in turn and a note of amusement flickered across his eyes.

'Hey, Jude, Lili! Up already?'

The little chair creaked when he dropped into it with his full weight. The two men smiled at each other, and Jude straightened himself and puffed out his chest. I was a small, red-faced thing again. Murphy rummaged for coins in the depths of his pocket.

'I'll buy you a coffee! Cookie, Lili?'

I didn't dare say yes, not between these big men who took only whisky and crack. Murphy got to his feet and the chair seemed to stand taller. He went into the coffee shop, rolling his great backside.

'He's a very old friend,' said Jude.

'I know. He's told me about you.'

Jude stared right at me for a long time and frowned. Then he pulled himself together and looked away. He didn't really have the right to act the man, not after last night, anyway.

'Yes,' he said, and lit a cigarette.

'Are you going to stay on the *Rebel*?' I asked.

'She's going to be doing tendering all summer, that's not for me.'

'Yes but this winter on the Bering Sea, pot fishing for cod, and then for crab?'

'I don't know yet. If I'm around, if Ian can run the boat again and if he'll still have me ... I 'spect so, yes. The *Rebel*'s a good boat, and Ian's not a bad skipper.'

Murphy came back with the coffees, a new smile stretching his face wider.

'Jude's a good guy,' he said, turning to me. 'Big Jude. You can trust him.'

Jude gave an embarrassed laugh and I went very red again. Murphy took my hands in his.

'Look at these hands. Shit, never seen anything like 'em on a woman. Look, Jude, they're as big as mine, and hard ... but they're all nicked and scarred. Don't you ever wear gloves?'

'Yes I do, but I don't run to change them the minute they get cut.'

'Need to take care of her, Jude, seeing as you work with her, look after her a bit. Given what her hands have been through, she could have been a goner and you didn't even notice?'

'Shut it, Murphy. *I* was the one who gave her tablets every morning. Me again who went to see the skipper to say she should stop.'

'Maybe we should be going,' I murmured.

We stood up and Murphy winked at us. Jude was standing properly upright now.

★

163

We go back to the boat in silence. Jude wants to find Ian to apologise to him, but he's out. Dave and Simon are not fully awake and watch us morosely. We grab some tubs and go back to work. The coffee in town seems a faraway thing, Jude and I are distant once more. Simon and Dave lug the tubs onto the upper deck and set to work in the sun but we stay in the shade under the standing shelter. Jude has been a sorry sight since he woke up from his bender. I notice him stop frequently and take off his gloves. He brings his hand to his mouth, blows on it, kneads it. With a pitiful grimace on his flushed face, he sucks his fingers miserably.

'Something wrong?'

'It's these fingers. I get this sometimes. I must have frozen them one winter when I was fishing on that trawler. They often hurt but this morning is worse than ever.'

Dave jumps on deck, a handsome athlete who's recovered his strength. He glows in the sunlight flooding the footbridge.

'Did Lili tell you how much we took?'

'She didn't tell me anything at all, except that I didn't want the coffee she offered me and you shook me like a madman but there was nothing doing.'

'Twenty-two thousand pounds, you were right. But the news isn't so good for the black cod. And *I* was right there.'

'Oh yeah?' Jude looks up.

'We're in trouble. We're up for a fine. Four per cent of the catch is the upper limit.'

'And what sort of figure is the fine?'

'At least five thousand dollars, as far as I know. Taken straight out of our share.'

'We won't have earned a cent the whole season what with the lost gear and the surplus black cod, and you're laughing. More than two years now I've worked my ass off for exactly nothing.'

I join Dave in the galley for a sandwich.

'Jude's not doing too good, is he? Is it because of last night?' he asks me.

'A bit. And also his hand hurts. He says he froze his fingers one time.'

'He should go to the hospital. We have to take the rest of the bait to the factory this afternoon, and break up all the ice and clear it out of the small hold. If his hand's frostbitten he'll never manage. And shit like that can be serious.'

'Yes, he could end up with gangrene.'

Ian takes him to hospital and they return a little while later: Jude doesn't have gangrene. The skipper yells at us, saying we have to get to the canneries quickly. I go to get Jude some painkillers with codeine from under my pillow. He washes down three of them, one after the other, with swigs from a flask he takes from his bag.

Simon and I had unloaded twenty-two thousand pounds of fish by hand and slept a scant two hours. I'm now kneeling in the hold, breaking up the ice with a pick. I'm not tired, maybe never will be again, maybe all it took was really wanting this, I'll never need to sleep again. We take out the boxes of bait and they fall apart in our hands. The slippery flaccid things slither into the cloudy water in the hold. The skipper roars.

''S'not our fault,' I mutter.

We paddle about in a brackish slop of melted ice and disintegrated cardboard, trying to collect up the squid. Our gloves have holes in them. Jude pauses more and more frequently, screwing up his face as if crying.

'Let me do it,' I say. 'There are enough of us to handle this.'

He digs in his heels. Dave sends down the pump to empty out the water. Ice has re-formed on the floor and up the walls. I grab the pick from Jude.

'Let me do it,' I say more forcefully.

He hesitates for a moment then goes up to the deck. Soon it's just me left in this hole, battling with the last encrusted bits of ice. The cold flays my fingers and it feels as if my fingernails are being pulled out.

'Lili! Come out of there now, it's done.'

They're calling me from up on deck. But I just can't stop. There's too much energy inside me.

'Come have some lunch, Lili!'

I pop my head out of my dark lair. Outside, sunshine. I blink. Standing around me, the skipper, Dave, Jude and Simon. I look at the four of them, one by one, and laughter gradually takes hold of me, sheer joy washes over me and I'm pitching my head backwards in the summer sky. I close my eyes. When I open them, the men are still there above me. They stare at me in growing astonishment, which starts to look something like tenderness.

'Oh, Lili, *what* is so funny down there?'

Ian and Dave take one of my wrists each and pull me up. I'm overcome with laughter again as I swoop up through the air.

'I'm flying!'

We untie the *Rebel* and she picks up speed. I crouch down next to the bulwark, and the sun ricocheting off the water warms my skin. My legs are muscled up under my soft cotton jog pants, which were white once upon a time and now feel like a second skin. They smell of summer heat. I have my eyes closed and when I open them, Jude is crouching a few metres away. My long thighs are a woman's thighs, I could swear he gets that.

'The sun feels good,' he says.

The weather changes as soon as we're back at the port. A fine rain has started to fall, and the mist coming in from the West has already engulfed the mountain and is gaining on us. The quayside gradually blurs. Ian has gone out again and we are back at work.

'I bet we're the last ones still working.'

'Could well be.'

'How many tubs do we have left to do?'

'Thirty-ish.'

'That's not many.'

'No but they have to be done.'

'Are we off to drag the gear tomorrow?'

'Yeah. Killing ourselves for no reward all over again. Be amazed if we find anything.'

'I won't be taking my girlfriend to Hawaii, for sure,' says Dave.

'Not this time,' Jude says. He's stopped work and has brought one thigh up to his chest, with his heel on the table and his arms crossed against the chill. 'My share's one and a half, how about you?'

'Same as you. But I'm not really a longliner. Crab fisherman, yes.'

'Can't say it makes much difference.'

I feel terribly heavy-hearted, pinned to my chair by the sadness of it. I've just grasped that this won't go on forever, that it won't last much longer, life on board, the men, the boat. Soon it will all be over, I'll be on the streets, my heart raw. The day drags on. Simon yawns, looking grey in the half shadows under the standing shelter. So will it never be evening . . .

'To think I'll hardly have enough to pay my ticket home,' Simon says.

'Are you sure you're being paid a half share?'

'That's what Ian said when I arrived.'

'For me it may be a quarter share,' I say.

'That wouldn't be fair,' says Dave. 'You worked as hard as us and you did your watches like everyone else.'

'Yup,' I say, 'it wouldn't be fair.'

'For the black cod at least . . . for the halibut, I wouldn't say.'

Simon doesn't say anything. Jude sits silently at the end of the table. I drop my hooks and fid, and look at them.

'I come pretty cheap, don't I?'

'I didn't say that to upset you, Lili . . .'

I chuck my gloves down on the table and go into the galley. I untie my hair and brush it for a long time till it falls in waves down my back. I go into the cabin, pick up my money and change my sweat-shirt, putting on the one with 'Fly till you die' written on the back, my favourite. I go back out, walk past the men with my head held high and my mane of hair loose, then I step off the boat without a glance in their direction. The rain is warm and my heart is leaden. They can work without me. I walk along the gleaming dockside in my green boots that make me feel very tall.

I have two beers in quick succession at Tony's, then leave and walk along the arcade to the Ship. The old place is full to bursting but I wriggle my way up to the big bar with its patina of grime, and stand beside an impassive old Native woman and her glass of schnapps. Some of the men are bawling out sea shanties, others lean over their glasses and I can't see their faces. It's so dark I can hardly make out the naked women in the paintings, they've melted into the shadows on the walls.

The waitress comes over to me, still wearing violent coloured make-up on her exhausted face. We smile at each other: she recognises me.

'A Rainier, please.'

She offers it to me on the house, and along with the beer a small glass of schnapps – which I don't like and knock down in one before she gives me more.

'Come to my place,' she says. 'We need to get away from their men's world from time to time. They won't fall over themselves for you once they've sapped all your strength to make money out of you, or used your ass to get their kicks. They're not saps, you can take it from me.'

'They're paying me a quarter share.'

'That's not even a thing, a quarter share,' she rails. 'They're just bastards, I'm telling you, dickheads. Don't let them walk all over you. If you hadn't done the work they'd have thrown you off fast enough. Be careful with them. You should never trust them. And most of all watch your ass.'

'I'm not scared. I can defend myself.'

The guys are thirsty, screaming for drinks. She leaves me with a wink, and goes to serve them. A man has come over and nods at an empty stool.

'May I?' he asks. 'Are you Native?'

'No. But yes, you can sit down.'

'I thought you were Native when I saw you go past in the mornings, a little Native girl from a neighbouring village who goes salmon fishing on one of the seiners on the pontoon.'

He talks in a soft deep voice, with a lilting, slightly surprised sounding tone and a faraway feel to it, as if he were a thousand miles from here. Judging by his boots, his hands and shoulders and the tanned leather of his face, he's a fisherman. He tells me he's on the big red boat outside the harbourmaster's office, the *Inuit Lady*. He's fished hard this year, and the three previous winters, for the sake of his wife who wanted to live in Hawaii. She's there now, but he has to keep working, endlessly, to pay the mortgage for a house he never sees, a home he doesn't even want to know because his life is in the Great North, not on some beach in a land of sunshine and idleness. His own life was in the forest.

His story is a sad monotonous drone, with the slow rhythm of a lament. He's a little drunk, and talks on and on.

'I was so happy when I was a trapper. Oh boy was I happy. Long days in the forest, in the cold and the snow and the silence. Oh I was so happy.'

His voice keeps repeating itself until it's just a heartbroken litany, little more than a sigh. He gazes blankly, looking dead ahead across the darkness of the bar through the opaque smoke-filled air. Perhaps he can see the huge trees, he's walking through the snow, which creaks under his snowshoes, and the wind in the treetops makes a sound like a muted foghorn through the vastness of the woods.

'You should go back there then.'

He swivels to face me.

'You don't get it at all!' he explodes, suddenly exasperated and on the verge of tears. 'I have to pay for the house ... It's my wife! And I have to pay all the bills for her set-up. I have to keep coming back to this misery. Maybe till I die. The Bering Sea in winter – you don't know what that's like, you haven't been through it, that torture. It really is torture, freezing sea spray, and constantly having to break up ice, or you die, your body exhausted, the friends you lose ...'

'I'm sorry,' I murmur.

'Would you like to come away to the woods with me?' he asks, softening.

The old Native woman smiles at me through the blue smoke of the cigarette she drags on with the tips of her lips. Men bay rowdily, sitting up on their stools. The waitress who's about to take over downs her whisky in one and orders another straightaway. My beer is empty and I want to get out.

'I'm Ben,' says the fisherman as I get to my feet.

'Bye, Ben. I'm Lili.'

It's dark outside and the rain hasn't stopped. I cross the street back to the docks. A man comes round the corner of the taxi office and walks towards me with a limp. I recognise him because I've often seen him at the square, sitting on a bench waiting for the days to go by. Sometimes he's drunk, but not this evening. He stops when we draw level and looks at me with dark eyes like two bottomless pits of black, the eyes of a shipwrecked soul. He says something barely audible in a halting guttural language I don't recognise. I spread my hands as a sign of helplessness, and he just shrugs and continues on his way.

I reach the boat and only Jude is left on deck, knotting gangions. I pour myself a lukewarm coffee, sit at the table in the galley, and sigh. In front of me, a pile of wispy ends of white cord. I start tying gangions, there's nothing else to do ... I'm not even drunk but tiredness crashes down on me and nails me to the seat. My eyes half close.

'Starting to feel not so warm out there,' Jude says, coming in and sitting at the table.

'I was falling asleep, you woke me.'

We go back to work on the gangions.

'You're making them too small,' he says.

'No I'm not.'

'Yes you are. Look ... Oh OK, you're right.'

'Did they all go out?' I ask.

'As you can see.'

'I was at the bar,' I say.

'Oh.'

'I had lots of beers. Met some people.'

'Mustn't listen to what everyone says. There are some bad men around here.'

'Not just here. I know all about them. Where I come from we have them too. I chatted with Sandy, the waitress at the Ship. She even invited me to sleep at her place.'

'Keep your distance. A lot of dope goes down at her pad. And she's a lesbian.'

'Maybe not,' I say quietly. 'Anyway, I can't see the harm in that.'

Jude must have been cold outside, he's sat himself very close to me. His thigh is pressed against mine. He clears his throat, hesitates. Then in his deep voice he stammers slightly and keeps his golden eyes pinned on the thread between his fingers:

'Why don't we take a motel room this evening, to get away from the boat a while? Life on board can get kind of suffocating. Just to change our headspace, take a proper long shower, maybe even a bath, watch TV, relax, or whatever ...'

'Or whatever?' I laugh.

He's thrown by my laughter. But still persists. His leg is now really heavy against mine. That's when Ian returns. Very drunk.

'Lili,' he cries, 'c'mere. I need to talk to you ... Come to the wheel-house with me.'

I follow him. His pale watery eyes are open wide, his face ashen.

'I called Oklahoma. I told my wife everything. We're agreed, we're separating. She's taking one kid and I'll have the other. We can get married, Lili. We'll go to Hawaii. I have enough in my account to get us a boat. We can go fishing together in warm seas ...'

I back away to the stairs.

'No,' I say. 'No, I don't want to get married, I don't want to be your wife. A wife. You already have one. I want to stay in Alaska.'

I've hurt the lanky man, the man who once told me 'passion is beautiful', long before I joined the crew of the *Rebel*. I head back down the stairs. He follows me, tries to stop me leaving. The galley is empty, Jude has gone – thirsty, probably. The lanky man follows me all the way to the cabin, wants to come inside with me. I push him away.

'Lili,' he says. 'Lili, wait.'

I'll be the one crying if this keeps going – if he goes on looking at me with those hangdog eyes – I'm the one crying. I push him away. I can feel his ribs with my hand. I catch one last glimpse of his tormented face, of this great tall forlorn child, before he goes back out. It will definitely be my fault if he drinks gin and tonic till he's rolling on the floor this evening. I retreat into the cave of my bunk, bury myself completely in my sleeping bag. I've unloaded ten tonnes of fish, I've fought the ice in the hold with a pickaxe, I've been a rebel and done the rounds of the bars, and met a sad trapper. My skipper wants to take me fishing in Hawaii and Jude wants to take me to a motel. Manosque-les-Sorrow still waits for me. That's a lot in one day.

The men have gone off to bars again. I sit alone listening to the water sliding against the hull of the boat.

Midday. We're waiting for the skipper. He arrives late, still drunk. He looks exhausted. The men say nothing, look away. We cut loose and the *Rebel* leaves the harbour.

Dave and Jude nod at each other.

All they say is 'Yes. He'd do better to sleep. He's tired', and they send him gently off to bed. They will take turns helming the boat to the waters where the lost lines must have drifted.

The sea is perfectly still, dazzling. We finish repairing the last longline under a wide-open sky, on the upper bridge. The full glare of the sun licks our cheekbones, burns our foreheads, dries out our lips. It devours our faces. Simon hums to himself, Jude is unreadable, his face tilted towards the line. There are seals lying on the rocks.

'I'd like to be a seal warming myself in the sun,' I say out loud.

Simon and Jude laugh.

For more than twenty-four hours we've been trawling a grapple hook attached to two hundred fathoms of line through the waters where we fished. The lines are nowhere to be found. Ian has joined us on deck. He's been icy towards us since he woke. Well, he's forgotten about me. Lili erased. All that's left is a crew member he shouts orders to.

'We'll head east and keep looking for them,' he announces.

That means travelling even further from Kodiak. Simon pales.

'But you said ... What about my flight?'

The skipper's quick to snap back.

'Do you really think that's how fishing works?' he barks. 'You do your eight hours and then go home, put your feet under the table and watch TV? Do you really think we burned all that gas for nothing, that we'll give up the search when those lines could be just a few miles away ... and that we'll pay compensation for them when we've worked ourselves to the bone? A nice jaunt out to sea and then guzzling the same amount of fuel again to get back in time for his lordship to catch a plane? You shouldn't come on board next time, kiddo, you should stay home in California.'

Simon squares up to Ian for the first time. He stands tall, white with rage, jaws clamped.

'You promised when I bought my ticket,' he says in a monotonous, barely controlled voice. 'That was the condition on which I came with you. I had your word.'

Ian bellows and slinks away. In the wheelhouse Dave has seen none of this. Jude isn't here either: he sees nothing, hears nothing and will say nothing. I suddenly feel contempt for the lanky man, and his role as master on board; for Jude, and the silence, the belligerence of these strong men, these all-powerful men who impress us with their experience, the mysterious knowledge they keep hidden behind those inscrutable faces, and the thunder of their voices when there's any urgency. A silence built as much on submission as indifference.

The two greenhorns exchange a weak smile. The skipper has disappeared into the wheelhouse. Simon belongs to the boat until he disembarks. Was it the pride of unloading the catch of halibut, of being promoted to Jude's position for the space of one night, or Dave's virile handshake in the morning that made him forget that? He stares at the horizon, a hint of anxiety lurking in those blue eyes, a hint he concentrates on extinguishing before it overruns him completely. I can't help him. I hand him a cigarette and we smoke in silence, without stopping our work. My eyes gloss over Jude and refuse to see him. I look at the sky. When will I set off for Point Barrow at last?

The grapple hook catches one of the lost lines the next day, on our very first try. Then another. The atmosphere eases. Ian promises to buy Simon another ticket. We finish the last longline and the tubs are all lined up on either side of the deck, then securely tied in place. For dinner this evening there'll be halibut cooked by Jude on an improvised barbecue. We go off to get some sleep and Jude calls us when it's ready. The sun has burned him, like a stronger spirit than the alcohol that fuels his nights.

We head back to shore and find the green mountains have tended towards mauve. Drifts of supple fireweed wave under the eagles' low flight. Jason once told me they're his favourite flowers. We don't have much time left on board together. The men's thoughts have already moved on. Ian hasn't said anything more to me about going fishing on the Bering Sea. Shyly, I venture to raise the subject. He's evasive but then relents.

'I'm going back to Oklahoma. We'll see. Maybe.'

'I've never worked so hard for so little,' Dave says when we're given our pay, and then adds, 'We'll bail ourselves out this winter, with the crab season.'

And he laughs.

Simon caught the first flight to San Diego. Jude pocketed his cheque without a word and left.

I don't get a quarter share but a half share. I have enough to buy myself some good shoes: they're on offer – Redwings. The best, according to Jason, and he wears nothing else when he isn't in his boots. I'm left with a few crumpled notes that I stow carefully under my pillow with my papers, some sticky sweets and the box of chewing tobacco.

And then everything happens very quickly.

The Great Sailor

I'd arrived here alone, from far away. *I want a boat to adopt me*, I'd whispered in the great windswept silence of my first nights as I lay on the floor in the wooden house, looking out at the dark sky – the Alaskan night, the vast wind, and I'm a part of it, I thought – gazing at it till I fell asleep. I want a boat to adopt me. And I'd set sail, I'd found my boat, a boat blacker than the darkest night. The men on board were big and tough, they took my bunk, threw my rucksack and sleeping bag on the floor, shouted, I was frightened, they were harsh and strong, they were good, so good for me, they were all the good Lord when I raised my eyes to them. I'd married a boat. I'd given my life to it.

Now I was walking along the quayside with my beautiful Redwings on my feet, proud of the sound of my footsteps on the tar road. It was a gorgeous day. I was hungry – maybe just a coffee and a bun at the local supermarket – then I was suddenly gripped with panic. What if everyone had already left? What if they'd all gone? It would kill me.

I ran back to the boat, demented. The decks were deserted, naked. The rain gear that we used to hang under the upper deck had disappeared. Except mine. The poor-quality, holey, mismatched yellow-and-orange rain gear from the Salvation Army. I froze, standing on the bridge in the blinding light, staring at those bare hooks. The season was over. They'd gone. I wasn't dead. I raced down to the cabin. The bunks were empty, a solitary abandoned sock still lay on the floor. Nothing else. Well, yes: my sleeping bag, my clothes rolled up hastily next to a dirty pillow. The boys had gone. We hadn't even said goodbye. I let myself collapse onto a bunk, appalled. I was an orphan. I want a boat to adopt me, I had murmured two months ago – an eternity ago – at the very start of this adventure. It was over now. I'd slept in the warmth of men's sleep. I belonged to them. My whole heart belonged to them.

Joey appeared in the doorway and screwed up his eyes.

'What the hell are you doing in the dark?'

He was holding a Budweiser in one hand and a cigarette in the other. Judging by his dancing eyes, he must have had quite a lot to drink already.

'Have they gone?'

'All of them. Got the hell out! You didn't think they'd stay till Christmas, did you? I've finished cleaning the cabin and the oven. Now I'm waiting for Aaron, to find out when we'll start setting up the gear – water tanks, fuel tanks, food stores … Don't stay in the dark, Lili, come have a beer on deck, Ronnie's not here. And we sure earned a break.'

I got up and followed Joey. He took a pack of beers from the fridge on his way past. The light on deck burned my eyes.

'Help yourself,' he said, handing me his pack of cigarettes. 'You can always help yourself without asking.'

'Thanks, Joey. When does the season start?'

'We should be leaving Kodiak in about a week. Salmon fishing has been open for a while but there was hardly any work for us in the early stages, not enough to fill a boat anyway, with what the seiners would have brought back each evening.'

He looks at me kindly.

'You'll see, it'll be an easy season for you, nothing like what you just did, a fixed rate every day for three months. By September you'll be rich, you'll be able to get your ass out of here and go find some sun.'

'What if I told Aaron I don't actually want to do this season?' I asked in a quiet voice, almost a whimper. 'I don't think I can face anything now, I just want to go to Point Barrow. Will he be angry if I drop out?'

Joey looked at me in amazement.

'But, Lili, no one turns down a season tendering on this boat. What the fuck do you want to go there for?'

'To see the end of the end.'

'The earth's round, Lili. It isn't the end of anything. There's nothing to see there, we already told you that. It's a soul-destroying place: unhappy people who're drunk or high – or both – all year long, who live on welfare and subsidised fuel, and they all dream of going someplace else. Eskimos who've lost everything, especially their dignity, and who'll eat you for breakfast. And how do you plan to get there, anyway? You can't afford a plane ticket with what you just earned.'

'I'll hitchhike,' I said with a shrug.

'The road stops just after Fairbanks, it'll cost you your life, all that for a scrap of rock that'll soon be iced over.'

'Beyond the road there's a dirt track for trucks supplying the pipeline.'

'You're crazy, but most of all you're tired. You need a beer and a few days to yourself. Two months you've been working day and night, or nearly ... You worked as hard as guys twice the size of you who've been doing it their whole lives. I'll give you your day off, and right away. We won't start anything before tomorrow. I'll tell Ronnie that I sent you out to get some air. He'll understand, he's a good boss, you'll see, he never yells. And he knows his job.'

'OK,' I said. 'Thanks, Joey.'

We drank a beer and smoked a few cigarettes. Aaron didn't show up, so I left the *Rebel*. I walked along the quay and past the Alaskan Seafood canning factory spreading its putrid smell across the town – the wind was changing. After that came the landing stage for the ferry, the *Tustumena*, which was moored up. I watched people walk up the footbridge, then continued along Tagura Road. I was heading towards the boatyard when someone called to me. I turned and saw two figures casting black shadows on the white road. One was colossal and seemed to swing from side to side, the other more elongated, with a red mane that blazed in the light like a golden helmet. They were heading in my direction.

I recognised Murphy, and I'd come across the other guy at the square. I waited for them with the sun warming the back of my neck.

'We were looking for you,' said Murphy, catching his breath.

'Me?'

'We have something for you.'

Murphy reached out his hand to me. In his chubby palm, between his open fingers, which were plump as a newborn baby's, was a small box decorated with lacquered red and black stripes. Murphy's friend took from his pocket a cameo in fake mother-of-pearl.

'Oh, thank you,' I said. 'But why?'

'Just a present,' Murphy explained, a warm smile creasing his face, which was still congested from the walk.

'But why?'

'Because we like you, that's all. We're happy you're here.'

They continued on their way and I was alone on the road once more. I stroked the polished wood and put the cameo away in the box. I was hungry and went into town, where the streets were busy: the fishing fleet was back. The doors to bars stood wide open as if there wasn't enough air inside. Shouts, laughter, wild uninhibited whoops and the occasional chime of a bell emerged from these dark lairs. I would have loved to venture into those shadowy dens, those wild animal cages, but I no longer dared. I hurried on whenever I passed one. The guys had left without saying goodbye to me, without a trip to paint the town red together. Even though they'd promised me as much. I felt so sad I wanted to die. I was hungry for popcorn, and turned down the street by the liquor store.

We almost walked into each other. Jude. The great sailor. Once again he'd lost the handsome rage of a fishing man, his shoulders were stooped. His footsteps had no self-assurance, as if he were in a foreign country, unsure how to walk or which way to go. The lion of the seas was back to being a bear.

'Everyone's gone,' I stammered.

'Yes,' he said. 'Bad season. Time to move on.'

'Oh.'

'Where are you headed?'

'I . . . I'm going to buy popcorn.'

He smiled, just. As if afraid of something, he closed his eyes, took a deep breath and puffed out his chest. He swept one hand slowly across his brow.

'Can I get you a drink?'

I said yes.

We went into the bar close to the liquor store and hovered indecisively for a moment in the sudden darkness, the shouting and smoke. Then he walked to the bar and I followed. There were two stools free. We drank a beer very quickly, perhaps frightened, not knowing what to say next. We'd left the boat, neither of us was part of anything now.

'Let's get out of here,' he said.

Outside, the light, the wind, people, and the liquor store. Jude went in and walked straight up to the stack of Canadian Whisky, not even looking as he grabbed a plastic half-bottle. Still not stopping, he went to the back of the store, opened a glass door and took a pack of chilled Rainiers. The whole process took less than a minute. The fat woman at the till turned her pale, heavy face towards him, then stared me up and down slowly. What was she thinking? I was intimidated by her and I blushed. We left the place.

'Would you like to go have a beer in the sunshine?' he asked back outside. 'I don't really like bars. Too much noise, too much smoke. And it all gets too expensive.'

'Yes,' I said.

'Huh? I've never been able to understand your voice. And I can hardly ever hear it.'

'Yes,' I said again, a little more loudly.

We left the bars behind, and followed the road to the ferry. We walked in silence, with the sun burning our faces. Low tide: the fresh, slightly bland smell of the water combined with the acrid stench from the canning factory's chimneys.

'It stinks,' he said.

'Oh, I like even this smell.'

He shot me a sharp look of surprise.

'I'd like to take the ferry one day,' I told him.

'I'll be on it in less than a week. I have friends in Anchorage. Might find a boat to work on too. Or if not, Hawaii.'

'Hawaii?'

'I have a brother there. He lives on the Big Island with his stupid bitch of a wife. I'd like to fish in the South Pacific.'

'I want to go to Point Barrow.'

'I already heard that on the boat,' he almost laughed. 'What the hell do you want to do up there? And how do you think you'll get there?'

'Hitchhiking, that's how.'

'You don't know what you're heading for.'

'I'm not frightened,' I said firmly.

'You won't get there in one piece. I know the kind of people you'll meet on the way, you all on your own on that deserted track. I lived in Nome for years, it's the same kind of place. Alcohol and drugs. And who gives a damn about the law there ... Looking out over the icy ocean, and in the other direction, forests going on for hundreds of miles, then desert-like mountains, the very end of everything. Do you think you can cope all on your own?'

'Maybe I should buy a gun.'

'Do you know how to use one?'

'No.'

Where I come from you can die too, I thought.

'I still want to go there,' I said in a quieter voice.

The yellow eyes on me again.

'Are you a runaway?' he murmured.

'I don't think so.'

We walked along the water's edge, the sun reflecting off the surface. Then past the smaller port, scarcely more than a wooden pontoon between its waiting fishing boats. I didn't know whether I should keep following him. He seemed heavy and tired, bitter perhaps. The sea, the real sea, was so far away; so far from us the open ocean and the great sailor squaring up to it. Instead, these overpopulated streets, the confusion in bars, and this man trudging wearily, his bag weighed down with beer. I kept going, though.

Soon there were no more houses, or boats, or anything, just a vast wasteland cluttered with rusted, broken crab pots, twisted sheets of metal and aluminium panels piled up on the very green grass and the mauve fireweed, just torn gill nets and rotting netting. He stopped, blew his nose with his fingers and spat a long way away. Once again, with some embarrassment, he ran a hand slowly over his forehead moist with sweat.

'We could sit down somewhere here,' he said with a shy smile. 'It's clean by the water.'

'Yes.'

We sat behind the pots. Ahead of us was the channel, and every now and then a boat travelling along it. I thought they could probably see us, our two bright red faces peeping above the grass, and they might be amazed to see these two beacons lost among the metalwork, close to the span of the large bridge linking the road to Dog Bay.

'We're almost under the bridge,' I said in a constricted voice.

He didn't say anything, there was nothing to say. He opened a beer and handed it to me, then lit a cigarette and was wracked by a spate of coughing. He spat off into the distance, with all the power of the man I knew, the man who shouted at the sea.

We drank all the beer. Quickly, because we didn't know what to talk about. We were too hot, and once the beer was finished we had nothing to keep our hands and mouths busy. He moved one arm towards me awkwardly, then put it around my shoulders, and rolled me against him.

He was lying on the grass with the sun beating down on his face. I looked at the light in his yellow eyes, the threads of tawny red in his irises, his heavy eyelids, the tiny blood vessels under his burned skin. I closed my eyes. Hard, so hard I kissed that mouth which felt warm and alive next to mine. He was burning underneath me. I was small and supple, undulating on top of him. He sat up, swung on top of me. He crushed me with all his weight and sighed. He was smiling. 'Oh God … God,' he kept saying.

We're walking along the white road, our cheeks blazing under an azure sky.

After rolling on top of me he'd sat up and said, 'We can't stay here. If someone saw us … Let's go to a motel, shall we?'

We sat up on the grass, and I wiped his saliva from my lips. He totted up the crumpled banknotes in his pocket.

'I don't have enough,' he said, then turned to me, embarrassed, and added, 'If you could lend me some I'll give it straight back to you this evening.'

I rummaged through my pockets. I had thirty-one dollars.

'Does it cost more than that?'

He looked at me indulgently, laughed gently.

'Y'don't go to motels much. That definitely won't be enough. But I know someone in the little harbour. His boat was there earlier, let's go see.'

The man was there, a forbidding-looking character standing very tall and upright on the deck of a small seiner equipped for trolling. His grey hair fell to below his shoulders and was held back by a faded blue bandana. A breath of wind made his hair mingle with his very long beard. He watched us come over without breaking into a smile, his steely white gaze never faltering. Jude spoke to him quietly, and I stood to one side, my cheeks burning more with each passing minute – either the beer or my shame. The man took a wallet from his pocket and handed over a banknote.

'Will that do it?'

He could have been made of bronze as he watched us leave, motionless in the sunlight, his sinewy arms crossed over his bony chest, his silver hair floating among flights of ash-grey birds. We made our way back to the road without a word.

'I'd really like some popcorn – I'm so hungry,' I muttered as we passed the cinema.

Jude went in and asked for the largest portion.

'Surely the plastic makes it taste bad, the whisky, I mean,' I said, remembering the whisky in his bag.

'That whisky's not meant to last long,' he said with a smile. 'It doesn't have time to take on the taste of the bottle.'

And now we reach the motel, one of two in town.

'Why not the other one?' I ask. 'Why not the Star?'

'Sometimes I go to the Star with buddies. Maybe ten of us to a room ... party time. The Shelikof's completely different.'

The women in reception scare me a little. I can't wait to be in the room, quickly, far away from all these people. But once there, I suddenly feel cold, and those big arms close around me. The rough palms cup my face. The wall feels cold against my back. The runaway is caught. I could almost cry. He pulls off my sweater, takes off my T-shirt. I cling to his head, his thick mane, his powerful neck. I watch him. I hold back a sob. Gently he pushes me towards the bed. Then he's very warm and kind.

'Tell me a story,' he whispers. He has a deep, slow voice, muted and softly husky. Like a cat asking for something. Tell me a story ...

Later he opens the bottle with his teeth and gulps some whisky, still on top of me.

'D'you want some?' he asks quietly.

'Yes,' I say even more quietly.

He drinks some more, leans over me and in his kiss is a mouthful of alcohol, a burning amber that chokes me. And then he's inside me again, the golden eyes not leaving me for a moment, he delves deeper, and deeper, until he burns my soul.

He's asleep and I'm watching him. A mixture of surprise and embarrassment. The heavy white chest slowly rises and falls. Curly, almost russet-coloured hair on his huge torso. A cough suddenly wracks his

187

body, breaking the silence in the room. A terrible roar, but even this doesn't wake him. I flatten myself onto the sheet, huddle under the duvet. A real lion is asleep beside me. Eyes half closed, and controlling my breathing, I watch. Outside at this time of day the colour and smell of the port are changing as the tide comes in. The evening wind, the seagulls, running through the streets. I'm hungry and I smooth a hand over my empty concave stomach, the sharp curve of my ribs. I reach out my arm furtively to the popcorn on the bedside table, gather five white clumps and stuff them into my mouth. They crunch against my teeth: the taste of butter and grains of salt on my tongue. The yellow eyes open. Startled, I swallow the popcorn down in one and give a disconcerted smile. A heavy arm wraps itself around my shoulders. He's coming back to himself and coming back to me. His thick fingers glide over my cheek.

'You're the best thing that could have happened to me in a very long time.'

I think about the docks and the seagulls. About running through the evening air.

'Such a long time since I've been with a woman.'

His hand comes off my cheek and picks up the bottle from the bedside table. He sits up and takes a long swig, then coughs.

'Want some?'

'Yes ... No ... A little.'

It's too strong. I don't like whisky.

'Will we see each other again?' he asks.

I'm still thinking about seagulls.

'I don't know. You're leaving soon, and I have work. The *Rebel*'s leaving as soon as the salmon show up.'

'We could still see each other, though. You could also come with me.'

'On the ferry? To Anchorage?'

'Anchorage and Hawaii. Or anywhere.'

I laugh quietly.

'No Point Barrow, then?'

'No Point Barrow.'

He takes the packet of cigarettes, lights one for me.

'Thank you.'

It will soon be nightfall over the port. The sky, which I've been watching through the window, has already lost some of its brilliance. Perhaps Aaron's waiting for me at the boat. Perhaps he's done waiting for me. A terrible weariness fills my heart: I don't want to go back on the boat, I'm tired and I want to belong to myself. Either at Point Barrow or running along the docks.

'Will you let me go?' I whisper.

He doesn't hear me.

'Will you let me go? I just like being free to go wherever I want. I just want to be left to run.'

I look away as my words come tumbling out, then I take a deep breath and look up.

'I'm not the kind of girl who chases after men, that's what I mean, I don't give a damn about men, but you have to let me be free otherwise I'll go. Either way, I always end up leaving. I can't help it. It drives me crazy if someone makes me stay, in one bed, one house, it turns me nasty. I'm unliveable with. Playing the little woman isn't for me. I want to be left to run.'

'Can we see each other again?'

'Yes,' I whisper. 'Maybe.'

So he invites me out to a restaurant the following evening. He lets me go – for now. And I run down to the port: it's not yet dark. Some guys are stumbling out of a bar. Murphy calls to me from the end of the street and I run over to him. He smiles broadly, revealing all his damaged teeth. I'm out of breath, choking and laughing.

'Breathe, Lili, where are you running from like that?'

I stifle the last blast of laughter with the back of my hand over my mouth.

'And Jude? Is that it? Did he leave the boat? What's he doin' now?'

Crows dive into steel containers where the supermarket employees have just emptied the day's refuse.

'All these crows . . .' I say.

And Murphy lets me go.

There's no one on the *Rebel*. The table in the galley is covered with empty beer cans. The ashtray is overflowing. Joey's forgotten a copy of *Penthouse* on the table.

Aaron gives me the week off. Jude and I will go back to the motel, but the Star because it's cheaper. Come in the afternoon, Jude said. The long plywood building is right on the road and trails of dust have left grey streaks on its white facade. I recognise the duffel bag outside a half-open door. Furtive glance at reception, no one there. I push open the door and see Murphy inside, slumped in a leatherette armchair – he was bored out in the street. Jude on the sofa, both men parked in front of the TV wreathed in smoke. Murphy has opened a tin of spam and he's putting hunks of it on sliced bread with mayonnaise. He's sipping a Coke because he's given up drink, yet again.

'Alcohol makes me mean,' he says.

'How about crack?' the great sailor teases.

'Oh, crack's even worse. But I can't afford it right now.'

I once said I liked vodka so Jude's bought some and he's drinking it straight from the bottle. Every now and then he mixes himself a drink with some of Murphy's Coke. Murphy's enjoying himself, commenting on the film.

'Of course it's ridiculous,' he says. 'Beautiful chicks with great asses, big tits and no brains, men stuffed with money, big houses … but it makes a change from the square and the shelter. The shelter's great, it would be paradise for you because there's hardly any women. A room with thirty beds all to yourself. But on the men's side, my God it can smell and snore, some nights there's forty of us in the dorm. Sometimes I really wish I could make the trip to Anchorage, to see my kids and grandkids.'

'You're a grandfather, Murphy?'

He laughs and nods, 'Forty-three years old and eight times a grandfather. I go see them sometimes. I stay with one of them or I go to Bean's Café. That's a nice place too, the food is good. There may be a hundred times more of us than at the shelter but they have space for everyone to sleep. And in Anchorage it's easier to get construction work.'

He takes a huge bite of bread, then drains a Coke to wash everything down. Jude is staring glumly at the screen.

'That's my real job,' Murphy says. 'Construction. I fish here every now and 'gain, it does me good, compared with crack and all that, and I never have trouble finding work on a big boat, a tough boat, seeing I'm big and strong.'

'You've never seen Murphy when he gets mad.'

'Yeah, and you're better off that way. I go crazy and with my weight . . .'

I've brought pizzas but the great sailor is sulking: I've been running through the streets. He bites into a portion of pizza then spits it back out in disgust.

'Did you find this in the trash?'

'You shouldn't talk to Lili like that,' Murphy says, looking at me kindly.

I turn away, rubbing and kneading my damaged hands. The great sailor's eyes blaze. He's watching me, laughing at my expense. He points at my swollen hands, my strange paw-like mitts, bigger than many men's.

'What sort of man would want to be touched by hands like that, I ask you?'

Murphy laughs, not unkindly. The TV blares. I say nothing. I keep interlocking and releasing my fingers in the hopes they'll lie still at last. But yesterday he said he wanted them on him the whole time, these hands of mine. The two men drink and eat, every now and then one of them coughs and spits into an empty can.

I think about the seagulls.

'I forgot something,' I say.

The great sailor turns towards me, the copper of his face dazzling in the shadowy room. He was distant, but now he's furious.

'Well, I have,' I say.

'If you yell at her she won't come back,' Murphy says, licking the mayonnaise from the spoon. He smiles at me.

The great sailor says nothing. He takes a long draught of vodka from the bottle. Lights another cigarette. Stares angrily at the screen. He ignores the pair of us. I get to my feet. I'm almost through the door when he calls out.

'But you'll be back?'

The note of anxiety in that gravelly voice. I turn round. The yellow gaze has wavered. He's hunched in on himself, fear in his eyes. A silent plea. I look away, embarrassed, then look up again and over to Murphy, Big Murphy in all his innocence, sprawling in an armchair, laughing at the film, his open mouth full of bread and mayonnaise. I want to fall at Jude's feet, put my arms around his knees, crush my forehead against his thighs, touch his face with these hands he's taunting me about.

'Yes, I'll be back.'

I hover in the doorway, between the thick air of the bedroom and the powerful sunlight outside. Soon I'm running but I decide against Baranof Park and the salmonberries and blackcurrants, and lying down in the grass and hearing the crows' rasping cries under the tall treetops. Instead I grab a quick cup of coffee on the docks. Already this man is taking my life from me, and it's not fair.

I come back out of breath. Murphy smiles but the other man doesn't so much as look at me. There's no spam left now, just bread and mayonnaise. The TV's still on and there's a different series showing, but it still involves shouting. I take some chocolate bars from my pocket to secure forgiveness. I sit down on the dirty carpet, curled up on myself. And wait. I contemplate the fact that the great sailor will be leaving soon, and I'll be working on the *Rebel*.

A hand has come to rest on the back of my neck. I close my eyes. The grip tightens, making me buckle. He's hurting me.

'Come close to me,' he whispers.

What the hell's he doing to me? I think helplessly. I turn to face him.

'What are you doing to me?'

'Come,' he says, softening – oh the velvet of his husky voice. 'We're going to take a bath.'

Murphy's gone to sleep on the other bed. Or he's pretending he has.

'Tell me a story. You're the woman I want to love, forever. Tell me a story ... please.'

He does me so much good, he wants to do even more for me.

'What would you like?' he asks. 'What could I give you that would make you happier?'

'I am happy, I have everything ... you make me feel good.'

Because he goes on and on about it, because he torments me on the subject for ages, because he won't stop making me moan until I've replied, I bury my face in his moist armpit, with its strong smell of salt and the sea, the great sailor's salty water still on my lips, and I – the seafarer with shapeless clothes spattered with blood, guts and fishy foam – whisper:

'I'd like something a woman wears. A real woman.'

He doesn't understand.

'I'd like a corset,' I blurt out.

He laughs.

'They're pretty,' I murmur, 'and they have a secret. You feel even more naked underneath.'

He frowns.

'Have you worn them a lot?'

'Once ... it made me so beautiful. No one knew. I felt like a queen under my Salvation Army clothes.'

'Will you come to Anchorage with me?'

'Yes.'

'Will you come to Hawaii?'

'I can't. My boat is leaving soon.'

'Well, then come with me. Anchorage ... a corset ... a motel.'

He punctuates each word with a deeper, slower thrust of his hips.

★

193

'Do you still like me?' he asks.

The ferry blares its horn. We're on board and the great sailor is different in a battered leather jacket and tired old cowboy boots that he'd polished anyway. His fishing boots, the Super Tuffs, are in the huge duffel bag dumped at his feet. Over his shoulder a worn bag hiding his bottle because alcohol is forbidden on the ferry. In his hand a plastic bag, a refuse bag full of fish fillets – halibut from our last expedition for his friends in Anchorage.

'Is that all you're bringing?' he asks. 'What about your fishing boots?'

The bridge and passageways are crawling with students, visitors from the lower forty-eight who've set off on adventures working in canning factories for the space of a season. It's raining but we find some room under the canopy on deck. We sit on the floor and watch Kodiak grow smaller in the distance. The great sailor very soon takes out his bottle. One of the young guys scowls, outraged, but then he's really furious when the halibut starts to defrost and leak: the bag is broken and the molten water is trickling onto the boy's luggage. The great sailor doesn't notice.

'The guy's not happy,' I say, tugging at Jude's sleeve. 'It's getting him wet …'

'He can go someplace else.'

'There isn't anywhere else.'

'Well, tough, then. I get the feeling this bottle's bothering him too. What the fuck is he doing here, anyway? This isn't the place for him if one little bottle drives him crazy.'

Then he's hungry and we head off to the restaurant. The great sailor has a formidable appetite: he orders a double ration of beef stew and we drink. It's hot, the room is cramped, its neon light too harsh, so the Formica table blinds me. Jude goes very red, as if he's choking. By the time we go back out it's dark and there are already people lying down to sleep. There are no spaces left on the reclining seats under the canopy.

'Let's go here,' he says, leading me further along the deck.

We spread my sleeping bag on the deck, which is damp with sea spray.

'You lie down now.'

He puts his own big sleeping bag over me, then he lies down, keeping the bag with the bottle in it by his head. He takes me in his arms. Above us the sky. Clouds scud past the white moon, a moon so smooth and white it looks like a face. The stars glimmer. From time to time light rain comes and tickles our foreheads. Everyone else is sheltered like sleeping sheep. Not us. We're on the crest of this black wave, in the cool of the drizzle. The great sailor draws me close, we make love under the sleeping bag. I laugh when he moves slightly and the wind sneaks along my back.

'I'd like to sleep please,' I plead in a tiny voice.

But the great sailor's never tired. In the end I cry a little, and then he kisses me and pats my backside. He sighs, grabs the bottle and takes one last swig as he gazes at the stars. He names them for me and the muffled sound of his words mingles with the to and fro of the waves. Then there is just his wave-like breathing booming in his chest where I rest my forehead.

The deck is deserted, the ferry motionless. It has been moored up for ages when we wake. The sun is already very high in the sky. I laugh as we hastily fold up our sleeping bags.

We're going to walk into town: Seward. It's a beautiful day and we're hungry. The last of the passengers are milling about at the foot of the jetty. We follow the only street, a straight road edged with low-slung houses, setting out from the sea and heading off far away between the trees into the depths of the forest. The first coffee shop fits the bill, and Jude lets his duffel bag drop heavily to the ground outside.

'Let's eat!'

We find a table by the window and I sit down. Two tables from us is the little student we annoyed on the ferry. He looks away but gets up and leaves when the great sailor throws the now completely flaccid bag of halibut at his feet.

A small chubby-cheeked woman brings us coffee, the big pink heart of her apron strained over her round belly.

'A full breakfast for me. The whole lot.'

'And pancakes for me.'

'So what are we doing now, Jude? Are we taking the bus to Anchorage?'

'I'll call Elijah and Allison. They'll come pick us up.'

'Elijah? Allison?' I ask, confused.

'My friends. I told them we were coming. They're expecting us.'

'I thought...'

'What?'

'That we'd be just the two of us in Anchorage.'

'Well, that *is* where we're going, isn't it?'

I walk off towards the trees, heading for the deep forest. The place is huge. I stop at the first bench, take out a cigarette. Tight throat. I shouldn't have left the island. The boat. We're going to stay with people. A tall dark pine quivers above me. I suck on a pine needle that's fallen on the table. A tiny burning sensation in my throat when I swallow it.

I didn't hear anyone coming but a man suddenly sits down beside me and puts a pack of beers down between us.

'Would you like one?'

I look up and the man studies my face. His dark, slightly slanting eyes are like two wet fish, his black hair like seaweed.

'No thank you.'

'D'you have a cigarette?'

I offer him one from the packet.

'Where are you from?'

'The ferry...' I wave vaguely in the direction of the jetty, its white landing platform blinding in the sun, the water twinkling.

'Where are you headed?'

'Anchorage... I don't know.'

'Are you a runaway?'

The great sailor has joined me and shoots a murderous look at the man next to me. The Native with the fish eyes slopes off with his beer.

'Don't get angry,' he says. 'We'll go to Anchorage, and I mean the two of us, just the two of us. But I can't afford to pay for a motel for five days.'

'Yes,' I say. 'Of course. I can't afford it either.'

'My friends are great. I always stay with them. I've known Elijah since he was almost a kid. We didn't choose the same path but that doesn't make a difference. They know who I am and it doesn't bother them.'

'Right.'

'A proper house every now and then does you good, don't you think?'

'I dunno.'

'C'mon, we better go now. Let's start walking. They'll be here soon.'

'Kiss me first,' I say. 'We won't be able to later.'

We walk back towards the road, drifting to and fro across the path. Him in his worn leather jacket, me in my Salvation Army jacket. Will we reach the sea? Will we come out of the woods? I don't want to get there. Neither does he.

But they soon arrive; their white car comes and parks on the verge. Elijah steps out first, smooth face, blue eyes under a crop of very light blond hair. He takes the great sailor in his arms and Jude returns the hug rather stiffly and awkwardly, and they both laugh. Allison climbs out of the car, one hand holding down her mass of auburn hair that the wind wants to tie in knots. She's smiling. She's pretty.

They're amazed by the great sailor's 'squeeze'. They were probably expecting a barmaid with copious breasts, a dancer from a bar, a brash fishing-woman ... Never this scared girl-child thing with her knife-hacked haircut. I stand their hesitantly in my faded Carhartt which was once my pride and joy. It flaps around me like a flag. I hide my hands in my misshapen pockets. Jude looks at me with no obvious indulgence and I can't help looking at the big dark woods behind them. We get into the car and I shrink on the backseat. I've lost my tongue.

As for Anchorage, the great sailor lied to me. There'll be no corset, no motel room we don't leave for three days. Elijah and Allison are young and beautiful. They have a house, a white bungalow with blue shutters, between other white bungalows; and a dog and a little six-month-old child. What about us, where are we from? I keep thinking, as I look at them over the course of three days spent sitting on a chair, a sofa, an armchair. Sitting for three days. In silence. Increasingly silent and sad. I can't get my tongue back, not a hope. I want to run away. Will the *Rebel* wait for me? I want to go fishing again.

I try to help Allison but when I empty the dishwasher a glass shatters on the floor.

'You sit down,' she says. 'You're on vacation.'

The men talk in front of the television, on the handsome leather sofa. Elijah looks at me kindly.

'Come sit down.'

I sit. The days are long. I always have to sit. On the sofa then on a chair at the table. Allison tries to get me to talk. My voice chokes, I stammer. I keep thinking about the *Rebel* and counting the hours.

In the morning, when everyone's still asleep, I silently open the glass door and slip outside. I sit on the closely mown grass and look at the rose bush in from of me, the latticework of the gate, the milky sky. Sometimes I see birds fly by. Bastards, I think, lucky bastards, they're flying. My eyes settle on the gate again. Oh, the need then to escape along the docks, alone, suspended in the clarity of this still, naked morning, on my own.

Elijah and Allison go out one evening and we're left alone together, at a loss. It's a beautiful evening.

'Let's go out,' I say.

We walk in the balmy evening air along the rows of white houses, all of them white. The straight roads are perfectly parallel, and they don't have names – just numbers. We turn a corner: the streets at right angles are just the same, but they are given letters. I look up at a skein of barnacle geese flying overhead. Their deep, hoarse cries travel across the sky lit gold by the evening sun. Jude has taken my hand. We walk on through the labyrinth.

'Elijah and Allison are nice,' I say. 'But can we be just the two of us?'

The wild geese have flown past, the sky is bare again. The great sailor doesn't answer my question.

When we've wandered around the streets enough we go back. Jude switches the television on again and hands me a beer. I sit down on the red rug and he comes over to me, tips me backwards onto the floor and lies on top of me. The powerful coppers of midnight light come in through the big picture window, illuminating the battlefield of his face. Soon I'm naked and white on the red rug. My tears well up. So does pleasure, like a blast of cold air. The milky skin of his huge shoulders. But what's happening to me, I think, I'm numb inside. He kisses me. I hold his face in my hands. His jaws and cheeks move as he kisses. It's as if he's still drinking.

'To get to sleep I've always had to be exhausted ...' Jude was saying softly when they came back earlier than expected. We didn't hear them open the door.

I sat up, startled. Jude covered me with his jacket. They jumped in surprise. Elijah went very red, Allison very pale. The baby was asleep in her arms. Then they laughed a bit. The great sailor was standing naked in the middle of their living room. I looked down at the carpet, and his large white foot buried in that red wool struck me as even more incongruous than the nudity of his colossal body outlined against the sky through the large window, his stiffened penis jutting from the patch of curly hair, which looked almost red in the coppery glow of the midnight sun, a fiery mane for an erection he didn't even try to hide.

Allison looked away, gave a little cough.

'How about we go to bed?'

The great sailor is annoyed with me. We daren't look each other in the eye any more. Only the couple with the dog and the small child are happy. As for us, we have nothing.

'I'm frightened of houses,' I tell him one day, 'of walls and other people's children, the happiness of beautiful people who have money. Please can we get away from here?'

We stay. When we make love it's terrible and sad. His beautiful eyes burn me and fill me with despair. He's more alone than ever, more alone even than the man who shouts at the sea. Soon he grows jealous, he's distraught when I leave him one night to sleep on a sofa, and keeps badgering me – Why? and, What did you do? and, Where did you go? Promise me you weren't with them, or with him or her ... But where? And why?

'You were coughing, it was so loud it sounded like you were yelling. I was too hot, you were crushing me. I wanted to sleep near the garden. I wanted to be outside. I opened the window a little to feel the night air ... I want to get far away from this place.'

We're in the little room that I escaped to in the night, when he was roaring in his sleep with a cough that tears through his chest. In all the loneliness of my insomnia and growing anxiety, I have wedded myself to a lion who's already devouring my nights, and will devour all of me one day. He lies on top of me and won't let me leave. He drives deep into me, pummels me, wants to make me cry out, as if he wants to kills me, his runaway. Keeping me forever. His congested face reddens on top of me, he gives a long moan, a hoarse heart-rending groan, a sob.

We're walking the streets in silence. A washout of a day. We've left the pretty house, and the suburbs of Anchorage stretch before us, grey and dirty in the rain. Spenard: a succession of dismal, uniform facades along straight avenues interrupted only by the harsh neon lights of a car dealership, the wasteland outside a warehouse, the brightness of a bar. He's thirsty, I realise. His bottle's been empty for a while now. We left our things in a cheap motel as grim and grey as everything else. But it's a roof over our heads. It's home for the night. And now we're walking. At the street corner, red and green neon lights – a bar. Jude straightens up and quickens his pace.

PJ's it's called. A girl stripped to the waist opens the door for us. She takes our dripping wet jackets and smiles. We venture deeper into the lair – a few men sitting in the shadows – and find ourselves a table. Another girl, in a corset, comes to take our order. Vodka and beer. Pink suspenders hold up black stockings, stretched to breaking point over long, chunky legs. A tiny purple G-string shaped like a butterfly twinkles over the smooth raised mound of her pubis. On the stage a full-bodied woman swings her hips, with one hand on the suspender she is slowly unclipping. Her huge red mouth seems to be kissing the mic. She sings and moans in a husky melodious voice. I watch her, fascinated. The great sailor has downed his vodka in one. He orders another. At last he talks after hours of silence.

'Is this the first time you've been to a titty bar?'

'Yes.'

'Does it bother you?'

'No.'

The girls laugh as they flit from table to table, their breasts moving with them, while the swivelling spotlight picks out gleams of gold on their legs sheathed in red, blue, black … He wanted to impress me, he still does: he calls the waitress over, whispers something to her, and shows her a banknote that he puts on the table. She winks at me and puts down her tray. Then she finishes undressing, slowly, not watching him but me, smiling at me as if to a sister. Her hips move backwards and forwards, flicking slowly at first, then faster and faster. The muscles in her back undulate in sinuous waves from her rounded shoulders to the supple small of her back, while her thighs quiver with each thrust. When she's naked – it doesn't take long – she takes the money.

'Thank you,' she says to the great sailor. 'Would you like something else to drink?'

He offers me another vodka and buys a T-shirt with the bar's name on it. When we leave the mist has descended and I'm cold. The avenue seems to go on forever, nothing but rain and cars. I've taken his hand, the sadness of wandering aimlessly has brought us together again. On the way, a liquor store: he refills one of his bottles of vodka.

'I'm hungry,' he says. 'How'd you feel about a pizza?'

A crummy café on the street corner offers its services. We cross over, Jude opens the door, and a bored girl turns her faded eyes on us. She yawns as she takes our order, pushes aside a lank lock of hair, sits back down, waits. We go back out and sit on the wet pavement while we wait for our pizza. Rain slithers down our cheeks. He lights a cigarette, the dull dirty light of a leaden sky weighing on his tired face. A face ravaged by alcohol, a sky full of misery. We're so cold.

The bottle peeps out of his bag. He spits on the ground and blows his nose with his fingers, then for the first time in a long while he really talks to me.

'Where's home?' he says. 'Where's my home? I don't have anything. I go from one boat to another, from the docks in Kodiak to the docks in Dutch. No wife, no children, no house. A motel room when I can afford it. But even animals have a lair.'

His shoulders have drooped, lacklustre curls of hair straggle over his reddened forehead, the lumpen skin of a man who's drunk a lot. He takes the bottle out of the bag and drinks from it, offers it to me.

He coughs. For a long time. When he finally catches his breath, he lights another Camel. The girl calls to us and we don't even react.

'I'm tired, you know, I'm so tired.'

The man with no lair isn't waiting for any response and I don't give him one. He's crushed by the world, this frozen desert, so merciless to the desperate, like the wan light of a fading day that disfigures and humiliates this face of his that's been so burned by life. And then I become aware of them, there on that corner of rain-swept pavement, a subtle quivering along my back, a rippling as light as breath: my wings – they've been there all along. I'm wandering too but it's not the same.

We take our pizza and set off along the grey avenue. It's still raining and the box goes limp in our hands. It's getting colder and colder but we're not afraid of anything now: the motel isn't far, a red light on the corner of a crossroads, the neon glare of a small yellow crescent moon swinging in the mist.

We go in, close the door and that's the end of the misery, we're at home. We draw the curtains against the dirty sky and the street. We slip between the sheets and hold each other close in the whiteness of the bed. At last I see him smile, that first shy and incredulous smile.

'You scare me,' he murmurs.

He rolls his forehead on my chest and stays there a long time. I listen. The beating of his heart, the muffled rumble of the traffic on the avenue, the rain ... Tomorrow I'll be gone.

'Tomorrow you'll be gone,' he says, as if guessing what I'm thinking.

'Yes.'

'I can't ask you to stay. Seeing what I have to offer.'

'I don't ask for anything. We each have to earn our own lives.'

'Women do like their comforts, a house.'

'Not me. I want to live outdoors.'

'Well, I'd like that.'

'And fishing?'

'Fishing is what saves my life. The only thing that's powerful enough to get me out of all this' – he waves vaguely around the room – 'but building a house for myself ... Oh my, I'd like that. We'd have a child and he'd be called Jude.'

'If you're looking at me, you haven't got yourself the kind of woman people dream about.'

'For a long time now I thought I wouldn't meet a woman at all.'

'I'm a runaway, I can't change that. I'll end up in some shelter.'

'Let's get married.'

'I want to go fishing again.'

He holds me close.

'We'll get married and we'll go fishing together.'

'I don't want to be on land. I think I'd rather drown.'

He sits back up to get the bottle, but without letting go of me. His chest crushes my face for a moment.

'You want a shot of vodka?'

'No. Yes. We both drink too much.'

'I drink the whole time, but you don't, your drinking's nothing.'

He takes a slug and kisses a mouthful of it to me. I cough and laugh. His eyes shine in the darkness and I can see the sheen of his teeth where his lip has curled back as he laughs too.

'Let's sleep now.'

'That's right. Let's sleep.'

Someone from reception knocks on the door at five o'clock. The dream is over already, we have to go back to the world, outside, the street. I extricate myself gently from his arms.

'Go back to sleep,' I say. 'I have to go.'

'I'll come back to see you,' he says. 'I'll write you from Hawaii and I'll wait for you. Always.'

Anchorage is blanketed in mist. My plane takes off into an opaque sky. But as soon as we gain any altitude, it's summer. I won't come back to Anchorage. The great sailor is still asleep, lying in the warm dip I left in our sheets. I still have the smell of his skin on me. The stewardess serves me coffee and a cookie but the guys in front of me ask for beer and talk about Dutch and a boat that's gone under. When the plane drops down towards the island of Kodiak my throat tightens, I'm going back to sea ...

Once I catch sight of the trawlers resting in the harbour, the ocean dotted with little boats, their foaming wakes, I know that I had to come back. My heart quickens, I'm going fishing again.

I pick up my bag from near the stuffed grizzly in the airport's tiny arrivals hall. Around me big men in boots are reclaiming theirs. I go out into the sunshine. It's still early. I walk up to the road, which is deserted. I stick out my thumb and eventually a taxi stops and the driver leans over to open the door for me.

'I'm going back to town,' he says. 'My fare's been paid, I'll give you a ride.'

I get in and put my meagre luggage at my feet. He's an ageless little man, with a pale puny bird-like head, washed-out grey eyes and a croaky, high-pitched voice. He offers me a cigarette. His hands are slender, translucent; they could almost be made of glass.

With the sea on one side, we drive along a road that runs straight all the way to the coastguards' base. Not a tree, the earth black and naked. Then comes Gibson Cove and the first cottonwoods before the scattered trees grow denser. To my right, the fuel docks and the silent giants moored alongside the first of the canning factories. They hurt my soul and tie my stomach in knots and call to me, just as loudly as Jude does. The *Topaz* is back. *Lady Aleutian* and the *Saga* have moved since I left.

The driver talks a lot and quickly: Angus, born and raised in Arizona, ended up in Kodiak thanks to chance and indecision. The ashtray is overflowing and books have been lobbed pell-mell on the rear seat. The radio interrupts him, a call for a fare.

'Drop in to Tony's this evening, I'll buy you a drink,' he says when he leaves me by the first pontoon. A tall man with lots of hair is waiting for him in torn jog pants and a sweatshirt, and with a refuse bag over his shoulder.

The *Rebel*'s deck is deserted. The sun is blazing down so I walk all the way to Dog Bay. Halfway across the bridge, I lean over the rail: below me, seagulls, the dark blue water moving in deep, slow undulations. I spit, copying what Jude would do, and continue on my way. The dense woods of Long Island look black, the mackerel sky very blue. I reach the small harbour, walk a few more paces and close my eyes: the smell of the water blends with the other smells from the thick forest across the road. I inhale the air for a long time and then, dazed by tiredness, I suddenly feel incredibly light.

I walk on as far as the *Milky Way*. Not a sound. Jason must be asleep still. I lie down on deck, the wood warm against my back. The water laps at the hull. Way up at the top of the mast a plastic crow stares at the mountains. The sky smells of seaweed and shellfish. I'm almost asleep when Jason emerges from the cabin, his hair awry, his face still swollen with sleep.

When I step into the galley Aaron is sitting at the table with a mug of coffee between his pudgy fingers. He tilts his head and smiles when I come in. A woman greets me with a brief nod, and goes out.

'That's Diana,' Aaron says quickly, and gives a little cough. 'Did you have a good time in Anchorage?'

'Yes, but it's good to be back.'

He clears his throat.

'I have bad news, Lili . . . I'm sorry, really . . . The boat's insurers haven't agreed to pay for your accident. Andy doesn't want to take you for the season now. He thinks your papers aren't in order. Too risky, he says.'

He's such a little man, sitting there stammering excuses, his eyes opened wide but focused on his crossed hands.

'There's nothing I can do about it,' he adds and his forget-me-not eyes come back to meet mine. As clear as a child's.

'But you can stay on board so long as the *Rebel*'s in harbour.'

I've found Jason at a bar, sitting with a pint of Guinness.

'Jason, we can go fishing together!'

He's thrilled. He throws his cap in the air with a ferocious whoop.

'That calls for celebrations, deckhand! We're going to paint the town red tonight . . . Two tequilas, that's two!'

I think about the great sailor. What will he say, what will he do when he knows? Sink the boat?

'Jason,' I say quietly, 'I'm in trouble . . .'

Jason expects the worst, hearing these words from a runaway.

'I have a boyfriend, a great, a very great sailor . . .' I catch my breath, keep talking confidentially. 'He's very jealous. He might kill us if he sees us together.'

Jason rolls wild eyes under frowning brows.

'Where is he?' he asks.

'Anchorage. And soon Hawaii.'

He roars with laughter and orders two more tequilas, vodkas, rum and White Russians.

'We'll be the crazies of the sea,' he hollers, sitting up tall on his chair. 'When are you going to teach me to breathe fire? When can we finally go hustle and get drunk in every port in Alaska?'

I go back to the *Rebel*, the port shimmering and dancing. I head straight for my bunk, bury myself in it and go under. When I wake in the morning Joey has put his sleeping bag over me.

★

It's a beautiful day and I'm eating like a hungry bear. Jason and I are repainting the *Milky Way*. When evening comes we climb onto the big bridge, sit with our legs dangling and pretend to be frightened. The wind moans as it swoops under the arches, while the sea surges back and forth far below. Our heads spin. Terns pass close enough to touch us, then they dive headlong giving piercing cries. Their shrill nasal notes mingle with the mewing of herring gulls. Once we're back on land, hearts thumping and pupils dilated, we reel with vertigo. And that's when we head off to drink rum and vodka. But I often prefer the innocence of a milkshake: it's like being a child, I tell Jason.

Today we took the *Milky Way* to the big harbour and moored up to the quay, in the area where they careen boats at low tide. When the tide drew out we scraped the weed and barnacles off the hull and painted it with a coat of antifouling paint. The tide came in almost too quickly, everything dancing and flying towards us with flashes of gold. And we were all orange and black, spattered with antifouling paint and silt, the paint even in our hair. Murphy walked along the dock and waved.

'Any news of Jude?' he called.

I stood up and knocked straight into the beam supporting the hull. Sprawling in the sludge, I laughed too much to get back up.

'He's fine,' I said, catching my breath. 'He's still in Anchorage and I'm going to join him in Hawaii as soon as I have the money.'

Murphy's silhouette was a dark shape against the sky, his radiant face like a giant sunflower. The sun dotted the underside of my eyelids with gold stars. The sea was up to our calves now, time to get back on board.

While we waited for high water Jason showed me a glass float hanging above his bunk.

'It's very old,' he told me. 'Nineteenth century, maybe. Or maybe the war, I don't know. It came from Japan, it must've been drifting for years before I found it. We'll find more when we're fishing – on the beaches in Uganik Bay and all along the west coast, Rocky Point, Karluk, Ikolik ...'

'Mm,' I said dreamily, fingering the irregular bluish sphere speck-led with air bubbles imprisoned in the blown glass. I wished I could be a float.

'Hold me ... hold me tight.'

The man with the ravaged, pockmarked face, the man who always hangs around between the square and the public toilets stops me and clings to me. I hug him with all my might.

'Thank you,' he says and continues on his way.

I meet Murphy coming out of McDonald's, burger in hand.

'You still working?'

'Well, yeah. We're off dungy fishing at the end of the month.'

'You work too much, Lili. Do what I do, take a vacation. Come live at the shelter, you'll have a mess tin of food every evening, show-ers and a dormitory all to yourself, or nearly. A shower – you could put on dress, go out to get drunk!'

I laugh.

'Anyway, my skipper's waiting for me, can't hang around.'

And now, so long as he can still see me in the distance, Murphy hollers, 'So did you do it? Did you finally get drunk?'

And I yell a reply across the streets and the docks, 'Not yet!'

The *Milky Way* was repainted and Jason was waiting for the pots, which were a long time coming. The *Rebel* left and I moved into the *Lively June*. I wandered aimlessly away from the Tagura boat yard, sneaking between the blackcurrant bushes when I drew level with Baranof Park. Sometimes I fell asleep behind a bush, under the big cedar tree or behind the giant hemlock. I was always woken by insistent hoarse cawing from crows perched in a circle around me in the red alders. I tried to get them to eat from my hand, but they didn't like popcorn. So I'd get up and go to the ferry jetty, where I'd sit and watch boats go by. The great sailor was still in

Anchorage with Elijah and Allison, in the pretty house with the red woollen carpet. I called him every evening from the harbour's one phone booth.

'Are you sleeping alone?' came his harsh voice on the phone.

I burst out laughing.

'Of course!'

'Hmm,' he said, 'every young dog in the port must be sniffing around you.'

'I may be going fishing with Jason.'

'Wait, who?'

'A guy from the *Venturous* who needs a crew member.'

'Are you going out to bars?'

'Not much. I prefer going to McDonald's for ice cream.'

'Will you come to Hawaii with me?'

'Hey, kid!'

A car horn sounds behind me. I'm counting my last few coins, sitting on my favourite bench, the one that looks out over the whole harbour. I turn round and see an old, once-white pick-up. Sitting at the wheel is Conrad, a pale-faced jig fisherman who used to stop by the *Rebel*.

'I'm gonna need you tomorrow. To help dig a trench for some pipe work. Twenty dollars for the day sound OK?'

'Yes,' I accept.

'Are you off fishing soon?'

'I don't know. Jason's still waiting for the pots.'

'I'll pick you up at seven tomorrow.'

He drives on as far as the B and B, then the truck gives a squeal of brakes. I see him step out in a cloud of dust. The afternoon is almost warm. A little man walks along the quay – small paunch out in front, drooping shoulders – and stops when he's level with me.

'Can I?' he asks quietly, gesturing towards the bench.

He opens his round eyes wide, his wilting mouth sketches a smile, stiff bleached hair hangs round his withered child-like face.

'Sure,' I say.

He sits down beside me and we watch the harbour in silence. The fleet of seiners is almost up to full strength. The salmon are keeping everyone waiting. Fishing has been closed for three days.

'Take this,' he says in a barely audible voice, handing me some crumpled pieces of paper.

He's jumped back to his feet and is already walking away. I open out the three foodbank vouchers and get to my feet to catch up with him but he's disappeared around the corner of the taxi office.

After giving the ground a quick going-over with a mini-digger, Conrad left me that morning with a spade, a spirit level, a ruler and a mountain of gravel. I just needed to level it all out. Over a distance of almost a hundred metres. He came back in the evening and found the trench perfectly level, ready for the pipes to be laid. My eyes were closing with exhaustion; his were unfocused, and also tending to close, and he gave off a powerful smell of whisky. He handed me twenty dollars, burped loudly and asked me to be at Fuller's boatyard at seven in the morning.

Conrad has a boat of his own, the *Morgan*, but it's been in dry dock since he ran into a rock a month earlier. I think he'd had too much to drink. My job now is to hose down the hull of the tiny wooden schooner several times a day to stop the planking shrinking and the caulk cracking. I scrape, sand, re-varnish and repaint. She's a glorious boat: twenty-six foot, slender-keeled to navigate deep waters, her hull rounding like a little girl's stomach for balance on rough seas, then narrowing down to the bow.

'She's the most seaworthy boat I've ever had. She was built the year Lindbergh flew across the Atlantic, 1927, imagine that! And she's good as new,' Conrad says proudly.

I scour the hull as if curry-combing a huge horse, then go into the cabin lined with oiled wood for a coffee and settle into the skipper's chair. I rest my hands on the antique wheel that dates back to Lindbergh's day, the small cast-iron stove hums behind me, and my eyes come to rest on the chart table, unrolled charts stained with brown – coffee?

Back outside again, working, I hear the ferry's horn every now and then and I run to watch it go past. One evening when I worked very late and was just finishing on the *Morgan*, I tried to catch up with it. I almost slipped on my way down the ladder and ran all the way to the water's edge, but the ferry was already passing the buoys at the mouth of the channel. I watched it disappear, waving my arms for a long time but my greeting was soon for the waves alone. The *Tustumena* had gone out to sea and was getting further and further from me. I turned and headed back. Along the way, old trucks cast golden shadows in the soft sunlight of ten in the evening.

One morning I'm perched at the top of the mast in a paint-spattered old jacket Jason has given me, and when I look down there he is: the great sailor. He's come to take me to Honolulu. He came on the morning ferry. And Conrad lets me go.

'Go ahead, kid, take a few days. Peggy says it's going to rain, you won't have to hose down the boat, and you won't be able to paint.'

We walk away from Tagura's small shipyard, along the gravel track, between the embankments smothered in fireweed and flowering salmonberries, the piles of rusted pots, torn gill nets, the carcass of an old truck and a dilapidated boat overrun with brambles. It's a beautiful day, the morning air still fresh and permeated with a wonderful scent of low tide, earth and the more subtle smell of rotting wood and rust. The great sailor is flushed and awkward, I dance alongside him, his wildcat eyes on my bare shoulders. He takes my hand, stops.

The bridge across to Dog Bay, big concrete arches over the wasteland where we once lay in the grass, lobster red under an azure sky. We reach the town and stop at the first bar. We drink beer and he goes off to spew it up in the toilets. He comes back and tries again but the beer won't go down.

'Come, let's go get a room now.'

We buy Canadian Whisky and vodka at the liquor store, and some cigarettes, fruit juice and ice cream at the supermarket. We go back to the Shelikof because it's nicer, and this time I'm not so frightened of the women in reception. The sun streams in onto the bedspread in our room. I'm hungry already so he feeds me ice cream, lying on top of me, his thighs clamped around my waist. He feeds me by the mouthful like a mother bird. The ice cream slithers off the spoon as he tips it towards my lips, and it runs down my neck.

'Hoo! That's cold,' I say.

He catches it with his tongue, the burning sensation over the ice feels good. I'm smeared all over and the sheets end up sticky. He takes the lid off a bottle with his teeth and knocks back some vodka, then kisses me, letting the spirit flow between my lips. I laugh and then choke.

'You're mine,' he says.

We sleep. Often but not for long. When he wakes he puts the TV back on, then lights a cigarette. He grabs the bottle and takes a slug. My eyes are closed, I'm pretending to sleep. I hear the long sigh he makes when he's had a drink. It's like being inside him. His great body is at rest beside me like a becalmed boat, a mythical titan moored up at a fuel dock. But I don't like his TV: it makes me want to escape, as if he's caught me in a trap; it makes me want to run along the seafront till I can't breathe. When I've drummed up the courage, I ask him to turn it off.

'You see, it's like those people, those voices are actually in the room with us, and I want to be alone with you.'

So he turns it off, then switches it back on moments later. He can't help it. I look out of the window and I can feel my restless body wants to run. I'm bored, but it feels good too. He huddles close to me and gives me another mouthful. He's bought some gorgeous juicy nectarines from California, some bread and chicken. He hands me a hunk.

'This chicken's so tender you can even eat the bones. And plus it wasn't expensive.'

Juice from the nectarines dribbles over my chin, down my neck, over my pale torso and into the grooves between my ribs. Like a good mother cat, he licks my skin and cleans me. His rasping tongue presses around my breasts. He tickles me. I laugh.

Then, lying in bed on sheets blotched with ice cream, he starts to talk.

'There was a river where I used to go fishing. The leaves on the trees made golden shadows dance over the water. It was black under the willows. We were kids ... My brother found an old kayak and we went on trips. A blanket in the bottom of the kayak, a slightly rusted can to make coffee, a bit of bread, a can of baked beans for when we didn't catch anything, matches. I had a knife and I'd sculpted its handle myself. A little totem with a crow's head at the end. I used it for cutting open trout. Their bright red blood ran over the blade and the crow would go red too ... It was great. When it started to get dark we'd make a fire. My brother collected wood and I gutted the trout and did the fire: I was the oldest. I taught my brother the stars. There were owls ... sometimes the beat of their wings as they took flight – my brother was frightened – and the deep hoot of an eagle owl, or sharp little calls or higher more plaintive cries. Then a sort of monotonous chant that sounded sad, so sad. One day my brother turned up with a bottle. A twenty-five-ounce bottle of old whisky, some gut-rot my father had forgotten in his truck. The old man must have been too drunk to remember it that day. We drank under the stars. It was wonderful. The pair of us puked up afterward. We almost burned the blanket. And I fell into the river. It was cold. We swore we'd never touch that shit again.'

I laugh. He sits up and frowns.

'Don't laugh,' he says. 'We didn't touch it again for at least two years. I was twelve, he was eleven. After that it wasn't the same. After that there were girls, local dances, all kinds of dances, and then bars and more girls. And we wanted to be men. The river, the stars – gone.'

214

I look at the sky through the window. I think about the river and its black waters, the golden leaves above it, dancing.

He smiles to himself.

'I grew up in the forest, you know. It was beautiful. Me and my brother would go on trips. My mother waited for us. For days and nights on end. We'd come back starving, covered in dirt and scratches, one fine morning or one dark evening as the shadows spread across the forest – the shiver of it on our skin – our foreheads burned by the sun, slashed by brambles, like a crown of glory. We were young lions.'

He pauses for a moment and then his deep voice starts up again, almost a sigh: 'Then there was beer ... it was over, we hung out in bars, chasing girls. Then I hit the road with my dad. We hired ourselves out as loggers. Back in the forest but it wasn't the same. We went from town to town, patch of country to hickburg village, tavern to bar, Maine to Tennessee, Arizona to Montana, via California. The forests of Oregon, the misty coasts along the Pacific ... We'd get incredibly drunk. Bars were our life. And heavy work, that kills you. We slept in shacks or motels, motels or shelters, shelters or shacks. For me home came to be a motel room.'

He smiles as he remembers. 'Sometimes we'd bring girls back, when we'd been paid, when we had a room. If we hadn't drunk it all away already. One time we ended the night in the local jail: we'd had a fight over a dancer.

'The sea saved me. I drank non-stop till I was twenty-eight. From the woods of my childhood to the forests of Alaska I was drunk. Then I got on a boat. Here. I liked it. Scarily much. I found I could only get drunk when we were back ashore. Yes, scarily much.'

And on the great sailor talks, on a summer's night in the great expanses of north Alaska, in that room gilded by the great coppery glow of the ten o'clock sun. He's lying down, he turns his weathered face to me and says, in his deep slow voice, his slightly hazy, softly husky voice, 'To get to sleep, I've always had to be exhausted, through with everything, always. With drink, with sex or with work.'

★

215

Evening comes and we shower. Standing pressed up to me, he's very tall. I wash him: his powerful arms, the generous caverns of his dark armpits, his chest, the pink flower of his nipples, hidden in the reddened thatch that spreads lower, growing lighter over his protruding stomach and disappearing into the dark V between his thighs where the strange animal nestles, an animal I wash with respect and something close to fear: it comes to life in my hands. Then his hard buttocks, the white marble pillars of his legs, his feet that always remind me of that red wool carpet – I'm stifling a laugh. I slide the flat of my hands over his body, all the way up to the anchor of his shoulders, which I cling to for a moment. The shadowy groove between the powerful tendons, the moorings at the back of his neck. He closes his eyes, smiles. I lather soap in his beard, run my fingers over the contours of his heavy eyelids, his brow bone and bushy eyebrows, his tall forehead. It's his turn: his big hands work slowly, soaping my back, my hard little rump, my feet – more gently. Then finally my hair. The shampoo spreads under the jetting water, stings my eyes ... he kisses me – the taste of soap. I laugh.

We go out after dark, walk down to the docks and sit under the memorial, in the shadow of the sailor lost at sea. Along the way he's bought more whisky – or maybe vodka. Or rum. Some chicken perhaps, the sort that's so good you can eat the bones. Coffee for the machine in the motel room. Cookies for me. We watch the boats in the harbour and he says something. I turn towards him, his face half hidden by the stone sailor's shadow. He pours me a drink while I look up and gaze at the statue for a long time: the wind and the salty air have eroded his features. Then I remember the woman, on a beach in the English Channel, facing the horizon with the same mask eaten away by the sea and the wind and the torments of endlessly waiting.

'Oh, Jude, the sailor lost at sea doesn't have any face left.'

'No ...'

'I saw a memorial in France: it's a woman waiting for her sailor. Her face is eroded just like this.'

Jude gives a short, bitter laugh.

'Women don't wait long around here, when they've had enough they go off to Hawaii or with some other guy. Or both.'

'Why do you say that? Anyway, you're the one going to Hawaii, not me.'

'Would *you* wait for me?' he asks pointedly.

'Definitely not! I'd sooner go fishing. With or without you. I wouldn't even want anyone to wait for me ashore.'

'There, you see?'

'You don't understand,' I say slowly. 'It's not the same! I don't want a house, I don't want any of that any more, not me, I want to live! I want to go off and fish like you guys. I'm not the waiting kind. No, I don't wait. I run. You go away often enough, you guys, you're always running. I want to go away to sea too, not to Hawaii.'

'Won't you come to Hawaii?'

'I will, Jude, yes. One day. But first I need to go fishing. '

He doesn't say anything more. I shyly move closer to him and stare at the dark horizon. He runs a finger slowly over my cheek. Then we go back to the motel and he turns on the TV. Turns it off. And on again.

He maintains that semi-alert state from his seafaring life at all times. Broken nights: he sleeps for a couple of hours, maybe three, then gets up and takes out a cigarette. Paces once around the room, goes to sit by the TV – putting the volume on low – or by the window. He smokes, grabs a bottle from the bedside table. He stares: at the moon when it's there, but always at the sky. And at the sea, sensing it behind the houses.

His urgent breath against my temple brings me sharply awake. His great body is lying on mine again. A burning hot coat. The TV is on its lowest volume, and as he leans towards me, shifting light from the screen flits over his face, playing with the irregular grain of his skin. His muted voice in the dark:

'Tell me a story ...'

But he tells me one again.

'There was a loon – most likely there were lots of them, but for us this was *the* loon ... you know, those birds that fly for miles, or at least they have huge wings … There was the lake where we went fishing when we travelled along the river. The sky and the water … it was vast. We caught beautiful carp there. Catfish too, Arctic char, bowfins. We were scared of that place. For a start it was a long way away and the kayak took on a lot of water. Basically, the thing was worthless. And when the wind got up … We were lucky, you know. The nights felt so much bigger when we made it all the way there. We slept on the shore. I'd build a fire, my brother collected wood. I prepared the fish – kind of our ritual. Now I think about it, that was the start of the sea. That was where it started, on that lake, a longing for the ocean. But I didn't know it yet. Of course, I didn't know anything yet.'

He props himself on one elbow, opens a bottle with his teeth and takes a slug. I can feel his warm breath, catch the smell of whisky when he draws me close.

'So like I said, there was this loon, these loons. They called in the night. Sometimes they made a sniggering sound that chilled us to the bone, especially when the moon lit up the lake and the shadows of the trees moved … then these harrowing, plaintive cries that grew deeper, coming closer over the water, so deep and dark – the water, I mean – and they would rise up towards the moon like a madman's laugh. We huddled together under the blanket. We swore we'd get the hell out as soon as the sun was up. In the morning there was just a heap of twigs on the shore, the place those night-time calls had come from. It was the loons' nest and there were these ridiculous little mewing sounds coming from it, which made us laugh at ourselves. Sometimes when I close my eyes, I can still hear those calls. And I get goose bumps. And the same shiver down my spine.'

'What about your mom?'

He gives a sad little laugh.

'We gave her a pretty hard time. I think she's getting a break now we're gone. My dad, he's the one who takes care of me. He's stopped drinking. He'd like me to stop too, but he doesn't talk about it. Anyway, I don't want to. He sends me dough when I'm really in the shit. One time he gave me a sleeping bag, a really fantastic one, he must have cleaned himself out buying the thing. That was when I was wandering the streets of Anchorage in wintertime.'

'Didn't you go to Bean's Café?'

'Not much. Sometimes for food. But I left straight after. I've never liked living in a herd. I preferred sleeping in the park with other bums. Or on my own. I'd dig a hole for myself in the snow. I wasn't cold in my sleeping bag. I was fine.'

I press myself up close to him. I'm under the snow with him. I wrap my legs round his. We're not cold now.

'One year when I wasn't fishing, I wanted to build a house for myself. My dad had bought this plot of woodland at an OK price. I'd had a good season on a trawler. I worked like a dog. The house was coming along, then winter came. The road was cut off by the snow. I stocked up on drink – I've always planned ahead,' he adds ironically. 'They found me weeks later, half dead.'

'Half dead? Of what?'

He doesn't answer. Lights a cigarette. Then in a murmur, 'When you shut yourself away with the monster . . .'

After three days we really do have to get out of bed.

'I'm leaving this evening,' he says. 'Come with me.'

'I want to go crab fishing first.'

'Who's this Jason?'

'A really young guy, on his own little boat,' I say lightly. 'You saw him walk past on the quay when we were working on the *Rebel*. He'd sometimes stop by at the end of the day. It'll be the first time he's fished alone, and as skipper.'

'Are you sleeping with him?'

'No! I just want to go fishing again.'

'Come to Hawaii with me,' he insists. 'We'll find a boat in Honolulu.'

'Not yet. I don't want to leave Alaska so soon.'

'Marry me.'

We head off to look at the harbour. I've left my long, long hair loose for the first time and I feel proud walking next to the great sailor, with my woman's mane flowing in the wind. He's proud too.

'Say something to me,' I say. 'Otherwise I feel so alone.'

His deep voice does me good immediately. So he talks, slowly.

'I want you to be with me always.'

A beautiful, kind thing to say.

We're alone on the beach. There's a very fine drizzle. Entirely, entirely grey. The birds and their cries have dissolved in the mist. We're cold but even so, we're having a go at making love on the wet sand, between two black rocks.

'Say something to me,' I say again. 'Otherwise I feel too alone.'

He's on top of me, moving forward slowly. The rain dribbles into our eyes, the rocks are torturing my ribs, our clothes get in the way.

'I feel alone too,' he says, then laughs a little. 'At least we tried ...'

We have to head back quickly because the tide's coming in and the route we took on the way here will soon be cut off. We sit on a fallen tree trunk at the very end of the beach by the path. He takes the bottle of vodka and the ice cream from his pack. He pours me a drink and gives me some ice cream, then hands me his Walkman to listen to. Tom Waits. From time to time he leans his head against mine to listen in – *We sail tonight for Singapore*.

A guy walks past, says a half-hearted hello.

'What the hell's he doing here?' the great sailor says softly. 'This is our beach.'

'Yes. Maybe we should kill him for it.'

'Come to Hawaii with me.'

'Not yet, not this evening, I want to go crab fishing.'

★

'You'll look after yourself, though,' he says some time later.

'Yes,' I say.

'You won't go to Point Barrow.'

'Not yet.'

'And if you don't have a boat left to go to, if Ronnie has to take the *Lively June* back out, you'll go to the shelter. You'll be safe there.'

'I can always find an old car to spend the night in,' I say nonchalantly. 'There's plenty of abandoned trucks on the edge of the beach near the Salvation Army.'

'You're crazy. I shouldn't go. I should stay and give you a baby.'

I laugh quietly.

'Why give me a baby?'

'To keep you away from rusting old cars!'

We wait for the ferry. The sun set hours ago, on the wide beach where we waited in the mist. We've taken refuge in his car, an old rust bucket that never moves from behind the shelter. He has his big hands round my face. In the harsh white light of a street lamp I look at his swollen features, his lumpy copper-coloured complexion, the moist gemstones of his eyes. I think he's beautiful, I think he's the most beautiful, the most dazzling, the greatest. He wants me to love him more, again. He'll never get enough of love, sex or alcohol.

'No,' I murmur. 'No, we might be seen. Not in this old car by the shelter, surrounded by mud.'

He keeps pressing me. So I love him with my mouth. In the end I cry. He, on the other hand, feels great. He sees the tears in my eyes.

'Do you hate me?' he asks, holding me to him.

'No. Why would I hate you?'

He has my face in his hands again. Those yellow eyes probe mine.

'I'm really sorry,' I say, not for the first time.

'You go to the shelter,' he says in the dark. 'Ask for Jude, my father. He runs the place. His name's Jude. Keep him up to date with what you're doing. He'll get news through to me. And he'll give you my news if my letters don't get through.'

'Jude, like you?'

'Yes. Jude too. And I'll be in Hawaii with my brother for a while. Ashore. Time enough to find work. I'll wait for you.'

'Does your brother live there the whole time?'

'Part-time. Jude has a house on the Big Island. He works in construction. Right now he's on a site in Kawai. That's where I'm going.'

'Jude's your brother? Him too?'

'Yup, him too.'

'So you all call each other Jude.?'

He laughs in that deep, feline purr of a voice he has, then hugs me to him and takes another swig of whisky.

'I'm Jude Samson. But I prefer to be called Jude. And we can make another little Jude together.'

It's started to rain again. Water runs over the windscreen in rivulets and these busy little streams hide us from the occasional passers-by at last.

Jude lights another cigarette.

'It was a long time ago,' he says. 'My grandfather was a logger in South Carolina. He was in a bad way, he'd been hit by a tree. He was probably going to die. My grandma, who was still young, went to pray to St Jude. She swore to him that every descendant would be given his name if her man pulled through. She lit a candle every day. He pulled through.'

'And are the women called Judith?'

He takes a swig and kisses me, his calloused palms cupping my temples.

'There haven't been any women since.'

The ferry blasts its horn in the dark; it's been sounding for a while. He has to go. He grabs his sailing bag and slings it over his shoulders. The wind buffets his dark curls of hair and the rain falls on our faces, cool and light. His face is streaming; it reminds me of a painting I saw as a child, Cain's children fleeing, possibly in a storm.

'You look like someone in a very old picture,' I say.

'Sisyphus?'

'Maybe him too.'

The great sailor. Yes, perhaps he is Sisyphus, crushed by the world, scorched by fury and passion, by alcohol, salt and exhaustion. Or maybe the other one, the one whose liver is pecked by an eagle for all eternity because he gave men the gift of fire. I'm not sure, but deep down it doesn't matter, he's all of them.

We reach the ferry and wait in the drizzle mingled with sea spray. A woman taking tickets at the end of the jetty asks if he has any alcohol in his bag. No, of course not, he says.

'You go now,' he tells me.

'I want to stay a little longer.'

So he kisses me quickly and fiercely.

'You're the best thing that could have happened to me in a very long time.'

'You already said that,' I mumble.

'I'll say it again. You'll catch cold. Where's your scarf?'

I lean towards him with the loosened scarf on my shoulders. The wind blows around us and he ties the scarf snugly for me. But the ferry's booming already so we say goodbye again.

'We should get married.'

'Yes. Maybe we should get married,' I say.

'We'll get married and we'll go to Dutch Harbor this winter to work on a boat.'

I head back in the fine rain. Later I hear the ferry from my bunk, its crying in the dark. I realise I forgot to plait his braid, a little braid he asked me to make for him.

In the morning I got up early. The sky had cleared and it was a beautiful day. I walked over to the taxi office and a woman came out of the toilets behind the office, then a man. They were both wearing filthy old overalls and holding hands. The woman looked very young, she had rounded burnished cheeks, untidy hanks of black hair and patches of yellow around her mouth. Maybe she'd been sick. She almost fell over but the man caught her and wedged her under his arm.

'Now stop moving,' he chided gently. 'I'll walk and you hold on to me ... like that, that's it.'

She laughed and let herself be led, her eyes half closed. He might as well have had a ragdoll in his arms. The man looked up and from somewhere in his rough-hewn face, in the puffiness that trapped his eyes, the limpid flash of two green irises ringed with red blood vessels made its way to me.

'So how's my friend Jude? Is he doing OK?'

'Yeah, he's doing fine. He's in Anchorage. Hawaii soon, and I'll be joining him ...'

'Say hi to him from us. Sid and Lena, tell him ...'

They staggered on, two black beetles silhouetted against the sky and the pale water in the harbour. They made their way slowly along the quay, stopped, seemed to hesitate, toppled briefly, then stood upright again, kept going, towards the square perhaps.

Birds call to each other, making strange cries. Fish jump, and sea otters and porpoises dance around the boat, chasing each other and forming groups in the iridescent spray. We're cradled between sky and sea as if between two arms. Jason yells, he's always yelling – he's frightened, he's never skippered before. He loathes me for running, leaping to attention at his least instruction, going red and puffy-faced when I haul up the anchor against the current. He'd pictured a graceful, light-footed elf on deck, the fire-breather. He pictured us evolving into two wild and beautiful pirates, the best fishing team in Uganik Bay, and soon in all Alaska. But I don't share his bunk, and crab fishing is miserable. Every night he's terrified the anchor will slip. I don't say anything and just keep running, but when he starts shouting I'm all fingers and thumbs.

'For God's sake, do it with class!' he roars when I have to tie up the *Milky Way* to cleats at Uganik's canneries.

There's nothing classy about me when I'm scared, I want to say.

The water pump's getting weaker: we have to keep refilling the tank. It's not long before we run out of fresh water. We fill the skiff with every empty container on the boat – cooking pans, bottles, coffee pots – and head for the green creek where there's a stream. We top the tank right up but the water pump gives up the ghost in Terror Bay. Jason's stopped yelling, he's close to tears.

'I'm going to make some coffee, Jason, and then we'll see ...'

A red-and-black tender has dropped anchor in the bay, the *Midnight Sun*. We get back into the skiff and the three crew members watch us paddle over with a mixture of amazement and kindness. We're distraught and we look lost. Jason can hardly speak, and I stammer out words that no one understands. The skipper emerges from the wheelhouse and he's a very kind man who comes to our rescue. A dark mane and full beard behind which I can make out a face furrowed with wrinkles. As he walks over to us he reminds me of a bear. Jason pulls himself together.

'Good timing! The *Midnight Sun*'s full and we'll be going back to town this evening to unload,' the man tells us. 'But we'll come straight back tomorrow. The boys can pick up a pump while they're ashore. But come inside.'

He makes some coffee, takes out some cookies, tells us to eat.

'Could I use the radio to order the pump?' Jason asks.

'Of course.'

'Thank you … have a drink for us in Kodiak,' Jason says before going up to the wheelhouse.

'I've had my fill of bars,' the skipper tells me as he pours me another coffee.

'Did you quit drinking?'

'I'd be dead if I still drank. I spent long enough trailing around the streets in my own piss and puke like a pathetic animal. I'm done with all that.'

His piercing eyes come to rest on me and he smiles.

'Have another cookie.'

He talks to us about God, then sees us back out onto the deck. It's late in the night and there's a full moon. Out there in Terror Bay I get a sense of this God of his. A seiner approaches the *Midnight Sun* slowly, the red line along its coaming dropping deep underwater.

'The *Kasukuak Girl* sure as hell is loaded this evening. She's the last one I'm unloading,' he tells us. 'Then I have to get going, kids. Catch the tide to get through Whale Pass OK. Wait for me here tomorrow. I'll have the pump.'

He pushes back the cover to the hold, grabs a salmon floating in slimy water and molten ice and hands it to me.

Jason gives it all he's got: jaws clamped and eyebrows knitted under his fraying bandana, he powers through the dark. The skiff glides over black waters that shimmer in the moonlight. Back at the boat Jason goes to his bunk without a word. I kneel on deck gobbling the raw red salmon like a happy animal. The pouch of roe splits open in my mouth and I run my tongue over this creamy fruit of the sea which breaks up and melts in my throat. The moon bathes the deck in light. The *Kasukuak Girl* has dropped anchor not far away, and I can see the red dot of an incandescent cigarette quivering on the bridge.

'I want to go on the beach, Jason, there may be some Japanese floats.'

The sun's already high. We had breakfast in silence. Jason hasn't said a word since I evaded the two scrawny arms trying to lead me to their bunk last night.

'There are grizzlies on the coast.'

'I'll be careful.'

So he takes me ashore and leaves me with a horn.

'Blow on it when you want to come back or if there's a problem. The minute I hear the signal, I'll be here.'

The skiff's gone and I'm walking along the shore. Driftwood is strewn about the beach – it's smooth and beautiful, bleached by the sea and the weather – but there are no blue glass balls that have travelled the seas for years. So I head off to find bears. I smell something behind some bramble bushes: an eagle lying dead, its forehead flattened on the sand, its wings spread and coated with dried silt. A sudden knife stab to my stomach, a burning blade, enough to knock me off my feet. I fall to my knees on the beach right beside the broken eagle, blinded by tears. I barely have the strength to blow the horn to call Jason.

The *Midnight Sun* is back with the new water pump, but neither the well-meaning skipper's pills nor his prayers or even Jason's herbal teas succeed in calming the pain. I writhe in agony on my bunk and I'm evacuated the next day. The small hydroplane that Jason calls for on the radio makes a water landing in the bay. Clutching my stomach, I curl up on the seat next to the pilot, looking out at the instrument panel and the sky, my insides consumed by bristle worms. I think of all the fish I've slashed with a knife, of those that have served as bait. I've sliced into so many still-palpitating white bellies, I've done so much killing, I have to pay. The sky dives into the cabin. Or are we diving through the sky?

The hospital doesn't keep me in. Poisoning, they said. It'll pass ... I go back to the *Lively June* sadder and poorer than ever. The *Rebel* is moored up, and Aaron grabs me on his way past – there's tons of work. They want me to join them and I just have time to go into town: a letter from the great sailor in poste restante. He's in Hawaii, on the beach, waiting for me. He's drinking rum and Budweisers. He's made a friend who shares his foodbank vouchers and his beer with him. Someone had their throat slit only a stone's throw from their tent the night before. The great sailor's hungry in spite of the foodbank vouchers. Come find me, he says again, of course I'll worry about you with all these rutting men who live on the beach and drink, but how do I know what you're up to with the young dogs in Kodiak? Come, Lili, come. We can finally make this ice-cream baby of ours.

I have ten days' work on the *Rebel*, spending every night loading cargoes of salmon from seiners. A woman on board: Diana. She's beautiful, and often helms the boat. She's fierce: we women don't have the luxury of making mistakes if we want to be accepted, she tells me – tough girl. We have to be the best. She's contemptuous of my hesitant voice, but when the wind whips up, fifty knots at one point, she disappears into her cabin and holes up in her bunk. Wiped out by seasickness. I sit next to Joey in the wheelhouse. White birds circle slowly in the bright halo around the mast light. We're out on the black ocean and Joey teaches me how to use the controls. It's great.

Some afternoons, when the boats are fishing, Joey takes the canoe and goes off to the beach. The huge forests of Afognak and Shuyak stretch far into the distance, over the dark cliffs that rear up between the pine trees. I daren't ask to go with him. He goes alone and always brings back strange and wonderful things, with the glowing serious face of someone who spent his childhood in the forest. Roebuck antlers or eagle feathers, branches polished by the waves, worn down to nothing more than a pure curve, the essence of what was once a tree. One day he finds a massive hard fungus, and promises himself he'll paint it and sculpt it when it's dry.

Our work begins as soon as it's dark. Diana and the men yell, and I'm constantly frightened. This is exile, I think. Everyone's asleep today, the sun's beating down on deck. Lying on my bunk with my eyes open in the half-light, I think about the tenders last night, the ones waiting in Perenosa Bay. You can't describe it to other people, you can't explain it to people who haven't seen any of this – yes – the big tenders in the night, huge steel boats with names that speak of life and death and epic journeys. Their thrumming engines, creaking winches, orange men labouring in the wind, faces streaming in the glare of sodium lights, a bizarre and disturbing film reflected on the black waters. No, you can't describe it. Who would understand?

One day we return to harbour and I feel cold inside my bones. I want to say, Let's go home – but there is no home, there never will be again. I have nightmares but we soon put to sea again. And then in Viekoda Bay I fall into the fish hold, salmon by the thousand marinating in dirty water, thick with mucus and blood. I've injured my leg and it throbs angrily as we motor through the night, trundling through the darkness to get to Izhut Bay where other boats are waiting for us to unload their catches and fill up again.

Kodiak Island has embraced me in its arms of black rock. I've come back to the *Lively June*, the key hidden under the overhang on the bridge, the same smell of diesel and wet rain gear. At the launderette I met Virgil, who plays golf and fishes for red salmon. I dragged my leg all the way to his boat, the *Jenny*. He prepared some coffee and made popcorn, and that made me feel better. I came back out and walked to the post office where the postal worker handed me a letter. I recognised the large handwriting. The old envelope was sealed with a sort of black paste – tar? I hurried off to Baranof Park, to the place under the big cedar, and lay down there to open Jude's crumpled letter spotted with fat and beer, like the last one. And I read it as clouds passed by in the great summer sky. I fell asleep and dreamt I was on the bridge of a boat, with a storm raging around me. Freezing cold waves crashing down on my bare head. There were men working alongside me, wrapped up in massive rain gear, the faceless men in Ian's film. Meanwhile I was practically naked, floundering in grey water that soon came up to my waist. But I was afraid of nothing, not exhaustion, not the cold. The men were pleased with me and I worked well. I'd become a real fisherman. When I woke, the sun coming through the branches had settled on my face. I sat up and saw some lupins in front of the little Baranof museum, they looked like dancing patches of colour. Then I walked to the road and crossed it. In front of me was the blue water and the ferry: it was setting off for Dutch Harbor again that evening. I could go to Dutch, I thought, I'd find work on a crab boat. But it wasn't the season. And anyway, what could I achieve on deck with this leg? This is exile, I thought again. I went back to the *Lively June* and packed my bag, then perched on the folding chair in the wheelhouse and waited.

Conrad knocked on the window; I recognised his angular white face through the glass, his pale eyes under swollen drooping eyelids, blinking occasionally as if wounded by the light. I opened the door and the thin line of his mouth creased into a smile that looked almost shy. His blue overalls hung off his bony body, he pushed back a filthy baseball cap on his yellow, tow-like hair.

"Parently you're in a bad way?' he said as he came in.

I told him to sit down. I'd just made some coffee. I handed him a cigarette and he went to spit his chewing tobacco into the bin.

'You should come to my place for a while. My house is at Bells' Flat, twenty miles from here. I'll make you poultices with plant extracts and they'll soon get you better.'

'Thanks, Conrad, but I'm happier here in the harbour.'

'I sometimes write political pamphlets. You can tell me what you think of them.'

'What do you write about?' I ask.

'Life.'

'You should show me them sometime.'

He shrugs. His mouth has reverted to its bitter, slightly sardonic twist.

'I could still really do with your help, as soon as you can, as soon as your leg's better. I have gardens to do, another trench to dig, and the *Morgan* still needs hosing down from time to time. It's not so dry, the wood's holding the moisture OK and the caulking joints haven't cracked, but it would still be safer. And it still needs plenty of linseed oil on the deck.'

'As soon as I can,' I nod. 'I'm starting to feel seriously broke. I'm waiting for a cheque from Andy but he always takes his time.'

'I won't be able to give you more than last time, you understand, with the work on the *Morgan* and missing a season. It'll still be twenty dollars a day.'

'Twenty dollars still means I can eat and put something aside.'

'Did you know there's a halibut opening coming up in a month? Twenty-four hours non-stop.'

'Yes.'

'You could get a job on a good boat, now you've done a black cod opening and the last halibut opening. You'll be able to make a bit of money.'

'I don't know if I ever dare go fishing again. Something always happens to me. What if I go overboard next time?'

He laughs.

'Fishing accidents happen to everyone.'

'Are you going to do the opening?' I ask.

'Dunno yet. I've never liked this twenty-four hours non-stop of theirs, a race. It's all about who does it better than the next guy and there's always some prick who ends up going under because he was trying to do more than his boat could handle.'

'Well, if I'm going to do it, this leg needs to get better. No one's gonna want a cripple on board.'

'Yup,' he says. 'If you come to my place I'll make poultices for you and they'll heal you right away.'

'I want to stay here.'

'And what would you say to us doing it together, this halibut opening? I'd give you a good percentage. Fifty-fifty. My quota's six thousand pounds. At over a dollar a pound ... I have secret areas I know for halibut. You take care of the tubs, baiting the gear, getting the lines in shape, the fish hold super clean, the ice – I'll handle the rest. Running the boat and finding the fish.'

'Have to see. If my leg gets better.'

He stands up.

'Do you maybe have another smoke? I have to go work now, a garden to do, I really like gardens. And I earn as much as I can fishing.'

Conrad's left. Water laps against the hull. It's dark and snug in the shadowy boat. Flies stray constantly over the windows in the wheelhouse, trying to find a way out. Sometimes I catch them and put them outside, but they always come back. Then they die and that upsets me. I turn to look at the sun-drenched docks, then decide it's time I started making my belt, a secret leather belt to fit snugly round my waist and into the small of my back like a second skin. A belt on which I can hang a knife, a very fine blade in a sheath I'll make myself.

A memory of Lucy, met one summer under the strong Okanagan sun. She was Native, this Lucy, she was my friend. Our cheeks were so red that day, the blue bruise of her black eye, her laughter and the brightly coloured pack beating regularly against my back, a white road up ahead, candelabra cactuses, the desert ... He'll kill me if I go with you, she said with a laugh. I'd miss him too much, anyway ...

but make yourself a knife, your knife, we're like wild animals, have to save your own skin.

I make a start on my belt, then take out my box of paints. I draw and paint winged men, mermaids, the great sailor in the half shade and me sleeping against his thigh. Maybe I will go halibut fishing. If we catch enough I'll go to Hawaii.

I came outside – blinding light – and walked along the deserted pontoon. On the colourful boat, the *Kayodie*, a tall blond guy with an anxious face came out of his cabin. He invited me on board with a wave of his hand so I stepped over the rail and sat down on the hood of the hold.

'I'm Cody,' he said.

'I'm Lili. What does *Kayodie* mean?'

'Coyote. They're incredible animals to the Crow tribe, kind of like crows themselves, with supernatural powers and insanely intelligent. The coyote's always around, in among us, he just changes his face.'

'It's a good name for a boat.'

'Yes. By the way, I noticed you limping since you came back and I have a remedy that should help you. It's a liniment for horses, it gets everything working right.'

He went into his cabin and I heard him rummaging through boxes. When he came back out he handed me a pot of translucent ointment.

'It's very powerful. Wash your hands afterward.'

'Great, thanks.'

'I follow regular healing courses with a Native American tribe in southern Arizona,' he explained. 'I'll be a medicine man one day.'

'Right ... and you're not fishing right now?'

'I fished salmon for a few weeks. Not great. And then we had one breakdown after another: the hydraulic reel died on us, then we got a bad tear in the seine when we caught it on a rocky seabed, and then Nikephoros was meant to do the season with us and he abandoned us mid-trip.'

'Oh, that's too bad,' I said.

'How about you?'

'I'm waiting to get better to go out fishing again. At least, I hope so. I don't have much experience yet but you have to start somewhere, don't you? Then I'm off to Hawaii for a while when I can afford it.'

'What for?'

'To meet up with someone.'

'Ah,' he said.

We sat in silence for a moment. The light danced over the water.

'Have you been here a long time?' I asked eventually.

'I came here after Vietnam. Actually no, that's not true, I travelled around quite a bit before settling in Kodiak. I worked with a buddy north of Fairbanks, prospecting for gold. When we fell out I drifted and strayed till I ended up here.'

'Have you ever been crab fishing?'

'No, never. I leave that to the others.'

'Oh. Where are you from?'

'From Vietnam,' he said, and his eyes flickered before becoming strangely fixed, then eventually refocusing. 'Well, not really, that was before ... it was after too.'

'Right ... Where were you born?'

He seemed to hesitate, looked at me with a note of surprise.

'I was born – I was born in the East I think, somewhere between Texas and New Mexico. Do you want a beer?'

'No thanks,' I said. 'I have stuff to do.'

The tide was on its way in, and the breeze and the birds along with it. I looked towards the port as I walked up the gangplank: the shutters on the wooden houses seemed to be watching me from the hillside. The coffee shop was white with sunlight. Higher up, the green mountains and their tide of flowers. Sitting at tables on the black asphalt pavement, the pretty waitresses, the ones who don't like me – and why is that? – smoked and laughed loudly. Their beautiful hair gleamed in the light bouncing off the water in the harbour. I walked on with my limp. I walked and walked some more, avoiding the square and the bars, and finally sat down on the jetty for the ferry.

234

Before me the blue waters of the channel, in the distance the woods on Long Island.

The *Rebel* was back in port. It was late and the sky was lit up with a patina like old gold. I met Joey on the pontoon, his grim forehead brightened for a moment and a twinkle lit in his dark eyes set deep under heavy brows.

'We don't have anything left to eat,' he said, laughing. 'I'm going to see if I can find something before my thirst gets the better of me.'

So I gave him the fish soup I'd just made. I'd been given a batch of salmon heads by Virgil, who fished red salmon in Bristol Bay. He was laid-back and laconic but there was something sophisticated about the way he spoke and dressed compared to the other rough-and-ready men here. The eyes floated on the surface but I thought of them as just another part of the soup, as good as the rest.

Joey came by again the next day when it was drizzling and the seagulls' cries were mournful in the mist. He rapped at the window. I was sitting in the shadows, watching the flies on the windows in the galley.

'You're coming with me for a beer. Nothing else to do in this terrible weather.'

'Was the soup good?'

Joey gave a strange smile and didn't answer. Diana probably didn't like the eyes, maybe he didn't either, despite being Native. I grabbed a sweater and followed him.

It was still early and Tony's was only just opening. We sat at the bar and Joey ordered two Buds. Across the room from us a white-haired man was having coffee with Susie. He was wearing a woollen three-piece suit and a soft felt hat. I spied the man who'd baited tubs opposite where the *Rebel* was moored two months ago, when the Kinks had sung about going away to sea. He was playing on a pinball machine in the shadows.

'Hi, Ryan,' Joey called over to him.

'Is his name Ryan?' I asked. 'He has a beautiful boat.'

'The *Destiny*? It was once a really beautiful schooner, but it's had it now. They'll go down together one day, Ryan and his boat. In the harbour.'

'Can't he do something?'

'Ryan's all washed up. Apart from his beer and his pinball, he doesn't really—'

A wild-eyed man came in, smooth bald head shiny from the rain, a thin beard hanging all the way down to his belt. Susie stood up and showed him the door. He protested briefly before heading back out into what was now driving rain.

Joey handed me a cigarette, then he talked to me about the forest. He really liked the tendering season in the summer, he told me, when he found time to get away from the boat and escape to the hills. It was like returning to his childhood, nestled in the deep woodland, buried in the island's musky soil. Back then, when he was twelve, he'd had a rifle, his life ahead of him, and all the forests, mountains and skies in the world ahead of him, open like a vast virgin territory which would only ever belong to him.

'Every kid around here has that same feeling. That's when men grow up.'

'And the women?'

'I dunno about women, not so much probably. It depends. My old aunties grew up outdoors. Maybe my mom did, I never asked her. Her childhood was nothing to do with me.'

'I liked running free too,' I said.

'There, you see? But later it goes, it has to go, you have to grow up, Lili. Beer takes over where the freedom left off, and work, marriage . . . kids. And then they'll start all over again, running through the woods, and they'll leave them behind one day themselves.'

'For the sake of beer and all that?' I asked sadly. 'Why do people stop running for the sake of bars and dope and everything that's bad for us?'

'I don't know, that's just how it is. So we don't die of boredom, I guess, or despair. And also there's the beast in all of us. It needs calming. If you knock it out things are easier.'

I drank a long draught of beer and sighed. Yes, the beast.

'But why?' I asked again. 'Why does it always have to come to an end, all that wonderful running through forests and mountains?'

'Because that's the way it is. The law of life. Things to worry about. Everything fizzles out over the years.'

'But it doesn't, not always.'

'Yes it does. Have another beer and stop making that face,' he said, laughing gently. 'You'll be like everyone else, you wait. You'll soon be running after something other than docks and boats. Life'll catch up with you one day.'

'Not me, it won't. Never me. I'll go fishing. For crab too, some day.'

'Be careful.'

'Of what?'

'Of everything. Of life, here, everywhere.'

We drank a lot of beer. Ryan, the little guy in the felt hat, didn't move from where he was. He abandoned coffee in favour of Bloody Marys and turned away from the pinball machine in order to slump on the bar, where he sat drinking morosely. Two strapping men who smelt of bait and salt rowdily offered each other Jägermeisters. Joey's shoulders gradually drooped.

'What is it that you want, at the end of the day?' he asked me, his sad dark eyes probing mine. 'At first you said Point Barrow, for reasons that made no sense at all, now it's crab fishing that's eating at you. And then sometimes it's Hawaii, for some guy, I guess . . . Be surprised if it was for a girl.'

'Most of all I want to fish. I want to exhaust myself over and over, I want nothing to be able to stop me, like – like a tightrope, yes, it's just not allowed to slacken, so tight it could snap. And then Hawaii . . . and Point Barrow some day.'

'You're all the same, you people who come here like visionaries. For me this is where I belong, I've never known anything else, I haven't travelled further than Fairbanks. I'm not searching for something impossible. I just want to live my life and bring up my kids. This island's my home! Mind you, I'm just an idiot, a dirty black Injun.'

237

'No, Joey, I don't like it when you say that.'

The bar filled up and we put down roots, our backsides wedged into our chairs, our elbows set permanently on the wooden bar. White-haired Ryan was still there opposite us. I smiled at him, waved an arm, like two sailors waving from the bridges of their boats.

'So,' Joey went on, his voice slowing now, 'you left your home to come fishing for adventure.'

'I left, that's all.'

'Pfff, there are tens of thousands of you, you've been coming here for more than a century. The first were a ferocious bunch, but you're not the same now. You all come looking for something that's impossible to find. Some sort of security? Hell, no, it's not even that because you seem to be looking for death, or at least you want to meet it face-to-face. You're trying to find ... certainty, maybe ... something powerful enough to fight your fears, your pain, your past – something that would save everything, you first of all.'

He took a long drink straight from the bottle, eyelids half closed, then put the bottle back down and opened his eyes.

'You're like all those soldiers who go off to test themselves in war, as if your own lives aren't enough for you, as if you have to find a reason to die. Or you need to atone for something.'

'I don't want to die, Joey.'

He looked away and started muttering: dirty negro Injun. I finished my beer, thanked him and went back to the *Lively June*. It was still raining.

It rained for five days and the swelling in my leg was going down. The blue line of bruising under the skin turned purple. Joey came by again the next day and I made him a coffee. His face was peaceful and sad once more.

'Be patient, Lili,' he said, looking out through the window casting a bleak white light over us.

A gloomy sky outside.

'Be patient. You want everything, and straightaway. We said some dumb stuff at the bar yesterday. That happens to me sometimes, I get angry with people who show up here. I almost preferred the real gold seekers. But you guys, you're looking for a metal that's a different kind of powerful and a different kind of pure.'

'Those are pretty big words.'

'But maybe deep down you were right too. The veterans – Cody, Ryan, Bruce, Jonathan and all the others – they didn't come looking for death, well, not necessarily. Nature is the best healer, as they say. What they found here, when they fished, was a lust for life, a brutal lust for life, a real struggle with real nature. Nothing or no one could have given them that. And there's most likely nowhere else on earth that could.'

'We don't all come from Vietnam.'

'No. We've had prisoners and outlaws who wanted to be forgotten. These days we have a bit of everything: people running away from a crisis or some fuck-up. The bottom line is we get lumbered with all the rebels and headcases on the planet who want to make a new life for themselves. And the dreamers too, like you.'

'For me it came on like an obscure longing,' I murmured. 'Going and seeing what happens at the very edge of the horizon, beyond the Last Frontier. But sometimes I think it was a dream. That it *is* a dream. That nothing can ever save anything, and Alaska is just a fantasy.'

Joey sighed and crushed his cigarette into the empty sardine-tin ashtray. He suddenly looked tired, he must have stayed up late, drinking, and his face bore witness to the fact uncompromisingly.

'It's not a fantasy. You can be sure of that at least. Open your eyes, look around you.'

'I'm looking. Oh, I'm looking.'

'Anywhere else a lot of you would be dead already. Or locked up.'

'But, Joey, why do you all keep running after something, why do we run?'

'Everything runs, Lili, everything moves forward. The ocean, the mountains, the earth you walk on. When you travel the earth it seems to move with you, unrolling in front of you from one valley to the next, mountains, then ravines with water tumbling into them and flowing off into a river, then running towards the sea. Everything's in the race, Lili. The stars too, night and day, light, everything running. And we're just the same. Otherwise we'd die.'

'And Jude?'

'Your great sailor had better keep on running. Otherwise that means he's drowned.'

Joey left. It was midday and he was going to the Breaker's but I didn't want to go to with him. I lay on my bunk and ate a tin of sardines. It was almost dark in the belly of the boat. I listened to the regular sound of rain on the upper deck, like a soft patter, the faraway lament of a seabird, and the kiss of the water against the hull. I pressed my forehead hard up against the damp wood. I was woken by hammering on the door. I'd fallen asleep and was dreaming again. I hauled myself out of my sleeping bag but there was no one on deck. A little fulmar lay on the soaking wood, a bead of blood appeared each time its tubular nostrils bulged as it exhaled.

'We're bored,' Murphy says.

'Yup, we're bored. We could make a trip to Anchorage for a change of scene. I could see my daughter, maybe she's found me some books at last. You can see your children, and grandchildren – maybe you got some new ones!'

'And we can go say hi to our friends at Bean's Café.'

''M guessing Sid and Lena would be up for it. You coming with us, Lili? We can all take the ferry together. The *Tustumena* will be here this evening.'

'I'd like to but I can't even manage that,' I reply with a sigh. 'Andy still hasn't paid me.'

We sit under the awning at the harbourmaster's office and watch the rain fall. The sailor lost at sea has drowned in the mist.

★

Ryan called out to me as I walked past the Ship.

'Come have a beer, Lili!'

I hesitated. His eyes had the same dark sparkle as the slate-grey waters in the harbour. He was almost good-looking with his ash-blond hair framing his face.

The ill-lit bar was almost empty and there was a different waitress. At the corner of the bar, under the pictures of naked women, three old Native women drank in silence. Ryan seemed to have forgotten I was there.

'What about your boat?' I asked. 'When are you taking her out fishing?'

He took a long time to answer.

'Some day maybe,' he mumbled laconically.

'Oh. Where are you from?'

'I come from the asshole of the world, somewhere in the lower forty-eight. But that was a long time ago. I've practically forgotten. And roll on the day when I totally forget all those asshole places. How 'bout you, what the hell are you doing here?' he asked but he wasn't looking at me.

'I came to fish.'

'Well, you've done that, then. When are you going home?'

'Um ... I don't know. Maybe never.'

'Don't you have a guy?'

'No. Well, not here. And even then ...'

'We don't want people like you here. We're fine as we are. We don't want tourists coming to have an experience, fucking our men and then going and telling people they've been to the edge.'

I stood up, knocking my stool over. I was flushed red, my lip trembling. I walked hesitantly to the door. I must have looked drunk.

The rain had stopped at last, and Murphy and his physicist friend Stephen had gone. A dishevelled, tired-looking couple were walking slowly up the hillside to the shelter where a glum little group of people was waiting for them on the steps. I walked along the quayside clinging to the sides of warehouses. I won't ever go to their bars again, I thought. I hurried back to the *Lively June*, almost slipping on the soaking pontoon. The little fulmar hadn't made it.

★

241

I repacked the bag that I'd unpacked that morning. Point Barrow or Hawaii, I wondered yet again. Men yelled on the docks, then came the rustle of wings of a bird taking flight. I holed up in the shadow of my bunk, an animal in its lair. I heard the tug and I waited for the wail of the ferry's horn. Which didn't come. The shadow of Manosque-les-Sorrow filled the cabin, the memory of another kind of fear and a smoky bar as my only horizon, someone in a black leather jacket and his clapped-out cowboy boots, a bedroom as dark and damp as a burial vault, the mattress on the floor, perhaps starting to rot. It was a nightmare vision full of dread, there may have been maggots crawling over it already, over the body of my shipwrecked man who was still waiting for me just like he was waiting for his killers, the syringe of insulin camouflaged between two bottles, the sad little dog also waiting for me to come back, one ear cocked towards the door whose wood was swollen with damp and whose hinges stubbornly refused to creak . . .

I woke at eleven o'clock, got up and dressed, brushed my hair: ready to go – but where? The sky was barely any darker than when I'd fallen asleep. In the end I pulled myself together and went back to bed.

In the morning the sun was out. Things were looking up.

I walk through the bland warmth of the streets, my leg heavy and painful. I've hurried past the bars, crossing the sleeping town, passing McDonald's and on to the post office: I've written a long letter to the great sailor. There's no mail for me. I come back out and walk to the little yellow house on its trailer that's still for sale. I sit on its wooden steps to rest my leg, and I fantasise that they're my steps. Oh, to have a tiny little buttercup-yellow house. I would put it on a patch of wasteland and it would always be there, for when I come home from fishing. It's a pretty thought and it fills me with joy. I get to my feet again and cut across the grassy plot, past Jude's old wreck where we took refuge one time, and climb the hillside up to the shelter. The door is open and to the right of the entrance a big thermos of coffee has pride of place on a table, surrounded by cups, sugar and a basket full of cookies. A man sits behind a desk, his forehead leaning towards a register. I cough and ask for Jude. The man raises black eyebrows over yellow eyes that I recognise. I blush.

'You're here for Jude?' he asks, laughing.

'Yes. Well, for the Jude in Hawaii,' I stammer. 'But I'd like to talk to the Jude at the shelter.'

He stands up and smiles at me. He's well built, shoulders like a lumberjack, face scarred, creased with wrinkles from hard work and with other, older marks, damage from a life of excess. He's noticed me looking at the thermos and cookies.

'Help yourself to coffee,' he says. 'I'm Jude's father. And you are Lili.'

'I don't think he's been getting my letters.'

'I spoke to him on the phone two days ago. He asked whether you'd been to see me. Otherwise, still no work. He talked about trying to find a job on a boat in Honolulu. He's waiting for you.'

The man has the same voice as the great sailor. I'm drawn to and embarrassed by the ageing leather of his skin. I turn away and look at the sun streaming onto the grey floor tiles. He goes over to the urn, fills a cup with coffee and hands it to me.

'Sugar?'

'No, thank you.'

'A cookie?'

'That yes.'

And as I reach towards the basket he can't help laughing.

'Compared to you, I have hands like a baby. Do you have work at the moment?' he asks.

'Maybe helping to dig a trench. As soon as I'm up to it,' I reply sadly. 'I hurt myself falling into the hold of the *Rebel*. I'm also hoping to do the next halibut day. As soon as I have some money I'll join Jude.'

'Do you have somewhere to sleep?'

'Yes. I'm on the *Lively June*.'

He smiles again. I don't understand why.

'Is your name June too?'

'No. My name's Lili.'

'Come to the shelter if you have any problems. There are hardly ever women here. You'll be fine. A dormitory and four showers all to yourself. And a meal in the evening.'

'Yes, I know – Murphy told me.'

'I'll pass your news on to Jude as soon as he calls. Mail sometimes takes a real long time, you know.'

With one last look at my hands he adds, 'See you soon.'

Back outside, dazzling sunlight and the little white road. I come across two men heading off to the Shelikof with their sailor's bags over their shoulders, and I continue to the port. A Chevrolet pick-up heading towards me grinds to a halt, creating a golden halo of dust. Andy lowers the window and calls me over. I panic for a moment but he smiles, the set of his mouth looking carnivorous in his square jaw.

'Are you working? I'm looking for people to repaint the *Blue Beauty*. There's a good three weeks' work.'

'When and where?'

'Be at Tagura shipyard at seven tomorrow. The *Blue Beauty*'s in dry dock next to the apron.'

He drives off. I forgot to ask him for my cheque again.

I'm repainting the engine room and Andy's paying me six dollars an hour. The others get ten. I can hear them outside, scrubbing the hull, reconditioning the propeller and replacing zinc plates eroded by electrolysis. They talk loudly; sometimes they get beers and the sound of cans being opened carries to where I am.

After a while I'm in such a blur I can hardly hear them at all: the Trike used to degrease the bilge and the engines goes to my head, and the paint makes it worse. I wrap a scarf round my face but it doesn't block the fumes. When I ask Andy for a mask he gives me dust filters, but they don't work either. Sometimes I go out on deck for a breath of air; the light blinds me and I stagger. I have a coffee and a cigarette under a sky that seems to suck me in. Andy's promised me I can paint the mast if I work fast and well. I go back to the engine room to finish as quickly as possible, before he sends someone else up the mast. When the others leave I stay on board alone.

A dull thud on deck wakes me at five o'clock one morning. I pull on some trousers, go up and find a tall man standing in the galley.

'Hi,' he says, 'I'm Tom – a new recruit for the job.'

I go back to bed, fully dressed under the dirty covers. This new recruit pops his head through the half-open door and asks me three times whether I'm not lonely.

I keep telling him I'm not, then I sit up on my bunk and say, 'You're weird. Excuse me for asking such a dumb question, but are you on coke?'

'Coke? Do you know anything about it? No, I haven't taken any for at least two weeks.'

245

'I don't know anything about it, you're right. You're just weird, that's all.'

And I go back to sleep.

Tom is back from a month of pollock fishing: bad fishing, he tells me grimly. Mauve bags under his eyes, the same colour as his irises, make his eyes look disproportionately large and exhausted in his emaciated face. I'm mesmerised by his expression. His protuberant Adam's apple moves when he talks, a peculiar sort of bird imprisoned by the tendons in his thin neck. He sits on the rail and his legs jig nervously as if he's going to jump down onto the deck any minute.

'I wasted my time yet again,' he says. 'Didn't make any dough. It was almost lucky that we tore the net, gave me a chance to escape. Now this work for Andy ... I'll earn a few cents before going fishing again. And I can't wait, to be honest. It can get more tiring being ashore, what with dope and booze. But what can I do with this hunger? This fierce burning inside me? What can I really do to calm it apart from crush it? Exhaustion. Anything I can do to achieve that. The more violent the better.'

'So you're a hero too, then,' I say dreamily.

Tom sniggers.

'A hero?'

'Well, yeah, a mythological god, I mean.'

This time he laughs out loud and slaps my shoulder.

Tom teaches me to lift heavy weights by using my thighs as levers. We train on the bridge of the *Leviathan*, the neighbouring boat. One day I move a 700-pound crab pot from the fo'c'sle to the rail in little stints.

'Now you can go crab fishing on the Boring Sea.'

'Why the Boring Sea?'

'Because that sea sure can be rough, with troughs of thirty foot or more, but it can also bore you to death when it's dead calm, a real desert ... enough to make you put a bullet through your head. Rehab, that's another name for it.'

'Why rehab?' I ask, baffled again.

'Because it's forced withdrawal, from dope.'

'Aha. Do you think I'll get to go there? Do you think I'm up to it?'

'Stick to your guns, never give up, you'll manage like anyone else.'

One evening when I arrive back from Baranof Park there are two men on the boat, sitting at the table in the galley. One of them has a bald head that gleams in the neon light while he prepares his lines of cocaine. His thin plaited beard disappears between his thighs. I recognise the man who was shown out of the bar a few days ago. He rolls up a dollar bill and takes a long snort, turning towards me with glittering eyes and a slightly crazed expression.

'Want some?'

'Oh no,' I say, but I'm thinking yes.

'I've seen you out on deck a lot,' he says, his eyes blazing. 'I'm Blake. And I could show you things you've never seen before, you know. I could really make you scream if you just come along with me.'

Tom laughs and I sit down with them. The two of them talk boats, skippers and dope. A letter from the great sailor in my pocket is burning my thigh. Blake doesn't offer any more cocaine but starts rolling a joint of weed.

'Want some?'

'No,' I say, embarrassed. 'I pass out afterward.'

'Lightweight!'

I flush with shame.

When I open my eyes the next morning Tom says 'Good morning' from his bunk.

'Good morning,' I reply from mine.

And I go off to make coffee, singing.

The hull is freshly painted and covered in antifouling, and the propeller flashes in the sunlight. Tom has left for sea on another trawler. He gave me a high five and said, 'See you soon in Dutch, I'll buy y'a drink at the Elbow Room, every crabber's favourite bar.' I carry on alone, working long hours and late. Then I walk across town to the B and B, feeling a little disorientated. My stomach hurts and I'm very thirsty.

'Are they freshly painted too?' the waitress quips when I put my hands on the bar.

I have paint on my face, and strands of my hair are stuck together.

'You'll die if you keep going,' the guys around me say, concerned. 'Gotta wear gloves and not use the Trike to clean up. That shit's poisonous.'

I just laugh at them and order another beer.

It's pitch black outside when I weave my way back to the boat feeling light-headed, I could touch the stars. I fall asleep at once and I'm up again at six. While I drink a coffee I eye the mast – soon it'll be mine – before going back down to the engine room.

My stomach ache wakes me one morning. I get out of bed and the world spins – I only just break my fall by putting a hand to the wall. At lunchtime I go into town and eat sitting by the legs of the sailor lost at sea. Crows circle around me and I treat each one to a piece of surimi.

I bump into Virgil outside the coffee shop.

'Are you drunk?' he asks.

'No, it's the paint,' I say, rubbing my eyes.

'You gotta stop – you'll end up a vegetable.'

The thought makes me laugh but when I open my eyes again he's vanished. Tears spring up, I suddenly feel lost and stand there on the pavement, idiotically. A car comes to a stop and Brian leans out.

'Where are you headed?' he calls.

'I dunno.'

'Get in!'

I fall back against the seat, it has a nice smell of Old Spice after-shave. Brian looks at me in the rear-view mirror. I close my eyes.

'Are you feeling bad? What sort of shit have you taken?'

'I'm not on any shit, a few beers in the evening, and I don't even do that every day ... and I'm gonna be late for work now. I really have to finish the engine room if I want to paint the mast, you know.'

I open my eyes when the engine slows and see that we're at City Docks, near the *Venturous*.

Brian makes a coffee using the handsome espresso machine. He hands me a cookie and gestures towards the half-open cabin door.

'Now you're going to lie down and get some sleep.'

'Would you take me on as crew for your crab season?'

'We'll talk about that later. Go sleep!'

On my way back to the shipyard I meet Andy. He doesn't look happy to see me in town at this time of day.

'The painting's making me sick,' I mumble. 'Everything's spinning.'

He relents and gives me the day off.

'Drink milk,' he says. 'Lots of it. Sleep. And come back tomorrow. The engine room needs finishing as soon as possible.'

'Will I really paint the mast after that?'

The next day a man drops his duffel bag onto the deck.

'I've come from a long way away,' he says. 'Andy just took me on to repaint the deck. I hope it's gonna be OK because I haven't had any papers for a while. I'm Gray, by the way.'

And he really is completely grey, from his face to the tattered clothes bundled around him. His head is hunched between sturdy shoulders and his eyes look strange, soft as ice in sunlight.

'But you're not painting the mast?' I ask anxiously.

He mops his brow and doesn't answer, his few wisps of hair wafting in the breeze. He picks up his bag, goes into the cabin and throws his things onto the bunk at ninety degrees to mine. He unpacks a few clothes and takes out a Bible which he puts under his pillow.

'I'm Lili,' I say. 'I'm repainting the engine room. Help yourself to coffee. And the mast is mine.'

★

'Have a good evening, Gray. I'm off to do a round of the bars. There are some pretty good ones here.'

His strangely twinkling blue-grey eyes contemplate me kindly but his thick mouth has a severe set to it.

'I went through all that a long time ago. It's evil, it's not good for you. I know what you need ...'

In the doorway his hefty frame creates a barrier between me and the beautiful evening sky, the orange crane and the shimmering water beyond the apron. I slip through a gap and escape.

The wind is up and two drunken women are hurling insults at each other outside the B and B, their hair flapping in the wind like exasperated animals. I open the door and they follow me inside. I recognise a man sitting by the window – Dean, who worked on the *Blue Beauty*'s propeller. He's drumming his fingers agitatedly on the corner of a table, his knees jigging feverishly.

'Hi, Dean.'

'Oh ... Lili.'

His eyes sidle from me to the window, uncomfortable.

It's Friday, his payday. I lent him two hundred dollars when Andy finally paid me. I know instantly that he won't be able to pay any of it back, not today, not ever.

'You see,' he says, 'I have barely a hundred dollars left. And I'm waiting for this guy ...'

This guy – crack or cocaine? I give a shrug and walk to the back of the bar. Gus, the diminutive taxi driver, is sitting bright-eyed on a stool, talking passionately. He waves his arms around, his small child-like hands whirring faster and faster like spinning tops.

'I'm so mixed up in all this stuff!' he wails in his high-pitched voice.

Slumped on the counter next to him is Ryan: an old man with his glass of whisky, his beard yellowed by nicotine, his thick white hair framing handsome regular features. Joy the Redhead brings me my beer this evening. The two drunken women eye each other menacingly across the room. One collapses onto the jukebox then drags herself back to her feet. She manages to get back to the bar and clings to it as if it were a buoy, her myopic eyes completely obscured behind her glasses, which got twisted in her fall.

'She'd give a blow job to absolutely anyone! Five dollars a shot – anything to get a drink,' rails the woman who stayed standing, her beautiful green eyes flashing. 'At least I give them for nothing!'

Dean and his dealer look away. Dean has a hangdog expression and glances over at me as if trying to apologise.

'Cool it, girls,' Joy barks in her powerful voice, 'or I'll throw you out!'

The old man with the white face sits drinking next to me. He hands me a little bag full of dried sausage.

We eat without a word.

'I'm Bruce,' he says eventually.

The 'guy' has left and Dean has snuck over to me. I offer him a beer.

'I'm real sorry, Lili, I can't give you anything yet, I don't have a cent left. And tomorrow I'll probably be in jail. An old problem with the booze. It's been chasing my ass long enough,' he says, then laughs as he adds, 'Gotta say, it'll feel like a vacation ... a week of rehab. Clean, fed, housed, TV thrown in ...'

He orders two tequilas and we laugh together at last.

Two men with black hair come over to us.

'You're the chick who ate the raw fish in Terror Bay, right?'

I remember the seiner that dropped anchor not far from the *Milky Way*, the night I had raw salmon.

'Are you from the *Kasukuak Girl*?'

'Eating raw fish ... she'd make a good squaw,' the older of the two says, laughing.

Dean has slipped away. Things are getting heated between Bruce and Gus, the cab driver with delicate hands. Gus is yelling now, and when Bruce says they should have dropped an atomic bomb on Hanoi right at the start of the war, Gus knocks his glass over.

'Cool it, guys,' Joy scolds from the far end of the bar.

'Why would you say that?' I ask in horror. 'Why an atomic bomb? It was horrible enough already, wasn't it?'

'That's just it,' he replies quietly, almost inaudibly, 'at least it would have been quick. It would have avoided the napalm, the horror and the madness that just kept on going.'

'But, Bruce, why does one kind of horror always have to be replaced by another?'

Bruce spreads his hands helplessly.

'That's just how it is. Because the horror's just there, always.'

I don't reply but sit watching Bruce: he's gazing into the distance, his eyes thoughtful – or perhaps empty.

'I'd give my life, do you hear me?' he mutters. 'I'd give my life, right away, on this very bar, if I could stop someone else going through what I went through. My life's over. But if what's left of it could at least help to stop a single person seeing that stuff, dying of it ...' his voice trails off, then he turns to me and says, 'This isn't your thing. You, you have to go fishing.'

A powerful hand is laid on my shoulder, startling me. I twist myself free and recognise Glenn, the skipper on the *Leviathan*.

'Are you the one working for Andy? He's told me good things about you. How would you like to come paint the *Leviathan*?'

He's a tall man with a razor-sharp profile and fiery eyes, one of which is smothered by a bruise that runs from his cheek all the way up and along his brow bone.

'Ah, no, I can't ...'

He's pressed his hip against mine. I get up and put on my jacket.

'Where are you going?'

'Back to my bunk. It's late. I have to start early tomorrow.'

'Tonight you're staying with me,' he says, putting a hand on my wrist. 'That's how it is.'

I extricate my hand and slip away.

Dean comes out of the Breaker's as I walk past the deserted square. He comes over to me with a skip in his step.

'I'll walk you back. This is no time for a woman on her own. And all the way to the shipyard, too.'

He takes my arm but I pull it free and throw my head back laughing under the pale sky of a summer's night. He takes my hands and we both laugh, then I push him away and head home. Dead boats are silhouetted against the sea all along the wasteland of Tagura. Waves lap against the rocks. The wrecks look as if they've been stitched onto the shifting canvas of water. Every now and then a bottle top gleams on the road, like Tom Thumb's trail. I climb the ladder silently, step over the rail and drop down onto the deck without a sound. The Bible lies open on the galley table and Gray is asleep in the cabin, breathing heavily.

I've come up to get some fresh air and Gray is on deck painting the border on the coaming. He uses his brush slowly and precisely.

'One day I'll have a house of my own,' he says dreamily. 'I'll only ever paint it with a brush. It takes longer but it'll be perfect.'

He breaks into song and intones the words, '*Red is so pretty . . . so pretty.*'

The morning sun slinks over his neck and a breath of wind lifts his sparse grey hair. He's a good worker, patient. Paint has run down the handle onto his thick fingers, coagulating the black hairs. He clicks his tongue in irritation, breaks off for a moment and looks at his hands gleaming red in the sunlight.

'Do you like the colour red, too?' he asks in his muted voice. 'How about blood red, do you like that?'

I swallow self-consciously and finish my coffee, then go back down to my dark lair. The engine room is almost finished.

My stomach hurts when I go to bed but it's no longer because of the paint. Gray's hot heavy breath comes so close to me when he turns over in his sleep, and so do his quiet groans, the occasional moan, the hoarse breathing when he dreams. I get up silently, roll up my sleeping bag and carry it up to the wheelhouse. There I can see the night sky and, because it's raining, threads of water trickling over the windows. I go to sleep on the floor, my perennial bed.

Andy puffed out his chest and smiled.

'Now you can attack the mast.'

253

So I've attacked the mast. Beneath me, nothing, but beyond that, hard surfaces: starting with the deck, then dry land far below. If I miss my footing I'll fall. Lili flat as a pancake, splatted on the concrete. Gray should be happy, seeing he likes blood. I have to sand down the whole mast so I wrap one leg around the mast to hold myself in place and the other leg hangs free. I stretch to reach as far as I can, until I'm almost horizontal. It gives me vertigo but I soon gain confidence and it gradually feels natural, like an animal instinct. My body knows the laws of the different forces without my even having to think about them. The others are far below: poor things, I think, crawling around on the ground like ants ... Poor, poor things. I'm up in the air. It really is better up here. A young seagull, a dirty grey creature, watches me from the cross-pole of the boat's antenna. We eye each other for a while, then I go back to work.

Gray and I eat together at lunchtime. He takes out a hunk of bread and blesses it, then slices it with his old knife, its blade concave from years of sharpening. A drip of paint from the coaming has run onto its worn polished wood handle. Gray eats the bread with peanut butter and spam, grinding it in his great jaws wordlessly. I've made us some coffee. My wrists are hurting, and I spend a long time rubbing them. He looks up and studies his own hands with his grey eyes.

'Do you think I have powerful hands?' he asks in a distant voice, turning them over distractedly. 'I'm not sure myself ...'

'Oh yes, they're strong hands,' I tell him. 'What I do know is mine are hurting, and so's the whole rest of my body.'

'Pain is good ... pain is so good, isn't it?'

I shrug my shoulders and go back to play with the empty space beneath me ... the pleasure and pride of being perched up on the mast. The wind whistles in my ears. If I get it wrong I die.

I finished the mast and repacked my bag. Gray headed off with his bag, a small slow figure dwindling as he walked away, his back permanently stooped. Was his bag really all that full? His Bible all that heavy? For a moment I felt sorry for him.

The *Blue Beauty* was going back on the water. I watched the travel lift move along the side walls, the boat resting on huge straps, hoisted off the ground like a nut shell. The machine lowered her very slowly onto the apron so she could slip into the slack water at high tide. The *Blue Beauty* seemed to come back to life when she touched the water and my heart constricted – I wished I could be a boat being put back on the water. I tore myself away from the shipyard, suddenly feeling very low. I was frightened: there was no more work for me, I was nowhere again. The great sailor was waiting for me – but was he still waiting? Would Andy pay me this time? And when?

There was that abandoned truck by the shore so I walked through the tall grass, snagging on brambles. The front door was ajar: I stowed my bag under the seat and shut the door. I suddenly felt lighter – of course Andy would pay me and I'd go to Hawaii. I rejoined the road and went back to town, I saw the tall burly guy with the bald head and the plaited mandarin beard coming towards me.

'Hey, Lili. Still not ready for me to make you scream today?'

I laughed briefly.

'No, not today . . . I'm bored, the *Blue Beauty*'s gone back to sea and I'm lost. I want more work. I need to earn enough for my ticket to Hawaii.'

'Let's go get drunk! And then I'll surprise you.'

'I don't want to get drunk or go with you.'

'You disappoint me, Lili,' Blake sighed. 'Go along the Western Alaska wharf if you really want work, there's gear work on the *Boreal Dawn*. She's just back from the Pribilof Islands and is setting straight back out to Adak.'

The Pribilofs and the Aleutian Islands . . . I thought of Jude who longed to go fishing again.

'I've stayed on the rock too long,' I murmured, repeating words Tom had muttered one evening after coming home defeated once again, a haggard puppet imprisoned in his own pitiful body, suddenly sickened by his life ashore, the bars, the dope, the madness and excess . . . that furious urge to escape himself to find some sort of equilibrium.

I walked to the canneries where the *Boreal Dawn* was moored up next to the *Abigail*, her engines off. I stood motionless for a moment, bowled over: weighty and silent, dark and majestic on the pale morning water, she was as imposing as a cathedral. She was heading off fishing again soon and was far too beautiful for me, a skinny little woman with puny arms. A bright, lilting laugh from a man on the quay mingled with the bird calls. I felt like crying, as if I was losing the battle. There were always too many men, everywhere, I'd never be able to live my life like theirs. And I'd probably never go to the Bering Sea. Yet again I felt the humiliation of being a woman in their midst. They were returning from battle, I'd just arrived from the backstreets of the port.

The crew were slouched on metal seats. One of them looked up and gestured for me to come down.

'There's tons of work if you want to make a few bucks.'

Tina Turner was singing her heart out on deck. My own heart leapt with a furious burst of happiness. I grabbed hold of the ladder and went down to join them.

Nikephoros stops me just as I'm leaving one evening. He offers me a drink and invites me to play a game of pool. I'm terrible at it but when another guy comes over wanting to show me how to hold the cue, Nikephoros goes crazy. He hurls his beer can across the room and it skims past the copper bell, just missing the mirror. Joy the Indian has a screaming fit. The man beats a retreat. Nikephoros closes his eyes and takes a deep breath, his nostrils quivering like those of a crazed horse. I make myself as small as I can and slink back to my beer. Bruce smiles at me from the other side of the bar.

When Nikephoros has calmed down he tells me he'll build me a boat, he'll introduce me to his mother in Greece and she's going to love me, for sure, and we'll get married there, and then we'll stay together till death do us part – and he'll kill anyone who doesn't show me respect.

'Greece,' he says again, his dark eyes filled with the sad softness of black velvet. 'It's been over twenty years and I still miss it just as much. The smell when you walk in the hills and close your eyes ... You know you'll recognise every plant, every herb, every flower you step on because the sun pounds down so hard and the smells are so strong.'

'Yes,' I murmur, 'and the cicadas.'

'And the cicadas too, shrieking in the heat and light of the sun. The sun like a white knife between your shoulders ...'

The room has filled up with the crew of the *Mar Del Norte*, a trawler that's had a good haul. Joy rings the bell: drinks all round.

'Do you want to go Hawaii?' Nikephoros asks me.

Yes I want to go there, maybe, but not with him. So I leave.

The big urn of coffee and the cookies are still there when I walk into the shelter. Jude the elder is in the hallway and turns his penetrating eyes to me.

'Good evening, Lili. Tough day's work? News of Jude?'

I blush, again.

'Not for a long time,' I say quietly. 'In his last letter he said he was working hard. As for me, the *Blue Beauty*'s gone back to sea. I've done some baiting at the canneries and I've heard there's work on the *Alutik Lady* in the next few days. Right now, though, I'm here to see if I could sleep at the shelter.'

'You're not on the *Lively June* any more?'

'I could be if I wanted.'

He pushes the register across to me and I fill in a form. There's quite a crowd sitting at a table made of three planks resting on a pair of trestles on one side the hall. The men tucking into huge plate-fuls of pasta and mince move up to make room for me. I'm back home with my family, among my brothers; I was a bit late for the evening meal.

'Just in time for dinner,' says my neighbour, an emaciated man with a huge hooked nose and horse teeth. 'But the food's gone cold, you should put yours in the microwave.'

'I don't know how to work it,' I mumble, embarrassed.

The others laugh amicably and the tired old horse gets up and does it for me. I devour my food. Jude watches us eat from where he stands in the corner of the room, arms crossed and wearing the indulgent smile of a father surveying his brood. He cooks the meals himself.

'Where are Sid and Lena, and Murphy? And the big physicist? Do you know?' I ask Jude before we go up to our dormitories, the men to the right in a close-knit herd, me to the left on my own.

'Not yet back from Anchorage ... it's summer, they have to make the most of it. Murphy must be with his kids. Or at Bean's Café. And

Stephen – maybe he finally found his book, you know? The book that'll help him change the theory of relativity.'

'Yes, I know, he told me about it.'

It rains for three days and suddenly feels like autumn – the fall, as they call it. What is it that falls? The leaves, the light ... our own fall? The summer sun has burned our wings and we fall back to earth like Icarus. The light on the water in the port is a slap in the face, I'm alone on the docks and the streets are deserted. A cab waits outside the public toilets and the driver, a hefty red-faced man, has fallen asleep, his head tipped back. I walk across the square, the bland smell from the canning factories is heavier on the air today, it seems to seep from every building, but stronger smells roll in from the sea. The wind appears to be picking up – a north wind? – and the tide's coming in. There are two scruffy men on a bench hurling insults at each other, and from the Breaker's open doors I can hear bursts of conversations, shouts and the wailing jukebox. I cross the street, hesitate, then go in with my heart thumping. I slip to the end of the row of old Native women sitting in the shadows, upright and dignified as they contemplate their glasses of whisky. The last in the line greets me with a nod and I nod in reply. Her face is still carved of marble. She takes out a cigarette and brings it to her mouth with the tips of her fingers. The waitress comes over to her, behind the huge U-shaped counter with names engraved into it.

'Your taxi's here, Elena.'

The woman gets up, and the fat red man who was sleeping in his taxi gently takes her arm and helps her to the door. The other women haven't batted an eyelid. They just nod.

'Elena sure is tired today,' one of them says.

'Sure is,' the other replies.

I order a Bud and some popcorn, take a cigarette from the packet inside my boot and settle on my stool. I'll just blend in with the old women. You never know, some of the men might even be fooled, then they'll leave me in peace.

259

A hulking great guy puts his paw on my shoulder.

'Are you a Native, girl?' he asks.

'No,' I reply, turning to look at him.

'I'll buy y'a drink ... Rick. Crabber before the almighty Lord and every living thing.'

'Lili ... Li'l Lili before the Eternal Father, and one day I'm going crab fishing on the Bering Sea too.'

The man looks startled.

'I'll buy y'a drink OK, but not to listen to you talk garbage. Tell me about something else, your salmon fishing, your herring season, how tough it is on the trawler you work on – but not crab fishing, you don't know what it's like. Men lose their lives out there. Don't get involved in that men's stuff ... You're not up to it.'

'I did a black cod season on a longliner,' I mumble.

'OK, sweetheart,' Rick the crabber says, softening. 'But what the hell do you want to go there for? What are you punishing yourself for?'

'You do it, don't you? Why can't I?'

'You have better things to do. Having a life of your own, a house, getting married, raising kids.'

'I watched a film with my skipper – huge crab pots toppling in the swell, the ocean boiling; it was like being right inside a volcano, the waves were enormous black scrolls, like larva, never-ending ... it was calling me. I want to be right in there. That's where life is.'

The waitress brings us two beers and Rick sits in silence.

'I want to fight,' I rush on. 'I want to look death in the eye. And maybe come back. If I can.'

'Or not come back,' he murmurs. 'What you find won't be a film, but reality, the real kind. And it won't do you any favours. It's merciless.'

'But I'll be standing on my own two feet? I'll be alive? I'll fight for my life. That's all that matters, isn't it? Resisting, going the extra mile, overcoming everything.'

Two men have locked onto each other in the back room. The waitress yells at them and they calm down. Rick gazes into the distance, a very slight smile playing on his full lips.

'That's what drives us all to do it,' he sighs. 'Standing up to it. Battling for our lives alongside the elements, which will always be stronger. The challenge, going to the edge, dying or surviving.'

He rolls a ball of tobacco and slips it between his lip and his gum.

'But you'd do better to find a guy, stay warm and safe away from all that.'

'I'd die of boredom.'

'I'd have died of boredom too if I'd had to choose an easy job.' He drinks from his beer before going on. 'But boats don't really give you a life, nothing of your own, ever. You're just used from one job to the next. And constantly repacking your bag, repacking the pathetic bag of your life. Always starting over, every time ... it's exhausting at the end of the day. Soul-destroying and exhausting.'

'It must be possible to find a balance,' I say, 'between security, mortal boredom and a too-violent life.'

'There isn't a balance,' he says. 'It's always all or nothing.'

'It's like Alaska,' I suggest. 'Constantly tipping from light into darkness. The two are always racing, chasing each other, always wanting to get the better of each other, and we tumble from the midnight sun to the endless night of winter.'

As I leave the bar a black van comes to a stop, raising a cloud of dust. Nikephoros and his van, looking glorious, the pair of them. He leans out of the window and calls me, the mermaids on his arms seeming to writhe in the arabesques of waves when he ripples his muscles.

'Come for a spin with me, Lili! We can take this baby through its paces.'

'I'm supposed to be going to the *Alutik Lady*,' I say. 'There may be some baiting work there.'

'I'll take you there afterward, we'll just go for a quick drive.'

I climb in, the music's blaring. He hands me a cigarette and pulls away with a screech of tyres. I settle deep into the purple leatherette seat and we drive through town like lunatics, jumping three red lights in a blaze of headlights and slaloming between two children cycling. Nikephoros is exultant. The air streams in through the windows, and he hands me a beer that he's opened between his thighs.

'You have a beautiful van, Nikephoros.'

'I just arrived from Acapulco. I earned plenty this year.'

'Did you have good fishing there?'

He laughs quietly, his black curls dancing over his protruding forehead and tanned cheeks. His wide mouth opens to reveal bright white teeth.

'I went to sea when I was a kid, I left Greece at fifteen – I haven't stopped fishing since. I've done all of the seven seas ... I gotta take a vacation sometime. In Acapulco I jump off the big cliff for tourists.'

With these words he peels off his T-shirt and tosses it into the back. The tattoos on his arms continue all over his torso. He puffs out his chest, ripples his pecs, looks at me and smiles. We've left the harbour, driven past the coastguard base, Sargent Creek and Olds River, and we're following the road due south.

'Where are we going, Nikephoros?'

'To the end of the road. There's only one road anyway. Either you go north or south. I'm taking you to the sun. How d'you feel about Mexico? I'll show you the rock in Acapulco and I'll do the high dive for you.'

'Do you dive a very long way?'

He laughs again.

'Around 115 feet. The hardest part isn't the height, it's calculating how long you'll take so you get there at the same time as a wave ... if you miss it you get smashed on the rocks.'

'Oh! I thought I was tough when I was at the top of the mast.'

We drive for a long time, to the end of the road, then Nikephoros parks the van in a clearing. Douglas firs mingle with spruce and hemlocks. Purple catkins on the red alders hang in heavy clusters by the side of the track. A smell of moss and mushrooms rises in the fragmented golden halo of evening light. The music has stopped and we sit drinking another beer and smoking cigarettes on the edge of the deep, dark forest.

'It's so quiet, Nikephoros. Aren't there any birds?'

He's not listening to me. Eyes shining, he's put one arm around my seat and with the other hand he's stroking his handsome hairy chest, like a silky pelt. His smile has gone very dreamy.

'I should get back, Nikephoros. I have to go see this boat.'

'You want a boat? Choose one, I'll buy it for you. We'll go fishing together. You'll be the skipper, I'll be your deckhand.'

'I want to go back, come on, Nikephoros, start her up.'

It must be at least thirty miles to get back to town. I peer into the dense woods.

'Are there bears in there?'

Nikephoros doesn't reply. He's lit another cigarette and puts a hand on my shoulder. I feel a surge of anger, as violent as it is sudden. I open my door and jump out, slamming it behind me. I walk away, kicking petulantly at the stones on the track.

The van starts up at last and crawls behind me.

'Don't be mad, Lili. Get back in, quick!'

'Go fuck yourself!' I tell him, hurling a stone into the ditch.

The Man from the South is hurt. I can hear him yelling at my receding back, 'Fuck you! Come on, Lili, just come back!'

I stride furiously along the track and he keeps coming, making the engine roar, then calming it. I hurry on, afraid he'll run me over in his temper when he overtakes, reverse back over me – only trying to block my route. Then I look up at him, and all I want to do is laugh. I get back in the van. He's smiling too.

'That wasn't respectful, what you did there, Lili,' he says sternly, his frowning face concentrating on the road.

'But I do respect you, Nikephoros!'

He lifts a hand to silence me and hands me a mango he's taken from his bag.

'Could you cut it for us?'

I take out the knife I wear around my neck, slice two lozenge-shaped halves from the fruit and pass one to him. He smiles and asks me to bite into mine first. I bury my teeth into the sweet orange flesh, the juice runs down my chin. I hand him his half again and he bites into it, his eyes half closed. We drive home in silence, with me sitting up very straight, and both of us smiling.

'Why did you leave the *Kayodie*?' I ask when we pass the fuel docks.

Nikephoros laughs bitterly, his beautiful mouth swelling into a contemptuous pout.

'Cody's completely crazy,' he says. 'We were having a party in Izhut Bay when it happened again – one of his flashbacks. He didn't recognise me, he thought I was a Viet and started waving a knife at me. Three of us struggled to control him. I jumped on the first tender that came along and scrammed. What would you have done?'

It's too late to stop by the boat when Nikephoros drops me in the harbour. The water's motionless, bang on high tide. I walk along the quay towards the shelter, breathing the smell of mudflats. I look up at the rippling, reddening sky and watch a harrier's swooping flight as it skims very low over the mountain, wheels on its own axis for a long time, then drops to the ground with its wings raised in a 'V'. After that I lose sight of it.

The *Morgan* has left the shipyard. She went back on the water one clear morning in September. We're going halibut fishing in two days. I'm on the deck, baiting, when Conrad comes reeling onto the boat. He doesn't see me. I can hear him cursing under his breath. Two crewmen on the next boat laugh at him.

'Hello, Conrad,' I say shyly.

He's embarrassed. I laugh. He slumps heavily onto the hatch cover and rubs his hand vaguely over his waxy forehead as if trying to gather his thoughts.

'We're going to fill up with gas oil,' he says, 'that should straighten me out.'

I offer him a hand to help him to his feet, but he falls back down and we both laugh. Eventually he manages to stand up and goes to the galley. The guys next door wave to me when Conrad fires up the engine, and I start untying the moorings. We leave our berth and almost plough into three hulls. The *Morgan* zigzags its way out of the harbour and heads for the open sea. Conrad turns her and grazes past the buoy. I'm happy. The seagulls are drunk too, crying and circling in the light around the large white tanks. Conrad has pulled himself together and backs us uneventfully at the docks. We are the only boat there, though. I unscrew the cap on the fuel tank while Conrad finally manages to find the key. A dockworker hands me the pump and I slip it into the aperture and press the button. A geyser of gas oil squirts over my face.

'Looks like the tank was already full,' Conrad muses. 'Let's get some water, then.'

I wipe myself with a dubious-looking cloth. Clouds are still hurrying over the mauve mountains and puffins skim the tops of the waves. Long bird cries hang in the warm air. We sit on the hatch to the hold and Conrad hands me a beer.

'I'd forgotten how much I liked you,' he says with a belch. 'But I have a woman now, a kind girlfriend – her name's May.'

'Like the springtime?'

'That's right, like the springtime. But that's nothing to do with us: you and me are different, we're both artists,' he says, waggling his head. 'I'd like to give you the steel, and you'd build something with it. Something big. Huge.'

'Why steel, Conrad?'

He gives a great groan then a cry. His face contorts and he grimaces in pain. He looks as if he's crying, but just as suddenly he laughs and hands me another beer. A truck brakes violently on the dock, a few metres up from where we are. We see a woman climb out, her hair billowing in the wind. Conrad goes pale.

'Conrad! Drunk again. You've got one hour to get back home! Not another drop of whisky or even beer.'

The woman leaves as abruptly as she arrived, and the place is empty again. Conrad has put away the beer, eyes downcast, back stooped.

'Was that May?' I ask.

'Yes, that was May. Like in springtime. Untie us.'

I untie the moorings and we head home to the harbour. It's time for the shelter to open its doors.

I notice Aaron watching me walk up to the shelter and give him a little wave. When I reach the shelter the radio's warning of a tsunami; Dutch Harbor's been evacuated already.

'Let's all go to Pillar Mountain,' I cry. 'We can watch it come in.'

The boys agree.

'It's not here yet,' says Jude. 'You have to time to eat first.'

A group of Mexicans pose for a photo with their backs to the port. They ask me to stand at the front: we all smile at the camera and I picture the wave behind us, so huge, and these dummies still laughing when they're submerged. Aaron interrupts what we're doing and takes me back to his place, like a naughty girl caught hanging round somewhere she's not allowed to go. There's a pond, trees and a little hydroplane waiting among the water lilies.

'Is that plane yours, Ronnie?'

But Aaron looks at me grumpily and out of nowhere a dragonfly settles on his head. Aaron's wife shows me to a clean, tidy bedroom. I wait till they're asleep to run away in the night. The night watchman at the shelter lets me in, although it's way past opening hours. The boys are asleep in their overpopulated dormitory. The tsunami alert is over.

Ever since that day it makes me sad to think about the shelter. The call every evening at eight o'clock ... all that food hot and ready, waiting for us and us alone, meant just for us, us bums. The big cream cakes, the urn of coffee and the endless supply of cookies. The showers and clean sheets, the warm friendliness of the men, their loud yet tender voices, and their strong smell. When it comes down to it, it's depressing to learn you're so weak, so fragile, moved and disarmed by a helping of food – the abundance of it, such abundance and such warmth, and then me, off crab fishing soon . . .

So then I tell myself I really will have to go back to taking my chances sleeping in rusted old vehicles. For the sake of my pride, for Aaron and the others, I really have to.

It was agreed: I would do the halibut opening with Conrad. He arrived at six o'clock – I'd been up for a long time already. We left in the grey dawn, the port apparently still asleep. Once we were through the mouth of the harbour, though, we could see all the boats that had set off shortly before us swarming over the ocean. The wind had picked up in the night.

Conrad stands facing the dials in the *Morgan*'s tiny cabin and helms us. I watch in silence by his side. Sprays of water sweep across the windows, a flight of grey birds wheels ahead of us. On the radio Peggy gives us a weather report: warning of gusty wind, ten-foot waves rising to fifteen feet, a thirty-five-knot north-westerly strengthening through the day ... then there are fisherman talking to each other. OK, Roger, they always say.

'I didn't know there were so many Rogers here,' I tell Conrad.

He raises an eyebrow in surprise and laughs, but I don't understand why.

'This is where we're going,' he says pointing to a chart he's unrolled. 'Have to pass Spruce Island, Ouizinkie Harbor ... Shakmanof Point ... At midday we'll set the gear. Rising tide. We should find them ... Can you take the wheel?'

'I've never used a wheel. We had a joystick on the *Rebel*, and mostly autopilot for the greenhorns.'

''S not hard. First make sure you know your course ... then you only move the wheel when you feel you're getting on top of a wave. That's when your steering has the most effect on your forward momentum.'

I keep my eyes pinned on the compass. I can feel the rise of the waves against the wooden hull, the surge against the counterforce of the wind, which is against us, the moment when the *Morgan* reacts to a manoeuvre. The boat bridled at first but she's obeying me now and feels alive in my hands.

'One day I'll have my own boat, Conrad.'

He laughs.

'Just keep going like that. Do you want a beer?'

'No, Conrad. Not at sea.'

'Well, I'll make you a coffee then.'

I stay at the helm alone. The *Morgan*'s prow cleaves the grey water. Waves flow over the deck again and again. If I had the ice-cream baby I wouldn't be here.

Midday. We have time to sound the waters. On a signal I toss out a marker and a buoy, then the anchor. The first ten tubs unwind without a hitch. A quick hose down of the decks. Before I know it it's five o'clock. We stop for a break and the wind picks up.

'To be expected,' says Conrad, 'halibut fishing. We won't get that to calm down.'

He's been drinking steadily since this morning and is growing wobbly. I stiffen, straining towards the sea like a bowstring, more alive by the minute, growing increasingly tense as the time to bring in the lines draws near.

Conrad takes the outside controls in the recess of the wheelhouse. When the buoy appears between two troughs in the waves, I reach out the boathook and pull it back on board. I slip the buoy line into the reel and coil it up all the way to the anchor which I heave on board. The first lines bring in black cod, which we throw back. They're already dead and float away belly-up, buffeted by the waves, pale forms that sink languidly into the water. Seagulls and fulmars follow us, shrieking and dive-bombing to try to catch the dead fish. A demented wake in an increasingly leaden sky. I coil up the lines.

A fine rain has started to fall and now the first halibut comes aboard.

'Haven't you been taught how to do this right?' Conrad roars when I drive the gaff into its flank. 'You're ruining the fish! In the head, you should always put the gaff in its head. Otherwise the cannery black-lists us and takes a discount off our whole catch.'

I don't reply immediately, but look away. Ashamed.

'Yes, I knew that. But I was worried I'd miss it.'

'Right, get the gaff and your hook. The hook's for releasing your fish from the fish-hook on the line. With one hand you gaff it to bring it aboard, and with the other hand you use your hook to lever its mouth away from the fish-hook, a quick tug and it'll fall of its own accord. There, that's right, you got it …'

The halibut are here, Conrad's shouting and I'm throwing all my weight into heaving the fish out of the water and swinging them over the rail. These giants of the sea thrash the air with their smooth flat bodies, sloshing backwards and forwards across the decks. There's no end of them coming aboard now. The swell has grown with the strengthening wind, and the *Morgan*'s rolling heavily. Two halibut are swept away over the bulwark. I lean out over the black water, my face streaming, I'm in a muck sweat. The anchor looms up out of the waves, then the buoy line and the last buoy. Conrad whoops for joy.

'You've earned your plane ticket, more than earned it – and your Hawaii vacation, too!'

He disappears into the galley and comes back out with a beer in his hand, his eyes blurry. It's getting dark and the wind hasn't dropped, far from it. For a moment I think we've fished enough, that the sea is getting angry and we should stop. Do no more killing. I'm sud-denly frightened: Conrad will be drunk soon, and that's probably another thing the sea doesn't like. I grab hold of a halibut and grit my teeth, my hair dripping with seawater and rain. I take hold of it bod-ily and try to lift it onto the cutting table, which is just a plank nailed between the handrail and the edge of the hold. The fish is far too big and starts to slip from my grip, the swell makes me lose my balance and swills around the mass of bodies covering the deck, tripping me up: we fall together. But I don't let go. A strange embrace with the wind and water slapping into us in gusts.

I've already cleaned three fish, kneeling on the deck itself to work on them, but the *Morgan* is drifting. Conrad comes out of the wheelhouse, throws his empty beer can overboard, belches and turns to look at me.

'Not like that: you gotta get it onto the cutting board.'

'Sometimes they're too heavy, Conrad.'

'Lie them down on the table, then take a knife. Drive it into the belly, up to the gills, cut through the gills, up again – this membrane, here, from this side, to the other. And then pull, take out the lot, the stomach, the guts, it should all come out in one go. Then the balls, at the bottom ... that can be the hardest part. All that's left is scraping it out with a spoon. Five seconds it should take you, max.'

'I know, Conrad,' I mumble. 'I've seen it done. But I won't manage five seconds.'

He's not really listening to me, he's toppled to the decks with the halibut and paddles about on all fours, cursing and yelling.

'You're drunk, Conrad,' I scream through the noise of the waves.

'Drunk, me?' he says, getting back to his feet. 'I'll show you ...'

And now he's climbing onto the rail, trying to walk along it, arms spread like a tightrope walker, swaying between the deck and the black foam-topped waves. The boat rolls dramatically.

'Conrad! Get down from there. Please, Conrad!'

He sways from left to right, loses his balance, flails his arms, and falls ... onto the deck. I can breathe again.

'Gotta stop drinking, Conrad, gotta stop drinking at sea,' I say haltingly. 'Go get some rest, Conrad, I'll deal with the fish and then I'll make some coffee. We'll have our coffee, Conrad, then we'll pull in the other sets.'

Conrad gets to his feet.

'I've been fishing all my life,' he thunders. 'All my life I've fished, and now you, a skinny little foreigner from some back of beyond place, want to teach me my job?'

'Yes, Conrad, no, go lie down, please.'

Conrad goes in. We're drifting.

The moon has risen, lighting up the decks strewn with bodies still wracked with spasms. Their naked white side, the sightless side, is turned towards the moon. It seems to undulate with the swell and

271

the bodies – almost corpses now – sweep the deck, slewed from one side to the other against the *Morgan*'s edges. The bulwark's too low, every now and then letting a body slip over the rail. If the fish is still alive it snaps furiously back to life, diving down into the depths from which it was torn. If it's dead and gutted, it's carried by the high, powerful waves. It sinks slowly, a white shape gradually fading in the darkness of the water. I gut the fish that I've managed to lie on the plank of wood. Even opened up, they still twitch. They need to die more quickly, they need to die before my knife gets them. Conrad's simmering on his bunk. Or is he still drinking? I'm wading about on deck. Slime and guts from the fish cling to the hair that's escaped from my rain gear. I try to grab a halibut in my arms – some of them are as big as I am – delving into its gills with one hand, the other clutching its smooth body. Then I have to heave it onto the cutting table but it escapes my clutches, convulsing spasmodically. I fall with it, smeared with blood. It's an exhausting struggle, clasping this fish and dragging it through the acrid smell of salt and blood. When I finally succeed, I bleed it, a deep jab of the knife in its throat, I cut into it from the arc-shape of the gills, which can clamp down on my hand and – even through my glove – take the skin off it. I gut the huge body that still puts up a fight, and the process makes a strange noise – the screech of silk being torn. The fish struggles, bucking furiously, its tail thrashing frantically and splattering me with blood. I run my tongue over my lips, I'm thirsty, the taste of salt ... The knife continues its fierce progress, turns in the very depths of the belly, comes back up the vertebrae all the way to the gills again. Then with one swift movement I tear out the huge parcel of innards and lob it into the sea. The seagulls circle, screaming, trying to grab the intestines on the wing or diving into the waves ... I still have to find the testicles, like two eggs buried deep in the abdomen, swaddled in cartilage and flesh. Scrape off the compact black blood that's collected along the backbone. The halibut squirms with each stroke of the scraper. I tip it down into the fish hold. It falls back onto the deck and gets lost among the others.

This hand-to-hand battle with the dying has me sweating copiously. Gusting waves lash my face, dribbling right down my neck, insinuating themselves inside my rain gear. The wind roars in my ears, it's blowing hard now. The *Morgan* disappears in the trough of each wave, and the moon tips behind the water only to reappear moments later. The ocean turned upside down, the sky toppled over. A small dark red heart carries on beating on the cutting board, palpitating in the imperturbable halo of the dancing moon, naked and alone amid the blood and intestines, as if it hasn't yet realised what's happened. And then I just can't bear it, I was about to throw it into the sea with the rest of the guts, but not that, no, I can't. My face daubed with tears and blood, that taste of salt on my lips – and blood too? In my distress I remember my first halibut, killed on the decks of the *Rebel*: I grab the heart and swallow – now I can feel this beating heart warm inside me, and within my own life I can feel the life of the great fish I've just hugged to me to make it easier to disembowel ...

What's Conrad up to? I'm scared.

I gut the biggest of the halibut kneeling on deck. Through heavy half-closed eyelids they watch me in disbelief – perhaps that's what it is. There, there, I murmur as I run my hand over each smooth body, still crying a little, eating each beautiful dying creature's heart. And then I stop falling over, and stop crying, and just do my job. The hearts that I gulp down one after the other form a strange ball in my stomach, an icy burning sensation.

The last of the halibut have gone into the hold, lying on their dark side so as not to mark the flesh. I've broken up the ice with a pick to fill their abdomens and cover their bodies, and I'm now back inside. Conrad's snoring on the bench seat. I light a cigarette and make some coffee, then I wake Conrad. He's feeling better so we head off to the next marker. Conrad grabs a beer.

We have trouble finding the buoy, a dull red dot that disappears between the waves. I stand against the rail holding the gaff, my swollen knees smacking against the hard wood to the rhythm of our listing. I reach out to gaff the buoy and almost manage it when Conrad steers us away again. When it goes wrong for the third time I push him out of the way without even thinking, and take the helm. He steps aside. I straighten the boat's prow and turn her slightly to starboard.

'Take over again, Conrad.'

I pluck the buoy from the water with a brisk flourish and grab the buoy line to slip it into the reel. The wind is head-on, skinning us alive. The rain has started again all the harder and the moon has shrouded itself in cloud. What the hell is the time in this dense darkness? Conrad is silent. The boat moves slowly in the same axis as the mainline. And still the halibut keep coming aboard. They're sloshing across the deck again, aggravating the listing, and swilling back in quick bursts to thump us in the calves. My battered knees knock the sides regularly. Conrad's at the helm, I'm gaffing. Our faces streaming under the dark sky, overwhelmed. Clouds chase each other, white birds circle and swoop in their shrieking flight. The line stops.

'Are we caught on the seabed, Conrad?'

The boat turns, imperceptibly. Both of us leaning over the dark water, peering into the eddies. Something is caught in the line, a big pale body. Conrad lifts it up. As best he can. A large fish tail emerges from the water, a blue shark caught in the longline.

'Pass me the gaff hook – and a knife.'

'A shark, Conrad. Is it really a shark?'

'Pass me a knife, for God's sake.'

'What're you going to do?' I ask.

'I have to free up the line, have to slice off its tail.'

'Will it die?'

'It's dead,' he says flatly.

I heave the amputated tail on board.

'Ditch it.'

'Not yet,' I insist.

The lifeless body sinks slowly. And the last buoy appears.

Ink black. It's very late. We've finished cleaning the last of the halibut, and the hold is three-quarters full. We let out the last ten longlines and I clean the decks.

'Stop that,' Conrad says. 'The sea will do everything for us. We should be having something to eat, I put a cod to one side. Come on.'

Our soaking rain gear is lying on the floor and Conrad has cooked the cod. I'm kneading my hands, which are slashed from my wrists to the tips of my fingers, and Conrad is picking his teeth.

'We have a choice now: either we go back to work straightaway or we take a few hours' rest.'

'It's your decision, Conrad.'

'Let's sleep. Two hours. We sure have earned it.'

He takes out a bottle of whisky and takes a slug of it then winds the alarm clocks. I pull my sleeping bag over my head, my cheeks itching with dried blood. I'm shattered, my body beaten. Two hours, I think. Two hours to sleep. How wonderful.

We're drifting.

I hear the alarm clocks but Conrad doesn't stir. A bit longer, I think, just a little bit longer ... I go back to sleep for another two hours, then I wake first. The fuel stove is purring and on it sits a coffee pot and the remains of some coffee as thick as tar. I pour myself a cup. My face is burning, and so is my body – it's too hot. Cold and dark outside the misted window, spattered with squalls of water. I go out onto the bridge, currently being washed by great sweeping waves. The air is raw, an icy burn in my nostrils and lungs, and on my skin. The wind seems to have relented slightly, the boat's drifting gently. The empty tubs haven't moved, secured tightly to the fo'c'sle. The huge blue shark tail which I tied to the anchor bounces with every jolt of the waves, a barbaric, ghostly figurehead. I go back inside and make more coffee. I shake Conrad for a long time before he surfaces.

'It's time, Conrad.'

Mechanical work. Automaton movements. Wind in our faces. The halibut have vanished with the turn of the tide. From time to time a solitary fish, its eye sockets empty, writhing with sandflies. It's still cold and dark. The water whips against us head-on and infiltrates our rain gear. Conrad crushes starfish angrily against the sides. Their huge monstrous mouths, which look as if they're suckling on the fish-hooks, split open on the dark wood. They litter the decks with shreds of pink-and-orange flesh. Conrad hasn't spoken since he woke, his face colourless, rinsed of life by exhaustion, his lips clamped in a thin bitter line. He occasionally stops the reel, lets the engine idle and looks at me in exasperation.

'Wait a minute,' he says and goes into the cabin.

The darkness is paling. On the misty horizon we'll soon be able to make out the dark shadow of the coastline, the dense black woods of Kitoi, to the north. Conrad reappears looking calmer, his eyes unfocused.

'I'll be back, Conrad ... it's my turn to go in.'

I find the bottle lying on his bunk, and hide it under the pillow.

The choreography of starfish lacerated on the bulwark has started up again. Conrad stops the line and goes back to the cabin but this time he takes longer. I glance through the window: he's found his whisky and is drinking with helpless abandon, head tipped back, eyes half closed. I can't restrain myself any longer: I storm inside and snatch the bottle from him.

'No, Conrad, no, that's enough!'

I go out and hurl the bottle into the sea. Conrad is ashen, a dribble of whisky still running down from his half-open mouth. He comes to with a start and curses.

'You stupid little hillbilly,' he screams, 'trying to teach me how to fish! Little idiot stealing my bottle.'

I hear a dull thud. The waves against the hull make a furious panting sound. I let myself drop down onto the lid of the hold. And then I cry. Greenish tears surround the *Morgan*, toying with the little boat. I think about the great sailor, about him lying on top of me and his lion-like breathing and his mouth feeding me drink, in Hawaii, which I'll never see, the ice-cream baby we now won't make. I sob in the rain in the grey dawn. The sky is heavy and malevolent. I'm aware of the beautiful giants of the sea underneath me, lying on their bed of ice, wrapped in their bloodied shroud. The engine purrs. We've done too much killing. The sea, the sky and the gods are angry.

I'm cold and hungry. I go into the galley and find Conrad kneeling with his face on the floor and his behind in the air as if prostrating himself at Mecca. But what exactly is his Mecca, and what's he doing here? Maybe he's sleeping? I sit at the table, grab the bread that has rolled onto the floor and take a bite out of it. Conrad moans softly.

'Come on, Conrad,' I almost whisper. 'We have to get back on deck, we have to haul the gear.'

I eat my bread as if it were the last scrap of food left on earth, the only thing that really matters. The boat drifts. Conrad's still moaning.

'Come on, Conrad …'

I get up, go over to him and pat his shoulder gently.

'Need to get the gear back on board, Conrad.'

'Have I lost you? I've lost you, Lili.'

'No, Conrad, you haven't lost me, no one can lose me, but we have to get back to the fishing.'

'I need help,' he wails, still with his backside in the air and his face crushed against the filthy floor.

I keep on chewing assiduously.

'We all need help, Conrad, but please, please get up. We have to bring the lines in right now; we only have a few hours left before midday.'

Conrad lifts his head. Still kneeling, he gives one last, long moan. I help him stand up and guide him over to the table, where I pour him a coffee.

'It'll be over soon, Conrad,' I tell him. 'We can go back to Kodiak and rest, I'll even buy you a beer at Breaker's if you like.'

'Let's end it all now. We can cut the lines. We've done enough. We're going home.'

'No, Conrad, we're bringing everything back on board. Just a few more hours.'

Midday. The gear is all on board. The fishing window is over and we're heading home. Conrad has given me the helm. He opens a beer.

'Do you hate me?' I ask him.

'What about you? Don't you hate me?' he replies.

'Next time we go fishing you teach me everything first, how to handle the boat, the hydraulics, how to use the radio too – basically everything. Then you can get as drunk as you like. If you'd fallen overboard, I couldn't have done anything.'

The wind will have dropped completely by the end of the day. As we reach the canning factories I call Conrad. He's fallen asleep on the bridge, butt naked on the white bucket that acts as a toilet. He takes the wheel disconsolately. A line of boats is already waiting to unload. I've readied the mooring lines and taken out the fenders. We moor up gently next to the *Indian Crow*. The queue of boats is long; it won't be our turn to unload until tomorrow. I will have gone by then, and I'll never know how many tonnes of prey our halibut hunt constitutes. Conrad has regained his assurance, the probing eyes of a landlubber and businessman. We sit down at the table and he takes out his wallet. His washed-out features are grim proof of exhaustion. He signs a cheque and hands it to me.

'Will that do?'

'Yes,' comes my murmured reply, 'that'll do.'

We were going fifty-fifty, that's what he said. We must have taken a good four thousand pounds, surely? Most likely more, much more. We were going fifty-fifty ...

'Thank you, Conrad.'

I step over the *Indian Crow*'s rail with my rain gear rolled up in a black sack. The bridge is deserted, but the radio's still on and the door open. I climb the ladder up to the wharf and start to run, taking huge strides, my legs carrying me almost in spite of myself, supple and powerful. Up ahead, the seagulls, the harbour – and on I run – the misty sky and the wind. Virgil is back. I climb over the rail and knock on the window, out of breath. He comes out and smiles at me.

'So, kid, was the fishing good?'

'Look at my hands,' I say, breathing heavily.

He takes my swollen hands and holds them in his.

'Good girl. Come have a drink, I'm paying.'

We walk into Breaker's, the place is screaming noisy and full to bursting. I go up to the bar, head held high, and put my beautiful fisherman's hands onto the counter, shapeless paws I can't even bend any more. I'm not afraid of anyone now, and I drink like a real fisherman. Tomorrow Hawaii and the great sailor.

Lili my love, you won't get this letter if you're on the plane tomorrow. It won't matter any more anyway. I'm quitting a job at a sawmill today and going to look for a cheap room on the docks in Honolulu. The money's not good enough and there aren't enough shifts. I'm one of the best workers in the developed world but the guy I was working for couldn't see what he had. If you get here before I leave I can do what I want most in the world: be with you. But until we meet up, if we ever do, come looking for me in the crummy dives, the seedy hostess bars and Pacific soup kitchens.

I'm going fishing again. I don't yet know where or who for. My pay cheque should be enough for a flight to Oahu, a little room and a week's stay. After that, I'll have nothing left. Just my hunger to fish again. There's no point sending me anything now — letters, money, food or rum. I'm happy. Broke, out of work, on the street soon, but with my one and only reason to live at last.

I wish I could have come back for the halibut window. But too little time and not enough dough. One guy told me about a huge fishing operation around Singapore (maybe for another day). I haven't yet been across the equator in a boat, or sailed beyond 180°.

Lili, I really wanted you to come. You're the only person who could still make me change my mind, change where I have to go now. I waited a long time for you. I have to go now. You're in my thoughts. All the time. I'll keep you posted. Maybe I'll work on a local boat for a few days. Maybe we can still meet up, hire a crappy little place at Waikiki or in Chinatown, and try to make a baby — our ice-cream baby. I'm sure you'll have news of me next week — I'll be trying to find crewing work. Unless someone suddenly tells me, Get your ass over here, we're leaving in an hour . . .

Come looking for me in Oahu, ask for Jude at Susan's auction house. Look after yourself. I'll keep you posted.
Jude.

The ferry's still calling to me, its horn blaring in the dark: Come, Lili, come. And here I am, grounded in the port. Boats come and go. The great sailor writes to me from Honolulu: Come, Lili, come. We can still make our ice-cream baby. And here I am tied to the docks like an ailing boat. Sitting on the wharf with the street behind me, the launderette, the overpriced showers, the coffee shop with the pretty waitresses; further on, the bar and the liquor store, then the Alaskan Seafood canneries. Before me, the harbour, the fleet of boats setting out and returning. Eagles soar in a too-white sky, seagulls come and go, calling, taunting or lamenting, a racket that drags on with a weary shrillness, swelling then dwindling mournfully.

And I'm good for nothing. Watching boats leave, tides die and come to life again, listening to the ferry boom twice a week: Come, Lili, come ... Rereading the great sailor's letters scribbled on the back of old bits of paper stained with grease and beer: Lili, my love, come ... Watching seagulls, eagles, boats.

The island has closed its arms of black rock around me. The green embrace of the hills looms over me, silent and bare. Flowering fireweed undulates like a tide of mauve. The shadow of a sailor who lay down on top of me never left me when he went off in that soft, soft rain, on a white ferry in the densely black night. It walks alongside me when I trail through these streets populated by great tall men in boots who live from one boat to the next, then reel from one bar to the next, before heading back out to sea with supple balanced steps.

Night falls again. It's high tide and I walk along the deserted dock, take the last pontoon and follow it all the way to the blue seiner, the *Lively June*. The much-loved smell of diesel and wet rain gear, of coffee and jam. I'm not hungry. I go to my bunk and lie down against the rough wooden flank of the prow. It's dark. I look up and see the lights in the port dancing and throwing shadows. I see a huge, dark sky through the portholes. I listen to footsteps reverberating on the pontoon, bursts of conversation, the soft panting of the rising tide against the hull. It's that time of day when the *Arnie* goes out, the sound of its engines surges then dwindles, and then I know the tug is beyond the mouth of the harbour. I lie there motionless with my eyes open and sigh. The ferry calling in the night. The evening he left, the evening the great sailor left, the ferry gave this same heartbroken cry, the faraway sound of a horn calling in the mist, sadly, so sadly. Come, Lili, come.

Will I ever leave again?

I walk another twenty metres along the dock. The old seiner in turquoise wood hasn't moved at all since we left. Aaron's old boat where he took me once when my promised crewing job had fallen through.

I find the key hidden under the rim of the flying bridge. The door is even more swollen, it sticks and creaks. I go down the three narrow steps and here I am back in the dark den. It smells of diesel as usual. I open a cupboard: there's some coffee left, a tin of fruit, three tins of soup. Some cookies. I lob my sleeping bag into the front of the boat, onto one of the narrow bunks, which grow closer and closer together between the damp walls, all the way to the bow. Balancing on the edge of a berth, I open out the folding chair and heave myself onto it. I sit looking at the monitors with my legs dangling. In front of me is the mountain, imposing and very green, below it masts, boats, the red tug that goes out every night – and that's when you hear its engine coming to seek you out even in your dreams – as well as the docks and the pontoon which leads up to the bars in town. All around, everywhere, seagulls. Overhead, eagles. Between them, the crows.

The road is white with sunlight. It's low tide and to one side of the road the embankment of earth and rock is stripped down to silt. At the end of the road three men are sitting on the green bank leaning against the small square building of the public toilets and the taxi office. Guys from the square. They're waiting. For days, weeks, whole seasons, until it's time for the shelter to open its doors at six o'clock in the evening, and then there's food, coffee, cookies, warm showers and a dormitory. From far off I recognise Stephen, the stocky, greying little man – he once told me he was a researcher, a great physicist – he's waiting for a book, the book that his daughter's meant to be sending him, but never does. What the hell's the girl up to, has she forgotten her own father? With him is a tall, thin gloomy Native man and a blond guy with a devastated expression. Fat Murphy joins them. They cast black shadows on the green bank. Eagles alight on the ground.

Guys from the shelter. They wait in the square and on the banks of the port too. They get pretty bored. They gave up on fishing long ago. Every now and then they go from one boat to the next to bait tubs; it earns them a few cents, for alcohol, or crack. Then they drink to pass the time. They scrounge off anyone coming back from the sea – if the fishing's been good people shell out without thinking. The guys from the square and the fishermen have the same faces: a little redder and more worn among the former, a few more Natives among them, and women too. The women are very tired, they fall asleep a lot, their heads resting on the shoulder of someone who hasn't toppled over yet, hasn't rolled under a bench or into a flowerbed, or to the foot of the embankment when the tide's out. Drink or crack. The great sailor was friends with all of them, they all knew him and respected him.

The great sailor used to take me to motels. He lay me down on a bed. And lay on top of me. Tell me a story, he used to say. Oh God, he murmured. The shadow of a fragile, incredulous smile flickered over his ravaged face. Tell me a story. You're the woman I want to spend the rest of my life with. I want to fuck you, love you, be with you always, just you. I want to have a child with you. Tell me a story …

He was big and heavy on top of me, slow and burning inside me. Yes, I whispered, yes. I had no stories to tell. Tell me a story. Yes,

I said. His eyes made of jewels on me, his eyes made of daggers and a savage kind of love, his yellow wildcat's eyes that never let me go until I foundered. I want it to kill me, I said. And then he would kill me, for a long time, his powerful sturdy thighs, his rock-like back, the spear he drove into me, plunging his love into my pale smooth belly, my narrow hips, like two wings pinned down, pinioned against those white sheets smeared with ice cream. Those feral eyes wouldn't leave me, as he harpooned me in that calculated way, the slowness of it, the burning. His mouth dived at my neck, a carnivorous kiss that made me quiver, my whole life going through me in a long shudder, all the way up to my throat, which might well have been tipped back, offered up to his teeth, with him as the lion and me the prey, him the fisherman and me the white-bellied fish.

It's night again and the tide draws out. A bird cries on the jetty. I hear the ferry's horn.

I met the great sailor at sea. He shouted at the waves, grey waves in the daytime, black if it was night – 'Last tub!' or 'Anchor over!' – and he bellowed against the racket of the engine, when our roaring wake swallowed the dark anchor beyond the end of the last longline, against the wailing of seagulls tracing the shape of our wake in the sky. The black steel boat picked up speed. And still the great sailor shouted. With his chest puffed out wide, his powerful, terrifying voice would give one final roar. He shouted, alone against the waves, standing up to the vast ocean, dirty locks of salt-stiffened hair blowing across his forehead, his skin red and swollen, his features burned, and his eyes yellow, lit up like a wild animal's. He frightened me then, he always frightened me, I stood in his shadow, ready to eclipse myself, to disappear if he took the smallest step back. I followed his every move, moved the heavy tubs of longlines that made me totter under their weight, hooked a bag of rocks to each one, tied them together with a sheetbend knot that he always checked, without a word, and never a smile.

★

I dreamed it was happening all over again. The cold, the water in our boots, the nights spent fishing, the sea dark and violent, like black lava, my face daubed with blood, the smooth pale bellies of fish that we sliced into, the *Rebel* even blacker than the night, roaring, ploughing deeper into icy velvet, guts strewn over the decks. Hours went by one after the other, time didn't mean anything any more. The great sailor shouted, standing alone, confronting the ocean. And I'd made up my mind that that was how it would always be, motoring on, through the ink and velvet of the night, behind us our wake of pale birds, and more of the same to the point of exhaustion – staying with this shouting man, so that I could see him and hear him forever, and follow him in his single-minded pursuit – but touch him? No, never, I didn't even think of touching him.

One day perhaps the season would end and everyone would leave the boat. But I'd forgotten about that.

Nikephoros swam out to sea. This evening his funeral will be held in the bar. An Orthodox priest will come. We'll all bring things to eat and we'll drink late into the night.

He'd smoked a few joints of crack with Brian, the sailor from the *Dark Moon*. They sat down on the jetty with the sun sinking behind them. Nikephoros crushed out his cigarette between his fingers and turned to Brian.

'I'm tired,' he said. 'I think I'm really too tired. I'm out of here. I'm going home.'

And he let himself slip down into the water. Brian couldn't hold him back. Nikephoros swam straight for the horizon. Brian dived in to catch up with him, tried to bring him back.

'Leave me,' Nikephoros said. 'If you're my friend, let me go.'

And Brian let him go. His red hair hanging limply around his dazed, defeated face. He didn't stop drinking for three days and didn't want to set foot on the *Dark Moon* again. He bellowed and sobbed and railed.

Ryan, the tired man who was baiting on his worn old boat one summer's day, scooped me up as I came out of the bar one of those evenings.

'Where are you going?'

I'd had too much to drink. I clung to the edge of the wharf, looking out at the black water, wondering whether Nikephoros had got home or was still swimming.

'I don't know,' I said. 'I'm scared to go back to the *Lively June*. Maybe I should try to find Nikephoros.'

With that he took my hand.

'Come,' he said. 'You're tired.'

We walked along the pontoon and I let go of his hand. A bird flew up from the mast when he stepped over the side of the *Destiny*. The rustle of wings made me shudder. Ryan reached out his arm to me and I followed him. It was dark and dirty inside the cabin. The radio was turned down low. I stood motionless in the dark, hesitating.

'Take your boots off.'

Ryan lay me down gently on a mattress cluttered with old bedding. He pulled his sleeping bag over me, took his clothes off and lay down next to me. My heart pounded. I was afraid of dying alone, like a rat, holed up in a cold bunk. I heard the *Arnie* setting off in the dark, the *Tustumena* calling to me. I huddled close to him. In the dark I put my hands on his tired face. He had a soft silky chest and his blond hair gleamed in the shadows. He didn't touch me.

'Sleep now,' he said.

I took his hand. Then he rolled over and I rolled over too, towards his huge back. I held him tight, my legs bent into the crook of his, hugging his big body. Something fell onto the deck. The wind was picking up again.

'It's blowing hard out there,' I murmured. 'Do you think it'll be a problem for him? Do you think he's home yet?'

'Who do you mean?'

'Nikephoros,' I breathed.

'Everything's fine,' he said. 'Just don't listen to the wind.'

He turned towards me, put one arm over me, covering my ear with his hand. I sniffled. The bunk was too narrow for two. I was a bit squashed and so hot I was suffocating.

'Ryan,' I said shyly, 'I'm waking you again, but it's making me sick to my stomach. I think I'm going to be sick.'

'You're not going to puke here?'

'No, no.'

'Well then, go out, put two fingers down your throat and puke overboard.'

I sat up. Perched on the edge of the bunk in a semi-torpor, I let my eyes wander. The lights from the docks looked pretty through the filthy old wooden window. I felt very alone. I got to my feet and fumbled in the dark till I found my boots.

I went to the very end of the dock and sat with my legs dangling over the black water. I dipped them in to cool them. Seagulls appeared as pale smudges on the jetty. Were they asleep? I thought of the great sailor. Of this bare world and us in it. 'Nothing, nobody, nowhere,' I murmured. But I was in the middle of it and still alive, still living. And strong. So strong. The lights from the port danced on the dark water.

I stood up again and walked along the pontoon, up the footbridge and along the quay. The town was deserted. I walked on to the jetty for the ferry; the *Tustumena* had left. I set off along the road to Tagura. Boats slept in the shipyard, resting on their stilts as if on ancient columns. The ocean glittered under the moon. The regular sound of the waves filled the world. I kept going, following the shoreline to the Salvation Army. And the Beachcomber on the other side of the road. The building loomed naked in the moonlight, but the large fresco on the wall that faced out to sea looked even wilder at this time of night. The boats and waves really seemed to be moving. They reminded me of Nikephoros's tattoos when he rippled his muscles under his skin. The rusting old trucks hadn't moved. I tugged at the door of the first one. It resisted and then opened, the window was broken. I curled up into a ball inside. It smelled of mould, and the seat was saggy and damp. I felt cold thinking about Jude, and Nikephoros, who was still swimming – where was he now? – and my shipwrecked man in Manosque-les-Sorrow. I could hear the sea sighing. Where were they all right now?

It was getting light. I'd been awake for a long time already. Curled up tightly, with my hands kept warm against my stomach. An orangey light came streaming into the truck. I looked out: an incandescent buoy cleaved the ocean, which seemed to be trying to hold it down. Up it climbed, and up, tearing itself away from the ocean, suspended on the horizon before rising still higher. The wall painting seemed to come to life, blazing with the yellowish light bouncing off the sea. I sat up and black and orange dots danced behind my eyelids. The tide was right out, the sea gone. Yes, even the sea had gone. A light breeze whipped up short waves far out in the bay. The sound they made as they died away on the beach reached me, a regular beat, and far in the distance that soft panting, like a summons, the chatter of a bird joining a group of oystercatchers, their red legs glowing against the white sand.

I stretched, my body was stiff. I was hungry. I walked into town, where life was starting up again in the streets. I bought a coffee and a muffin from the coffee shop on the quay, which was just opening. Sat down on my bench. A crow came over, then another, waiting for some muffin. A shadowy shape lay on the memorial to sailors lost at sea. Sid, Lena? Maybe they were back. Or perhaps the Native with the slashed face? Someone. For a moment I thought of Nikephoros. I didn't dare go to have a look.

I gathered up my few belongings on the *Lively June* and packed my bag again. Point Barrow or Hawaii? It didn't matter much now. The one would always lead me to the other. The *Tustumena* would be here in two days. I thought I might wait for it on the quay, and sat myself down on the jetty. It was a long wait. I was hungry for popcorn.

I walked for a long time, to Monashka Bay, then Abercrombie, the end of the road. I kept going and reached the cliff. I walked into the wind, hoping it would take me with it. A flight of fulmars skimmed past, almost touching me. Their shrill cries wrapped around me and then were gusted away in the roar of the wind, the wild panting of the rising tide as it crashed into the cliff face. I looked far into the distance. Before me, the ocean. It quivered all the way to the horizon and stretched to the very ends of the earth. I wanted it to swallow me up. I was reaching the end of the path. Now I had to choose.

I waited a very long time. The sun went down. In town there were bars, glowing red lights, men and women, living, and drinking. I wanted to get closer to the water, but my foot caught in the root of a stunted, twisted little pine tree. My fall threw me so far I thought I was flying, but at last I touched the ground. Pain in my knee and a gasp of fear shot through me like a burning lance. The cliff edge was only metres away. I folded my knees against my chest, put my arms around them and pressed my forehead onto my thighs so I couldn't see any more. The sound of breakers filled my head. I thought about the great sailor waiting for me in the dust on his island scorching with light. Or perhaps he'd gone to sea already, standing square on the bridge of a boat, bellowing instructions over the bow line that dived furiously into the waves, flights of white birds sobbing around his head, like a halo, a wild halo.

Wave after wave broke against the cliff. I huddled in a corner in the rock, the same one that Jude had hunkered down into one evening, and drunk his rum – the Abercrombie evening. Bundled up in my sleeping bag, I thought about fish carried on the currents. It must have felt so good to be a fish right then. And we went and killed them. Why? I closed my eyes. Under my eyelids, Jude. He was walking, not very steadily, the scorched skin of his face partly hidden by dirty hair, the beautiful yellow eyes gazing beyond the queue of people, beyond the men and women waiting for their bowl of chilli – beyond the land. His great flushed forehead turned towards the open sea, towards the South Pacific where he would go fishing one day. Then he was in a dark bar. Semi-naked women with heavy curves, pinned in the halo of a red spotlight like poor deformed butterflies, swivelled their bulky hips and jiggled their huge bare buttocks in a simulation of lovemaking – and he drank in the view greedily, a glass of cheap rum at his lips. Did he still remember our ice-cream baby?

The ocean advancing towards me. The gaping sky. The vast world. Where to find him? So dizzying I couldn't breathe. Shadows around me stirred with the wind. Dead trees. I was frightened. The thundering roll of the ocean seemed to be amplified with the onset of night. The sky opened up like a chasm. I thought I heard the pained cry of a loon piercing the darkness. Coming from so far away … everything was moving away from me. Everything was too big and wanted to crush me. I was alone and naked. The bird's manic laugh resonated in the roar of the world, as if this were its very heart.

I'd found what I was looking for. I'd found it at last, a loon's cry in the dark. I went to sleep.

I dreamed. There was something lying on the ground. A branch perhaps. I leant down to pick it up. It looked like the neck of a wild goose. Or the loon's perhaps. Or was it a sand sculpture? I tried to grab hold of it, but it crumbled between my fingers. There was no way to restore it to any sort of comprehensible reality. The thing falling apart in my hand seemed like life itself, but also the death of my shipwrecked man, and of Nikephoros, and of the great sailor one day.